THE SPIRIT OF THE FAMILY

THE SPIRIT OF THE FAMILY

Josephine Boyle

This first world edition published in Great Britain 1999 by
SEVERN HOUSE PUBLISHERS LTD of
9–15 High Street, Sutton, Surrey SM1 1DF.
First published in the USA 2000 by
SEVERN HOUSE PUBLISHERS INC., of
595 Madison Avenue, New York, NY 10022.

British Library Cataloguing in Publication Data

Boyle,   Josephine
          The spirit of the family
          1.   Ghost stories
          I.   Title
          823.9'14 [F]

          ISBN 0-7278-5491-7

One

"So you're really going to do it," said Helena.

"Yes," said Julia.

Helena watched her going grimly about her business. "Why now? Why not years ago?"

"Cowardice," said Julia.

"Oh nonsense, you've always stood up for yourself."

"Shouting and screaming is easy, it's action that scares me."

"But now you're not scared any more."

"Of course I'm scared!" said Julia. She was tall and very slim, with brown hair in a long bob. "Nell, it's 1995 and in a few months' time I shall be thirty. Thirty! If I don't do it now I never will. I'll be finished."

"How can you be finished when you're so clever!" Helena exclaimed, hugging the pregnancy which excused her from having to be clever too. "I mean, you know about computers, and speak French and German, and you're so brave! You go into London every day and travel on the tubes and buses all by yourself. I can't remember when I last dared do that."

"I always come back," said Julia.

"Are you taking it all?" Helena asked as the pile of belongings on the landing grew larger.

"Not books and pictures; I'll fetch those another time."

"If things go wrong you'll have to bring it all back," Helena pointed out, her brow furrowed with worry.

"Then I'll take it somewhere else."

Helena saw another crammed plastic carrier dumped outside the bedroom door. She was shorter than Julia, and dumpier, even when not pregnant.

1

"When are you going?"

"This afternoon. The taxi's coming at three."

"Won't it be more expensive on a Sunday?" Helena niggled again.

"I've got to go to work in the morning."

Helena witnessed the transfer of Julia's toothbrush and face flannel from the vanity basin to the toilet bag to the suitcase with near awe. There was such a terrible finality about it.

"Father hasn't been dead long," she said.

"It's a year. A whole year. I daren't leave it any longer."

"Shouldn't you have told her?" asked Helena reproachfully.

Julia turned, crossed her arms and looked at her oldest sister with weary exasperation.

"Well, all right," Helena conceded the unspoken argument, "but I shouldn't like to be you when she finds out. Gosh, I hope she doesn't ring us! When's she due back?"

"Two or three weeks, depending on when they have the final row," said Julia, resuming the packing.

"We'll be down at the cottage," said Helena with relief, "and I can tell Philip to switch off his mobile. Well, I wish you luck of course, but I can't help feeling – I mean, if it were somewhere local but, well, I mean – Hackney!" Her face expressed utter bewilderment.

"I hope you'll be comfortable, Jule," said Bernice anxiously, "the bedroom's a bit on the small side."

"I'm sure it'll be lovely," said Julia, smiling and gripping her fingers together like a shy little girl who'd come to a party. It was the only thing which gave her away. Her face was pale and oval and discreetly made up, her expression was calm. She looked a nicely-brought-up, well-educated young woman who coped easily with a good job.

The long living room had a high ceiling, and the fireplace had been bound with hardboard and gagged with a gas fire. The wallpaper was the gentle floral of DIY superstores, circled with borders at picture rail, dado and skirting board as if to stop the walls from falling in. The pine table and chairs in the back half weren't old enough to have started coming apart, but in the front half the striped bed-settee was no longer pristine and the white fitments rested their damaged joints against the walls, proving that easy home assembly is one of the great lies of our time. Bernice's teddy bear collection populated every corner like a harem awaiting its proprietor's choice for the night, and her CDs apparently lived on the floor.

"It's a nice room," said Julia.

"I'm so glad you think so," said Bernice, beaming.

"I suppose this was the parlour," said Julia, looking round with what she hoped looked like admiration. "I wonder what sort of grate's behind that hardboard? Do you think it's got brass, or steel, or something nice like that?"

"Shouldn't think so. I mean, these houses aren't posh, not like the huge ones at the other end of the park."

"I like those coloured tiles in the hall. Who washes them?"

"We do," said Bernice. "It's supposed to be every Saturday, according to the agreement, but nobody actually comes to see that you do. Oh, and the bathroom's on the half-landing, and we clean it after use and do the floor every other day, but actually Win upstairs usually gets in and does it first."

"What's she like? I mean, would she complain if you didn't clean the hall?" asked Julia with slight apprehension.

"I don't think she'd make a fuss unless I left it a month. She's reasonable about most things. We're lucky with neighbours, really. The squatters next door are so quiet you'd never guess they were there, and the other side are a Bangladeshi family who never say a word to anyone."

"What about the basement?"

"Keeps himself to himself," Bernice assured her.

She was stocky and plump, with hair styled to look as if she had just got out of bed and a round, endearingly parrot-beaked face. Julia felt she could be quite comfortable with a flatmate who was so inarguably less attractive than she, albeit one with

3

a boyfriend who occasionally stayed the weekend. How had she managed it? No, mustn't be unkind.

"You won't mind, will you, Jule?" Bernice had asked when their new arrangement was first being discussed.

"Of *course* not," Julia had insisted. She hoped the walls were thick.

They went through the curtained-off kitchen area into a small, gloomy lobby which had once been the back part of the entrance hall, and thence into a small bedroom. This is My Room, Julia told herself. She looked out of the window. This is My View.

It consisted largely of concrete pillars, but in the shade below was a minute square of paving with shaggy grass in the middle; the sort of thing the sentimentally patronising call brave cockney gardening. There were plants in the leaning greenhouse in the left-hand corner, and around it clustered containers of a second-hand nature, from rusty tins to a cracked sink, waiting for the bedding plants still sheltering under glass. The garden itself was bare of all but a stringy, emotionless passion-flower tied to the new fence at the bottom, and beyond that boundary it was mayhem.

Up on the flyover, traffic passed loudly, incessantly, and in a great hurry. At ground level, invisible vehicles came roaring down the slip road and thundered past the fence. Oh.

Julia turned and studied her room. It was about twelve feet by ten. There was a fireplace with a mirrored overmantel across one corner by the window, with a chest of drawers in front of it. A wardrobe was squeezed into the other side. The chair under the window was draped in printed sunflowers and the curtains were sunflowered too. The bed was beside the door, wearing hand-woven cotton from Oxfam. A teddy held out welcoming arms on the pillow.

"It's lovely," said Julia brightly.

"Phew!" Bernice pulled a funny face expressive of extreme relief. "I was so afraid you wouldn't like it."

"I feel bad about turning you out of your room, though," Julia apologised.

4

"Oh, that's all right. There's only room for a single bed in here, and the bed-settee suits me better these days." She giggled.

They collected Julia's belongings from inside the front door, carried them through the living room and kitchen and dumped them on the dimly lit tiles in the lobby, about three yards from where they'd been before. While Julia started to unpack, Bernice nipped down the road for a take-away.

During that half hour, Julia sat alone in her new home and psyched herself up. It's going to work. I'm going to be independent. I'm going to be self-confident. And I am going to stop being afraid and sad and become happy like other people are. Her smooth, expressionless face looked as if she'd never been afraid or upset in her life. It lied.

Bernice returned with a grease-stained carrier bag and pushed the containers into the oven. She produced a tablecloth covered with bright orange flowers from a drawer.

"I always use this for Indian," she said, "it doesn't show so much. Put it on the coffee table, will you, Jule? Do you like *As Time Goes By*? I do. Oh, the cutlery is under the draining board, and you'd better take some kitchen towel in to mop ourselves up with." Take-aways were obviously frequent in this household; a plastic bag full of washed aluminium foil hung on the wall, labelled 'Guide Dogs for the Blind'.

The living room was brilliantly lit by the evening sunshine streaming down the length of the park. Julia pushed up the rickety sash and drew the striped curtains across the bay to lessen the onslaught. The action made her feel proprietorial.

"I've drawn the curtains," she told Bernice, in case she was encroaching too much too soon on her territory.

"Fine," said Bernice absently, looking for clean plates; there seemed to be a shortage.

"Do tell me if I can do something," said Julia. She hovered politely, hugging herself with tightly crossed arms. She felt huge, gangling, clumsy and in the way.

From the kitchen window she could look straight down

the passage beside the back addition and into the greenhouse. An old man was shuffling about with a battered galvanized watercan. His clothes had the set-into-folds appearance of the seldom cleaned and his checked cap was grey – certainly greyer than when it was new. The hair straggling down his neck was white, as was his moustache. His shirt was striped, his cardigan was brown and his trousers were a navy pin-stripe. His boots had once been black. Only his face, neck and hands relieved the dinginess of his appearance, for they were pink – and not a healthy, weathered glow but roaring blood pressure colour.

"Who's the man in the basement?" asked Julia.

"Mr Rillington," said Bernice, pulling a large tin tray out from beside the fridge and putting it on the table.

"He looks terribly old."

"He is." She looked for the oven gloves.

"Does he look after himself?"

"That's a matter of opinion. He thinks he does. They sent a social worker round once because he'd left his milk out, but he'd only had a bit of a cold and told her to mind her own business."

"That wasn't very nice. Most old people would moan if nobody noticed. Someone must have reported it, and they only meant to be kind, didn't they?"

"Yes," said Bernice, looking uncomfortable. She dropped the foil containers onto the tray. "Come on, Jule, it's nearly seven o'clock. Put the telly on."

The evening started from there.

Breakfast seemed to cause Bernice a certain amount of angst as well, as she wielded the frying pan with a great deal more energy than skill. "Do you like bacon well done?" she asked with anxious hope.

"Actually I don't often eat it," admitted Julia, feeling utterly ungrateful. "You don't have to do this for me every morning, you know, can't we take it in turns?"

"I think it'll be best if we just grab for ourselves, if you don't mind," said Bernice with obvious relief.

Julia opened the sash to air her bedroom and the noise and fumes burst in upon her. After only fifteen minutes she decided that the exercise was merely changing one sort of smell for another, and decided that she preferred her own. It felt strange taking her working suit out of the rather macabre art nouveau wardrobe and doing her make-up in the mirror above the fireplace. Well, no crushing herself into a commuter train today – work was less than three miles away.

The flat door was opposite the bottom of the staircase, and had once been the entrance to the parlour. The hall had never been spacious or elegant, and its back half had been shut away to provide access to Julia's bedroom. What remained suffered from dull cream paint and dull cream wallpaper, and seemed to wince under the light from the frosted glass strips in the front door.

As Bernice pulled their door shut voices sounded at first floor level.

"Morning, Bernie!"

"Morning, Win. Morning, Harry."

The couple pattered down the stairs and the steps, with hardly a check in their speed whilst opening the front door. They were in tracksuits and trainers, which explained why they sprang straight across into the park, but not why they had bulging bags with them. Tennis, perhaps?

"Who are they?" asked Julia as they followed them out into the world.

"The Grosvenors."

"Aren't they energetic!"

"Yes, they're always out and about. Sometimes they don't get home until eight o'clock."

"They look a bit old to be working."

"Oh no, they're retired but they're still out all day. Don't know where," said Bernice vaguely. "I expect they've got involved with some sort of voluntary work; people like that often do, don't they?"

The terraced houses had been pleasant enough homes in their prime and had a superb view from their front windows, but they weren't of the same class as those on the other edges of the park. Many were peeling and dirty, others gutted, with rubble and dried-up bags of cement in their unwalled front gardens. Some windows had the dusty, faded cloth of long hanging, and some the permanently pinned-across sheets of squatters. But gentrification had started and much of the street was on the way up, with white paint, door-phones, burglar alarms and metal shutters. Further along, pastiche period flats were already occupied.

The terrace of four which included their flat was in a fairly parlous state, one even having bricked-up windows and a hole in the roof. The basements were barely below street level and the ground floor was reached by nine stone steps. A bay ran down all three floors, but the front doors were narrow and not particularly elegant. Ornament was minimal, unlike the exuberant extrusions of foliage which decked most old villas in South Hackney, but a stone set above the porches of the second and third houses identified this undistinguished development as Ermintrude Villas. It seemed that whoever now held its fate in their hands couldn't decide whether to ignore it, patch it up or pull it down.

The journey to work was so bizarre that Julia couldn't take it in. She blindly followed Bernice's lead, up and down a foot-bridge over the motorway, through streets of workshops and small factories to a railway she had never even heard of, and finally onto the Docklands Light Railway, with which she was at least familiar.

The jerky toy train crunched and screamed around the bends of its elevated track and into Canary Wharf station. As they walked out into the open the wind came gusting off the river to blow construction site dust into their faces.

"There's a man up there," said Bernice with surprise, looking across at a building which had consisted of girders and concrete floors for what seemed a very long time.

"Gosh. Do you think he's lost his way?" said Julia.

"He's got a helmet on. Perhaps they're getting started on it again, after all, they keep telling us the recession's over."

"Hope so," said Julia. Supposing it wasn't? Supposing the firm went bust and they were both out of a job? Supposing she had to go home again?

In the foyer of Jones, Brown and Wilkinson, a long-established firm removed thither from Eastcheap and therefore clinging nostalgically to punctuation and conjunctives, a silvery trickle of water stirred the blue-tiled pool in the miniature rainforest and gave three circling carp the only excitement of their lives bar feeding time. A few weeks ago the caretaker had swanned off for a week in the sun and forgotten all about them. On his return, he had been told in a few well-chosen words that those blank fish hadn't come home from a school fête tied up in a blank plastic bag, they cost X blank quid each, so don't ever do that again. Whereupon the caretaker made it known to everyone that he wasn't a blank zoo keeper and someone else could blank do it instead.

So Bernice did. She had not been with the firm all that long, but already seemed more of a permanency than Julia. Bernice dived into relationships head first; Julia felt safer with a toe dipped cautiously in the water.

Bernice took the packet of fish food from under the reception counter and advanced on the pool, greeting the ready-raised heads. "Hello, darlings! Here comes your breakfast."

The staff arrived in ones, twos, dribs and drabs, and were subjected to the teasing of the automatic doors, which pretended to the last second that an unbroken stride would bring noses into contact with glass and then whisked themselves away at the very moment that face was lost by hesitation.

Julia opened the appointments book and made sure pens and pencils were at the ready. This is the first day of the rest of my life.

"Morning, Jason. Morning, Damian. Morning, Miss Standish. Hi Candice!" Candice liked you to say 'hi' to her. It went with her high-flying, mid-Atlantic image. "Good-morning

9

Mr Jones." You didn't say 'hi' or even 'hello' to Mr Jones, he was the Boss of Bosses.

The telephone sprang into shrill, warbling life and the first appointment charged at the doors, coming through with face intact. He was a smiling, pin-striped briefcase bearer.

"Bill Austin. I have an appointment with John Ash."

"Would you like to sign the visitors' book, Mr Austin? I'll just let Mr Ash know you're here."

He handed the pen back as if he'd signed her autograph book.

"If you would like to take a seat over there, Mr Ash will be down directly."

He gave her an indulgent smile and an ingratiating wink. "Thank you, dear."

Not at all, duckie. Bernice was on the phone. Julia picked up the other. "Good-morning. Jones, Brown and Wilkinson."

"Julia? It's Helena. Is it all right to ring you at work? You didn't give me your new number."

Mr Ash emerged from the lift and followed his outstretched hand across the foyer to his appointee.

"No, that's quite all right," said Julia, in the bright, obliging voice she didn't usually waste on sisters.

"I just wanted to let you know about Philip's first meeting, so you'd be sure to be free. It's going to be the Tuesday, not the Wednesday – apparently the hall was double-booked. Now you will come, won't you? A junior minister will be there and all the local Tory councillors."

"I beg your pardon?" said Julia with great politeness, for the benefit of Messrs Ash and Austin.

"Well, all right, the candidates for councillors, and of course we'd like all the immediate family to be there, it's such a landmark in Philip's career."

"Oh yes?" said Julia in a deeply interested voice. The lift doors closed on the two men. "For goodness' sake, Nell, do I have to? I have absolutely no interest in politics and I don't think I could stand watching Mum being mother-in-law of the candidate."

"Oh please, Julia," pleaded Helena anxiously, "it'll be me who gets the ear-bending if you don't. It's just one evening, surely you can spare that?"

A small group from Brussels arrived at the desk and was greeted by Bernice at her sweetest. The other phone rang.

"I'm afraid I'll have to get back to you on this, madam. I'll let you know as soon as possible."

"You'd better," said Helena with feeling. "I suppose I'll see you next Sunday?"

"Thank you for calling. Goodbye."

That night it was fish and chips.

"You don't mind, do you, Jule? It isn't just that I'm not much of a cook, but I don't really feel like doing it after a day's work."

"Oh yes, I do understand," Julia agreed immediately, with no intention of changing Bernice's lifestyle or of being a nuisance to her in any way whatsoever. "I'll cook sometimes, if you like. I quite like it, and I'm not too bad, really."

"Oh, wonderful!" Bernice was overjoyed.

Tonight the evening started with *Coronation Street*, but as nothing else appealed on the four channels available to them they opened a cheap bottle of plonk and talked.

"How long have you been here?" asked Julia, feeling quite remarkably happy. Free at last! Free at last!

"Just a few months. Win said an old woman and her son were here before. He was one of those rather sad men who'd devoted his entire life to his mother, but she died last year. He was going to stay on, but it turned out that she'd got a surprising whack she'd never told him about tucked away in a building society, though he'd been working to keep her for years. So he went off to Jaywick and bought a bungalow."

"Did she die here?" asked Julia, realising that her own room must have been that rather selfish old woman's.

"No, in Homerton Hospital. You should have seen some

11

of the stuff they left behind, Jule. I shoved it all in the box under your bed when I redecorated."

Of course the box had to be dragged into the living room, and the ludicrous horrors of past taste exhibited and laughed over; streaky repp curtains, hideous cushion covers and numerous other fixtures and fittings which Bernice had found impossible to live with, including kitchen curtains of red and black checks dotted with yellow roses and lined with black-out material.

"I mean, they must be fifty years old, Jule!" Bernice exclaimed with the utmost glee.

She had left the Deco light fitting in the living room, because after years of being out of date it had suddenly come into its own again, if only as a conversation piece or a good laugh. Also, she feared any attempt to move it could have messed up the wiring, which, she whispered as if the authorities were listening at the door, was probably in a thoroughly illegal state.

Julia finished the first day of the rest of her life with a bath and a quiet read in bed.

The bathroom was not a place which invited you to linger, but the gas heater meant the water was hot. The mattress had been bought by Bernice and was therefore comfortable, but the original stood upright under the stairs, guarding the locked door which led down to the basement.

Julia propped herself up with pillows and opened her book; Bernice had thoughtfully provided her with a shelf of literature. There were several *œuvres* brought out in time for previous Christmases, bearing commendations from well-known names to the effect that they had laughed till they cried or been moved to tears, and that either way they could never bear to be parted from them ever again. But there was also a Jilly Cooper, several Catherine Cooksons and Danielle Steeles and a promising trio of bodice-rippers. She didn't generally read that sort of thing, of course, but if that was all there was . . .

The Spirit of the Family

Outside the closed curtains the traffic was still going wherever people needed to go while others were settling down for a night's rest. No doubt she'd soon get used to it. She decided not to open the window until she had.

Two

J ulia lay looking at the ceiling. The floral cornice had been painted too often for its design to remain clear, and the centre rose was the same. Bernice had put up a big round paper shade, and the box under the bed held the corroded Edwardian brass circle with glass beads which must have dripped for at least twelve inches towards the breakfast table and caught in the maid's hair when she laid it. At least, she presumed this must have been the morning room.

Outside, the traffic thundered on. She'd slept a bit, but mostly watched the headlights creeping round the sunflowers to spy in at her. Now it was past six o'clock and the daylight was doing the same. The night was over.

She sat up and took another look at her new room. Bernice's taste was easy to get accustomed to, and with her own belongings scattered around it could get to feel like home. She'd soon get used to the noise, and if the headlights were too disturbing she'd buy an eyemask.

How different from home life in Cawarden Gardens, Worcester Park, where only the birds and the milkman made noise before seven thirty; here there was the grinding of lorries, the howling of juggernauts, the macho whizz of private cars getting ahead of the new working day. Someone somewhere was shouting. Further away, an early train brayed along the North London Railway. More traffic. More muffled shouting.

"Go away! Go away!"

I know just how you feel, sir.

"Go away, I tell you!"

There was a rattling sound beneath her window, then the

14

crack of wood upon wood. She shot out of bed, pulled back the curtain and pushed up the sash. The garden was empty, but the thudding and shouting continued and there was no doubt that it came from the basement.

She put on some clothes and tiptoed as quietly as possible through the living room, where Bernice was only a curled-up ball under a quilt on the bed-settee. She unbolted the flat door and let herself out into the hall, then put the front door on the latch and went down the steps into the tiny wasteland which had once been a garden.

In the similar mess next door, a young couple were standing and staring over the low wall at the bay window of Mr Rillington's flat. The man was tall and thin with a ponytail, the woman had long hair and the face of an undernourished child in a state of trance. She was wrapped in a blanket like a squaw.

"He's woken the baby," said the man.

"I think there must be an intruder in there, he's been shouting at him to go away," said Julia anxiously. "Should we call the police?"

"Does it all the time," said the man.

"Oh. You think it's all right to leave him, then?"

"He wakes the baby." The young man stood silently for a listen. "He's stopped." He put a protective arm around his partner and they disappeared under next door's steps.

After a moment's conscientious listening, Julia went back inside. This time the closing of both doors woke Bernice, who emerged yawning and blinking like a cartoon squirrel. Her reaction to Julia's story was like that of the man next door's.

"Yes, he does have funny turns occasionally, but they're soon over. I expect he gets bad dreams, poor old man. Be a darling, Jule, and put the kettle on. There's no point in going back to sleep now."

By seven thirty, when the shouting started again, Bernice was up in the bathroom. Julia went and reported on the situation through the door.

"I'm in the bath, Jule. Look, if he really sounds upset give

15

the Grosvenors a ring, they're always up early. The bell's on the wall by their curtain."

At the top of the few stairs from the half-landing, the Grosvenors had put up an old green velvet curtain with a notice hanging on it. Its frame had a regal flavour, being constructed of gilt plastic, sequins and a certain amount of fake red velvet, and the typewritten message it cradled with such ceremony was brief.

'The Grosvenors live here. Please do not pass curtain but ring bell. We like our privacy. Thank You. WELCOME!'

The banisters running along the landing had been backed by a continuation of the curtain, and the whole set-up seemed very likely to ring up on a pantomime.

Julia found a mock ship's bell mounted on oak stuck to the wall, as Bernice had said. She struck two bells.

A door opened at the front of the house, followed by brisk, muffled footsteps coming along the landing, then the curtain was drawn back to reveal Mrs Grosvenor in trousers and sweater, chewing. She was a thin, brisk, sharp-looking woman in thick glasses, with frizzy white hair discoloured by either its original shade or the remains of a semi-permanent rinse.

"Oh, I'm so sorry," said Julia, flustered. "I forgot you might be eating." Social *faux pas*.

Mrs Grosvenor swallowed and grabbed her as she turned to go.

"Come here, love, no need to stand on ceremony with us. What can I do for you?"

"It's Mr Rillington. He's making the most awful noise down in his front room; I think he must be ill. Do you perhaps have a spare key?"

"Can't say as I have," said Mrs Grosvenor dryly. "You won't catch Joe Rillington handing out door keys, he lives in that basement like a clam in its shell. Never asks no one in, these days."

"Oh, sorry, he's all right, then?" I shouldn't have stuck my nose in. They'll think I'm a real busybody.

16

"I didn't say that," Mrs Grosvenor demurred. "If he's ill, the least we can do is find out. Harry!"

"My friend said she tried to help him once and he was really horrible about it."

"Yes, I expect he was," said Mrs Grosvenor without surprise. "Silly old man. Still, we're all going to be silly old men and women one day – if we're lucky. Harry," she said, turning to address her husband as he came padding along the landing in grey shell suit and trainers, also chewing, "this young lady says Mr Rillington's kicking up hell's delight and won't answer the door. Should we go see what he's up to?"

Mr Grosvenor dispatched his mouthful and beamed at Julia. He was big, florid, and walked with the dignified roll of the heavyweight.

"Hello, love. Yeah, suppose we ought to go take a look at the silly old bugger. Hang on, I'll lock the lounge."

He went back down the landing and there was the sound of a Yale lock slamming, though the television continued to carry on chattering beyond it.

"We have to lock each room separate," Mrs Grosvenor explained apologetically. "No reflection on you and Bernice, you understand, but you never know who might get through the front door, or up from Mr Rillington's. If only the agents would let us put up a proper partition. We've been on to them often enough, but they say the owner won't have it."

"We're partitioned off," said Julia.

"Oh, the last people did that ages ago. Nobody from the agent's actually bothers to come here, you see. I mean, we all take our rent down there, don't we? Lazy lot."

They descended into the front garden with the usual brisk patter of feet down stairs and steps. Harry hammered on the door beneath and shouted, "Mr Rillington! You all right?"

Mrs Grosvenor went and looked in the basement bay window, which was sunk within a personal dry moat clogged with dead leaves and moss.

The heavy lace curtains were impenetrable. Win knocked on the glass. Another bout of roaring broke out, and then there was the sound of something hard being struck with something even harder. A huge, fluffy, black and white cat sat on the front wall and watched the goings-on with interest.

The Grosvenors knocked and shouted again. The roaring moved away from behind the window and began to advance on the door.

"Does he drink?" asked Julia nervously.

"Don't think so," said Mrs Grosvenor. "Never heard no bottles or cans go into the dustbin, not even late at night. Must admit, the last time he did this I actually went and looked in his bin, but there wasn't nothing there. Very clean, nicely-packed bin, matter of fact, not smelly at all. Everything wrapped up in plastic bags. Not many men are as particular as that, specially old ones with short tempers."

The abuse on the other side of the peeling door sounded pretty paranoid.

"It's only Win and Harry, Mr Rillington," shouted Harry, "we live on the top floor, remember? You've met us lots of times."

The voice denied that vehemently.

"Yes you have, Joe," Win insisted, with the hard-edged voice of one who wasn't standing any nonsense. "Once upon a time we used to come and look at your garden, and we always drop in a Christmas card. And Harry put in the new glass for you when those boys heaved a brick through."

"You're lying," shouted Mr Rillington. "I know who you are."

"Oh dear," sighed Win, as her husband continued to present his credentials and ask for admittance. "He's not quite right in the head, really, but he manages perfectly well and I don't see why he should be dragged off to do nothing but watch telly all day. It's only now and then he gets upset."

"How often?" asked Julia, peering through the frosted glass in the basement door at the pink and grey blur within.

"Last time was about February. He said he wasn't going to put up with no more of it, he was going to call the police. I managed to persuade him not to – they'd have had him put away in no time."

"Who does he think you are?"

"You tell me. I had a word with my doctor about it, last time I had to go see him, though I didn't tell him who I was talking about – didn't want to shop the poor old feller. He said it was senile paranoia – you know, that's when you think everyone's talking about you and out to get you. Sad, ain't it?"

"If he had a brick thrown through his window, that seems a perfectly sensible thing to think," said Julia, with an appalled, vivid understanding of what it must be like to be Mr Rillington, old, alone, persecuted, frightened; she'd experienced imaginary horrors, too.

"Oh, it started long before that." Win pushed Harry firmly out of the way. "Joseph Rillington, you stop making that noise or I'll knock this here door down, then you'll have to get someone to come and mend it. This is your last chance. If you don't shut up, I'll go and get your Florrie."

The shouting suddenly stopped.

"Always shuts him up, that does," said Win simply.

"Who's Florrie?"

"Don't know, love. I just know he's scared of her."

"How did you find out?"

"I picked up an old bound copy of *The Sunday at Home* down there once, and inside it said 'To Florrie from her loving mother'. 'Oh,' I said, 'who was Florrie, then?' and he went white as a sheet and pushed the book under a pile of newspapers."

"He didn't answer your question, then?"

Suddenly, Julia experienced a surge of irritation and self-criticism. Why does my half of a conversation so often consist of feed lines for the other person? Haven't I anything interesting of my own to contribute? I'm the new Julia now, and I really must make more effort to be assertive.

But not in this particular situation, she realised. There was little point in trying to have a two-way conversation with Win Grosvenor – she had a master's degree in assertiveness.

19

She hadn't even heard her final question, anyway; she was shouting a few last instructions to the presumably cowering Mr Rillington, to the effect that he should make himself a nice cup of tea and have a little rest, because there was nothing to worry about at all. Right?

By the end of the week, Julia was beginning to get used to the traffic, though only with earplugs, eyemask and closed window. She had conceived quite a strong affection for the room, now her make-up was on the chest of drawers and her ornaments on the overmantel. The clothes wouldn't all go into the wardrobe, which contained Bernice's already, but there were hooks on the back of the door and on the wall under the stairs. The rest of her belongings were piled on the lobby floor. A stopped gas pipe sticking out of the wall by the fireplace had been disguised with a plaque which told her 'Yes you can', and so far it really appeared that yes, she could.

Bernice's boyfriend turned out to be a big surprise. Rather uncharitably, and with a 'plainism' which she felt ashamed of, Julia had expected him to be of a similar status in looks, perhaps with unfashionable glasses, a weedy physique, no conversation and a silly grin. He was, in fact, a perfectly normal male, with just enough muscle in the right places, a cheerful face with brown eyes and a nice mouth, brown hair which was not too short and not too long, and clothes which suited him without any evidence of his having made too great an effort. He arrived on Friday evening, carrying a zip-up bag.

"Julia, this is Tom," said Bernice, pulling him into the living room where Julia was sitting with her feet on the coffee table, in a short, straight, office skirt which wasn't designed for such a position.

She swung her legs down quickly and got up, toes searching for discarded shoes.

"Hello, I'm Bernice's new flatmate. I hope I'm not going to be in the way."

He shook her hand. "Shouldn't think so, that is as long as you're sleeping in the other room. Nice to meet you."

They all went out for a drink in what Julia feared was rather a rough pub, then brought back sweet and sour chicken, fried rice, crispy noodles, mixed vegetables, pancake rolls and another man called Jim. On Saturday they had a long walk all around the park, which turned out to be very nice indeed, and came back mid-afternoon to save the joint Julia had put into the oven. Jim turned up as it was going onto the plates. On Sunday morning Bernice announced that they were going out on a picnic with a group of friends.

"Why not come with us? Jim's coming."

Warning bells started to ring. "No thanks, Bernice, I've got lots of things I want to do today." The last thing she wanted was to be paired off, especially with Jim.

She tidied her room, caught up with her washing and ironing and ate lunch in the open bay window.

Then she went for a walk in the park. ("Julia, how could you be so ridiculously foolhardy! All on your own!") The open ground stretched for miles on every side so if there were criminals lurking she'd have plenty of warning and time to run, but as far as she could see there were only people jogging, cycling and walking dogs. Brightly dressed kids from every corner of the globe were roller-skating and skateboarding, and far away across the grass a solitary figure was performing the dignified ceremony of Tai Chi.

It was respectable enough for Surrey.

She came back down Victoria Park Road. The tower blocks of the Trowbridge Estate hung behind the terrace, looking as if they were deciding whether to mug it. The houses seemed unaware of being under threat and in their own little world, turning their backs upon noise and ugliness and looking only upon greenery. Take no notice, they seemed to say, they may go away. Even the road in front of them, now relieved by the flyover, was rarely disturbed by traffic.

As she approached the house she could hear Mr Rillington kicking up rough again. Oh, great. The banging and shouting sounded as if he was taking on an army.

"Get away from that! Go on, get away from it! If you touch

21

a thing in here I'll call the police! And don't you try and hide in there, I can see you. Why can't you leave me alone? Go away! Go away! Go away!"

The squatters were in the garden. The girl stood holding a fat baby in a print dress and tiny earrings, with a scarlet bow on top of its fluffy head. Her partner stepped over the dwarf wall between the houses and bent down to look in the bay window.

"Yo, man," he called mildly.

"Go away!" roared Mr Rillington.

"You want to talk about it?" the squatter suggested. "Get it off your chest, right?"

"Can I do anything?" Julia offered. Must be a helpful girl – or was she being nosy again?

The squatter turned. "We're just going out," he said. The trio started down the road towards Hackney Wick.

Right. Seems it's up to me. Julia took over the baton and raised a jolly, reassuring voice.

"Hello, there, Mr Rillington! This is Julia Nutley from the flat upstairs. Do you need any help?" The shouting stopped. She could hear a budgie shrieking and ringing its bell. She knocked politely, called "Hello" several more times, then moved to the window and gave a friendly and reassuring wave, just in case he was looking through the camouflage of worn Nottingham lace.

There was a crash of breaking glass and something tore past her arm. The small bronze bust of Shakespeare ricocheted off the low wall onto the street and lumps of dirty stucco exploded in all directions. She jumped onto the steps and stood there for a minute in a state of shock. After all, she was only trying to help. Behind the broken glass, the lace had fallen back into place and she could just make out a bright pink face beyond it. She addressed it with tears in her eyes.

"That's a very silly and dangerous thing to do, Mr Rillington. You might have killed me, and then the police would have come and taken you away. If you want to go on being independent and living in your own home you'll have to behave yourself, won't you?"

Oh dear, I sounded remarkably like my mother when I said that. The next missile crashed through, being a large varnished footstool with barley sugar legs and a faded Berlin woolwork cover.

Now angry as well as frightened, Julia shouted "That's very naughty, Mr Rillington! I'm going to tell your Florrie about this!" Then she ran up the steps and, by force of habit, went to finish her pathetic snivel in the privacy of the loo.

Gosh, this room's depressing. I bet I'm not the first person to use it for a good cry.

Whether or not it was due to those dread words, there was no more noise that day; Joseph Rillington's latest funny turn was over.

Julia spent the evening alone with the television, her own choice of programmes, no interruption of her concentration and no live-in critic pulling everything apart. ("Really, I don't know how they have the nerve to turn out stuff like this, it's utter drivel. Turn it over, Julia, let's see what's on the other side. Oh good heavens, not him again, try ITV—")

She was remarkably happy.

Bernice and Tom got back at ten, equally on top of the world.

The next morning, Harry Grosvenor went and stuck a piece of hardboard over the broken glass, with no protest from within.

The weather seemed to be setting in for a long, sunny period, despite its being so early in the year.

Everything was going really well.

Three

"What's going on?" asked Bernice.
It was a very warm evening; in fact the weather had been kind for some time, adding to the enjoyment of the VE Day 50th Anniversary beacon-lighting in the park and the 1940s music which had set Win and Harry dancing. As the girls plodded down the road from the foot-bridge they saw two parked police cars, and a lot of people well ensconced for that enjoyable and timeless occupation, watching.

"What's going on?" Bernice repeated with little-girl wonder, this time addressing a large man in filthy jeans and a checked shirt who up until five o'clock had been mending a roof, but who was now free to stand and stare for as long as he liked.

"Found a body," he said with cheerful satisfaction.

"Not poor Mr Rillington!" said Julia, horrified. "Did someone break in?" It was the inevitable assumption for a Nutley, and she felt sick with fright. "Just think, it could have been us! If we'd been home the intruder might have got into our flat and attacked us as well."

"Nah," said the man, "nuffing like that. Seems he's been dead a while. The bit of board had come away from the broken window, and when the lady from upstairs went past she smelt him."

"Oh, that's dreadful!" cried Bernice, near to tears. "I should have looked after him."

"Look," said Julia quickly, trying to talk down her own erupting guilt, "you know what happened before. If it's anyone's fault it was his, for keeping people away. And throwing things at them," she added. She'd only been trying to *help*.

"He was ill," said Bernice, sniffing, "he couldn't help it. He was nice, really," she added plaintively.

"No he weren't," said Win Grosvenor, coming up behind them. "Oh, he weren't too bad once, but for the last few years he's been about as friendly as a pit bull. Still, it's no way to die, all on your own. Poor old man."

By the time Mr Rillington had been removed the girls had little appetite left for the evening meal which Julia was preparing. She looked down into the wilting back garden and noticed its neglected condition. She'd failed Mr Rillington and she'd failed his plants.

"Bernice, I think we ought to water the garden. He'd hate to see everything dying like that." Death had immediately transformed Mr Rillington into a sympathetic lover of living things, and no doubt more endearing traits of character would soon be discovered which no one had noticed while he lived. "Is there a way round?"

"Only through the basement."

"Couldn't we get over the back fence with a ladder?"

"I suppose so, but we'd better ask the police first."

They did. They were told they certainly couldn't, not until forensic had finished.

"It's the flowers," pleaded Bernice, "specially in the green-house. They haven't been watered for days."

"Sorry," said the policeman, shaking his head. "But I'll tell you what, I'm a gardener myself. If the boss says it's all right I'll give them a freshen-up."

Bernice asked again the next morning, as the boss had obviously said no.

"They still say we can't go in," she told Julia. "Apparently it's going to be fumigated today."

"But Mrs Grosvenor said he was pretty clean for an old man."

Bernice pulled one of her elaborate faces. "Well, he was there for some days, you see, and it's been hot . . ."

"Oh."

They were silent for a minute, digesting the information and finding it tended to turn their stomachs.

"I never noticed anything, did you?" said Julia after a minute. "I mean, he was right below us."

"By the bay window, apparently. Well, you did mention about the dustbins smelling, didn't you? The policeman says there's quite a mess in the flat, and the sink in the back room's been smashed with a poker. They thought that was the weapon used by whoever attacked him, but now it seems he must have done it himself. All that shouting and banging you heard, remember?"

"He was after Them."

"Yes."

The next day, hardly a plant in the garden was not dehydrated. Something had to be done and someone had to do it. Julia went and knocked up next door.

"Can I get over the wall from your side? I want to water the garden."

Although it was so early, the young man was dressed. Or perhaps he hadn't been to bed. Or perhaps he didn't undress for bed. Goodness. He conducted her through the dark passage which led from the front to the back of the basement, past piles of belongings and through a spicy smell which tickled nose and brain. Julia didn't know whether it was pot or merely joss-sticks, her limited experience having shielded her from both.

The squatter opened the back door and waded out over long grass with a pile of broken concrete on it.

"We're going to make a patio for the baby. Over there's the herb garden, and once we've cleared over here we'll put in some vegetables."

"Do you like gardening?" asked Julia, encouraged by his willingness to talk.

"Organic, of course," he said. "It's all going to be organic."

"Are you going to have a compost bin?"

"We're going to make it an ecological site where we can care for the earth." It was disconcerting how he didn't actually pick up on Julia's remarks. She felt as if her contributions to the conversation were pebbles disappearing down a well.

There was very little of Mother Earth to be seen. Against the fence a few dark pits had been punctured through the grass and plants sat in them in a state of shock, despite illustrated labels hanging on them for encouragement. The young man put an orange plastic milk crate against the crumbling wall and helped her over.

The air was full of the roar of traffic and the stink of fumes, and Julia could feel the aged greenhouse shaking. The putty had largely fallen out of the grey wooden framework and lines of dusty moss had settled along the panes of glass. The tomatoes were drooping. The cucumber plants were lying down. Most of the bedding plants were dead.

She refilled the can by the lavatory at the end of the back addition and went down the passage which led to the back door. Through the window she could see an unmade bed with the clothes pulled back to reveal a sagging, striped mattress with cotton tufts. Their kitchen was right above it; she could hear Bernice washing up.

She watered a few geraniums which were bearing up pretty well and performed an act of faith upon an obviously dead pot of busy Lizzies. As she returned past the back addition she glanced into another window. There was no curtain, and she could see the jagged remains of a sink and an arched tap dripping slowly onto the the floor.

Julia felt panicky, turned away quickly and went down to the fence. The poor climber was covered with enough grey film from the traffic to kill the strongest of passions, but the amazing thing was that any plant could flourish in such conditions. Everything seemed against it, but in fact, even the split concrete path was being colonised by wild flowers and positively savage ivy, creeping over the neighbours' wall.

The black and white cat suddenly sprang onto the wall from the other side and gave a pathetic miaow.

"Oh, hello," said Julia. "Hasn't anyone been feeding you?" She looked at the door and saw there was no catflap, so presumably Mr Rillington used to let it in and out himself. It didn't look neglected; no doubt it was a tough city cat who could look after itself. Mrs Grosvenor had taken the budgie upstairs.

The squatter's head suddenly appeared over the wall. "Things happening."

The girl was standing in the front bay of the basement, looking out over their personal rubbish dump into the road. The fat baby dribbled on her shoulder, chewed a lump of her hair, took it out of its mouth for a moment and sang a brief joyous gurgle at Julia.

"Two women," said the girl.

"Are they relatives, do you think?" asked Julia, watching them locking up their car, carrying bags into the front garden and disappearing under the front steps. One was blonde, one grey-haired, and both were dressed in trousers and blouses.

"They look surprisingly human for relatives of Mr Rillington's. Wonder why they never came to see him before? Or perhaps they did? I'm not often here during the day. Have you seen him get any visitors?"

"He used to complain about our baby crying," said the squatter. "Knocked on the wall."

"He had a bit of a nerve, didn't he?" said Julia, laughing and endeavouring to make them laugh too, desperate to induce some sort of reaction from the couple. It felt as if she had stopped existing, as if she were a disembodied spirit in a world which ignored it.

"They've come out again," said the man.

"Only one of them," said the girl.

The grey-haired woman was opening Mr Rillington's dustbin and looking inside. She had put on an plastic overall.

"Looks as if they're going to have a turn-out of his things," said Julia. "Wonder if they know about his cat? It'll run wild if someone doesn't give it a home soon."

"We better take her for a walk in the park," said the girl.

"Yeah," said the man.

"What's your baby's name?" asked Julia. Let them try and avoid a straight answer to that. The young man turned and looked at her as if she had suddenly initiated a totally unexpected attempt at a deeply intimate relationship which might threaten his whole mental and physical integrity.

"Gaia," he said. Julia seized the hour.

"My name's Julia. What's yours?"

He made another effort. "I'm Luke. I call her Fern."

Julia didn't try to extract her real name. It was probably something uncool like Jennifer.

Ready for work, she waited on the front steps for Bernice, looking at her watch. They were cutting it fine this morning. The blonde woman came out of Mr Rillington's flat with a scarf over her hair and her face smudged with dust.

"Hello, I live on the floor above," Julia plunged in, heartened by her small, assertive victory of the previous few minutes. "I was wondering if you knew that Mr Rillington had a cat. The lady on the top floor has been looking after the budgie, in case you're wondering where it is, but no one seems to have taken responsibility for the cat. Perhaps you could take it away with you?"

The woman shook a heavily loaded duster over towards the park before coming back and answering.

"Well, that's not really anything to do with us, love. You could ring the Cats' Protection League, they do a lot of rescue work round here. Shall I give you their number?"

"You're not relatives, then?" said Julia, immediately feeling silly.

"No, we're from the council. We have to go through his things and try and find out if he's got any relatives or friends who could take his effects and arrange the funeral. Do you know?"

"No, I've only been here a short while, and as far as I've heard, no one knows a lot about him. I should think Mrs Grosvenor on the first floor is your best bet."

"We'll have a word," said the woman.

Next door, Luke carried a battered buggy up the basement steps and unfolded it between a bag of cement and a broken bicycle. Fern waited with Gaia in her arms, her hair, beads and dress dragged downwards by the pull of gravity, her head drooping like a depressed madonna.

"They're from the council," Julia informed them, determined to keep things moving. "They suggest we contact the Cats' Protection League, that is if we can catch him. He does look pretty aggressive, doesn't he?" She laughed invitingly. The black and white monster was prowling round the dustbins with an air of menace.

"Come here, Bubastis," said Luke with little conviction in his voice. "It's ours," he added, though Bubastis's lack of response to his invitation didn't seem to back this statement up. It seemed more likely that Luke, Fern and Gaia were Bubastis's humans.

The trio walked up the road and entered the small gate into the park. Julia watched them drifting across the grass in their own little world, neither speaking nor touching each other, moving through East London in an envelope of more rarified air.

That evening, while Bernice opened tins, Julia went up to tell Win Grosvenor that the budgie was still her problem and was invited in. The Grosvenors' living room was once the master bedroom, directly over the front half of the girls' living room. Harry was out at the pub; she hadn't gone because they'd had a busy day and her dogs were barking.

"Well, it don't worry me, love, it's quite nice to have him, really."

"Does he talk?"

"Not yet. He's been a bit under the weather, though he got quite frisky with his bell this morning. I think he likes it up here. Much nicer than that dark old basement."

"It's a lovely view," said Julia. The window looked out on the same picture as theirs but from a better angle; over the park railings, through the trees, straight down the infinity of sloping grass towards the distant world of Bethnal Green.

"I know, we always sit here. Looks a lot better than it used to, I can tell you. When I was a kid it was full of barbed wire and trenches and Nissen huts and all that. There was a prisoner of war camp down the other end, and all the railings had gone, so it was a total blooming mess. The bombs didn't help none, neither."

"You didn't live here then?"

"No, I was born in Bow. Harry comes from Clapton. We rented an upstairs in Hassett Road a lot of our married life, but then the landlord wanted to sell so we took the lump sum he offered us and looked for something else. I didn't really fancy going on the council, it was all tower blocks then, and anyway the young couples with kids got the first go, but this was cheap and pretty nice for the money. I don't know why it's still so cheap. Well, I do really," she added, "look at the state of it. I don't know who the owner of these houses is, but you can't get repairs done for love or money."

She raised her hand and pointed across the park. "See them houses through the trees? My Gran and Grandad lived in one of them, in the basement. Every time I walk along Victoria Park Road I look down into that area and think, 'Wonder if Gran's making bread pudden today?' Where do you come from, love?"

"Worcester Park," said Julia, and felt herself very near to being overcome with shame.

"Oh yeah, where's that? South London way, ain't it?"

"Yes," she admitted.

"Don't know south London," said Mrs Grosvenor, shaking her head as if it were the South Pole.

"Are those photographs of your family?" asked Julia, changing the subject.

Mrs Grosvenor seemed to receive a surge of inner energy, like a Peugeot standing on tiptoe when the ignition is switched on. She stepped forward eagerly and pointed at the large wedding group which occupied centre stage on the mantelpiece. "That's our Shirley. She was married at St John's over in Lauriston Rd. That's me, there, and that's Harry. Good-looking feller then, weren't he?"

He was, in a way, though unlikely to set Julia's heart racing.

His lost attractions consisted of a lot more hair and a lot less paunch.

"And that's *her* daughter's wedding. She's a lovely girl, but you can keep him. Got two lovely kids."

"Do you see them often?"

"Well, they all moved out to Leytonstone, but they do visit now and then, and of course we go over there whenever we feel like it. It's nice their way; well, it was till they started flattening it for the new road. And they got forest land just round the corner, but I still like the park best."

"I've seen you go in there every morning for your run," Julia ventured, trying to contribute to the conversation.

"Oh, that's not for exercise," said Mrs Grosvenor strongly, exhibiting a vocation for putting people right. "I mean, it does set us up for the day having that nice brisk walk, but it's mainly a short cut to catch the bus. We could pick it up at the Wick but the fumes are something awful."

"You both work, then," said Julia, meekly offering her next feedline. I'm doing it *again*!

"No, we're both retired, so by the time we've finished paying for photocopies and things, there's not a lot left. Still, I've never gone in for posh clothes and that. My daughter don't approve. She always dresses lovely, my Shirl, and she likes me to put on a nice frock when I go over."

"Why do you need lots of photocopies?" asked Julia resignedly, feeling the reference had been dropped into the conversation on purpose to be picked up, and that refusal to do so might, as they used to say, offend.

"We're researching our family history," said Mrs Grosvenor immediately. "It started because of the name. When Harry was a kid, he was really bucked to find out it was the family name of the Duke of Westminster, and he'd always wondered if they was related. So when we finally got time we thought we'd have a quick look-see and find out if they was."

"And were they?"

Mrs Grosvenor leant forward and gripped her knee so hard

and unexpectedly that Julia jumped. She stared at her earnestly through her pebble lenses.

"Love, believe me, it weren't as easy as that. We'd thought you could just go along to some office somewhere, and they'd look it up in an old book, or perhaps on a computer, and say oh yeah, your great-great-great-grandad was a distant cousin of the first Duke, or something like that. Not a bit of it!" Her hand was removed to be waved in the air in a gesture of dismissal. "You have to root it all out for yourself, starting with the relations you know and going back to who their parents were, and then their parents, and so on and so on, and all about their brothers and sisters and whatnot, and who married who, and where they went to live, and where their kids were born – well, I won't bore you, but the long and the short of it is that we got hooked, and now we've gone into my family as well, and I can't see us ever getting to the end."

"And is Harry related to the Duke of Westminster?"

"We're still on the track of His Nibs," she said darkly, "but I don't reckon it'll be long now."

"Goodness," said Julia, quite impressed, "I must tell my mother."

Except for the upsetting business of the very dead basement tenant, Julia had been enjoying herself over the last weeks, but the next weekend advanced on her like a familiar shadow creeping back over her life. She'd left a note against the clock on the drawing room mantelpiece; 'Staying with friends,' but any moment now, retribution could fall.

On Thursday night, she made herself sit down and write a letter. What tone should she use? Light and jocular as if it were no big deal?

'Dear Mum, With a daughter of twenty-nine still hanging on and making a nuisance of herself, you must have been wondering when you were going to get your life to yourself at last.'

Of course she wouldn't have. Sensible and straightforward, to show how grown-up and able to take care of herself she was?

33

'Dear Mum, I have been thinking things over for some time, and have decided that the moment has come when I must stop being spoilt by your wonderful care and stand on my own feet.'

She might swallow that, but she wouldn't like it.

After a painful couple of hours' composition and another disturbed night, the letter went into the Canary Wharf box on Friday morning.

Tom turned up again on Friday night. The evening meal was easy enough, as neither he nor Bernice were the sort of people to let conversation flag, but by ten o'clock the two of them were sitting on the settee in front of the box with an unmistakable tension between them, and Julia was beginning to feel *de trop*.

"I'll have a bath and read in bed," she said.

"All right," said Bernice, looking up over Tom's shoulder with a bright smile. "I think the meter will need feeding. Have you got any change? The box is almost empty."

Julia tried to soak her worries away, but found she was only stewing them. Quite apart from having a head full of anxieties, the bathroom was such a gloomy place, created at a time when cleanliness was next to godliness and not intended to be any more fun. She had begun to feel uneasy whilst locked into its claustrophobic privacy and tonight the feeling was worse than ever. Whatever was going to happen tomorrow?

Four

Julia sat tensely on the edge of her bed, staring at the alarm clock on the dressing-table. The post in Carwarden Gardens came at about eight o'clock and it was now five to. She had time to wash and get some clothes on, at any rate; the psychological disadvantage of repulsing attack in a nightdress should be avoided if she was going to acquit herself adequately in the fray. She hurled herself into jeans and shirt and put on a long cardigan as additional armour. The clock now said nine minutes past. Her stomach was turning over. She hoped Bernice and Tom were awake. No, come to think of it, perhaps it might be better if they were asleep. They wouldn't be very pleased if they were interrupted.

Of course, she told herself at eight sixteen, she may not mind at all; I could be getting myself into a stew for nothing. I mean, it's a perfectly reasonable thing to do. I'm not off to smuggle drugs into Thailand or to join a kibbutz in Israel. (Do people still do that?) I might as well go and make some breakfast.

She stamped upon the lobby floor as loudly as was possible in rubber-soled slip-ons then listened at the door. The telephone started to ring.

She waited for seconds, but nobody seemed to be going to answer it. Well, if they were – well, you couldn't expect—. The telephone hung on like grim death. She heard the dull thud of impatient feet hitting the floor within and tripping over something. The ringing stopped.

Oh, oh, oh, supposing it's Tom answering, whatever will she think, whatever will she say? Oh my goodness, I should never have sent that letter, well, not to arrive when he was here, anyway. Why do I never think ahead? Why do I always manage to make my messy, incompetent life even worse by not stopping and thinking and making proper plans—

The door opened to reveal a flushed, dishevelled Bernice pulling a just-long-enough tee shirt down over her broad thighs, and a Tom dressed only in underpants putting the receiver down on the table and returning to bed.

"Oh hello," said Bernice with an embarrassed smile. "It's your mother. I hope it's not bad news."

"Depends on how you look at it," said Julia tensely, advancing on the table in the curtained bay window and trying to avoid looking at the occupied bed.

"Hello, Mum, did you have a nice holiday?"

"Who the dickens was that?" Mrs Nutley's voice was outrage personified.

"A friend of Bernice's. He's just dropped in."

"At *this* time of day?"

"He's been jogging in the park."

"Where does he live?"

"I don't know. How was Auntie Jean?"

"Don't change the subject. What the dickens do you mean by running away from home as soon as my back is turned? And *what* do you mean by running to somewhere inhabited by the very dregs of East London? How *dare* you keep me in the dark? I suppose you were too ashamed of the place to let me see it."

"Of course I'm not ashamed of it," said Julia in what strove to be a steady, reasonable voice, "and of course you can come and see it any time you like. I said so in the letter, don't you remember? Come today, if you like." Better get it over with. God, this was horrible; she was shaking.

"You're completely unfeeling, Julia, the others would *never* have treated me like this. If only you were another Helena; a nice little family, a husband she can be proud of and a wonderful future ahead of her."

Julia couldn't remember a time when Helena hadn't had a mysteriously wonderful future beckoning her. News about

Helena was spread around to every aunt and uncle and cousin as soon as it broke, resulting in excited discussion and wildly optimistic conjecture, even when details were not yet able to be revealed. It was difficult to remember just what the openings had been, and what had become of them, but the certainty remained. Fate was going to fix everything for Helena.

"Do you want to come this morning?" asked Julia, feeling the hurt solidifying in her throat and sinking down to become yet more fossilised, buried heartache.

"You expect me to put my life in danger by venturing *there*? You really expect me to—"

"Well, I'll be here all day. Come if you like. The address is on the letter and it's just round the corner from the Tunnel Approach motorway. Goodbye." Her voice was flat and hard. She put down the receiver.

She turned to face Bernice and tried to ignore Tom tucked in beside her. "Sorry, my mother may be coming this morning. Will that put you out?"

"Oh – no," said Bernice. Tom groaned and turned over.

"Of course, there is the park," Mrs Nutley eventually admitted, allowing a plea of mitigation to follow her verdict of guilty, though immediately following it with a rider, "but I suppose you'd be taking your life in your hands if you were silly enough to step inside."

She rubbed a dirty mark off the window with one finger. Her face was pink and plump and her hair grey. She wore large, light-framed glasses. She was short, like Helena. Of the Nutleys, only Julia and her father were not. ("Julia's such a beanpole.")

"It's beautifully kept," said Julia. She retrieved her mother's cup from the television and refilled it from Bernice's teapot. She'd had difficulty finding it – mugs and teabags were the usual method of brewing up.

"What a waste of money when it'll only get vandalised," deplored Mrs Nutley, looking at the curtains, turning them over to find out whether they were lined, pulling them up to see if the hems were weighted. They failed on both counts.

"Considering its size," said Julia firmly, "and the position and everything, it's every bit as good as any other park. It's got tennis courts and shrubberies and lots of carpet bedding, and even an old English garden."

Mrs Nutley turned her back on the bay window and looked at the walls instead. Her hands straightened a picture.

"It could do with redecorating."

"Only if Bernice wants to. It's her flat."

"That tiny little bedroom," Mrs Nutley exclaimed incredulously, "there isn't room to swing a *cat*."

"It's much the same size as my room at home." Ow, oh, too late, now I've done it. "Have another cup, Mum—"

The chin rose, the corners of the mouth turned down, the resentment came up like footlights. "I just don't see *why*, Julia. Daddy had it all done up for you only a few months before he died, and I've never intruded on your privacy, except to clean and tidy it, of course. Why the dickens you want to give up the comforts of a lovely home to live in this poverty-stricken manner is beyond me. In my day, we all stayed happily at home until we married, and it would never have occurred to us to throw our parents' hard work and self-sacrifice back in their faces."

Not love, Julia noticed. Hard work and self-sacrifice are the great virtues. We don't mention love.

The spoon ground round and round in the cup, as if sugar took longer to dissolve under such appalling conditions. Julia pulled anguished faces at the park, a half-filled skip and her mother's Rover.

"Is the car all right?" Mrs Nutley asked sharply, starting and raising her head like a dog which smells cat.

"The wheels have been stolen."

"What?! Oh really, Julia, that's not funny! You're always cynical and sarcastic these days, and you were such a nice little girl."

"Mum, Helena left home when she was twenty-two, Rowena

went when she was twenty-one and Belinda when she was twenty-four. So why all this angst and hand-wringing when I want to become independent at twenty-nine?"

"Why should you want to be independent? The others are married, with proper homes and families, but what have you got, apart from your little job? What will you do if you get made redundant?"

Oh thank you so much. There goes all that self-image I've been laboriously pumping up like muscles. You're quite right, Mum, I am pretty useless; that's why this belated effort to prove I can look after myself is vital, because if I leave it any longer I may never be able to do it at all; this is my last chance. Prince Charming isn't going to come for me now. It's very unlikely that I shall ever be married and I've pretty well stopped caring. Pretty well.

"And *you* could have been married, too," Mrs Nutley accused her virulently, complete with pointed finger.

Julia had a sudden vision of that James Thurber cartoon with the kangaroo in court. 'Perhaps *this* will refresh your memory!'

"I always liked Brian," Mrs Nutley seethed on, putting some CDs straight. "Nice-looking and well-mannered and very high up in the Young Conservatives. He's on the council now."

"I only went out with him three times," Julia remonstrated, irritation rising. "Why do you have to remember every piffling little date as a big romance?"

"And he wasn't the only one you could have had." The teddies were lined up tidily along the mantelpiece. One was required to present his label for inspection. Well done, Ted, you came from Harrods.

No, you also approved of Geoffrey, Grant and Sean, the sort of men only married by desperate girls. People said that didn't happen any more, but you'd only got to look at couples' eyes, see the disappointed lines carved into their faces, even among what her mother called ordinary, normal, decent people. The only thing that didn't happen any more was lifelong resignation to unhappiness, witness the divorce rate.

Her mother finished her rundown of Julia's love life and looked at the room again, unfortunately finding it unchanged. "Well, it's certainly not my taste; I hate cheap wallpaper, you just can't mistake it. Supposing you want to invite friends home? It'll look as if you can't afford anything better."

"I can't."

"Don't be silly, you've always been used to the best."

"I didn't pay for it."

"Well of course you didn't, that's what I said before – you've never needed to pay for things at home. I really don't understand what this is all about, some sort of principle, I suppose." Yes. "You're trying to prove something, though I can't think what." Yes, yes, yes. "And I suppose within a month or two you'll be wearing awful clothes and giving up washing and sniffing cola." Her fingers were drawn across the television and examined for dust. Mrs Nutley had no repose. Just being near her was bad for the nerves.

"You know perfectly well the word is coke." Mum, for both our sakes, shut up before I lose my temper.

"*Well!*" Flashing eyes, shake of the head, close inspection of a postcard from Bernice's cousin in Tring. "Don't you come crying to me when you get burgled or attacked outside your front door. You always think it isn't going to happen to you, but the Jerrolds in our road had their home absolutely stripped while they were on holiday, and remember Susan Hickey – she got mugged just walking along the Ewell by-pass."

"You'd better move somewhere safer then," said Julia with her eyes closed.

"You stand here in this awful place and tell *me* to move!" Mrs Nutley practically yelled.

Shut up, shut up, shut up—

"I've lived in that house ever since I was married, and its value has gone up every single year."

"It must be the only one in the country, then."

"You don't know you're *born*, Julia, just you wait and see how it's going to be living in poverty."

"Please stop it, Mum."

"Don't you realise I'm going to be worried out of my mind thinking about you in this awful place? How will I know what's happening to you?"

"That's why I asked you to come and see it, so you wouldn't worry," Julia said, fighting a sudden, quite terrifying urge to strangle her.

"Well, you needn't have bothered," Mrs Nutley snubbed her and rattled the meter money box to see if it were full.

"No, I needn't, and I wish I hadn't," Julia said, clinging onto her self-control. "I should have walked out and not told you where I was going, or better still, told you a pack of lies."

"You did just walk out! You've never been the same since you got that job. It's changed you, Julia, and not for the better."

"Everyone normal gets a job – if they can find one."

"You had found a job! It wasn't as if Daddy didn't pay you for doing his typing and form-filling and income tax and little things like that."

"It wasn't going *out* to work, was it?" argued Julia. "It was just staying at home with Mummy and Daddy."

"And what's wrong with that? Did you dislike us that much? Were we too boring for you? There are many, many people, Julia, who would be deeply grateful for a good job as a doctor's secretary. The ingratitude of it! I am absolutely certain that you broke your father's heart and brought him to an early grave. I just hope you can live with it, that's all."

"You mean, you hope I can't live with it," retorted Julia, but tears filled her eyes. "That's a wicked thing to say, Mum. Dad never even hinted that he was upset over it. In fact, I think he was glad for me to have the new experience."

"I presume you'll be coming to Belinda's for lunch tomorrow. It should be at Helena's, of course, but she's away."

"No, Mum, not this week. I've got something fixed."

"What! You're not coming?"

"Helena's not coming either."

"Helena is on holiday! *You* aren't on holiday."

But up to now, it's felt as if I am.

*   *   *

41

At last, flesh and blood could bear no more and Julia lost her temper, precipitating the row she'd tried so hard to avoid. It was a humdinger. Bernice came home in time to hear the last screaming insults from both sides as a short, plump woman in a flowered two-piece shouted over her shoulder on the way to the front door.

"Don't ever come to me for help again, Julia, because as far as I'm concerned you've shut yourself off from the family for good! After all I've done for you! If your father knew about it! And it's not as if you didn't know better, you've been surrounded by the very best from the moment you were born. And you cast it all aside to live in a dump like this!"

Julia followed her out into the hall, eyes closed, hands over ears, quite unaware of her embarrassed flatmate standing on the front steps.

"Go away!" she screamed. "Just go away!" She might have been poor Joe Rillington. Still with eyes closed, she turned and went back into the flat.

The stunned and totally ignored Bernice watched the car drive off towards Hackney Wick and that gateway to the salubrious south, the Blackwall Tunnel. She shut the door. Julia was in the kitchen.

"What happened?" Bernice asked in a hushed voice.

"Oh, hello. Don't ask," said Julia, back turned, blowing her nose.

"I never realised it would cause such a *row*. I'm so sorry, Jule."

"Oh, it's not really the flat," said Julia, washing the tears of rage from her face under the kitchen tap. "She's been rowing at me for most of my life. Anything'll do. If she hadn't been moaning about my moving out of home it would have been because I was still in it. Reason and consistency have never been my mother's strong points."

"How awful for you!" Bernice unloaded the weekend shopping onto the table very quietly, so as not to add to Julia's distress.

42

"Where's Tom?" Julia tried to get back to normal.

"Getting some beer. We're going on the river. Why don't you come, it'll cheer you up? I think Jim's coming, and one or two others."

"No thanks. I'm not fit to be with at the moment."

Once they'd gone she had another long, agonised cry, then flung herself into violent activity, cleaning her new nest. The pale bedroom dust rose and invaded her eyes, nose and throat.

She pushed up the window sash and the noise roared in at her. Along the concrete parapet slid the roofs of cars and the cabs and bodies of lorries, and above them the tower blocks hung in the invisible fumes. She shook out the duster, her contribution to pollution a drop in the ocean compared with such professionals.

She pulled out the bed and dusted the box. Bernice had opened it to show her the horrors inside, so all that white fluff must have accumulated since then. ("Julia isn't such a useful little housewife as her sisters, I'm afraid.")

The hoover roared around the floor, banging against legs and skirtings and flaking off a piece of paint. The layers were brown, brown, cream and white, the final skin of Bernicean cheerfulness bedded on conventional gloom.

She pushed the box back, its cardboard flaps dancing up and down like a fan. She supposed she ought to clean behind the old mattress. She certainly should, she discovered. It would have been used by the old woman or her son, and the dust which clung to it had to contain particles of their skin. What an appalling thought – every single person leaving bits of their bodies wherever they went, perhaps to remain there for years, or decades or even centuries. She slammed the mattress down onto the tiles and sucked the dust into submission with the vacuum cleaner.

Beyond that locked basement door, poor Mr Rillington suffered years of paranoid delusions and died all alone. I'll probably end up on my own, too, with nephews and nieces paying me duty calls once a year, bearing pot plants which will die within weeks of being left in my care, and bright smiles which will die as soon as my front door is closed.

This was no way to spend a sunny Saturday afternoon. Why wasn't she out on the river with a boyfriend, like Bernice?

'You could have come, Jule,' Bernice's voice said reproachfully in her head.

But I don't fancy Jim, she argued, there was no spark there, nothing which made me want to spend even five minutes in his company, let alone a day.

It doesn't always have to be It, Jule, it was only a nice day out.

Yes, I know, but supposing he got the wrong idea and made a pass, and I had to say no, sorry, or even worse, no, I don't, actually – though that's a lot easier to say than it used to be; there's a sensible excuse for celibacy these days, it doesn't have to mean prudery or cowardice. But to be honest, I'm just no good at this dating business, and I don't think I even want the trouble of bothering at the moment. Certainly not after my last fiasco.

The guilt which Mrs Nutley invariably brought with her still sat on her shoulder, pointing out her inadequacies. I've no reason to feel guilty, it's my life and I'm doing nothing I haven't every right to do at my age. I will not be blackmailed any more. I'll get myself something special to eat and watch a video. I am going to have a nice, self-indulgent time.

The cat was mewing on the other side of the partition; she must have shut it in when her mother left. She went through the flat into the hall and opened the front door.

"Bubastis, Bubastis, come on, puss, out you go."

I'll go out again, too. I'll have another walk in the park. Or I could go up to Oxford Street.

"Bubastis! Bubastis!"

Or I could watch a film on television, unless it's all sport. I don't know what I want to do, really. To be honest with myself, I'm feeling a bit lonely. I've been looking forward to freedom and solitude nearly all my life, and now I've got it—

The cat brushed past her legs as it left the house. Her eyes fell from the shining, inviting park to watch it as it made its exit.

Only nothing went down the steps at all.

Five

"D id you have a good day, Jule?" asked Bernice. Her face was red. The sun and wind had imprinted the shape of her teeshirt on her body, and its outlines were revealed at neck and shoulder every time she moved. On Tom the lines were drawn at waist and mid-thigh, and there was a strong smell of sun-screen lotion about both of them.

"Yes, thanks." Julia's long, angular body was curled up in a chair by the open bay window, and she was reading one of the indispensably funny Christmas books. The evening sun lit up her hair and reddened her right cheek. The left remained pale, a fact which would have told an observant detective that she had been there for a long time.

"We went down to the Thames Barrier and then we went to Greenwich." Bernice disappeared behind the curtain but went on talking. "It's the most beautiful view from the top." Thudding and rustling accompanied the dumping of the picnic remains on the table. "We could go over there after work one day. How about that, Jule? Shall we?" The kettle was filled. "You want tea, Tom?"

"Got a beer?"

He was sitting back on the settee with his knees wide apart. "Poor old Jim was pretty disappointed you didn't turn up."

"I never said I would turn up," said Julia, glancing up from her book. She wished he was wearing more. She looked down again as if she couldn't wait to find out what happened next to the famous TV personality during her early years; ('When I crawled miserably back to my humble desk I discovered to my deepest chagrin that I hadn't a single bloody paper clip left. The big boss was already baring his pointed fangs ready to take a large bite out of my *derrière*, so in a state of blind panic I snatched a safety-pin from my handbag and speared my painfully-typed pages together. He grabbed them from my trembling hands, glared like a foul-tempered traffic warden who had eaten something which didn't agree with him and gave them to the bishop. Unfortunately, I had omitted to notice that on the fourth page I had substituted an F for a D, with the result that the passage read—')

"What did you do with yourself?"

"I went to Oxford Street. The fumes were awful." ·

"You'd have been better off on the river, then."

Julia pulled her hair round to shut him off.

"Have you been cleaning, Jule?"

"Just my room and the bit outside."

"Thought so, the broom's on the lobby floor."

"Oh sorry, Bernice, I forget to put it away."

"That's all right," said Bernice, beaming round the curtain. "Did you have a nice time shopping?"

"Yes," said Julia. ('When I crawled miserably—')

She'd been reading the same page ever since she got home. She'd been all right while she was out, fairly all right, anyway, because the irrationality of the incident shrank considerably when surrounded by thousands of sweltering shoppers and tourists in the last word on silly clothes. She looked at Tom's brilliantly patterned knee-length shorts, which bore the comic-strip word 'Powwww!!!' across the front. If, she told herself, there are people in the world happy to wear clothes as blatantly awful as that, there can be no such thing as invisible cats. At that moment, it seemed like logic. She realised Tom was still looking at her and quickly removed her eyes from his shorts to the page.

"What are you reading, Jule?" asked Bernice, dumping a mug beside her. "Oh, that. It's so funny, isn't it? Have you read the bit where she was eating curry in a posh restaurant and wanted to wipe her nose and pulled her spare panties out of her handbag instead? I nearly died. Did you buy anything?"

"An electric fan."

"What a brilliant idea!"

Julia picked up the mug, took it into the hall, opened the front door and stood at the top of the steps. The grumble and whine of the motorway soared over the roof and away across the grass ahead.

The steps went straight down and out into the street. It might have leapt over the side without touching the steps at all, and there was plenty of rubbish to hide in, but she definitely hadn't seen it go out of the door.

She had called Bubastis, felt him brush past her legs, then nothing. He might have changed his mind and gone back upstairs, but if so he certainly moved fast.

They sat in the open bay window, drinking beer and tea and eating crisps and biscuits. Then as the westering sun turned the room into an oven they moved out onto the steps, in traditionally relaxed bed-sit city-dweller style. Apart from the absence of drugs, it fulfilled all Mrs Nutley's worst nightmares. Through the open window of the next door basement someone was singing about peace and love. Farther down the road a teenager was repairing and occasionally revving a motor cycle, to the sound of loud music. Someone somewhere was burning a barbecue. In the other direction the iron curtain had been lifted in one of the new flats, and the shrill chatter of a dinner party could be heard going on inside.

"It's stifling," complained Bernice. "Shouldn't be surprised if there was a storm."

"Heard any more about Mr Rillington?" asked Tom.

"No."

"Wonder who'll move in."

"Someone who doesn't know about the smell and the fumigation and the cleaning up," said Julia, gazing into the distance. I wonder where that cat went.

"We could plant flowers, now," said Bernice brightly.

"They'd only get nicked," said Tom. There was a touch of Nutley there.

"What do you think the park was like when these houses were built?" Julia asked.

"Doubt if it was ever Kensington Gardens," said Tom, stretched out along the slope of the handrail.

"Wonder who lived here?" mused Bernice, holding his hand to her cheek.

"Jack the Ripper," he said.

An amorphic white something leapt out of the dark front garden and onto Julia's lap, purring and paddling its prickly feet. She squealed in terror.

"Hello, darling," crooned Bernice reaching out to stroke it. "Whose lovely pussy are you, then?"

"He belongs to the squatters next door. I thought he was Mr Rillington's." Julia's voice sounded strange. Tom turned his head and looked at her.

"He didn't have animals, except for the budgie. Fancy not wanting a beautiful, handsome pussy like – ouch!"

Bubastis departed for his night's hunting.

"When's the old boy's funeral?" asked Tom, still staring at Julia.

"When they've found his family, I suppose."

"Suppose he hasn't got one? I suppose they'll shove him in with a crowd of people he never met in his life."

"Oh, I do hope not," said Bernice, sounding as if she were about to cry. "Perhaps we could take up a collection or something along the road—"

"Don't be daft, woman," Tom said with affectionate exasperation, "most of them never even exchanged a word with him, and the ones who did didn't like him. And do you know how much it would have to be? When my mad Great Auntie Bunty died, the family had to fork out a thousand quid, and that was cheap."

"Was she really mad?" asked Julia, her voice shaky.

"Well, I thought so; it was the only excuse for the way she carried on. Still, every family's got a mad one. Wonder which family's got Mr Rillington?"

* * *

There wasn't a storm, but the air remained hot, humid and oppressive all night and got even worse as the rising sun climbed across the flyover and into Julia's bedroom. She tried having the window open, but the noise defeated her. The traffic roared on, not continuously, but whizz, whizz, ten seconds silence, approaching and increasing roar, decreasing roar interrupted by a line of whizzes, two seconds near-silence, approaching roar – it's Sunday, for God's sake! Where are you all going at such a lick at six o'clock on a Sunday morning?

The fan hummed. She'd hardly slept at all. She was hot, sticky and bad-tempered and she'd probably got bags under her eyes. And she'd been so busy yesterday that she should have gone out like a light.

There are no invisible cats. Cats move very fast and very quietly, that's all. I ought to be able to lie in on a Sunday, surely. I do, I mean, did at home, I mean in Worcester Park. That isn't home any more, this is, and I'm not going back.

If only she'd brought a glass of water in with her last night. Supposing she opened the kitchen door and walked in on the soundtrack from a sex video? Sex was all right when you were doing it yourself, but when it was other people it was not only embarrassing, but plain ridiculous. Oh, I do want a drink.

In the distance, she heard footsteps tapping across the hall tiles. Thank goodness.

She pulled on her dressing-gown, tiptoed into the kitchen, where last night's washing-up basked in the morning sun, poured herself a glass of water and returned to her room.

She drew back the sheets of sunflowers. Sunbeams shone between the grubby tower blocks like searchlights. An immense Danish juggernaut skimmed along above the parapet. Can't you think of something better to do with a beautiful Sunday? Wonder how long Tom's going to be in the bathroom? She reached for the TV personality's bestseller.

'So His Grace stared at my ill-typed pages, glared at me over his pince-nez, woffled his moustache and—' For heaven's sake, when is this you're writing about? You're not forty yet. '"Miss Cadwallader," he grated through clenched, gold-filled teeth, obviously about to eat me alive for his episcopal breakfast—' Get real, Miss Booboo Cadwallader, formerly Annie Bugg.

She slapped the book shut. There are no invisible cats in the real world.

The door opened.

"Jule, I've brought you some tea."

"Oh thanks. Is Tom still in the bathroom?"

"No, he's asleep."

If she'd known it was Bernice up there, she needn't have been so coy about waiting. When she got back to her room, Bernice was looking out of the window, sipping from her own mug. "Goodness, that poor garden."

"Bernice, it was you who went up to the bathroom earlier, wasn't it? I heard footsteps out in the hall."

"No. Probably that cat got in again."

"In shoes?"

"Shoes?"

"Yes, they clicked quite loudly on the tiles."

Bernice shook her head and smiled. "Cats have claws, Jule, and a big one like Bubastis must have big claws."

"It sounded more like a Great Dane with hardpad," Julia insisted, feeling panicky. "Anyway, I didn't see Bubastis when I went out there."

"Well, you *don't* see cats, do you, not if they don't want you to. What are you going to do today, Jule? We thought we'd play tennis in the park. If you want to come too, we could rustle up a fourth, though I know Jim can't make it."

"Oh! Yes, I think I'd like that," said Julia, brightening. No Jim, eh? What a nice, constructive thing to do with a summer Sunday. Better than a Nutley Sunday lunch.

And there were no ghost cats in the park.

Well away from the flyover, the Victoria Park tennis courts might as well have been in Worcester Park, or any other much sought after middle-class suburb. The flower-beds were yellow and white with narcissi, children played, some of them very

nicely, old people sat, dogs were walked, lovers were all over
each other. Beyond the railings, new housing and old looked
through fresh greenery at the young enjoying themselves, like
chaperons around the edge of a Victorian dance floor.

It was one of the nicest days Julia had ever spent in her
life. No one bothered her. No one told her what to do. No one
checked her behaviour against a list of rules and regulations.
No one warned of consequences. No one gave a damn what
she did or said, and not just because they'd been drinking,
but because they weren't the sort of people who considered it
their place to criticise others. This was how Sundays should
be; relaxation in the company of people you liked, not the
polite endurance of the same old faces in the same old places,
rounded up by order week after week to sit at the same old
tables with nothing left to say to each other.

The rustled-up fourth was a young man called Chris who
showed no sign of personal insecurity in the shape of coming
on too fast, and they all finished up in the garden of the
Victorian pub at Queen's Gate.

Julia carefully angled herself so that the giant star blasting
through the hole in the ozone layer wouldn't give her much
more than a kiss.

"If skin cancer doesn't get you, something else will," Tom
pointed out.

But I wasn't brought up with that sort of philosophy. The
avoidance of danger was drummed into us from day one. If
it wasn't safe, avoid it, if it wasn't nice, ignore it. And one of
the things we were supposed to avoid and ignore was places
like Hackney and people like Tom.

They left Chris to prepare for early rising and wandered back
through the park. Their shadows stretched before them as if
they were eager to reach Hackney Wick, with its tower blocks
and its motorway and its railway, canal and factories. Ahead,
the four dilapidated houses of Ermintrude Villas stood between
spruce conversions like paupers between uniformed beadles.

They drifted into the living room, which was stuffy with
baked air, and Tom pushed up the sash. Bernice sat down on a

floor cushion with a happy sigh and gathered the nearest teddy into her arms.

Julia took off her trainers and socks and swung her feet up onto the settee. She leant forward to move a dented cushion to one side, but before her hand touched it the centre of the dent rose and the cushion rocked, slipped and fell to the floor. Something soft and tickly drew itself across the soles of her bare feet as it departed.

Julia gave a shrill scream of alarm, drew her feet in against her body and rubbed the soles frantically to get rid of the sensation.

Tom lost his balance on the window-sill. Bernice sat bolt upright and dropped her teddy.

Julia rushed away from the settee and into the bay. Outside, the restlessness of city night hummed in the twilight like a generator. Tom looked at her with outraged reproach.

"Would you mind giving me fair warning before you do that again? I nearly went out of the window."

"Sorry," she said, abjectly apologetic. "I thought I felt something." An invisible cat, for heaven's sake. A ghost cat. The ghost cat of Victoria Park.

She remembered the distant clicking across the hall tiles. If that was a cat it must be the size of a puma. The ghost puma of Hackney; how's that for a new urban legend? Her knees were trembling. She sat down on the window-sill. The other two stared at her.

"Whatever was it, Jule?" whispered Bernice.

Julia very nearly told them, but stopped herself in time; it was too shaming. Anyway, if you had problems, or worries, or fears, no one really wanted to hear about it. ("Don't make a fuss, Julia, pull yourself together.")

"Nothing. I'm all right," she insisted.

Tom's expression was incredulous.

The fan whirred on top of the overmantel, in the nearest thing to darkness the flyover permitted. She turned restlessly. I must to get to sleep, I've got to get up in the morning.

The air was swept around the closed, stuffy room. She could see the reflection of passing headlights dancing on the blades as the fan turned left and right.

I'll have to try and read myself to sleep. She turned on the bedside light and picked up *Just for the Hell of It* by Booboo Parabola, or whatever her name was. No, not tonight, I need calming, not annoying.

The fan turned and looked at the window, lifting the curtain edge curiously. It jerked and swung round, breathed straight at Julia, turned again to stare with interest at the door, as if expecting someone to come in. Back to the window. Round it came again—

I don't see how it could possibly be a ghost – no, don't think about it now. That's a really weird wardrobe; all those swirly, distorted tulips. They look like the sort of flowers you'd see under the influence of drugs. I really like the sunflowers, though. Did I hear something out in the lobby?

The room looked at her. The overmantel mirror trembled very slightly with the movement of the fan above, and the wire dangling before it had a constant, infinitely small vibration along its striped, woven length. The fan reached the end of its swing and jerked round to push more air in her direction. It was a busy little soul. She was glad of its activity and company; if there was stillness the power of the house might force its presence upon her.

It wasn't just that the house was old. No, it really wasn't that. Was it?

She experienced a sudden, agonised homesickness for 1930s Tudor.

Six

Tom departed early, before breakfast.

Julia was very quiet over hers. Bernice chattered away between her orange juice, yoghurt, honey and scraped toast. They emerged from the house into another still, fine day.

Bubastis was sitting on the garden wall, an expression of intolerable smugness gathered together into the centre of his fluffy head. Bernice stopped and attempted to pet him. He put up with it for a few seconds, then left.

"I *love* cats," said Bernice with the yearning tone of voice which would have gone better with 'I *love* Tom.' "It would be nice to have one of our own, don't you think, Jule? Trouble is, who'd keep it company all day? It would get so lonely, poor thing."

"We had one once and I really think it hated us all. The more you tried to be kind to it, the more you could see the sheer contempt in its eyes."

"Goodness," said Bernice, wide-eyed. "Whatever had you done to it?"

"We hadn't done anything to it," said Julia. "That was what got me down. It had just decided from the moment it came in the door that it was too good for us."

Bernice shook her head knowingly. "You just weren't cat people, that was the trouble. They can tell. If you *are* a cat person they come straight up to you and give you all their affection." Julia shuddered as if an invisible creature had walked over her grave.

The girls walked up the road, turned left into the rubbish-strewn piece of nothing which led under a disused railway line, and climbed the concrete slopes of the foot-bridge. It was a strange, surreal, alienated place. High on its long gallery, they passed over the concrete bearpit where metal predators rushed and howled. Farther along, the disused railway crossed on its own rusty, overgrown bridge to meet a derelict signal box. Among the warehouses and car workshops ahead, the North London Railway waited on its dirty brick viaduct.

Bernice looked as if she was struggling with a difficult decision. She finally made it.

"Have you spoken to your mother again, Jule?"

"No."

"Well, it's probably better to wait a bit," she agreed. "She'll come round, I expect. You've just got to give her time. It must be painful for her to have the last bird fly the nest."

"Yes," said Julia. After all, a cat might get it.

They descended into the chopped-off end of an executed road. Again, it was a strange place, out of time and not quite sure of its identity. Over there, the high-rise blocks of the Trowbridge Estate, here, a flock of finches twittering among rampant shrubs and weeds beneath the concrete stilts.

"Oh isn't that beautiful?" enthused Bernice.

Mind the cat, birdies.

"Good-morning, Jones, Brown and Wilkinson. Oh yes, I'll pass you over to her."

Bernice smiled and indicated that Julia should take the receiver. Julia's stomach lurched. This was no place to have a row with your mother.

A messenger tramped in wearing full leathers and helmet, bearing an A4 envelope decked with striped tape. He was closely followed by a pair of young men as impeccably groomed as Mormons.

Julia picked up the phone, cooed, "I won't keep you a moment, madam," cut her caller off from the human voice and connected her with Greensleeves on synthesizer. Two minutes later—

"Hello?"

"Whose idea was that stupid tape you played at me?" asked Helena.

"Oh, hello, sorry about that. It's supposed to keep you soothed and entertained whilst waiting."

"Whatever made them think it would? Look, you are coming tomorrow, aren't you?"

"Well, I don't think—"

"But you must! She'll never forgive you if you don't."

"Have you spoken to her?" asked Julia apprehensively, twisting hair round her fingers.

"Of course I have, she was straight on the phone as soon as I got home. I didn't have to say a word for ten minutes. How was it?"

"Absolutely awful. She said I'd caused Dad's death." Tears threatened.

"Oh, you know mother – she doesn't really mean it."

"That's no excuse. If she doesn't mean it, it's even worse to say it. It's hurting people for no reason at all."

Bernice, who was on the other line, mouthed "German" at her and proffered the receiver.

"Now you are coming, aren't you, Julia? Promise?"

"All right, but don't blame me if the meeting's wrecked," said Julia wearily and changed phones.

Walking west over the concrete foot-bridge, with the sun pounding straight down the park to hit them in the face, Julia narrowed her eyes and looked at the houses perched above the deep excavation of the motorway. You probably wouldn't hear the traffic so much here. It was further along, where the road sloped up and the houses down, that it became unbearable. She could just see the backs of the neglected Ermintrude Villas, with several broken windows and at least one shattered roof. Why didn't the owner do something to halt the deterioration of his investment?

"Is the lease due to run out on our house soon?" she asked Bernice as they turned the corner and walked down beside the glorious green park.

"I don't know," said Bernice, looking puzzled. "I'm only on a short tenancy."

"It rather looks as if it might be soon, don't you think?" said Julia as they approached home. "Whoever owns these must have redevelopment plans already on his desk."

Bernice stared at the cracked frontages as if she'd never noticed them before. "Oh look, there are the Grosvenors. Goodness, don't they look excited?" she added as Harry danced across the road and shadow-boxed a lamp post. "Hello," she called as they came within talking distance. "Have you had a good day?"

"Have we had a good day!" Harry asked Ermintrude Villas. "Have we had a good day!" he asked the park in ecstasy. "Show 'em, Win. Go on, just show 'em." He danced along the broken path and up the steps, turning to serenade Hackney with the first two lines of 'The Sunshine of Your Smile'. He was remarkably light on his feet for a man his size.

"Come on up, loves," said Win, unlocking the front door and trampling over circulars and second post. "He's just got to share this with someone quick, or he'll burst."

The girls were nearly carried bodily up the stairs and deposited on armchairs in the front room. As they invaded its solitude, the startled budgerigar shuffled down its perch and went very thin so that they couldn't see it.

Win could be heard plugging in the kettle, then she came rushing back to sit with Harry on the settee and produce a piece of paper from a Public Record Office carrier bag. "Now!" she said. "Tell 'em, Harry."

Harry took it from her hands, held it before the girls' eyes and said with touching pride, "Look at that."

They couldn't make head nor tail of it. It was an A3 photostat of a form; a mixture of official print and scrawled handwriting.

"It's the Census," Harry explained with glee. "If you look up here at the top, you'll see that it's in the parish of St George, Hanover Square, and over here on the left it says Park Street. And all these names are people that was living there in 1841, and right down here near the bottom of the page is Mary Jane Hoskins, sixteen years old, parlour-maid. I been looking for her for months. And you know who she is?" He paused, grinning and rubbing his hands together. Win sat smiling with crossed arms.

"Course they don't, get on with it."

"That girl was the mother of my great-grandfather, William Robert Grosvenor. I never could find her first marriage or his birth certificate or his christening, and she was a widow by 1842 – at least, that's what she *said*," he said with great meaning. "That's when she married a horsehair man called Albert Izzard and went to live in Bethnal Green. She had loads more children but she never changed the name of her eldest; he was always William Robert Grosvenor born Middlesex."

"Well!" said Bernice in an interested voice.

"Then I found out she had an unmarried sister called Hoskins – she was staying with them in 1861, you see, so I worked through all the Hoskinses in the 1851 name index; that took a while, I can tell you, but no joy. Then I looked for my great-grandad's birth certificate under Hoskins and found it, but he was born at Queen Charlotte's in Marylebone Road and there was no father mentioned, which meant he was illegitimate."

"Oh dear," said Bernice, with a sympathetic giggle. "Never mind, it's a long time ago, isn't it?"

"That don't bother us none, love," Win broke in with near-scorn. "Most of the noble houses of England was founded by bastards, and I ain't talking about their characters, neither."

"But I remembered my grandad saying she was in good service," Harry continued eagerly, "so I started looking through all the streets where the nobs lived, and today I found her at last in Park Street, in the house of a banker. And whose house was just round the corner? Go on, ask me! The Marquis of Westminster's!" he announced in triumph, without waiting for the question.

"There!" nodded Win, "Makes you think, don't it?"

"You mean," said Julia very cautiously, not sure if they were serious, "that he might have nipped down the street and made love to Mary Jane?"

"Well, not necessarily His Nibs hisself," admitted Harry, fully accepting the unlikelihood of such a scenario, "but he had lots of family, didn't he? Must have been plenty of randy young Grosvenors coming and going and perhaps visiting the banker over the way, and one of 'em might have noticed this pretty young maid bringing round the tea and cucumber sandwiches and thought 'I'll have a bit of that'. It happened all the time."

Harry danced to the family tree on the wall and gave it an affectionate punch.

"Excuse him leaping about, loves," said Win, "but it's a bit like finding the holy grail, this, you know. Harry, come and fetch in the biscuits – I don't see why you shouldn't have a treat today."

"They're really into it, aren't they?" whispered Bernice. "Did you understand all that? What's a horsehair man?"

"Don't know," said Julia. "It sounds like The Wizard of Oz. Just look at that! I mean, I haven't the slightest idea who my great-grandparents were, and I never met my mother's parents."

Above the sideboard, the lines of descent of the Grosvenors and the Smarts zigzagged up and down the family tree; along branches bearing strings of long-dead brothers and sisters, reaching further to long-lost cousins with different names, travelling way out to the most distant twigs, where all information bore the suspicious stigma of the question mark.

"I didn't know any of my grandparents," said Bernice. "I've got a few great-aunts and uncles, but I don't know what they did when they were young. It's so sad, isn't it, the way people get completely forgotten, even by their descendants. It's as if they'd never been alive at—"

"Go away! Go away!" roared Mr Rillington. His voice was angry and panicky and strangely hoarse.

Julia's hands shot out and grabbed Bernice's. They sat as

rigid as statues, staring into each other's eyes, breathing fast with their mouths open.

"I know you're there! Go away! Go away!"

Not from down in the basement. The voice was near.

Bernice's contact lenses swam in tears, and her breath smelt of peppermint.

"Go away! Go away! I can see you! I know you! Go away! I can see you! Go away!"

They crumpled together in a heap as the bird rang his bell for an encore.

"Oh," panted Bernice, still clinging to Julia, "that was *awful*! I nearly died of fright."

"I think I have died of fright," said Julia, barely able to speak. Her heart was beating so hard, and in such a misplaced position, that she felt quite ill, in fact, she realised with sudden panic, extremely ill; she didn't know whether she was going to choke, vomit, faint or go into a fit.

The strongest possibility seemed to be the second. She fled along the landing and shut herself in the bathroom, only just flinging herself down in time before the crazed lavatory bowl.

Once the worst of her misery was over, she leant carefully back against the wall with eyes closed, and bent legs across the black and white checked linoleum. The room was too narrow to straighten them. She could have eased herself a little more by putting her feet under the bath, but it was very difficult to get any sort of cleaning implement under it, and who knew what mouldy soap scum, lively silverfish and lost teeth lay between its clawed feet.

All I want now to make my joy complete is – no, don't even think of it.

She opened her eyes, trying to judge whether her body could be trusted to return to decent continence. It still had an uneasy hint of movement about it; queasy stomach, thudding heart, light, swimming head. She fixed her gaze on the crazed tiles ahead. Breathe deeply. It's all over. It was a mistake, there was nothing to be afraid of at all. Just a budgerigar. Not even a non-existent cat, just a live budgie.

How still rooms were, especially old rooms. How they watched you.

She felt six years old and about to face the adult world again after the shame of digestive disaster. ("Oh there she is, poor little mite! Are you better, Julia? Did you have a tummy-ache, then?")

Nothing around her moved, the room just sat there, waiting. It was its very stillness which seemed to make it alive. It watched her with its door and its window, with the frosted fanlight onto the landing and the tall, corroded, brass taps.

She looked up at the shadeless light bulb and the window with patterned paper stuck over the bottom sash. Oh, the deep sadness of neglected houses. The howling melancholy of cracked walls and rotten window frames, of the day-before-yesterday's up-to-date. It was a *horrible* room.

There was a light knock on the door.

"Jule? You all right, Jule?"

She scrambled to her feet, not wanting to look at the bathroom any more, not to be seen by it, and above all not to feel it. She struggled with the bolt which had been painted too thickly to open or close with considerate midnight discretion, and emerged, steeling herself for Bernice's well-meant sympathy.

"I'm all right," she said hastily, "it was nothing. *Honestly*," she insisted as Bernice showed signs of being about to put her arm around her.

They went back to the front room. The tea tray was on the table, and a plate of custard creams and digestives stood beside it. Next door in the kitchen, Win sounded as if she was telling Harry off, though she probably wasn't. She had that sort of voice. The birdcage was swinging backwards and forwards.

"My goodness, you're lively, today, aren't you, darling?" said Bernice. "You *are* feeling better up here in the light! Oh!"

What's the matter?" asked Julia, who was studying the family tree again. Gosh, fancy having a distant cousin who was hanged!

"Jule, I think he's dead!" She sped from the room, crying the bad news.

Julia hurried over. As she viewed the minute corpse the cage swung again, and then she was struck full in the chest by the pinpricks of invisible claws.

With a horrified intake of breath she fled to the bay window and only stopped herself from leaping out by gripping the curtains. I'm going mad. My imagination's getting out of control like it did when I was little.

Nonsense, Julia, don't tell such silly lies. You ought to be ashamed of yourself.

"I'm not telling lies," she insisted tearfully, "it happened. I felt it."

You felt nothing of the kind. Don't ever say things like that again, I don't want to hear them.

So bury it. Keep it secret. Live with the burden of knowing that you are mad and get the horrors, nightmares which wake you screaming, irrational dread which says there are monsters in the garage and demons in the cupboard under the stairs, and that sometimes you hear things. Keep the secret because it is so shameful that no one wants to know.

Seven

S o she still didn't tell them. They were too busy exclaiming about the poor bird to notice that she was looking even more ill than before. Tea and biscuits helped, and provided an excuse for not trying to talk.

During the evening, Bernice cried quite a lot about the budgie, but came to believe it had flown straight to Mr Rillington and that they were happily reunited. She cooked at the same time, eventually producing beans on toast, solid fried eggs and strawberry yoghurts.

Julia sat pulling obsessively at her shiny hair, and gazing at the turned-down but not turned-off television, wondering whether to tell her. Would putting it into spoken words make her feel better or worse? She didn't know Bernice's views on the afterlife – apart, that was, from her beliefs in a place where grumpy old men and their budgies could take happy flight together.

She shivered and worried about it most of the night, kept the bedding tucked round her in spite of the heat, watched for the denting of her bedding, waited for the soft caress of fur or the sharp stab of claws and listened for the clicking footsteps in the hall. She must find somewhere else; this was only supposed to be temporary anyway. Her stomach turned over at the prospect of another plunge into the unknown so soon, and without even a companion.

Next morning, she, Win and Harry were pressed into service as mutes, and Bernice led the funeral party through the squatters' home and over the wall, with a gold-ribboned shoebox balanced in her hands.

"I thought we'd put him here," she said, attacking the earth at the foot of the fence with Mr Rillington's trowel, borrowed from the greenhouse. "Oh, sorry, dear." She patted the passion-flower's root back into the earth and moved a couple of feet along.

Once the unfortunate bird was laid in the dusty soil and marked with a temporary cardboard tombstone reminiscent of a seed packet, the mourners climbed back and recessed through Luke and Fern's domain.

Win and Harry hurried off to find out how many randy young Grosvenors were alive and kicking in 1841, by means of Burke's Peerage. The girls made for the foot-bridge, Bernice openly expressing an almost pleasant tristesse, Julia painfully torn between two things to be apprehensive about; the impending meeting and the dead cat.

Bubastis sat on the wall and watched them all go.

I should be looking round for another flat by now anyway, I'm taking advantage of Bernice, occupying her bedroom. Of course, it doesn't have a double bed, so she might not want to move back. I wonder why it's never gone for her, when she's what she calls a cat person; you'd think it would have gone straight for her. Unless it wasn't there before. Why should it turn up now? What's happened?

Well, Mr Rillington's died, but he didn't have any animals. Perhaps he did once. Perhaps it's an ex-pet of his who's come looking for him and found him gone.

No, if he's dead the cat wouldn't need to come looking for him. Perhaps he'll turn up next. Perhaps when we go home we'll hear him shouting 'Go away', and this time it won't be the budgie. I'll have to move.

That evening, Julia obeyed the call of family duty with extreme reluctance. The constituency was on the other side of the park, in an area even less like suburban Surrey but at least conveniently near a tube station.

Once upon a time, such a meeting would have taken place in a Gothic mission hall built of corrugated iron. There would have been an ancient iron stove in one corner, a harmonium in the other, exhortations to lay the burdens of poverty, unemployment, sickness and despair upon the Lord, a haze of smoke and, unless free refreshments were provided, a thin turn-out. The only ingredient still present was the last, as the tea, coffee and biscuits were for sale in aid of party funds. The free hand-out was dead.

The battered concrete and glass hall of the Community Centre was sprinkled with about forty voters, some of whom looked uncomfortably far to the right of the party and about to slip off the end into the area beyond the political pale. Even the smoke had gone, as No Smoking notices were in evidence, one of them amended to forbid a different indulgence.

Mrs Nutley was in full plumage and her obtrusive, clumsy bustling drew all eyes. Julia knew that her behaviour was undoubtedly going to cause acute embarrassment to her family, offence to most of the rest of the audience, and dangerous provocation to the shaven-headed, boots-on-seats contingent at the back. She winced as her mother settled herself down in the centre of the front row, with unnecessary moving of chairs and a loud remark about what John Major had said to Philip. The elderly couple at the end of the row stared at them all like basilisks. I wish I were dead, thought Julia.

All four daughters were there, only Julia not resembling a Mrs Nutley clone, and also Helena's children, dressed up to the nines and in danger of being targets for every red-blooded street kid between the hall and the car park.

Helena's appearance was a work of art. Her pretty, peaches-and-cream face and well-cut brown hair were absolutely right with her good but understated clothes. Her round green hat was taste epitomised. Her tights were innocent of snags, her low-heeled courts were saved from too bald a statement by gilt twiddly-bits at the front, and a long blue and green chiffon scarf trailed down the front of her pale blue crêpe tent, like the fortuitous pieces of drapery which hide anatomical embarrassment in classical paintings.

Rowena and Belinda, who had left husbands baby-sitting,

managed a few discreet, supportive words with Julia while their mother's attention was otherwise occupied. They were incredulous at her daring and largely sympathetic, but Julia wouldn't bet on that sympathy being available under all circumstances, such as the regular summons to Sunday lunch. There was something other-worldly about the older Nutley girls, a breath of the past, before the last vestiges of fifties prissiness went down under the wave of the permissive society. They were too tidy, too nice, the sort of women who surface giving unquestioning support to caught-out public men.

The platform party consisted of Philip, Helena, the local Conservative agent and a very junior minister who was there to persuade the voters that the Government not only cared about their unwinnable constituency, but believed it was not unwinnable at all. He very nearly said so, but wrapped it up in enough verbiage to deny the media a useful quote after the inevitable defeat. Then the future candidate took possession of the laminated lectern with the gold decal springing off.

From then on, Julia shut off, rejecting the acute embarrassment she knew the speeches would cause her. It wasn't difficult; she had plenty of other things to think about. It wasn't a cosy cat. It scratched you. It frightened birds to death. Whose was it? Where was its owner? Walking about on the hall tiles? Applause broke into her worried thoughts and she joined in, smiling faintly at the bowing Philip.

The ordeal was not over after the question-answering (mostly about Europe, crime and immigration). The candidate's family were then expected to mingle with the voters and charm the pants off them. Julia stood stirring her tea in an invisible funk, smiling as if she were approachable and avoiding eye contact in a way that proved she wasn't. A brief glance up into the middle distance caught Mrs Nutley making for her through the scattered groups with someone tall, thin and familiar in tow. Oh really!

Her mother spoke to her for the first time that evening.

"Julia, you remember Brian. I'm sure you two have so much to talk about." The parcel delivered, she hurried off.

He had the grace to look embarrassed.

"Hello, how are you?"

"All right, thank you. So you're on the Council?"

"Yes. Sorry, Julia, this wasn't my idea."

"I'm sure it wasn't. No hard feelings."

"No. Thanks." He looked immensely relieved.

He drove her home. "Don't kid yourself, Mother," Julia said under her breath as Mrs Nutley waved them off.

Ermintrude Villas obviously shook Brian. He leant forward and looked up at the crumbling houses bathing in the street lights.

"Would you like me to see you in?" he asked.

"No, thanks, my flatmate's at home. Goodbye. Good luck with the cuts. Don't let them cap you out of existence."

He laughed uneasily and let in the clutch.

Suddenly alone in the night street, the nerves she had been holding down all evening burst out and became full-blown terror. Her hand was actually trembling as she turned the key in the front door. In the twilight of the hall it trembled even more. She could hear the television beyond the flat door, but couldn't find the keyhole. The metal tapped against the lock like a stutter.

Soft sound hissed in her ears as her heartbeat increased and the awakened adrenalin hurried blood along her arteries. It seemed as if it was outside her head instead of in it. Shhhh – like the swishing of waters, the insidious approach of the incoming tide slithering over flat sands. Shh, shh, shh, with the rhythm of the heart, the rhythm of movement, down, round, away—

Down the carpeted stairs, round the newel post, away along the tiled hall with a tap, tap, tap, through the partition into the invisible lobby.

The key slid home. As the flat door slammed behind her she gave a sob.

Bernice jumped round on the settee. "What's the matter?" she asked.

Julia stared, but couldn't speak.

"You look awful, Jule!" She got up in a hurry while Julia sat down with a thump, because her knees wouldn't hold her.

"I thought I heard a noise out in the hall and it gave me a bit of a start." That's right, good old English understatement.

"You mean someone's broken in?" whispered Bernice.

"No. It was a sort of swishing coming down the stairs, and then there was tapping like I heard before going along the tiles. It definitely wasn't a cat."

It's coming out, I didn't mean to let it come out, after all she's got to stay here. I'm being so selfish, I'll backtrack – her throat tightened, she felt tears in her eyes. Oh *damn*! She was crying.

"Oh Jule," Bernice was beside her, giving her a hug.

"I'm all right," Julia protested instantly, with the automism of long training. You were always all right and nothing was ever wrong. "You know what it sounded like?" she burst out, continuing to break all the rules. "Someone coming downstairs in a long skirt."

"You mean a ghost?"

Julia didn't like the word. She sobbed again. Bernice's eyes were wide open. Julia waited for her to join the panic.

"Well," Bernice said after a moment, breathing hard, "if you heard a long skirt, then it's not Mr Rillington. Perhaps it's the old woman who lived here before."

"Why should she come downstairs when she lived on this floor? And she didn't wear long skirts, did she?"

"Shouldn't think so; she can't have been *that* old."

Julia tried to calm down and mop up. She's taking this very well, she thought. Here's me going to pieces, and she's just sitting there all subdued and thoughtful. You'd expect emotional old Bernice to scream the place down but she's taking it better than controlled, inhibited old me.

But she hadn't actually experienced anything, she told herself, and she didn't know about the cat yet. What would she say when she heard about the cat?

How on earth were they going to cope with this?

For that evening, they coped with lots of coffee and talk

until midnight, regularly stopping and listening for sounds in the hall. Then Julia tried to cope by attempted rest in a fully lit room with a motorway outside. She almost liked the traffic tonight; it was real, crude and totally unethereal. Once the sun rose she slept for an hour; then it was breakfast, and unexpressed relief that only two of them appeared to be taking it.

So here I sit in my good navy business suit chosen by my mother (oh, the shame of it), with my well-cut hair and my face that gives nothing away, and I fold my hands on my shoulder bag and keep my feet and knees together so no one can see up my skirt, in the way my mother taught me. And I am a nice, good girl who goes through the working day conscientiously and without apparent effort.

But all you 'customers' of the Docklands Light Railway, sitting or standing with your newspapers and paperbacks and blank faces, you don't know that every time the phone rings or another stranger walks through the automatic doors, even now I worry that I won't be able to deal with them.

And on top of that, you've no idea what's happened to me now. You don't know that for the last few days I have been aware of a ghost cat in my home, and that last night I heard someone in a long dress come downstairs and walk past me with her heels clicking on the tiles.

Supposing I stood up and told you about it, would you say goodness, how interesting and ask for more? No, you'd think I was mad, dive deeper into your reading matter; and the train conductor would come down the car in her jaunty blue uniform and keep an eye on me until I got out.

Bernice looked at her across the aisle and pulled a face.

Julia sat still, composed, looked out of the window at the water beneath the rails and thought, my home is haunted.

It was like having an illness which didn't show. Outside you looked perfectly normal, inside something terrible was attacking your mind and emotions. Most of these people would be happy to go home that evening; she would be scared stiff.

* * *

They crossed the foot-bridge. It had been another hot day, followed by another beautiful evening. The smell of the invisible fumes rose around them. They coughed and sneezed.

"There was another pollution warning this morning," Bernice said. "Lucky we don't have asthma."

The backs of Ermintrude Villas were decrepit and sad, their foundations grimly gripping their truncated gardens above the abyss. From an open window came the gabble of a television.

There was the beautiful, sunlit park.

They walked up the steps, opened the front door and stood in the hall. Upstairs, the bathroom door was open and letting light onto the landing outside the Grosvenors' locked bedroom.

The front door closed. The worn brown carpet lay untrodden on the stairs, dust hung along sunbeams thrusting their way through the door. The painted partition looked more obtrusive than ever. The tiles needed sweeping.

They listened, but didn't tell themselves or each other that they did so. Again, Julia had a sense of the building waiting, watching; of controlled energy which might or might not be released. The stillness; silent motes drifting in the stuffy air, the sound of traffic outside.

The flat door opened and closed.

"Well, it seemed all right," said Bernice, with a relieved chirp in her voice. "I didn't hear anything, did you?"

"No," said Julia. She pushed up the sash.

The same cheerful, cluttered flat with the same lovely view. Get the television on and the kettle boiling, as quickly as possible.

Julia examined the cushions. That one? Something had imprinted itself upon it – just an elbow? Bernice did a quick tidy and plumped it up. Julia kept her eye on it. Bernice handed her a mug of tea.

The beautiful green, tree-filled park. The twittering of sparrows across the road. The vibrant hum of the city about and beyond. Homecoming cars passing, parking or taking cover behind the flats, where the expensive could find greater security.

"Are you quite sure, Jule?" asked Bernice, as they sipped tea and stared out of the window.

"Oh yes. Absolutely sure," said Julia briskly, not allowing herself to feel. Feelings must be screwed up tight and pushed into the cupboard where the unmanageable was kept. When the rule is that everything is always all right, there has to be a place to which the not-all-right can be consigned.

"Well, you seem to have got over the shock, anyway," said Bernice carefully. "Nothing upsets you for long, does it? Miss Standish told me once you reminded her of a madonna, with your long straight hair and calm face, sort of permanently tranquil."

Julia gave an incredulous laugh but let it pass.

"Look, Bernice, I expect you'll be wanting your room back soon, won't you. I mean, it's awfully nice of you to let me stay this long, but—"

"Oh no, I like you being here," protested Bernice immediately. "The only problem is knowing where to put everything. I suppose we could get another wardrobe and put it in the lobby."

"What about the old mattress?"

"Oh, there'll be room – it's not as if anyone uses the basement door."

"I hope not."

"And they wouldn't need doors if they did," said Bernice in a carefully matter-of-fact voice. "It's never happened before," she added, in a more uncertain tone.

"Hasn't it?"

"No. It looked a bit grim when I first came, of course, but once the painting was done and the really awful things shoved under the bed it was lovely. Just what I wanted."

"Even with the traffic?" Julia couldn't help asking.

"I never even noticed it; my family lives on the North Circular at Henley's Corner."

"Perhaps I've brought in a bad atmosphere."

72

"Oh don't be so silly, Jule! I just said, everyone says how calm and reassuring you are. I wouldn't mind being more like you, I'm so scatty."

"You don't want to wish anything of the sort. Bernice—" She paused, struggled with the mental cupboard door and then felt the words come tumbling out. "Look, there was something else – I haven't said anything about it before. There really is another cat around, but it's not a real one. I heard it miaowing and felt it brush past my legs, then I felt it on the settee, then up in Win and Harry's it jumped at me. And I shouldn't be a bit surprised if it frightened the budgie to death. I don't understand it. How can animals be ghosts?"

Bernice paused to take that on board. "Well," she said at last, looking rather pale, "I don't see why they shouldn't have souls, too. And I don't suppose they'd be anything to worry about. Animals aren't nasty like people."

"But it scratched me! Look!" She heaved her blouse up to show the faint red marks.

"Oh!" Bernice looked alarmed.

"It might belong to the woman with the long skirt," said Julia, getting up and going over to the window, hugging herself because her panic was rising. Her voice became lighter, her words came out faster. "I wish I knew who that was; I don't think I'd be so frightened if I did. Do you think the Grosvenors have ever heard her? They've been here for ages. Are you sure you don't want me to go? I mean, Tom could move in with you, couldn't he? I get the feeling that he's not easily frightened, even by ghosts."

"He works away," said Bernice in a quiet, little-girl voice. "I like your company, Jule, and we've always got on well, haven't we? I'd be sorry if you went. I'm sure we could find room for your things somewhere."

They went and looked at the lobby, pretending the discussion was all about cupboard space. They played the game, measuring, discussing, acting as if Julia's only worry was getting clothes out of boxes and onto hangers. They pushed the mattress even harder against the basement door, and there was about five feet. A wardrobe would go in.

"Or here," suggested Bernice, pointing to the partition – a mere three feet.

Julia looked at the pile of unpacked boxes on the tiles and didn't want to unpack them at all.

In the hall beyond, there were sounds of movement.

"Let's ask Win and Harry about who it might be," said Bernice, dragging them out of their defensive role-playing and back into the mire.

Footsteps moved across the hall floor. Not the muffled thud and squeak of plastic soles, but the tapping of heels, coming down the hall, coming through the partition into the lobby. Right beside them there was the sound of a door opening and closing, while the upended mattress remained against the locked entrance to the basement. The sound of feet descending uncarpeted stairs died away until they could hear them no more.

The girls fled.

Eight

"Wherever are they?" asked Julia tensely.

They were sitting on the window-sill, more out of the room than in it, continually leaning forward to look down towards the Wick for the appearance of two energetic figures in athletic wear carrying bags.

"I want the loo," said Bernice, agitated, but showing no sign of moving. "She won't be out there, will she?"

"How should I know? Last night it was after ten o'clock, today it was six. I'd always thought they had regular habits."

"She might go up and down all day when the house is empty," said Bernice in a thin voice. "Because you walk out of a house and leave it empty, you assume it just sits there until you come back. Perhaps it doesn't. Supposing buildings have their own life, and go on living without any people in them?"

That Bernice should come up with such a thought was deeply alarming; it wasn't her at all. It was the sort of disturbing premise that might arise in Julia's anxious psyche, and she found it only too easy to believe.

Because we create things, we think they're inert, but we feed our energies and lives into them as we use them. Buildings begin clean and lifeless, but then we start charging them like batteries, with our breath, sweat and heat, with our voices, our emotions, our loves and hates, our joys and sorrows. And the older a house grows, the higher its charged-up power becomes, and the more likely it might be to discharge that power. Think of what might be stored up in the fabric of Carwarden Gardens, Worcester Park, for the eventual alarm of future residents.

"Do you think anyone's claimed Mr Rillington yet?" Bernice said suddenly, watching pigeons scrounging among the weeds and rubbish below. "I wonder where he is now."

Julia gripped the window-sill, afraid she might fall out and down into the mossy area, and hear someone within tell her to go away, go away.

"In the mortuary, I suppose," she said shortly.

"I hope I don't die like that," said Bernice, looking across at the park and fiddling with the curtains. "All alone, and lying on the floor for days so that I start to go off."

"How many brothers and sisters have you got?"

"Six, and fourteen nephews and nieces."

"Well, you should be all right, then," said Julia, unconvincingly brisk. "Was he married?"

"Don't know. Jule, supposing it wasn't just senile paranoia? I mean, I had a great-auntie who used to accuse us of stealing her things, and creeping into her flat when she was out to change the time on the clock or paint the walls a different colour. But when she used to say her mother and father had been to see her, how do we know she wasn't telling the truth?"

"We don't," said Julia, feeling panic rise again.

"And when Mr Rillington was shouting at people, how do we know they weren't really there, and really threatening him, or insulting him, or—"

"There they are!" Julia interrupted with relief. If Bernice had carried on a moment longer she might have gone to pieces, because she was putting her own fears into words.

They stood out on the top step, with flat and front doors open, like nervous bridesmaids awaiting a bridal couple at the people-charged doorway of an old church.

"Hello, girls," said the bride cheerfully, stomping up the steps. "Well, we've got a nice long list of possible culprits and traced at least some of them who were in London that year. There's a few off abroad with the army and navy, so that's them off the hook, but—"

"What's the matter, kids?" asked Harry, looking at their unusually serious faces.

"Would you mind coming in for a minute, please?" Bernice invited in a small, polite voice.

They sat the Grosvenors on the settee. The girls perched uneasily on the edges of chairs. The sun flooded in and bathed them all in molten gold.

They told their story, first Julia, then Bernice, then both together. They watched the Grosvenors' cheerful faces set then fall, become alert then sceptical.

"Well, I ain't never heard nothing no time," said Win firmly. No negative could have been stronger. "Have you, Harry?"

"Nah, not a thing. Mind you, with Win talking all the while, I wouldn't have had much chance."

She hit him with the back of her hand.

"But we both heard it at the same time," Julia said pleadingly. "Was Mr Rillington married?"

"Never mentioned it to me, did he you, Harry?"

"Never."

"Don't mean he wasn't, though. You reckon it could be his wife, then?"

"How old was he?" asked Bernice.

"Sort of ninetyish."

"Oh well, he'd have got married in the twenties, wouldn't he, when skirts were right above their knees."

"The old lady who had our flat before," Julia suggested. The Grosvenors were being so nice and patient, like parents; well, some parents. ("What the dickens are you talking about, Julia? Don't be silly.")

"They come here just before we did," said Win. "Used to have a real big house in Highbury New Park, but it got too much for her, trying to get the rent out of the lodgers."

"Did she wear long skirts?"

"No, well above the floor. In fact, for her age, I always reckoned they could have done with being a bit longer. Of course," she considered, "during her last couple of years she didn't get out of her dressing-gown much, and she used to go up to the toilet in it."

"That old woollen wrap-around didn't swish none," said

Harry firmly, "and she'd always got slippers on by then, not heels. Interesting this, ain't it?" he asked them, beaming.

"Shut up, Harry," Win scolded, giving him a stroke of the elbow. "Can't you see the poor kids are scared?"

"Who lived in your flat?" Julia asked, appreciating her awareness of their state of mind but hating to have it put into words. Oh look, Julia's frightened. Ha! Ha! Ha! There's nothing to be frightened of, don't be silly.

"Young couple with three kids. Council rehoused them in one of them." She nodded out of the bay window towards a rearing stack of glass and concrete beyond Victoria Park Road.

"I bet *her* skirts didn't touch the ground," said Harry. He moved a cushion quickly to field Win's elbow. "Permanently bruised ribs, I got," he informed them.

"So who is it?" Julia almost begged. "It really does seem to have something to do with Mr Rillington, doesn't it, what with it starting as soon as he died."

"Don't have to follow. It could be someone who lived here long before him. When was these houses built, Harry?"

"Well, they was here by 1880, because my grandad's uncle lived in this road for a bit. He was a greengrocer in Well Street," he added conversationally.

"I wish there was some way of finding out all the people who've lived here since it was built," Bernice said without hope.

The Grosvenors looked at each other smugly. Harry laughed. "What makes you think there ain't?"

"You mean you *can*?" exclaimed Julia.

"Looks like a trip over to the Kingsland Road, dunnit, Harry?" said Win. "OK, loves, we'll have a day at the Borough Archives and see what we can come up with."

"And in the meanwhile, any time you're scared or just nervous, give us a shout, or even a scream if you like. We'll be down in a flash," Harry assured them.

The Grosvenors moved out into the hall on a wave of grateful thanks.

"Here we come, so move over," Harry shouted.

Back in their flat, Julia said shakily, "I don't know how he's got the nerve. I mean, she may not have a sense of humour."

"He probably doesn't really believe us and he's trying to cheer us up. Anyway, I don't think it works like that," said Bernice, putting on the television quickly. "Whoever it is, they may not even know we're here. It won't be 1995 for them, will it?"

"I wonder what year it will be?" said Julia.

They used the bathroom before night came. It was still and quiet in there, compared with the solid barrage of traffic outside the blind, closed window, and neither of them bathed because they were unwilling to discard the last barrier between themselves and the charged air.

The sunset bled all over the sky, red and orange and yellow, and the last light drained from the park as if leaving by the same gates as the people.

The television chattered on. They watched things which didn't interest them and filled time with things they wouldn't normally have bothered with. Bernice washed all the china and pans and put them away, then Julia rinsed underwear and tights, pressed some blouses and brushed her suit.

Bernice closed the curtains and the room quickly became stuffy. They sat on the settee in their dressing-gowns, pretending they were watching a film slotted well after the nine o'clock watershed and excessively violent, even with cuts. And even the violence had a certain comfort in it, because it was physical.

When they could no longer stop yawning, they parted for the night, hugging in a way which had never been part of their relationship before. Unused to embraces instigated by real emotion, Julia broke away quickly and went and sat on top of her bed in a mixed agony of embarrassment, gratitude and an apprehension which would need constant attention and control if it were not to degenerate into abject fear.

She wanted to watch the traffic go by, to enjoy the reassuring company of people who had never experienced ghosts, who would laugh at the very mention of the supernatural, but if she opened the curtains she would have to turn off the light. The lorry drivers perched up high in their cabs might look through her window and see her sitting in bed. Her eyelids insisted on drooping. She got under the covers but remained sitting upright; lying down, she would be at such a disadvantage. If something was going to come and curl up on her bed she wanted to be ready to jump out of it, and if footsteps were going to clip along the tiles behind her bedroom door she wanted to be ready in case they came on through it, and she felt a long skirt brush against her face as she lay on the pillow.

She held her head between her hands, trying to shake such thoughts out of her brain and juggle all other thoughts together to take up space and allow them no room to get back in.

She resisted sleep. ("Go to sleep at once, Julia, you'll be good for nothing in the morning. I won't have you going to school looking like death warmed up, what will your teacher think of me?")

At ten past two, there was a crash out on the motorway. She went and looked out, with the curtains pulled round her to hide her nightdress. The continuous row was interrupted but not stilled; it merely changed its tempo into braking, crawling, impatient avoidance noises and accelerating off. There was another crash, as someone hit an obstruction he wasn't expecting and therefore wasn't looking for. Within minutes sirens converged from both directions and flashing blue lights hovered above the parapet, though of the accident itself she could see nothing. When people are having to face an ordeal like that, whatever am I afraid of?

She sat down in the chair and leant her forehead against the glass. The garden below was a dark well, with the roof of the greenhouse glistening in the flyover lights. It contained mostly corpses, now. The watering had come too late and there would be no colourful planting in the tins, pots and discarded household receptacles this year.

Was anything happening in the silent basement beneath her feet? Were They there? Again she felt the secret treachery of buildings, the floor which seemed solid but hung over a void, the ceiling which seemed a firm lid on security, but which had the whole weight of the sky trying to break it in.

Something moved in the garden. Not the piebald form of Bubastis, slinking in and out of the shadows, but large and dark, and moving towards the ivy-covered wall which hid the Bangladeshis' garden.

On top of everything else, a burglar; and in a district like this, which Mrs Nutley had informed her with the full authority of her Tory tabloid had the highest figure for violent crime in London, it was very probably a violent burglar.

Her heartbeat went mad. He can't get up the basement stairs, it's locked and the mattress is in front of it, but he could get up to the first floor windows, no problem.

She put on dressing-gown and slippers and hurried to tell Bernice, glad to have an excuse to seek her company. She found her sitting up in bed, bestowing grateful affection on a mug of hot chocolate.

"What, with lights on, front and back?" she asked incredulously. "Surely not!"

"There's no light in Mr Rillington's, and he's almost certainly aiming for there. In fact, come to think of it, he's probably been in already, because he was making towards the fence."

"Oh dear, and it must be full of all his most treasured possessions. I think we'd better wake Harry."

They didn't greatly enjoy crossing the tiles, climbing the stairs and waiting for a Grosvenor to answer the summons they beat on the ship's bell. It seemed impertinent to trespass past the bathroom and actually knock on their bedroom door – they liked their privacy.

Harry emerged tying his dressing-gown belt, his thinning hair made fuller by tousling. He rubbed his eyes, listened to their story and looked at their frightened, unrested faces.

"All right, ducks, I'll just get me trousers on."

"Are we being silly?" Julia whispered anxiously as they waited, guilty at having been thoroughly inconsiderate and destroyed someone's rest. ("What the dickens is the matter with you, Julia, waking me up like that? Poor Daddy's been out half the night already with a desperately ill patient, and I need all the rest I can get with a house to run and four children to look after.")

Well, aren't I one of them? Look after me.

"Of course not," Bernice whispered back, "and he told us to call him."

You had to admire Harry's behaviour in a crisis. He went out of the front door first, tried the basement door, removed the piece of hardboard from the window and shone a torch through. Then he went down to the corner and up to the back fence, where he climbed over, swept the garden with light and did the same to the back doors and windows. On his eventual return he reported that there was no sign of disturbance at all.

Unfortunately, a member of the Emergency Services working on a piece of heavy lifting gear with a high vantage observed his escapade, and within minutes he was explaining his behaviour to a couple of PCs, while the two girls tried to support their champion.

"You *thought* you saw a shadow in the backyard," one of the policemen repeated, looking at Julia as if fully aware of the feminine derivation of the word hysteria.

"I did see it," insisted Julia, looking certain to the point of haughtiness. Inside she was sobbing miserably with humiliation. It was like one of those anxiety nightmares; out in the street in the middle of the night wearing only a nightdress and a thin, summer dressing-gown, trying to justify herself to a couple of strapping uniformed males and acutely conscious of her lack of knickers.

"Well, if there was anybody there he'll have gone now, but we'd better look inside. Have you got a key?"

Harry patiently explained the situation, picking at a splinter in his palm which he had lifted from the back fence. The policeman removed the hardboard, shoved his arm through the broken pane and unlocked the sash.

The girls sat on the top step, tired, frightened and feeling lost to reality. A sparse trail of lamp posts lit the path across the park, and in the distance Bethnal Green exuded a pale orange glow which wiped out the stars, though the moon watched them closely.

Julia wished fervently she hadn't started this charade; after all, if the intruder was going away, why not leave it till the morning? Don't go pushing your nose into other people's business, Julia, you'll only make a fool of yourself.

By the time it was all over and the basement returned to a mild degree of security, it was more than time for a cup of tea. Bernice pulled over her bedding and shut it into the settee, and while the kettle boiled, Julia slipped into her bedroom and dressed, though socialising in *déshabillé* didn't seem to worry Bernice and Win at all.

"What's it like down there, Harry?" asked Win with interest.

"Not too bad, apart from the broken sink — those two from the council seem to have tidied up. Think they've gone through all his drawers, though, and there's a suitcase out on the bed. One of the cops looked inside in case the burglar had packed stuff in it, but it was just full of papers."

"So they've probably found out all about him," said Julia.

"Maybe. He'd had a smashing time before he died, there's a pile of broken bits and pieces on the table and the photograph over the mantelpiece has got its glass broke."

"That's of his mum and dad," Win came in smartly with her know-all voice.

"What did his mother look like?" asked Julia with interest. You could understand a lot about a person from getting to know their mother.

Harry opened his mouth.

"Bit snooty," said Win, "like she had a bad smell under her nose. I could go another cuppa, loves, if you wouldn't mind. We ain't going to get no more sleep tonight, are we? How's the crash doing?" she shouted as Julia took her mug behind the curtain.

"Can't see much from here," she called back. Through the kitchen window, the power of the lights above the flyover was beginning to lessen in the thinning darkness.

"We could see a lot better from our bedroom," Win shouted. "Lorry had gone into the back of a car, then while we was looking, a couple more vehicles went into the back of the lorry."

Julia's eyes fell to the greenhouse, the vegetable mortuary. A shape passed across it and disappeared behind the back addition. It made no sound.

"He's back!" Julia exclaimed in a hoarse whisper.

Harry got there first, flinging up the sash and leaning across the draining board to shout down into the shadows.

"Hey, you, come out of that! I can see you!"

He waited a second then turned to Julia, while Win and Bernice hovered behind his large body in a state of frustration and alarm respectively.

"Bloody neck!" he said furiously, and rushed from the flat.

"Be careful, Harry!" Win yelled after him, then climbed onto the draining board and hung out of the window.

Julia hurried through into her bedroom, hoping to catch a glimpse of the intruder before he escaped over the fence. This was horrible, really horrible.

It was nearly five o'clock. The first weak, cold, pregnant light slid over the parapet and seeped down into the garden. It was a damn silly time of night to burgle.

She held her breath as something dark came round the corner from the back door and moved across the grass. It was nothing like a burglar. It was roughly cone-shaped with a flattened top. On either side of it hung dark, clumsy shapes which swung and bumped against its sides, and pushed it off balance. It moved slowly. It stopped and twisted and waited. It untwisted and moved on, still slowly. The base of the cone brushed across the long pale grass from one side to the other, but disturbed not a single blade.

The dark thing reached the fence and moved on, twisting yet again to raise a paleness to the window of Julia's room, even as it melted silently through the orange-stained wood.

She went back into the kitchen, standing in the doorway and holding onto the frame to stop herself falling over. Win was still balanced on the draining board, furry slippers and varicosed calves sticking out into the room, head and shoulders on the other side of the window-sill, shouting at her husband. From the next door garden came a mild, plaintive protest.

"Yo, man!"

"Are you all right, Harry?" shouted Win. "Hello, loves, sorry about the noise but we think there's a burglar in the basement."

"That's serious, man!" observed Luke's voice.

Julia moved through the dividing curtain on wobbly legs and sat down beside Bernice on the badly-packed, lopsided settee.

"It isn't a burglar," Julia whispered, her eyes dead with shock. "It's a woman in a long coat and a big hat, carrying two big bags. She's just walked right through the fence."

Bernice gasped, reached out and took her hand. They sat helplessly in the middle of their collapsed domestic idyll, staring at each other before the cold gas fire.

In a few hours the world would go to work. They would have to smarten up and walk away from all this as if it had never happened, and be sweet and polite to all kinds of people, and cope with every state of mind from idiocy to blind fury on the telephone. They would have to behave as if everything were normal. Everything is absolutely all right, Julia.

And when they heard it, it was only another nail in the coffin of their peace of mind, and only one more threat to the quiet life they were entitled to, and their fear was only one more uncomfortable emotion and unpleasant experience, turning their lives into an ordeal rather than a pleasure.

Within the flat with the door closed, any sounds in the hall were muffled. If an invisible skirt did swish against the banisters, if non-existent shoes did descend the carpeted treads they were unaware of it, but they heard the clipping footsteps on the tiles, along the hall to the back of the house, and they heard a door opening and closing, and very faintly, the thudding of shoes on wood.

"Harry's down there." Bernice spoke with the utmost horror.

"Come on," said Julia, suddenly unable to bear her situation any longer; frozen, frightened, cowardly, useless and waiting for Prince Charming to come and save her, as if all positive action in her own defence were denied her by reason of her sex and class.

In the dead morning, before the sun had appeared to bring it to life, they found Harry climbing out of Mr Rillington's bay window, the lace curtain trailing out with him and decking his head with a torn bridal veil. His heavy legs reached across the mossy ditch and hauled him up into the front garden.

"Are you all right?" Julia cried, appalled at what the experience might have done to an elderly, overweight man.

His face was expressionless as he clapped dust off his large, plump hands.

"Yeah," he said after a moment.

"Did you – er—"

"—hear anything?" Bernice completed the question.

"Yeah," he said. He guided them away from the window with one hand on each of their shoulders and sat down with them on the wall by the pavement.

"Footsteps going down the basement stairs?"

He fumbled in one of his trouser pockets.

"What happened when they got to the bottom?" asked Julia. What a dangerously funny state he was in. Calm but not calm. Preoccupied. Going through the motions. No, more like shock. A state of shock. Have we, she thought anxiously, a blanket large enough to wrap up Harry Grosvenor against shock?

"Nothing," said Harry. "Just stopped. Wherever she was going she'd got there. Like that old Variety catch-phrase. 'Well, I'll go to the foot of our stairs.' Remember that?"

"No," said Julia apologetically.

"Well, well," he said, "who'd have thought it, eh?"

Win came out on the front steps.

"You didn't get him," she said.

"No one there," said Harry, searching his trouser pockets again.

"You've given it up," she told him.

"He heard the footsteps," Bernice explained, "they went down the basement stairs again."

Win looked at him sharply. "Oh he did, did he? OK mate, inside, you. Tea is what you need, and this time I'll let you have sugar in it. Would one of you girls put the board back?"

"Oh, great," said Bernice under her breath. They rose with extreme reluctance and advanced upon the basement bay window. Look out for flying objects. Go away, go—

"What's that?" Julia squealed. "Win! Harry! Listen!"

The Grosvenors came back, listening with the faces of people who didn't want to hear anything. Within the basement the sound came again, not unlike an incompetent burglar wielding his tools.

Harry made a valiant move forward but Win grabbed him by the sleeve.

"You know what that is, girls?" she said in a low voice.

"Tools? Definitely something metal," said Julia. I'm going to move. After a night like this, I'm definitely going to move.

"Yeah, it's metal all right. It's six o'clock in the morning, and someone down in that there basement is cleaning out the range."

Nine

They didn't even bother to look inside – they knew there was nothing to see. Quietly, they climbed the steps and went into Bernice's flat where, without a word, she went and put the kettle on.

"No more for me, thanks," said Julia in a flat, stunned voice.

"Never say no to a cup of tea, us," said Win, folding her arms tightly across her dressing-gown.

For minutes they sat in silence while china clinked behind the curtain, then Harry drew a deep breath and said "Well."

"Yes," said Julia.

"Makes you think, dunnit?" said Win, drew another deep breath and let it out with a puff.

"However many of them *are* there?" Julia protested almost with anger. "And you really mean you've never heard anything at all until these last weeks?"

"Not a peep or a thud," said Harry. He made no jokes about Win this time. "Only disturbance we ever got was the traffic and poor old Joe Rillington having one of his blow-ups."

"Could be they was all downstairs with him," said Win grimly.

"Yes, that's what we've begun to think," said Bernice, pushing round the curtain with a tray of mugs. "Here we were, complaining about the noise and all the time—"

"Wonder if she's still at that range?" said Harry, spooning in a lot more sugar than was good for him.

"Should be just about done now," said Win. "My gran used to reckon on half an hour to get it all clean and the fire

88

ready to cook breakfast. Anyone feel like going and having a listen?"

Nobody volunteered.

"Don't blame you," said Win, and went for the tea. "Well, girls, let's hope the day gets better."

It took its time. The North London Railway was having problems, and the train stopped for ages among industrial buildings, rusty railway lines, overgrown watercourses and scrub in the half-used no-man's-land of Stratford Marsh. They got into Jones, Brown and Wilkinson's by the skin of their teeth, and the firm's minibus drove the top brass in from Tower Hill just as the diary was opened.

"Morning, Miss Standish. Morning, Mr Ash. Hi, Candice! Oh gosh, I haven't fed the fish. Good-morning, Mr Jones."

"Good-morning. Jones, Brown and Wilkinson."

"Julia, it's Rowena."

"Oh yes?" said Julia. I know what this is about.

"It's my turn for lunch on Sunday, and you are coming this week, aren't you? I mean, last week was about as much fun as a funeral." Rowena's tone was accusing. "The children started playing up and Mum gave them a telling off, Belinda was nearly crying, the rack of lamb got burnt and then Dennis lost his temper and Mother said she could see he didn't want her there and drove off in a huff. She was really hurt, you could see she was. Belinda sent her some flowers, but she didn't even ring up and say thank you."

The reception hall was momentarily empty.

"Yes, well, sorry about that, but it's not my fault, is it? Look, I've left home now, and one of the advantages of leaving home is that you don't have to be dragged back into the womb once a week, whether you like it or not. And please don't ring me at work any more – I've given all of you my home number. I hope you can understand the position," her voice became honeyed and reasonable as the doors sprang apart.

"No, I can't understand it. It's all very well for you," said Rowena with an inflection which said it wasn't all right for her, nor, probably, the rest of the world, "but some of us still think that responsibility to other people matters. *I* think it's important to hold the family together; I don't want to end up on my own, and that's what you're going to do, Julia. You'll have no idea how awful and frightening it will be to have no loved ones to fall back on until it's far too late."

"I have an inkling. Look, it's a long way and I haven't got transport." She was whispering now, while Bernice greeted a postman like a long-lost brother. A woman with a briefcase approached Julia.

"We'll meet you off the train. Or you could spend Saturday night with Mother and come down with her."

"I'll let you know," said Julia quickly, and put the receiver down. "Good-morning, madam."

It was non-stop all day. Bernice and Julia worked side by side without a moment when they need acknowledge the shadow over their spirits, their home and their lives. Coffee was drunk at the reception desk, and they took their lunches an hour apart. Only back on the Docklands Railway did their macabre problem once more become the centre of their concern, and dread came down on them like a blanket.

"I wonder if Harry and Win are home yet," remarked Julia as they left the foot-bridge.

They knew they wouldn't be. Their steps grew slower. They said what a lovely evening it was, and wondered if they should go for a walk in the park. They stood on the few feet of path at the bottom of the steps and looked up at the closed bay window, where no one was sitting to enjoy the view.

"I suppose it can't hurt us," said Bernice at last.

"I hope not."

"In fact, we might even get used to it."

"Might we?" said Julia with little conviction.

"Do you know anyone else who's had this trouble?"

"The subject didn't often come up in Worcester Park," said Julia.

"It didn't get mentioned much at Henley's Corner, either." She didn't notice the question remained unanswered.

They walked up the steps. The hall was silent, stuffy and empty. They looked into it but didn't enter.

On the mat lay an envelope addressed to 'The Occupiers'. Bernice opened it and read it out loud.

"'Dear Sir and Madam, Following our conversation after the discovery of the body of Mr Joseph James Rillington, I can now confirm that a relative of the deceased has been found, and we hope they will be willing to take responsibility for the funerary arrangements. However, since Mr Rillington appears to have died intestate—'"

"Here, I don't think this is for us, it's for the Grosvenors," Julia protested.

"'—there could be a period of some months,' Bernice went on quickly, 'before all his affairs are settled. You will be informed as soon as possible by the borough solicitors and Messrs Cyprian Smith of your position. Please ring this department at the above number if you need clarification. Yours sincerely, p.p. squiggle.'"

Bernice folded the letter and put it back in the envelope. "Well, it said the occupiers, didn't it? Can't help it if we opened it by mistake. I expect they found out all about him from that suitcase of papers. Wonder who the relative is?"

"The terrible Florrie?" suggested Julia.

The front door was still open. Neither of them made any movement to enter their home.

"Wonder what she's like?" Julia said.

"Funny that about the estate agent. Mr Rillington's flat isn't anything to do with the Grosvenors, is it?"

"Perhaps they said they'd keep an eye on it."

"Well, in that case," puzzled Bernice busily, probably trying to occupy her imagination, "why didn't they give them the key, it would have saved all that climbing in the window."

"We'll have to go in soon, you know," said Julia.

They continued to stand still, looking upwards. Supposing they were on the stairs when it happened, would they feel anything? Would the passage of an invisible resident through their bodies cause sensation, and what would that sensation be?

Or supposing next time they saw something?

Bernice gave a little gasp. Julie turned. She was looking down and turning left and right.

"Bubastis?" she said. "Where are you, puss? Come on, darling, don't be shy. Come to Bernice."

They looked for him over the side of the steps, in the crannies of the front garden rubbish, up and down the road, across in the park.

Bernice looked ill. Around her eyes, where her sunglasses had protected the skin, there was a pale, blueish tinge. "It knows I'm a cat person," she said lightly. "The poor thing wants affection. It's nothing to be afraid of, really." Her voice was getting higher.

"I'm not a cat person. It must have known it wouldn't get much affection from me."

"Oh you *are* affectionate, Jule, it's just that you don't show it. It wouldn't have come to you if you hadn't been kind and understanding—"

"Oh please stop it, Bernice," Julia pleaded. "Please stop pretending everything's all right. You don't make things right by saying they are, or by refusing to take notice of wrong things. Something is terribly wrong with our house, and it may always have been. For goodness' sake, let's admit it properly, now, while we're out of it and in the open air."

"Are you frightened, Jule?"

"Yes, are you?"

"Oh, yes! But not so much of the cat. Animals are kinder than people."

"Don't be so sloppy! Animals kill each other, including their own children at times, and a lot of them kill people, including ones they've known all their lives."

Bernice went quiet and dropped her head. Julia felt instant, familiar self-dislike. That was the trouble with habitually holding things in; there was such a nasty explosion when they finally got out.

"Sorry," she said with anguish.

"It's all right," sniffed Bernice, "you're upset. So'm I. Shall we go for a walk?"

"All right." All right, all right, we use that expression all the time, and it's rubbish. Very little in the world is all right and we know it. This compulsion we have to affirm it is – that's the giveaway.

"The front door's open," Bernice pointed out tearfully. "We might get another burglar."

"There wasn't a burglar."

"Oh no," Bernice remembered in a subdued voice.

They walked round the park; not a pleasant early evening stroll, a relaxation after a day's work, but a brisk, anxious march more suitable for a frosty morning. They forced their pace as if to escape their thoughts, strode over the acres of grass and circled round to return past the tennis courts, where four black girls wearing every colour but white were lobbing bright yellow balls across the softened tarmac.

Ahead, everything facing west was washed over with glowing, amber light like a glaze. Brick and stucco glowed, concrete glowed, vehicles gleamed and glittered. The tower blocks were turned from tired off-white to honey, and their windows sparkled and rejoiced against the softening blue sky. Even the dirty houses beyond the park railings seemed to dance in dappled sunlight and look as if they were absolutely all right.

They came out through the little gate and crossed the road. The upper bay window was open and Win was seated within, cuppa in hand.

"Sorry about the letter, Win," said Bernice, "we thought it meant us."

"Well, I suppose it did really, didn't it? I'm glad the poor old boy's going to get buried at last. It seems real indecent to keep him in a cold drawer for weeks."

"I should hope he was kept cold," said Harry with feeling.

"What was all that about the estate agent?" asked Julia. She was sitting opposite Win at the table in the window, her hands gripped together. She kept shivering, though it wasn't cold there, it was warm, bright, alive.

"Well, we was wondering about that, too," said Win. "Perhaps it's the landlord. Now he's got rid of his long-term sitting tenant he may want to shift us all."

"Oh dear," Bernice said with alarm.

Julia looked at her incredulously. What, now? You want to stay here in these circumstances? With the ghost cat? With the invisible sitting tenant? No, walking tenant; restless, on the move, always going somewhere with something to do.

"Anyway, we'll drop in on the agent some time and see what he says. You heard anything today, girls?"

Their stomachs turned over in unison.

"We've only just come in," said Julia. "I mean, it was such a nice evening—"

"Yes, I know, love," said Harry sympathetically, "don't blame you. Want to know where we've been today?"

"And what we got from it," added Win, opening her shopping bag and slapping a green ring-binder, a dog-eared notebook and a sheaf of scribbled-on pieces of paper onto the dining table. She picked one up.

"You want to know who was living here in 1915? Or in 1910? Or right back in 1896? Or—"

"You've been finding out who lived here! Gosh, that's so clever of you!" exclaimed Bernice. "What book was it in?"

They laughed, Harry indulgently, Win with near-scorn.

"I told you before, love, nothing in this game is that straightforward or easy. No, we been going through the Post Office directories and that. Not complete, by any means, but what we've got so far is this."

She held up a sheet of A4, revealing that the back was printed with an advertisement for replacement windows. What they really needed, thought Julia, was a replacement roof, or even walls. Or even better, a replacement home. I want to move, I want to move, I'm living in a nightmare.

"Right," said Win with enthusiasm. "Applications to Hackney Council for permission to build and drain. In June 1880, a builder called Tomkins put in plans for four houses. This here road was done by lots of different builders, by the way; put up in bits and pieces from about 1850 onwards. Oh, and it was on land belonging to the Crown, so the builders bought leases off Her Majesty Queen Victoria, through a government department called Woods and Forests. Now," and another piece of paper was disinterred, this time A5 and advertising a church Jumble Sale at Eton Mission.

"In 1882 the tenant was called Tarrant. In 1895 it was Baker. In 1900 it was John Jarvis. In 1902 it was Abraham Ingersall."

"John Jarvis didn't stay long, did he?" asked Bernice with wide eyes. "Perhaps they were hearing things right back then."

"Didn't have to stay long, ducks," said Harry kindly, leaning forward to explain, "people hopped in and out of houses all the time. Say you couldn't get on with the neighbours, or you changed your job, or you suddenly got a rise and could afford something better, then you gave notice, paid the rent, upped and went – no sweat about selling the house and clearing the mortgage before you could move."

"They didn't always pay the rent before they upped and went," said Win meditatively. "When Dad was out of work we moved regular, six hours ahead of rent day. Twelve o'clock at night, everything into the hand cart and off to the next lot of cheap lodgings where no one knew we was broke."

"Remember the tally man?" Harry asked her. "My Mum used to hide in the toilet and get me to go say she was out."

"Anyway," said Win, "in 1908 it was still Mr Ingersall, and he stayed there right up to when old Joe moved in. So there's our possible suspects; Tarrant, Baker, Jarvis and Ingersall."

"Though who they was and what they did with themselves while they was here, Gawd knows," Harry pointed out.

On their way down they took the opportunity to use the bathroom, taking turns to stand sentinel. They walked quickly downstairs, keeping close together. Julia stood with her back to the flat door while Bernice fumbled with the key. Inside—

"Shall we eat out?" suggested Julia.

"Well, if you like," said Bernice uncertainly, "but it'll mean going through all that business of coming in again. And if we do that today, what do we do all the other days?"

"Yes. Well, it's my turn tonight. I'd better see what we've got."

Bernice put on the television, but came and hung about in the kitchen while Julia was cooking. She raised the leaf of the calendar on the wall and peeped at the picture which would keep them company all next month.

"Oh look, it's a dear little Shetland pony with its foal, isn't that lovely? Well, we've had a nice few weeks together, haven't we, Jule?" Julia looked at her incredulously. "Oh, I know, but that's only been a few times. If you add up the frightening times and compare them with all the nice ones, it's really been a good month. June next – that means the house is nearly a hundred and fifteen years old."

"What do you mean?" asked Julia, searching the back of the fridge for onions.

"Win said Mr Tomkins started to build it in June 1880. Or perhaps you count the age of buildings from when they're finished."

"She said they were going to try the Census. Apparently that will tell us everyone who slept in the house on the nights of Sunday the 3rd April 1881 and Sunday the 5th April 1891."

"How strange," said Bernice with awe. "It'll be like looking through the windows and spying on them. Do you think we ought to?"

"Yes," said Julia strongly. "If I have to live with someone invisible I'd at least like to have some idea who they are, and whether they really are Jack the Ripper."

"You do have some depressing ideas," said Bernice unhappily. "It's almost as if you wanted to expect the worst."

"I like to get the waiting over," admitted Julia. "I just

can't stand things hanging over me." ("I'll speak to you later, Julia.")

"Well, I think she's more likely to be a poor little over-worked skivvy. If she were, we could have sympathy for her and perhaps make her feel better, even welcome her into our lives."

"Welcome her into our lives! Bernice, you expect everything to come up roses, which is just as extreme as my pessimism. You must get some terrible let-downs."

"Not terrible, just a bit sad," Bernice admitted meekly, "and at least I've had the happy expectations first. You almost seem to go out of your way to make yourself unhappy."

"Do I? Yes, I suppose I do," admitted Julia. "Very hard habit to break."

"But you must break it!" Bernice cried. "You're so clever and such a nice person, Jule, and you're wasting your life. Look, next time Tom and I have an outing you really must come with us. We'll get someone else to make up a four-some—"

"Not Jim," said Julia quickly.

"Well no, not if you don't like him. Don't you want a boyfriend, Jule?"

Julia's cool face didn't change expression. She looked down. "I don't want a boyfriend found for me," she said.

"But you could get one yourself easily, you're so attractive. Much prettier than me," Bernice said candidly, and obviously didn't expect to be contradicted. Julia didn't insult her by doing so.

"Being pretty isn't the same thing as being attractive," she said, and left it at that, with all its corollaries unspoken. The tears were heavy behind her eyes.

Somehow they got through to the weekend, which was to be Tom-less. Not without interruption; the footsteps were heard occasionally. The cat was heard yowling in the yard – but perhaps it was only Bubastis. On Saturday, Bernice suggested plans for getting through Sunday.

"The Grosvenors are going to their daughter's at Leytonstone, and I want to see my parents, so why not come with me, Jule? They'd love to meet you."

"That's very nice of you, but if I go to see anyone's family it ought to be my own."

"Oh yes, that'll be nice!" Bernice enthused.

"Probably not, but it might score me some points," said Julia, with little hope.

Bernice left at about ten past ten, loaded with a bag of gifts for her family, from a Power Rangers comic to a potted azalea.

"Will you be here when I get back?" she asked on the step.

"What time?" asked Julia. "I don't want to be the first person in, either."

"Definitely before dark," Bernice promised. "Say, eight o'clock? I usually stay much longer, and I don't want to disappoint them."

"All right, eight o'clock. You will be on time, won't you?" Julia added, with a hint of pleading.

"Promise," said Bernice earnestly. "Have a lovely day, Jule."

Julia opened her window and let the traffic in. She made the bed hastily, wondering what to wear, what would escape irritating comments. ("Hello, Julia, that's a snazzy outfit!" "What the dickens have you got on, Julia?")

She heard the Grosvenors run downstairs and knock on the flat door.

"Back this evening, love. Have a nice time at your sister's."

"Thank you!" she shouted through the hall partition. She began hurrying, nervous of being left alone. A church bell started to ring. She closed the curtains, put on blouse, skirt and sandals, and looked in the long mirror inside the wardrobe door. ("You mean you went on a public train with bare legs? Are you *asking* for trouble?")

On a scorching, early summer day there is nothing wrong

with bare legs, she practised saying. I will wear exactly what I want, she insisted. All I have to do is let it all flow over me, she told herself.

The bell stopped, as if it couldn't compete with the traffic.

But I'm going to have quite enough hassle already. Just walking in the door is going to cause an outbreak of civil war.

Low-heeled shoes, tights. She changed hurriedly, looking at her watch.

It was gone a quarter to eleven now; the bell had started again. Victoria only on Sundays. What was the best way to get there? The North London Line to Stratford? Bus? She rushed into the hall and consulted the local timetable which had been pinned up on the wall since London Transport obligingly pushed it through the door.

She had barely started to work out what went where and how quickly, when she realised she should have gone long since and not pushed her luck.

Ten

It was a dreamy, fatalistic feeling, of inevitability, of now-you've-done-it and serve-you-right. It reminded her of the time she fell into the sea before she could swim, and of the slow, strong, green reality blocking her senses, and pushing her around, and denying her any say in what was happening to her.

The swishing whispered down the stairs, louder and more confused this time, followed by the clicking on the tiles, again not clear and rhythmic, but a kind of incompetent tap-dance. Then a murmur of low, subdued voices and an indistinguishable complaint with a hint of tears. While the front door remained unmoved she heard it open and close, and the heels tip-tap down the steps outside and fade away. Perhaps down the road. Perhaps into the park.

To church?

Outside, she walked on weakened legs, afflicted by all the symptoms of irrational fright.

I don't remember whether I shut the door.

I don't know whether I'm going to the bus or the train.

Where are they going? Eton Mission?

Her legs gave up and sat her down hard on grass. She didn't know why she was in the park, or where she was going, or above all, what on earth was happening to her.

She put her head down on her knees.

The bell had stopped. All the congregation were safely gathered in. Did they get all the way to the church? Did they go in? Did the other worshippers hear them?

All she'd wanted was to grow up, to be independent, to have

some sort of home which wasn't associated with minority, inferiority, dependency, criticism and constant chipping away at her self-confidence. She'd really thought she'd managed it, but it was all spoilt now. Something frightening had happened and was still happening to her in that home, and she was in danger of becoming more of a wreck than ever. It had squatters – no, worse than that – sitting tenants, and she and Bernice were the intruders.

And what time would they be back?

At Dorking Station, Bradley got out of the tank-like estate and opened the passenger door like the gentleman he was. The kiss was gentlemanly, too, and totally without meaning. Her second brother-in-law was tall and saturnine, and never failed to go through the motions of courtesy, but somehow good manners did little to hide the fact that he appeared to be impressed by nothing and fed up with everything. Julia had sometimes wondered if it was all meant to be dry humour, but if so, it seemed to have got out of his control and become totally and corrosively serious.

"Hello, Bradley, how's things with you?"

"Things with me are much as usual," he said, with the wry smile which was his main social response. "I get up, I go to work, I come home, my children waste my substance with riotous living, I pay the bills and I go to bed. I hear you've taken to *la vie bohème*."

"Oh, do you?"

"Yes, I do, indeed I do," said Bradley with great emphasis. He swung the wheel. "I've heard about it from Rowena, from Belinda, from Helena, and at intolerable length from your mother. I have had Philip asking me whether there is any danger of your turning socialist, and whether your new address indicates that you have done so already. I have also been cornered in the garden by Dennis, where he had fled to escape Grace's nagging of his children, and asked if it was true that you are a secret druggie who has finally come out and gone to live in a squat. To be honest, I don't much care if I never hear about your new circumstances ever again, but I can bear to listen just once to your version of things and try to understand it."

The acute anxiety and distress which had accompanied Julia all the way down to Surrey accomplished a blessed, merciful metamorphosis and became relieving anger.

"Oh, how very kind of you," she said in an icy voice, her invisible fury safely belted into the constraint of the high class family car. "But as it's none of your business I'll refrain from boring you until we come face to face with Mother in a few minutes and can no longer escape the subject. Though you, Dennis and Philip can rush out into the garden again, if you prefer, while we have our next row."

Bradley left the tidy tarmac and aimed the bonnet at rural Surrey.

"Don't be pompous. I'm not getting at you, it's all the others yacking on and on. Tell me what it's really all about."

"All about?" repeated Julia irritably. "When did you leave home?"

"When I went to Oxford."

"At eighteen."

"Yes."

"And did your parents ask what that was all about? Did they demand to know why you couldn't bear to live with them any more, and why you couldn't pursue higher education in the next street?"

"Not that I remember," Bradley said in a humouring voice, swooshing between luxuriant hedgerows and sounding his horn at an untidy rabbit.

"And after Oxford, did you go back home to live?"

"No, I got a job down in London, lived in a flat in Croydon and stayed there until I got married."

"Your parents must have made a real fuss about that."

"Of course they didn't!" said Bradley. Leggy, wild-looking children pulled the white farm gate open as he approached, and pushed it shut again in his wake.

"I bet they were deeply offended that you'd taken charge of your life and even chosen a wife without consulting them."

"What sort of people do you think they are?" said Bradley, starting to get niggled.

"Like mine," said Julia, her temper showing in a tremor on the last word. She unbelted, opened the door and was captured by Rowena's gate-openers who had sprinted in behind them, and by Belinda's younger brood who came leaping out of the ex-farmhouse door. Her nephews and nieces liked her – she was different. Most of the time, Julia liked them; there was a latent rebellion about them which augured well for their mental health.

Mrs Nutley was helping in the kitchen. She hadn't been asked to do so but had assumed, as always, that her place was there. Rowena came and gave Julia a Nutley-type kiss one inch from her ear, with lowered eyes, tense mien and sticky cook's hands held far away from any unwanted embrace.

Mrs Nutley wore her baleful, offended stare, and appeared to suffer from the kiss of greeting as much as Julia did. Her eyes immediately abandoned her as being unworthy of further viewing.

"And about time too, we expected you an hour ago. We can make the gravy now, Rowena, I don't think the joint's too badly spoiled."

She opened the oven, broad bottom jutting out just where Rowena was trying to get past to the fridge.

"Were you held up?" asked Rowena. "There's been an awful lot of weekend work on the track lately." She didn't look at Julia. She stood waiting with a large, cut-glass bowl of lemon mousse in her hands, her eyes fixed on her mother's back, her whole body imbued with tension. She was, Julia knew, trying not to offend and not to scream.

"Well, it was fine once they'd found a driver. Shortage of staff, apparently."

"People won't work on a Sunday these days," said Mrs Nutley with contempt.

"I expect they would if they hadn't been sacked."

Rowena's agitation increased visibly. She pulled an exasperated face at Julia and mouthed "Ssshh!"

"Can I do anything?" asked Julia in apology.

"No thanks, we're all right. No, mother, please don't try to lift that, it's very heavy!"

Mrs Nutley heaved the tin onto the table and proceeded to bully the meat with a fork, a knife and a basting spoon. Rowena slammed the lemon mousse onto the draining board and picked up a cloth with which to wipe splashed juices off the floor.

"Go and ask Bradley for a drink," she said tersely. "I've got quite enough help already."

Drinks were in the garden – a sweeping expanse of close-mown lawn with a sprinkler doing the rounds of its unnaturally vivid half-acre, surrounded by roses and herbaceous plants which had enjoyed an upbringing guaranteed to allow them to shine. The younger children were playing boisterously down the far end by the plantation of ornamental trees, while those who were approaching the years of general disillusionment were slumped around on the garden furniture, whingeing.

Philip and Dennis smiled, kissed, teased and patronised.

"Julia! Lovely to see you! What are you drinking?" asked Philip. Julia was interested to recognise a new image being developed; the statesman who is yet a man of the people at heart.

"Probably a pint of mild and bitter, or a half of lager," said Dennis jovially. "How are the East Enders, Julia?"

The rest of the afternoon didn't improve. Everyone got a bit or a lot of Mrs Nutley. The children's clothes and hairstyles were disapproved of. Helena was told how to manage her imminent fourth child, and was warned that she should never have arranged to have it in that hospital, they had a bad record for cross-infection. Belinda got told that her thirteen-year-old son was turning into such an uncontrollable little tearaway that he must be on drugs, and got hysterical. Rowena got a migraine but continued to carry on conscientiously as hostess.

Julia got a bit of everyone, and their opinions on how her life should be run. She asked for a lift to the station before six.

"But we haven't had tea yet!" said Mrs Nutley angrily. "You're spoiling the party."

"I have to get back. I promised to do something tonight."

"Who with?"

"A friend."

"A friend!" Good heavens, what do you need one of those for? "Well, we can't stop you, but I preferred it when people cared about each other."

People meaning family, not friends and the rest of the world.

Dennis dropped her at the station. He was a headmaster, and given to hairy pullovers and balding.

"It's been lovely to see you and welcome you back, Julia. Don't leave it so long till next time," he said kindly. "We're always here if you need us."

"I haven't been to Africa," said Julia. On leaving the white farm gate she had abandoned the effort of trying to be nice and now sounded downright rude.

Dennis understandingly ignored Nutley Minor's cheek and went on giving wise, friendly advice. "You're looking quite stressed, you know. I suppose you've found out that looking after yourself isn't all it's cracked up to be. We all need someone to care for us. Now remember, Julia," he said with his head on one side in a generous attitude, "we're always here to help. Any time at all."

"Thanks." A fat lot you know about looking after yourself. You have this misguided impression that you protect and look after Belinda, when what you really do is provide money with which she protects and looks after you. And you'd be pretty surprised if I did ask you for help. You wouldn't have a clue what to do about my problem, apart from moving me back home to mother. Or finding a good man to look after me.

And would that really be so terrible, she asked herself, as the train started to move her towards Hackney Wick.

There was, of course, no real need for hurry. It was merely avoidance tactics, both of an unseemly bust-up and a general

105

nervous breakdown. She certainly didn't want to go home yet, if at all. Bernice wouldn't be back until eight, and she'd forgotten to ask when the Grosvenors would bus across the Lea Marshes from Leytonstone and walk briskly down Kenworthy Road.

But there was nowhere she could go to kill time. Her south London school friends had either moved away, or were married into the semi-purdah which lasts until all children are at school and/or husbands have become less attractive. And with the sole exception of Bernice, she had made no close friends since. Her social failure faced her yet again.

Cities are all right to be alone in during the day, but as evening approaches they become less comfortable. Those with things to do and places to go are doing it with others. Women on their own attract attention. Men on their own assume aloneness means loneliness, and that they are required to banish it. The predators come out.

Instead of the nicely prepared and laid family tea, she bought something fried in the station buffet, where the only thing she would appear to be waiting for was a train. Whatever did respectable, lone women do before the coming of railways? Not much, probably.

But by 1880 the country was swarming with railways, smoky, dirty, smelly, noisy, as bad as motorways. The back windows of Ermintrude Villas then looked out on a railway viaduct, and although the garden was longer, the smoke blew into it and suffocated the plants, and ruined the washing on the line, and blackened the windows, the paintwork and the brickwork. The housewife or servant worked constantly to clean off the black film, only to have it constantly renewed.

With that much cleaning to do, you'd be up and down stairs all day . . .

I do not want to go home.

She got a bus to Aldwych, then a 26 all the way to Hackney Wick. It was a slow, sleepy journey through the warm evening and the touristy streets, using up time, though not enough. The foot-bridge across the motorway was quite frightening, because there was nobody else about. In fact, she shouldn't have come this way, but hadn't been thinking. If one of Hackney's criminal classes were to step on the other end and advance upon her, there would be nothing she could do but run, and he would catch her long before she found any sort of help in the empty industrial ghetto at the other end.

And there might be one of them waiting under the railway viaduct. Or round the corner. Or across in the park; a whole gang might be waiting across the road in the park. Oh, Nutley family, I know I've been to see you, all right. My self-confidence has gone back weeks.

The windows were all closed. She unlocked the front door. The stillness of the house seemed to seize her by the throat and stop her breath. She shut it again and sat down on the steps, shaking. The first hints of sunset flushed over Bethnal Green.

I'm afraid to go into my home alone. Even when Bernice and Win and Harry are in I'm nervous and listening all the time. Alone in bed, I'm too scared to turn out the light and can't sleep.

I must move. Bernice can come too, if she wants to, so I won't be abandoning her.

She gazed across at the dry, springy grass. A few more hot days and it would be turning brown.

Was it difficult finding a flat? Did you have to be very alert and very street-wise to make sure you weren't being done? Did you have to sign an agreement, and would the agent make a fuss if you sat down and read it very carefully first, and then objected to terms you didn't like? She thought they almost certainly would object – after all, the advantage was on their side. Everyone wanted reasonably priced accommodation and it was hard to get.

I don't know anything about all that, I'm inexperienced, ignorant, utterly useless, and worse than that, scared. At twenty-nine. ("Really, Julia, how the dickens do you think you are going to survive on your own – you haven't the slightest idea of how to look after yourself.") No, I haven't

107

had up to now, but at least I'm trying to learn. I'm trying to be brave. Please appreciate that I'm trying to become responsible for myself and give me credit for it. No, you won't do that, because that's not the way you've ever wanted me to be, it wasn't the role you'd cast me for. And the reason for that is—

Everything suddenly slotted into place.

All groups of people, including families, needed to compare themselves with the less successful, and to indulge in head-shaking and sighs of "Whatever shall we do about poor X?" Someone had to be the dumbo, the scapegoat, the object of pity, in order to make the rest feel good about themselves.

And if I resign from that position, then someone else will have to take it on. And it might just turn out to be you, mightn't it, Mum. Without someone to belittle and nag and put down you'd have no status, because the other three don't really need you any more and you aren't anything in your own right. You're still playing head of the family, but Philip is gradually taking over the rôle. Being the person who tells others what to do is all you know, and because your entire terms of reference are bound up with being that person, just being Grace Nutley can't be done. How dreadful. There is no Grace Nutley. No wonder you're frightened. No wonder you're self-assertive, and aggressive, and intrusive.

Bernice appeared round the corner and waved. She toiled up the slope, carrying a bunch of garden flowers and a couple of carriers.

"Hello! Did you have a nice day?" Her eyes begged Julia to say that she had.

"Not too bad." Why inflict her problems on poor old Bernice.

"Look what Dad gave me from his garden, aren't they absolutely gorgeous? It would be so nice to have the front of our house blooming like this."

"Do you want to stay here?"

"Well – well, yes, I like it. It's home."

"But we aren't the only residents."

"It might stop. I mean, if it's to do with Mr Rillington, they'll be burying him soon and it might all stop, just like that." Bernice's visit home had made her more positive, unlike Julia's.

"Or alternatively, he could become one of Them himself and it'll be worse than ever. I'm exhausted, Bernie, and I can't see myself sleeping properly in this house ever again." Julia certainly did look pretty worn, and Bernice's eyes still had dark circles. She looked uncomfortable and stepped around the subject.

"Are you full up?"

"I had a huge lunch, but I didn't stay for tea."

"Oh dear, did it all go—" Bernice started, then stopped at the tense, defensive expression on Julia's face. She was learning. She proffered one of the carriers. "I bought a takeaway."

They opened up the flat and organised it back into their own occupation. Bernice put the Indian into the oven and went up to the loo. Julia flung the orange cloth over the coffee table and knocked over a fat white teddy in a tartan waistcoat. She sat McTed up again beside the hearth, along with the metal candlestick with a whimsical crescent moon on its shaft he had brought down with him.

She pushed the switch on the television. Nothing happened, and she started to panic at its lack of response before remembering she hadn't put the plug in that morning.

She bent down among the piles of CDs and video tapes and the clatter of metal came again. The moon candlestick remained upright, smiling, glancing at her out of the corner of its eyes while she heard sharp, slightly deadened blows, crunching, crackling, the rattling of metal on metal, the clang of an implement being restored to its place.

Julia crouched, petrified, with the plug in her hand. Her spine seemed to have locked and set her skull uncomfortably far back on her neck, looking up.

Creaking. The armchair was covered by a cotton throw bought from Bernice's Worldwide Fund for Nature catalogue, but something rubbed against squeaking brown leather. How could she know it was brown leather?

Now there was a tapping and rattling of wood, small sounds from small objects. A popping and bubbling. A long, exhaled breath.

In Bernice's bright, girlish world of flowers and stripes and teddies and pot-pourri, the smell of pipe smoke stole into the air.

The key turning in the front door was like another enemy creeping into the house to stab her nerves. Even the immediate sound of Grosvenor chatter didn't heal the wound in her self-possession. She knelt completely paralysed with fright, unable to get away from the invisible person who poked his fire, and sat down in his chair, and lit up a smoke.

Knocking came on the flat door.

"Anyone home, girls?"

The armchair was empty. The cushions didn't rise, as with the cat, they had remained unpressed during the sounds.

Julia got up and opened the door, standing looking into Win's rosy face. Her own presented her usual cool, expressionless barrier against the world, but her breathing came fast and her heartbeat thudded beneath her thin blouse.

"You all right, ducks?" Win was in her Sunday best. A flowery dress, a white acrylic cardigan in case of a change in the weather, beads and earrings. Even her shoes had an inch of heel.

"Can you smell anything?" asked Julia. Her throat closed before she got to the last syllable, so that the question finished on a strange hiccup.

Harry leant over Win's shoulder and sniffed.

"Pipe tobacco," he said decisively. "You reckon it's another intruder?" He was pretty smart himself, in slacks, checked jacket and tie.

"I don't think there ever was an intruder," croaked Julia. "I think it was one of Them. Just like this is. I heard him in here. He poked the fire and sat down in his chair and lit up his pipe. It definitely wasn't one of the women on the stairs."

The Spirit of the Family

Win put her arms around Julia's stiff, unresponsive body. "You mean the woman on the stairs, love."

"No, women. This morning there were several of them. I think they went out to church."

Win squeezed her harder, with a sympathetic "Dear oh Lor'!"

I don't like being cuddled, it's not what I've been used to. Touching means other things, not comfort. Touching means pulling into shape and pushing into position. Cuddle touching is false, an act for the benefit of others watching. I will not respond to the false. I will not deceive my feelings and emotions into expecting feelings and emotions in return. I will not be conned.

"Bring her upstairs, Harry, she's white as a blooming sheet. Leave the door. And better open the window – get rid of that stink."

"Takes you back, dunnit?" remembered Harry, sniffing nostalgically.

"Yeah, but you ain't going back, not to smoking."

"I don't need tea," Julia protested as they tried to lead her to the stairs.

"Then have a Scotch," said Harry persuasively.

Win was still holding her. I'd like her to let go but it would be so rude to say so. I mustn't hurt their feelings when they're being so kind, and whatever would we do without them?

She wondered what their daughter thought of them, and whether she looked forward to seeing them. Win was probably as forceful a mother-in-law and grandmother as Mrs Nutley, but appeared to get away with it.

Bernice came jumping down the stairs. "Hello! Nice day?"

"Oh hello, didn't know you was in. Yes, thanks, ducks," said Win. "Julia's just had another little upset. Someone smoking in your flat."

"Another burglar!" Bernice cried.

"No, a bloke you can't see."

"Oh my *God*!" Bernice nearly screamed. "Oh no! Oh Jule, whatever shall we do?" For a moment there seemed a dreadful

111

possibility that she might collapse, too, but gradually her normal life-view reappeared. "Oh, dear. Sorry. I mean, oh, *dear.* Still, they haven't actually done us any harm, have they?"

"Not yet," said Julia, stony-faced, "but what are they going to do next? That's the awful thing – we've no idea what to expect next."

"I suppose we could try accepting it, couldn't we; you know, see it as part of our lives instead of an intrusion. And he has gone now, hasn't he?"

"I'm not promising," said Julia.

"You want to sleep upstairs, girls?" asked Harry.

"No, we'll be all right," Bernice said bravely.

"That's the spirit," said Harry, grinning and feinting a punch to the side of her head.

The steps went along the hall at ten. The Grosvenors didn't hear it through the blasting of their television.

"Can't we move?" begged Julia.

Eleven

A few days later, Luke waylaid them as they came home from work. It appeared that someone had been round from Cyprian Smith's, and moving was definitely on the cards.

They felt sorry for him and his little family. At least they could afford to pay for another flat – he had to find another squat fit to bring up a baby in.

"But the Grosvenors are sitting tenants, too, aren't they?" said Bernice as they climbed up the front steps. "I bet they don't go without a fight, ghosts notwithstanding."

The death of solitary Joe Rillington was affecting far more people than might have been expected.

They found out about his funeral from the local paper. Every Thursday morning, Harry sat in the bay window with as much breakfast as Win would allow him and scoured the *Hackney Gazette* for interesting news, past and present. This Thursday he descended immediately to knock upon the girls' door, and inform them that the funeral service for the late Mr Joseph James Rillington would be held at the Sankey Road Strict Baptist Chapel, Walthamstow on Saturday.

"Funny day for a funeral, but it means you two will be able to go, if you want. Win and I'll step over there for old times' sake, but I dunno where the church is, I'm sure. Never heard of it. Still, to be honest with you, the only bits of Walthamstow I ever really knew were the Stadium and the Granada."

They invited him in and searched for the A to Z, which Bernice found at last under Teddy Mary, a well-worn, rather sinister giant in a print dress, named after the great-aunt who had given it to her.

"Here it is," she said, running her finger across the squares and squinting. "Goodness, it's quite a way."

"There'll be a bus, love," he said, "or even a train."

Julia studied the notice. "It says, burial afterwards at Abney Park Cemetery, Stoke Newington, so we'll have to get back on the bus pretty quickly if we're going to make that."

"Oh. Yeah, that's true."

"Perhaps there'll be room for us in one of the cars?" she suggested.

"Doubt it," he said, screwing up his face. "In my experience of funerals they work out exactly how few limos they can squeeze everyone into, so I reckon we may have to give the service a miss and just turn up at the cemetery."

They decided to club together for flowers.

"Pink," said Win decidedly. "You can't beat pink."

"Are you going to ask the squatters?" asked Julia as they handed her their money.

"I don't reckon they could afford it, love," she said, stuffing the notes into her bag, "so I won't embarrass them by asking. Right, I'll order something nice on our way out. We're going over to the Archives again, so we may have more to tell you tonight. How did you sleep?"

"Oh, not too bad," said Bernice brightly.

The footsteps had gone down the hall several times. They had sat together on Bernice's bed, solaced by cheap Bulgarian Sauvignon and Sara Lee chocolate gateau, but eventually dropped off.

"Funny what you can get used to," said Julia, and was indeed surprised at herself, though hardly amused.

It might be all right once he's buried, she told herself. She didn't quite see why, but it helped to have something to hold on to. Whatever it was, it would stop then.

And tonight, after a quiet and uneventful evening, she went back to her own room, really pleased at how brave she was being.

* * *

She awoke with a violent jump. The electric light looked puny in the first light osmosing through the curtains. The fan purred and jerked. The traffic came and went in the irregular, repetitive way which is supposed to create the most irritating sound pattern in the world, but neither of these had woken her. It was the gentle tinkling, as of an oriental windbell, sometimes soft as if brushed by a gentle hand, sometimes a sharp crash, as if struck.

The apprehension was already back with her as she opened her eyes.

It must be caused by the fan – something being agitated by its busy wind. She studied and eliminated the curtains, the clothes flung over the sunflowered chair, the beads lying still on the mantlepiece, and all the other movable, blowable items scattered about the room. 'Yes you can' remained immovable on the truncated gas bracket. Oh, can I.

Beads – it definitely sounded like beads. Not a bead necklace, though, nor a curtain; that rattled and this tinkled. It must be very small beads. She'd seen something recently with lots of small beads.

It lasted about half an hour. She didn't go back to sleep.

"Bernice, that box of stuff under my bed – could we put it somewhere else?"

"Is it in your way?"

"No," said Julia. "I just don't like it. It's the feeling of not knowing where it's been."

Her mother's vocabulary. Put that down, Julia, you don't know where it's been. Don't touch those, you don't know where they've been. Don't have anything to do with *him* – who know's where he's been? Since it was almost impossible to know where anything in the whole world had been in the past, it was not surprising that she had put the whole place off limits.

"All right, then, we'll move it out into the hall tonight."

"The front hall," Julia suggested with some force.

115

"Oh," said Bernice, looking puzzled. "Supposing it gets stolen?"

"Who'll care? Are you going to tell Tom?"

"I suppose we'll have to. But I can't see him being too upset; you know Tom, he's pretty happy-go-lucky. And we'll all have a lovely day in the park on Sunday, won't we?" she said with a bright, comforting smile.

"You what?" exclaimed Tom, dumping his bag on the floor. They explained what.

"Get off!" he jeered.

"We're trying to," said Julia. "We've had enough."

"Rubbish!" he declared in the required macho fashion, but with rather less force.

They gave him the full details.

He sat up late in front of the television, drinking Carlsberg.

"Aren't you tired, Tom?" asked Bernice, yawning.

"I just want to see the end of this," he said blandly. He fell asleep at two, without making any attempt to undress. Bernice pulled a face at Julia. They left him sprawled across the settee and tiptoed away into the bedroom. Julia picked up the funny book. Bernice leafed through yet another catalogue which had arrived that morning. You could now get bed linen covered with sunflowers as well, she told Julia with delight.

"How do you think it will be tomorrow?" asked Julia as her eyes drooped. "I've never been to a burial. My family goes in for cremation and tidy little pigeon-holes in a Wall of Memory."

She remembered the sheer ridiculousness of posting her father into his box. She hoped a celestial correspondent had collected him. It was difficult to imagine Dad in an afterlife, he had been so up to his neck in this one; always out looking after people, or on his way to look after people, or preoccupied with thinking about people who needed looking after. His science was not only above all things, but also the measure of all things, for he acknowledged nothing outside it. Even while she was working for him, there had been little personal communication. Dictation was made. Instructions were left on the desk. And for other things the recommendation was to ask your mother. She'd hardly known him at all.

"We have burials. There's quite a row of us in Hendon Park."

"What's it like? All grisly like in Hamlet?"

"Oh no," Bernice reassured her. "Everything's covered up with that artificial grass, so you can't see any of the earth they've dug out. And if there's already another coffin in there they cover that up, too. It's very nice and tasteful, really it is."

Tom was a bit under the weather and taciturn next morning and made little complaint when they went out. The sun was flooding the park with brilliant promise for another warm day, and the grass was beginning to brown.

A lot of buses went up the Kingsland Road and stopped outside Abney Park Cemetery, so they were there in plenty of time. The sight of lodges and pylons straight from a Pharaoh's funerary temple was rather shocking. It was as if you had started out to a decent, Gothic, traditionally English ceremony and finished up on the back lot at MGM. The central gates were already open in readiness for the hearse, and a man was hovering between them and the lodge. Ahead, the entrance courtyard split into orange-sanded roads which wound off into the trees, through a mysterious world of monuments and undergrowth.

"Better ask where it is," said Win, "or we'll end up running after the procession." She was wearing a straight black skirt, a high-necked white blouse with a lot of nylon lace and the same heeled shoes she had worn to her daughter's. The hovering man went in and out of the lodge to produce a plan, complete with X marks the spot, and they set off like an expedition to the interior, with Win bearing the map ahead of them.

"I think this is the wrong way, Win," said Harry presently, as they approached a derelict brick chapel which looked alarmingly like a giant crustacean.

117

"Gosh, I do hope so," said Julia, her scalp beginning to crawl. If there was anything bound to get her head swimming with vertigo, it was being under a church spire, and this one was very tall indeed.

"No, this is right," said Win with utter certainty. "We go straight past the chapel and turn right, then cut through that little path there."

They neared the arched porch under which black carriages had drawn up, and where waiting horses had tossed their plumed heads. From within, there suddenly came a deafening rattling and banging which gave Julia, and probably at least some of the other three, a shock she could have done without.

"Only pigeons," said Harry, turning round and grinning. "They hit the corrugated iron on the windows."

"Ah," said Bernice, smiling. She walked on quite fast, though. Julia followed, resolutely refusing to look up.

Win did get lost, which meant they all did. Her sense of direction was reasonable, but many little pathways shown on the plan were no longer available, due to undergrowth, and on top of that, some of them had graves across them. They struggled between upright obelisks and draped urns which surely could not have been installed until all members of the family had come home, and were frequently blocked by smug, square pepperpots which seemed to be the most popular style of memorial. Eventually, they reached the grave by an extremely roundabout route. It was on the north side, one row back from the road which went all round the outside of the cemetery. It was indeed covered by sheets of mock turf, and a very large grey slab topped with theatrical flourishes was propped against an intentionally broken pillar too massive to suffer from the liberty.

They only just made it in time.

The hearse could be seen turning the stone-crowded corner ahead, its lack of speed not only for reverence's sake, but for safety. They moved to the other side of the road and stood there with folded hands and sympathetic faces as the procession approached.

There were two lots of flowers on the coffin. One was their little round pink cushion. The other was a sheaf keeping itself firmly to itself within an envelope of cellophane.

There was only one car behind, and only one mourner in the centre of the back seat. A large, square woman sat in what might be described as state, wearing a lot of clothes for a hot day, mostly black. The funeral director glided from the hearse to open her door and she got out, leaning on his hand, to stand with bunioned feet turned out while the coffin was removed.

They all four stared at her, then switched their gaze hastily to the emerging deceased as she suddenly turned. Her face had an extraordinary lumpiness about it, and the hair just about showing beneath her velour hat was streaky grey. Everything about her was remarkably unattractive, both the things she couldn't help and the ones she could.

The minister emerged from beside the driver. He might have been Strict, but still looked human and rather nice, and after giving them an anxious summing-up and deciding that they did belong to his funeral, he made a bidding gesture.

They went and stood at the graveside. Bernice was right; the bottom was covered and however many relatives lay down there, they were decently invisible. It didn't take long to consign Joseph Rillington to the ground, most of the ritual having previously taken place in Walthamstow. Words were spoken, earth was scattered, the meagre flowers were laid on the bank of imitation grass.

The woman shook hands with the minister, then looked across the grave and nodded. Her eyes were pale and slightly protuberant, and her thin mouth took cover between the strange, pasty bulges of her face, thus avoiding any obligation to smile.

The funeral party embarked once more and continued on its way, disappearing round the next bend with even more care than the last.

"Dear me," said Bernice, pulling a face, "I suppose that must have been Florrie."

"She had eyes just like old Joe's," said Win, holding her handbag to her bosom. "Give me quite a turn. I got the feeling I was trespassing, didn't you?"

"Yeah, I certainly did," said Harry with a touch of resentment. "For a moment I thought one of the bearers was going to pull out a shotgun and see us off the estate. What a miserable old cow. Here, what you doing, Win?"

Win had climbed past the open grave, and, straight skirt notwithstanding, whipped a notebook out of her bag and started scribbling. The girls remained in the sandy road, well back from the green grass hole into which Mr Rillington had been squeezed, and Julia noticed a couple of men in jeans and teeshirts waiting further down. Oh goodness, gravediggers.

"Look at all them names!" Win cried excitedly. "But they can't all be in there, surely! I mean, there ain't room."

"How many can you get in a grave?" asked Julia nervously, hoping nobody would tell her.

"Win!" Harry said sharply. "Better leave it."

They looked up. The gleaming black backside of the limousine was reappearing round the corner, like an overweight dowager easing herself towards a chair. Once more they stood politely at the side of the road with funeral faces and behaviour, while the car whispered to a halt beside them. The passenger was seen to lean forward, then the window slid down and framed her bun face and dreadful hat.

"Excuse me, are you by any chance Win, Harry, Julia and Bernice?"

She said 'bay,' thought Julia. I've never heard anyone pronounce by as bay before, not even in Worcester Park.

"That's right," said Win, stony faced. "We was Mr Rillington's neighbours."

"Eoow, how kind of you," said the woman with great condescension but not a sign of cracking her face, "I wondered where the other floral tribute came from, the names were quite unknown to me." Only she said quate.

After distressing emotion tend to come relieved giggles. Julia didn't dare to look at Bernice in case she was having the same trouble.

"My name is Lily Wright. Would you care for a lift home, I am going in that direction? Or have you your own transport?"

It was like the lady of the manor bestowing largesse on tenants. No, not quite, thought Julia, perhaps just going through the motions of etiquette to prove she knew them; like her mother, only with more dignity.

"Well, don't mind if we do," said Win, pushing her notebook back into her handbag and preparing to board.

She and Bernice took their places on either side of Lily, who stuck firmly to her central position, and Julia and Harry sat opposite. Julia succeeded in looking at ease outwardly, but failed totally inside, *vis-à-vis* this Medusa.

"Nice day for it, anyway," said Harry with modified cheer, "nothing worse than a burial in the rain."

"Quite nice," said Lily, indicating she was used to better, and looked out at the passing monuments as if they were likely to wave at her. "There is some very high class statuary in this cemetery," she told them.

"Yeah, and it's nice to be able to see them again proper," chattered Win. "We come in here a few years back before they cleared it up, and it felt like looking for the source of the Nile. We was looking for one of Harry's people, but we couldn't get near him. Stuck away on the edge under enough undergrowth to hide an army, and even the roads was full of mud and potholes. Of course, it was a common grave, so there probably weren't no stone to see, anyway."

"A common grave? Oh *relly*?" said Lily, fixing her fishy eyes upon Win. "And do you have relatives in here, too?"

"No," said Win, "mine are mostly in Tower Hamlets, and they're common graves, too. But we put my mum and dad out at the City of London, and they've got a real lovely stone. Beautiful black marble with little glittery bits in it, and a rose carved in the corner. And the lettering's all gold."

"One always likes to give one's parents the best, even when

121

they've never been used to it. Our grave cost a great deal of money. And of course, opening it for each family member has always involved a large outlay. Particularly this time," she added with some pride, "as the cemetery is officially closed to burials except for very special cases."

"Couldn't the others come today?" asked Julia with a certain tartness.

Lily's gaze hit her face like a left hook. "There are no others. I am the last of the line. I am the daughter of Mr Rillington's sister Agnes," she boasted. (You've heard of sister Agnes, haven't you? Well, of course you have.)

"Oh dear, how sad for you," Bernice exclaimed.

Win opened her mouth but Lily beat her to it.

"The estate will therefore come to me," she stated, black-draped legs astride on the soft, grey upholstery. "Mine was a most superior family, very rich and very well-respected. You would not believe the achievements my family has to its credit."

"No, I don't reckon I—" Win started.

"My grandfather, old Mr Rillington, had a very large drapery business in Mayar Street; all the local professional families used to patronise it. Some customers came from Highbury and Islington, and even from the City and the West End."

"You mean it was better than Sel—"

"His father, who started the firm in Clerkenwell and moved out in 1875, had kept his own carriage, and he himself purchased one of the first motors ever seen in Heckneh."

"Oh yeah? I remember when—"

"My grandfather was a councillor for some years, and received a testimonial from the Borough on his retirement. And he was also a churchwarden at St John of Jerusalem, a very fashionable congregation and not too high. I do not care for churches which are too high." The car nosed out of the Egyptian entrance into Stoke Newington High Street, and the driver put his foot down. "Driver! I am not accustomed to speed! I'm afraid a delicate constitution is one of the burdens of good breeding. As my dear mother said . . ."

She remained metaphorically on her feet for the entire journey back to Ermintrude Villas, her loud, slow, refined pronouncements bludgeoning them with the Rillington Saga while they sat within the purring black limousine, asphyxiated by her eau-de-Cologne. The hearse had disappeared and the driver, who had been told to remove the earpiece of his radio, was a bit sulky. Every attempt by Win to turn the monologue into a conversation was mercilessly mown down in a way that, in a non-superior family, would have been considered bad manners.

"Do you remember the shop?" Bernice said, turning to Lily with charming ingenuity and managing to get through.

"I most certainly do. I was taken there on numerous occasions to buy my wardrobe."

"They sold furniture as well, did they?" said Harry.

"No, they did not," said Lily coldly. "I was referring to dress. The establishment was about halfway down the west side, a very handsome building put up by my great-grandfather. Unfortunately it was destroyed by firebombs in 1942. I can remember my dear mother picking up the newspaper from the mat and exclaiming, 'Oh, Lily, your inheritance has gone up in flames!'"

"So you must have come to Ermintrude Villas, too?" said Bernice with interest. Julia saw what she was up to.

"No, my parents and Uncle Joseph did not speak at that time."

"Really?" said Win, perking up and getting a word in despite Lily. "Had a row, did they?"

Lily flinched as if she had received a painful dig in the family honour.

"The Rillingtons were extremely well-bred people," she admonished. "We as a family have never engaged in altercation of any kind. Family loyalty was upheld by every member as a sacred trust."

"How come you wasn't speaking to old Joe, then?" said Win bluntly.

"It was due to a misunderstanding; he could be somewhat

difficult. After the death of my dear mother I called on him and offered to let bygones be bygones, but it was not accepted. *However*," said Lily in a more threatening voice, turning her head so that her words bounced off Win's impertinent, plebeian countenance like batons at a demonstration, "I nevertheless wrote to him regularly on his birthday and at Christmas, with appropriate good wishes."

The arrival of a large black limousine with a uniformed chauffeur outside Ermintrude Villas caused a certain amount of interest among Hackney residents using the park, washing their cars or looking out of their windows. The slow unloading of Lily provided an equally absorbing spectacle, and her expression as she studied the outside of her uncle's disintegrating den would have delighted anyone interested in human nature.

She made as if to descend the first step. Harry caught her under the elbow and steadied her.

"It's all locked up," he said, "and I reckon the agent's got the key."

"Oh," she said, looking severely put out.

"Never you mind, love," said Win. "Harry, give her a hand up the steps, and we'll all have a bite to eat."

Lily Wright could get no further than the ground floor, so post-funeral refreshments were served in the girls' living room, from which Tom was fortunately absent. There, she quickly got into her stride again, boasting of her ancestry and inheritance.

"I thought he didn't leave a will," said Julia, feeling she could happily fight to the death to stop this snooty old bat that Mr Rillington seemed to have disliked from getting her hands on his few personal possessions.

"The estate was entailed in my grandfather's will," Lily squashed her, and all of them.

Oh, the dignity she put into the word! *Your* family has never inherited anything by entail. *You* don't come from a commercial aristocracy with a great inheritance passed on from generation to generation. *Your* petty little family

Testaments or Grants of Administration never dealt with such glories.

A sip of tea allowed in a quick question from Win, whose face had screwed up into permanent determined resentment some time ago.

"Where would that be, then?"

"Where would what be?" asked Lily, recovering from the sip.

"The estate. Big house in the country, was it? Lots of servants?"

"You misunderstand me," said Lily, flushing. "I refer to pecuniary estate. And the houses, of course."

"What, old Joe owned property?" exclaimed Win.

Lily looked at her as if she were stupid as well as working-class. "We are sitting in it," she said coldly. "Ermintrude Villas has belonged to the family since well before the war. Were you not aware that he was your landlord?"

"No, we bloody wasn't!" said Harry with amazement, "—begging your pardon."

"The agent never said," said Win, looking outraged. "Well, fancy old Joe sitting down there pretending to be a tenant like us, and there's us worrying that his flat was in need of repair and bad for his health, and the top floor with a leaking roof and blocked up plumbing, and we couldn't get nothing done about neither of them nohow, and Harry having to climb up and do it hisself – cor!! And we used to take him in bits and pieces sometimes in the old days before he went mental, because we reckoned he'd only got his pension to live on!"

"Hear that?" said Harry, turning to Lily again and sitting with hands on knees, staring at her. "All them years your Uncle Joe was taking our money and giving us sod all in return. What did he do with it, eh? Stick it in the bank? And so now you're our landlady, eh?"

"I am the new proprietress of these properties, yes," said Lily, distancing herself from the seaside image.

"Well, nice to meet you, Lily, and I honestly hope we're going to have a good working relationship. We're regular payers, by the way, and so are the girls, so you've got nothing to worry about there."

"The business of payment will be nothing to do with me," said Lily, "and I must warn you that I may choose to realise my assets." Julia had the impression that she had been practising saying that for many years. "In which case," Lily went on, fixing her fishy eyes upon Win, "it might be advisable to start seeking other accommodation."

Win stared at her, too. "Oh yeah?" she said.

It was quite a business getting Lily Wright back down the front steps. It appeared she could not use public transport, due to her feet, so a minicab had been called, but they were all left waiting on the front path for some time. The atmosphere was strained, particularly that exuding from Win, and even Harry seemed put out and very nearly tetchy. Lily ignored them and examined her inheritance.

"He never done a thing to none of them, not the whole time we been here," explained Harry emphatically. "Them window frames up there, I done them meself, cause they was rotting. I climbed up and put a few slates in, too, when the rain was getting in. That window there," he indicated Mr Rillington's bay, "I put a new piece of glass in when it got broke, and that bit of hardboard was from after he threw things out. He wasn't all there by then."

"What happened to them?" asked Lily, weighing up whether her feet could cope with the three steps down to the basement.

"What happened to what?"

"The articles which came out of the window," said Lily, ignoring the fact that Joe's hand had propelled them.

"Couldn't say," said Harry, looking grim.

A long, flashy Toyota swept round the corner from the Wick, shot up the road past the house, braked sharply and backed again. All the windows were wide open so that the driver could share his taste in music with the world.

"Car for Walthamstow," he shouted above the din.

"That's right," Harry said, going over to lean in the window and speak in confidence. "I should keep that music going, mate, she loves it. Oh, and she's a bit of a speed freak, too, so give her an exciting ride, won't you? Might win you a good tip." The driver winked. "Right on, man."

Twelve

"That wasn't kind, Harry," scolded Win, as the Lily-bearing minicab was heard doing an exciting three point turn in the scrap of road before the railway viaduct and the foot-bridge. "Supposing she gets hurt?"

"She won't," said Harry. "Wait till he gets her onto the Lea Bridge Road," he added with satisfaction.

"He might go via Hackney Marsh," said Win.

"Nah, you can't get up any sort of a speed in Leyton High Road. Lea Bridge Road it'll be."

They strolled up the steps and back into Bernice's flat, to sit down and start a belated post-mortem on the last rites of Joseph James Rillington.

"Well, this is a turn up for the book," said Win, weighing the teapot and raising the lid when it proved disappointingly light.

"She wasn't very nice, was she," said Bernice regretfully, taking it from Win's hand and going behind the curtain.

"How come she's the last, and the one who collects all the cash?" said Julia. "There seemed to be enough names on that stone for the Rillingtons to populate Hackney all by themselves."

"Wonder if she's got any children?" asked Bernice from behind the curtain.

"No ring," said Julia. She always noticed that.

"Well, I'm going right back up there as soon as possible to take another look," said Win with obvious excitement. "Then a bit more follow-up in the archives, and we might start seeing what's behind all this."

"Here, they ain't our family, you know," protested Harry. "What about our lot? We was just getting somewhere with Mary Jane."

"The Grosvenors and the Smarts'll wait," said Win firmly, "I've just got to track this lot down first. It's like an addiction, love," she said, turning to Julia. "Once you gets on the track there's no leaving it till you reach the end." She squeezed her arm comfortingly. "Don't you worry – we'll find out what this is all about."

"And will that stop it, do you think?" said Julia hopefully.

"I don't know about that," she warned. "Right, girls, as soon as we've taken off all this," she indicated their concessions to funerary convention, "Harry and me are off to Leytonstone for the weekend. Our Shirley wants us to stay over, being Bank Holiday, and she's got Trish and him and his people coming up as well, so we can't say no without looking rude to them. Now you've got Tom to look after you, and I don't suppose you'll have any trouble anyway. We'll be back during Monday evening. Reckon we'll have had enough of that lot by then." She grimaced. "OK?"

"We'll be quite all right," said Bernice.

"Yes," said Julia, and immediately became paralysed with apprehension.

The weekend shopping in the afternoon was made easier than usual by Tom's car. They climbed up on to the flyover and swept past the grubby backs of Lily Wright's houses on the way to Tesco's at Bromley.

Julia had not expected to come off that howling racetrack, alight in a supermarket car park and find herself next to an abandoned piece of rural Essex. In fact, it had always been the first bit of rural Essex on the way out of London, on the Lea by Bow Bridge; river, trees, eighteenth-century watermills, towpath, lock gates. In the past, the view had also included monastic ruins, but building had long ago wiped those out and translated a large number of the monks into cardboard boxes in a Plaistow warehouse. Even now, the wharf stacked high with waste paper, the view of the sewage pumping station and the gasworks and the District Railway and the line from Fenchurch Street to Southend crossing overhead only seemed to accentuate its anachronistic charm.

"Look at it!" she exclaimed. "Take a photograph from a careful angle and it might be a Constable."

"Yes, isn't it pretty," agreed Bernice, as gratified to have given Julia pleasure as if she had built the whole thing herself with her bare hands. Quite apart from the horrible situation in her flat, which was at least as embarrassing as inviting a long-term guest at the very moment the loo goes out of commission, the problems in her friend's family had worried her a lot over the last weeks.

She liked Jule so much, she was such a nice person. She was good-looking and graceful, and polite and helpful, and free of the abrasive idiosyncracies which make working with some people unnecessarily trying. And yet she was aware that underneath that shiny brown hair, and behind that tranquil, madonna's face, Julia was not a happy person at all.

She didn't greet the world's small joys as gifts presented to her by life and intended for her enjoyment. She didn't look forward to things with confidence that they would arrive and deliver their sweets into her hands. She didn't seem at home with that greatest of excitements, the male sex, or even to aspire to enjoy it. Everything seemed to be approached with distrust, with testing, with an expectation that it would be snatched away at the last minute, or, being tasted, would turn to dust in her mouth. Despite her cool, self-confident appearance, there was a tenseness about her, a refusal to accept anything at face value, except the likelihood of disappointment. And there was the tendency towards apology and self-deprecation, and the apparent assumption that if something was denied her, it was almost certainly her own fault. It was all so sad.

On Saturday night, friends came round to partake of Julia's cooking. They were a couple from Camden Town, the female partner being a childhood friend of Bernice's. A second male was brought in to make up the numbers.

"Not Jim," Julia had requested.

"Chris?"

"Yes, Chris is all right."

Everyone expressed delight at the inside of the flat while remaining politely tacit about the outside and the bathroom, and they raved quite genuinely about the food. If the steps had come down the stairs they couldn't have heard them through the music and conversation.

"That was a lovely evening, wasn't it?" asked Bernice as they washed up enough to leave room for eating breakfast. "That meal was absolutely delicious, Jule. I bet Chris is wondering whether to offer you a permanent position."

Julia didn't say anything, and Bernice winced and went back to collect more glasses. She must remember not to *do* that. Tom was leaning out of the open sash window into the twinkling darkness. She came up beside him and put her arms about his waist.

"I can hear someone crying," he said.

"Oh dear, is it in the park? Perhaps we ought to call the police."

"Seems to have stopped now, but it was nearer than that." He sniffed. "Someone's smoking. Probably at the upstairs window."

"He's given up, and anyway they're out," said Bernice, her tender, happy mood immediately vanishing. "Tom, it's one of Them again. Look round, quick. Can you see anything strange happening?"

"Them?" he exclaimed incredulously. "What are they, nine foot high ants?"

"I'm serious," she said, her voice growing higher. "Look around, please!"

Julia came round the curtain, the sponge mop dripping onto Bernice's teddy apron.

The happiness of the evening evaporated and fear rushed in to fill its place. Tom stood in a state of disbelief while the two girls looked, listened, turned their heads, afraid of being taken by surprise. There was no denying that the pipe smoke was there again. They backed away from the armchair and stared suspiciously at a squashed cushion in the corner of the settee.

Then Tom glanced down, around and at the window, puzzled and then visibly alarmed.

"Is it the cat?" asked Julia in a rising voice. Her nervous hands were squeezing the mop over the carpet.

"Well," he granted after a few seconds thought, "it could have been a cat." He slicked his hair back and looked the room over again, this time with anxious concentration. "Hey, there it is again," he said, turning to the window, "a woman crying. Can't you hear her?"

They hurried through the hall with nervous glances up the silent stairs. They stood on the steps and strained their ears through the roar of the traffic and the music of neighbours pounding through the warm, lamplit darkness. They could all hear it, now; a woman in distress, though it was difficult to pinpoint where. It seemed to be around and above them, but after some minutes' search they had discovered only one thing about it. It faded as they moved away from Ermintrude Villas.

They stood in the minute front garden, looking through the dark, dirty window of the basement. The woman was still weeping, and there was still no indication of where she was. Somehow the thin, high, sobbing voice floated separately among motorway whine and hissing reggae percussion.

"I am *not* going in there," said Julia fervently.

"We haven't got the key, Jule. I suppose it isn't someone real?"

"It sounds bloody real to me," Tom retorted, peering in. "Got a torch?"

"No."

"It could be one of the Bangladeshis."

"It's not on that side."

"What about the squatters?"

"Give them a knock in case."

Tom went over the wall. The girls stayed in the garden,

tense, tearful and yet again, scared. Their conversation was short and brusque.

"She's not screaming as if she's in pain," said Bernice, in the tone of one thanking God for small mercies. "Doesn't sound clear enough for the front room. Could be the back one. That was Mr Rillington's bedroom."

"Which one is the range in?"

"Don't know. His kitchen's at the back under the bedroom."

Julia shivered at the thought of that dark hollow beneath her bed. "Why at this time of night?" she protested.

"Do they have any time?"

"They cleaned the range at six in the morning."

"Well," said Bernice, "some people always had to be punctual."

"You mean, a servant?"

"Maybe. Jule, do you think They are Rillingtons?"

"I don't see how they could be. According to those directories, they weren't here until 1932. That doesn't go with long, swishing skirts."

"Oh, I hate all this," Bernice whispered with agitation, "it's so sad and so dreadful, and such a shock, too. I always felt there must be such things as ghosts, because so many people seemed to have seen them, but I never, ever thought . . ." She shook her head.

"I did, too," admitted Julia. There was so much negative emotion flying about everywhere, that some of it was bound to hang about in dark corners. In fact once – hello, she'd thought that was well at the back of the cupboard; she'd never envisaged that being allowed out, ever. Cram it back in. Tom reappeared.

"They hadn't heard a thing," he said, rolling casually over the wall. "I stuck my ear up against their weirdo posters, but nothing. Seems to be all right now."

"It's not all right," said Bernice, tears running down her face. "It will never be all right. This poor house is so full of sadness that it's dying of a broken heart."

Bernice's twee habit of animating the inanimate didn't seem silly this time; in fact, Julia felt her words were in tune with what she'd already sensed herself. The house seemed diseased. It had held infection within it for decades and now the sickness was coming out. Its all-wrongness was emerging into public view; the secrets, the sorrows, the shames, the things which the neighbours must neither hear nor see, must never, ever know – they were all getting out at last.

"It must not get out," said the voice close to Julia's ear. She turned her head, found nothing there and went completely to pieces.

For minutes she sobbed and screamed and begged to be allowed to go home, and asked where Mummy and Daddy were, and said she couldn't stand it any more and they must let her go at once because she was going mad, going mad!

She was persuaded into bed and wrapped in blankets, and plied with whisky and hot water. Bernice stayed with her for hours, while Tom sloped off to the bed-settee.

Julia jerked out of an exhausted doze to hear him knocking on her door and saying someone wanted her on the phone. The sun was up and Bernice was gone.

She turned off the radio which had burbled companionably into her ear for the last few hours, then went to tread the embarrassing journey from kitchen door to bay window, around the doubly occupied bed, trying to forget the awful spectacle she had made of herself the night before.

"All right?" he asked gruffly.

"Yes thanks," she said coolly, not looking at him. "Hello?"

"Julia, you are coming to lunch today, aren't you?"

"No. I told you I wasn't. Sorry."

"But that will be two you've missed," protested Belinda, "and Mother will be furious. How long are you going to keep this up? Don't you like your family? I mean, we all go along with this arrangement, so why shouldn't you?"

"That doesn't sound very enthusiastic. If you're all just going along with it and only doing it because you should, it sounds as if you secretly feel like I do."

"And how *do* you feel?" demanded Belinda.

"Claustrophobic. I feel I've been repeatedly forced into the company of people whom I should like a lot better if I saw them voluntarily and less often."

"Oh thanks a lot!" said Belinda.

"Well, it isn't what I want to feel about you, and if it weren't for all this togetherness by order I probably wouldn't," Julia tried to explain. "I can see things in nearly every member of my family which I like and could enjoy, but it all gets spoilt by this suffocating obligation to like and enjoy them all the time. It's like Christmas once a week."

"What on earth are you talking about, Julia?" Belinda said wildly. "And surely you don't include Mother? After all she's done for us? How *can* you not like your own mother?"

"Have you really looked at her, Belinda? Have you listened to her opinions and the awful, tactless things she says to you and the children? Have you ever heard her say anything kind or encouraging or positive? Every time we meet I start off determined to make allowances for the way she is, and to be patient and let it all go over my head, but after five minutes in her company my spirits have taken a dive and the most positive feeling I have about life is that I would rather like to be dead and out of it. I have lived with Mother for twenty-nine years, ten of them with only her and very occasionally Dad, and the last one as the sole person sharing the house with her, and she's got steadily worse. I have put up with her, and gone along with her, and given in to her, and lost my self-confidence and my freedom in doing it. In some ways, I really think I've come close to losing my sanity. You *know* I'm right," Julia urged, desperate to be understood. She saw her mother with such clarity that it seemed unbelievable that Belinda apparently did not. It was the difference between seeing things as they were and as they ought to be. "Have you really not noticed the continual barrage of negative opinions, and the scorn for everyone and everything? Her inability to see anyone else's point of view, because she never listens to it? The way you

135

can never quite do things right for her? The way you can't win because she doesn't want you to?"

"She's not that bad," said Belinda, audibly shocked.

"She has been to *me*," Julia insisted with anguish.

"Don't be so silly," said Belinda, falling back on her mother's clinching catch-phrase as she felt the alarm aroused by sudden recognition that something is unpleasantly and inconveniently true. "You're paranoid, that's your trouble."

"And who's fault would it be if I were?"

"Yours. Mother's all right if you know how to take her. Anyway, it's awful to talk about your mother like that. I mean, you just don't."

"I just did because it's true!"

"Yes, I heard you, and you shouldn't even if it were! She needs you, Julia! She's all alone in that big house."

"She can move to somewhere smaller."

"But she couldn't bear to leave – not when she's spent all her married life there."

"Other people have to do it. Or she could take in lodgers."

"I will treat that very silly remark with the contempt it deserves." Belinda's hysteria was very near the surface, now. Julia's totally unexpected defection had put all responsibility for their mother onto her sisters, and they had found it neither easy nor pleasant, but then neither had Julia. "It's just not fair of you, Ju. if you don't turn up this week we're all going to catch the fall-out, and it'll be another horrible, spoilt day."

"Well, if it is it will be down to Mum. It's her that makes the bad atmospheres and stresses in our family, Bel, not me, and I don't see why I should continue to be blamed. Why don't all the rest of you start standing up to her as well? She might even improve." She suddenly remembered the audience behind her and was overcome with embarrassment. "Well, good luck, anyway," she finished lamely. "'Bye."

The two faces above the sheet looked stunned.

"Sorry," said Julia.

"That's all right," said Bernice in her most little-girlish voice.

"Are you ready for some tea?" asked Julia distantly.

"What a good idea," said Tom. He was looking at her as if she'd turned into a toad.

She could hear a low-voiced discussion on the other side of the curtain. She filled the bowl with water and put more china in to soak before she took their mugs in, plus a two-for-the-price-of-one packet of chocolate chip cookies she'd fallen for in Tesco's. She needed a bit of comfort eating.

"You're not going out to lunch, then," said Bernice, still about six years old.

"No."

"Would you like to come to Kew with us?"

"Are you sure you want me?"

"Of course."

"All right. Thanks." She went through the curtain and poured her own tea, then heard Tom's thoroughly fed up voice ask "Hasn't she got *any* friends of her own?"

"Not round here," said Bernice apologetically.

Julia whisked her mug out of the room, shut the door, sat down on her bed and tried to control the gush of tears, but the pain in her throat was so bad that she had to let them out and sob into the sheet with her pillow over her head.

He doesn't want me to come, and I don't blame him, who wants a perpetual gooseberry? I don't think Bernice does either, really, she's just being kind. But if I don't go with them wherever shall I go? This is the place I was hoping to make my bolthole, and now I'm afraid to stay here alone.

It's all gone wrong. You blame your problems on your surroundings, and then find they've grown into you and that you're carrying them around with you wherever you go. Perhaps all this is my fault, too.

By the time she'd dried up it was too late for breakfast. She dressed and looked into the overmantel mirror. A cold wash might improve things. Were they up yet? If not she was cut off from the bathroom.

She decided to walk into the kitchen humming in case. Tom was reading a paper at the table and you could almost see the black cloud over his head. Bernice was packing bread, fruit, sausage rolls and last night's leftovers into a plastic shopping bag. Julia went up to the bathroom.

She hated the first floor this morning. No one up there, no one friendly and reassuring likely to pop out of one of those closed doors. It was all still, and silent, and holding its breath. The ship's bell was too motionless to stay that way for long, it was inviting an invisible hand to strike it. The landing behind the old green curtain would not be able to contain itself much longer, but would creak and crack under the pressure of a footfall. The bathroom which seemed to enclose her too eagerly and too completely, would certainly not behave itself when it possessed such a repertoire of self-expression in the forms of water, gas and metal. The sounds of old and unreliable plumbing have reduced many a nervous stranger to a wreck.

She was out again in minutes, fleeing the violent downrush of water from the bracketed, high-level cistern, just as she had done as a child. Quick, or it will get me.

Tom was sitting in the window now. In the kitchen, she avoided Bernice's eyes and started on the rest of last night's washing up.

"What time are we going out?" she asked.

"About mid-morning. We'll buy a bottle of wine on our way, once the off-licences are open. You all right, Jule?"

The marks of tears stay for hours. Immediately she felt another storm coming on. She dropped a cup back into the water and beckoned Bernice urgently out into the lobby, where she leant against the closed door and faced her, tears and all. The sentence started all right, than soared up into an anguished squeaking.

"He doesn't want me to come, does he?"

"Of course he—" Bernice started, distressed.

"Don't!" Julia choked, rejecting the well-meaning lie. "He really hates me."

"Well, it's not you, Jule, but I think he wanted us to be – he doesn't often see me, you see, and—"

"Right! Well of course I won't come, then. I mean, I

138

wouldn't dream of being in the way—" She hit another top note of overwhelming and shaming distress, born of memories of childhood rejection, inadequacy and subsequent self-dislike.

"Oh, I'm sorry, I'm sorry," said Bernice, dissolving into tears herself and putting her arms around her. Julia went rigid and pressed her hands against her ridiculously distorted face. "It's your Mum you're crying about really, isn't it, Jule? I mean, we couldn't help hearing, you know."

Julia nodded. It was both, but not getting on with your mother was more easily admitted to than being wounded by rejection. Everyone had parent problems, but not everyone suffered the shame of being a social misfit.

"Do you really not like her at all? I mean, I know things start getting difficult once you're in your teens, but before that . . ." Belinda was not the only person to find Julia's clear-sighted recital of her mother's faults disturbing. You just didn't *say* that sort of thing.

Julia shook her head, rubbed her palms into her eyes.

"But I expect you love her, in spite of everything?" Bernice assumed confidently.

"I don't know," said Julia, stuffed up and sniffing. "I don't think I do, really, but then she's never wanted to be loved. I used to need her, of course, but she wasn't too keen on that either. In fact, I never really found out what she did want from me. I'm not very good at loving, actually, I can't seem to get the hang of it. I seem to disappoint people."

A bell started to toll. Julia turned her head sharply towards the partition. "What time is it?" she whispered, glancing at her watchless wrist.

"About quarter to eleven, I should think."

Julia gripped hold of Bernice and looked upwards, listening. "I think they're coming!" she whispered.

Indeed they were. The swishing and padding down the stairs, a voice, another voice answering, the clicking on the tiles, the front door opening and closing.

"They've gone to church," said Julia, tense with fear. "I wonder why he doesn't go too. I thought whole families always went together then."

"But we don't know when it is," said Bernice. Her own reddened eyes were wide and she swayed slightly.

The bell rang on, calling the congregation out of their homes and to prayer.

They gave Tom a short, undetailed report. Noises, they said. Much as before, they said. "I don't want to know," he answered shortly. "I reckon you're both going round the bend." He went up to have a bath.

They went on packing the picnic.

"I can't stand much more of this," said Julia. "No, correction, I don't think I can stand *any* more of it. I'm sorry about last night, Bernie, but we really must go round to the agent tomorrow and find something else."

"It's Bank Holiday, they won't be open."

"I bet they will. Property hasn't picked up that much, even now, and they'll be angling for customers with regular jobs and good money."

There was no answer on Chris's phone.

"Shall I try someone else?" offered Bernice.

"No, I don't mind going off by myself." It wasn't huffy self-pity, she meant it. The situation was going to be intolerable, but she must get out of the house.

"Do you think they'll be back from church before we go?" asked Bernice uncomfortably.

"Not if we leave now," suggested Julia, looking earnestly into her eyes and hoping she'd agree.

"Right," said Bernice, grabbing everything on the table. "Get your things."

Tom came down and went to turn on the radio, ignoring their frantic bustle. He looked moody.

"Not now!" they shouted in unison.

"Oh for God's sake!" Tom exploded. "I'm fed up with all this neurosis *à deux*! If you have to have a flatmate why does it have to be a raving neurotic who has screaming fits and hates her mother and thinks there are spooks everywhere and follows you around like a dog?"

"It's all right, I won't come," said Julia hysterically. "I don't want to anyway."

"Yes you are, Jule," insisted Bernice. "You don't understand, Tom, she's afraid to stay here on her own."

"That's not my problem, is it?" Tom said with exasperation. "All I want is a day out with my girlfriend and no hassle. Is that too much to ask?"

"Of course not, and it will be fine, won't it, Jule? Now we'd like to get off," Bernice said anxiously. "Are you ready?"

"Not quite," he said. "See you outside."

He came out with his sports bag and they drove off just before ten to twelve.

If They did return from church, nobody heard them.

Kew was hot, busy and beautiful, and Julia went off for several little excursions on her own, feeling like a leper. She'd have to go as soon as she found somewhere else.

But the situation had a different resolution. Tom dropped the girls back home then left, Bank Holiday tomorrow notwithstanding. They knew he wouldn't be back.

Thirteen

"I've wrecked your life," said Julia, devastated.

"Of course you haven't," sobbed Bernice, "the ghosts aren't your fault, are they?"

"I don't mean that. I mean barging in here and getting in the way of your private life. It was so kind of you to give me somewhere to stay, but I've no right to hang on any longer."

"You're not going, too!" Bernice protested.

"No, no." She couldn't go without Bernie. Of course not. "If you can still bear me as a flatmate we'll move together. I wonder how soon we could find somewhere else?"

There was no question of sleeping in separate rooms. On the other hand, Julia couldn't possibly have brought herself to get into sheets used by Tom, and even worse, by Tom and Bernice. This hadn't seemed to occur to Bernice, who was still overwhelmed by emotional loss, so she sat on top of the cover in her dressing-gown and stared at the television. Behind the striped curtains, the metropolis hummed through the open top sash.

"Goodness, isn't it hot?" Bernice's eyes were still swollen, and an occasional hiccup burst from her throat. She was drinking ice-cold orange juice, eating biscuits and fanning herself with Tom's newspaper. "What about bringing your fan in here, Jule?"

"Come with me?" begged Julia.

They opened the door into the dark lobby and flushed it out with light from the kitchen before venturing any further. Julia's hand stole round the doorpost into the bedroom as if expecting to meet another before it could turn on the light. While she unplugged the flex and reached up across the fireplace, Bernice stood with both hands on the door, holding it open in case it should slam shut and imprison them. They were no longer motivated by reason. Panic was driving them; apprehension of what might happen next.

They actually backed out of the lobby, and when the kitchen door was closed, Bernice put a chair against it, though they knew that was irrational – nothing could shut Them out of their own home.

"If he sits down and lights up again tonight I think I'll die," Julia declared vehemently.

"No you won't, Jule. He can't hurt you."

"Do you think she'll come down again?"

"Might do. Do you think it was her crying?"

"There are several women," said Julia.

"Jule, look!"

Bernice pointed urgently. Something moved the fringe of the throw on the armchair.

"The cat!" she whispered.

A dip appeared at the bottom of the bed, and a light shock ran throughout its frame. The dip started to move up the bed, down, up, down, up, advancing on them with stealthy, sinister friendliness.

At the moment it seemed about to lavish insinuating caresses on their feet, they leapt from the bed, Bernice towards the window, Julia towards the kitchen, and at once there was nothing there. The tumbled bedding was still.

Julia hit the wall with her fist, swearing. Bernice kicked the armchair. They raged with frustration and misery and sheer tiredness.

"And you can shut up!" Julia shouted at the television.

They pretty well abandoned sleep and finally had breakfast at the ridiculously early time of six thirty.

"Shall we go over and see if the estate agents are open?" suggested Julia wearily, as they put their used china onto the draining board.

"All right," Bernice conceded, rubbing tired eyes, "though I bet they won't open until tennish. What are we going to do with the rest of the day, grit our teeth and stay put?"

"We'll sit out in the park," decided Julia. "It's so near it's like having our own garden. We'll take books and suntan oil and food and rugs to lie on, and stay there until Win and Harry come home."

"But supposing somebody rings up?" said Bernice. He might. He might have thought better of things now, and want to make up—

"We'll leave the front window open. It'll be quite safe, with us just across the road keeping an eye on it."

They washed in the sink, and the unavoidable visit upstairs was a mutual one, taking turns to exchange the creepy loneliness of the bathroom for the vulnerable sentry go on the landing. Julia ventured into her bedroom to collect clothes, but took them into the kitchen to put on.

"Let's hope it doesn't rain," she said.

"It won't," said Bernice confidently. "There, now everything's ready to pick up when we get back. We're going to have a lovely Bank Holiday, Jule."

The traffic was still on the go outside the kitchen window. Happy Bank Holiday, lemmings. Happy noise and pollution spreading, happy fume-making.

"Of course, if we had a car, we could go out into the country," said Bernice with a certain wistfulness.

The traffic noise mingled with the sound of birds and the rippling sound of a fairy harp. Julia dried up, stared at the concrete landscape and wondered if the view was any better before it was erected. It was probably just houses and factories and the railway, not a lot to weep for, really. But before that it would have been fields and river and marshes, and maybe attractive buildings like the mills at Bromley. Far too late to gentrify and conserve and get back to that distant golden age.

Another stroke across the fragile harp. It was like beads. Like touching a fringe of beading on a lampshade.

They turned to each other in dumb panic.

The beads were struck again, and left gently tinkling. Something swished and slid. The girls moved to the kitchen door but no further.

A metallic clang and a thud.

Another swish and an impatient sigh.

The bedroom door was open, and the bedroom window. They heard a juggernaut roar along the flyover, even as they pressed back against the kitchen door jamb so that they needn't look into that occupied room.

Now a series of gentle thuds accompanied things being laid in their places on a soft, padded surface.

Second after second they listened to the sounds of the past, being played back on the walls which had recorded them; afraid to move, afraid to run away, above all deathly afraid to step forward and look through that open door. They might see nothing, but on the other hand, they might find themselves looking into a strange room, with strange furniture, and brown paintwork and green repp curtains and a bead-fringed lampshade hanging from the gasolier above the table. And who knew whether they might not be able to get out of it again?

The traffic drove on through an early summer morning in the 1990s, while within a hundred yards or so, a long-skirted maid laid a breakfast table in 1910.

"How did you know it was 1910?" asked Bernice hoarsely.

"It felt like 1910."

The Drive, Victoria Park, constructed for the promenade of the middle classes, was busy with cyclists, runners, and a few wild, gaudy rollerbladers, and the girls kept well over to the side.

"You mean you imagined what was going on in there and that was the sort of period you thought it might be."

"I suppose I did," said Julia uncertainly. "That thudding noise – what did you think that was?"

"Laying the table, and she dropped a fork."

145

"What was she laying the things on?"

"A cloth with something thick under it."

"What colours?"

"Well, I don't know *that*," said Bernice reproachfully.

"It was white on red," said Julia, panting as they strode briskly past the Victorian pub which had seen them on a happier day.

"Oh," said Bernice, looking wary. "Did you – have you any idea what she might look like?"

"No."

"Perhaps we should have looked."

"I don't think we'd have seen anything if we had."

They marched on, getting hotter and more tired, but unable to slow down. "Do you think there's a lot of this about?" Julia wondered, appalled at the thought.

"What, like measles, you mean?" Bernice said without laughing.

"You see," Julia pursued the alarming idea, "if there really are people in the house and we can't see them, how do we know the whole world isn't full of ghosts, clinging to the places they used to know, and walking around among the living, and trying to go on with lives which ended years ago?"

"How can they be?" Bernice said with a degree of shock. "People go to heaven when they die. Why should they stay down here when there's a much better place to go to?"

"But they may not all know it's there. Or they may know but feel they won't be at home there – if they weren't very good, I mean. Or they may even be trying to avoid hell," Julia added with a thrill of horror.

"I don't believe in hell," said Bernice with immediate repulsion. "If I were God I wouldn't send people to hell."

"Not even if they were mass murderers, or someone like Adolf Hitler?"

"I'd try to make them better," said Bernice in an emotional voice. "Anyway, whoever They are, they go to church, so they must have gone to heaven, mustn't they?"

Julia felt a violent surge of irritation. Bernice's eternal sweetness and other-worldliness sometimes verged on the head-in-sand. She went for the jugular. "What about people who've been horribly cruel to animals, like bull fighters, or fox hunters, or vivisectors, or people who starve and abandon puppies and kittens?"

Bernice's face creased up with distress. "Well," she said hastily, before more unbearable images were brought up before her eyes, "I think I might send them back to live as animals, so they could see how it felt."

"If you did, you'd have to arrange for a whole lot more animal cruelty, wouldn't you? And then the people who'd done that would have to come back and go through more of it, and you'd have God sponsoring an unending cycle of cruelty. Still," she relented, as she saw the expression on Bernice's face, "nobody would be afraid to die if you were God."

"Just think," Bernice said tearfully, hanging on obstinately to her positive view of the world, despite Julia, "all this grass we're looking at may be crowded with past East Londoners walking around and enjoying the sun. And dogs, too, spirit dogs leaping about and having a wonderful time."

Julia shuddered. I didn't see that. They were there and then they were gone, and I *did not see* them. She increased her pace even more.

"What would they think if they saw the park now?"

"They may not see it as it is now," said Julia in a strained voice.

"You mean They don't see us?" said Bernice, trying to keep up. "Not even the cat?"

"Well," Julia admitted reluctantly, "the cat does."

The estate agents' was near the top of Mare Street, in the part open only to pedestrians and southbound buses. All other traffic swerved away just before the old town hall and the even older stone tower, standing churchless at the entrance to the great, green graveyard. Modern shopfronts might have deceived the eye, but if you looked above, sash windows remained bedded in stucco and old brickwork, and the sheer narrowness of the thoroughfare betrayed that beneath those buildings the traces of a thousand years might be found. Cyprian Smith's had been there for at least a hundred – at least, that was what they claimed – but the frontage was largely plate glass and the logo of a national building society appeared everywhere, even taking first billing on the facia.

The pictures in the window were almost entirely of Victorian houses, either run-down and ripe for modernisation or completely gentrified with new paint, window boxes and a high price. There was also a large number of rents available, though many were for the restored houses, at several hundred pounds a week.

The interior was right up to the minute; curved counters and desks, cream walls with blue and jade green stencils, blue and cream carpets and upholstery. The young man at the nearest desk smiled good-morning at Bernice, and said, "Be with you in a moment, sir," to the people who had come in behind them. He was evenly tanned, with short, dark, curly hair, and dressed in the bottom half of a grey suit, a crisp, white shirt and a blue and red silk tie. His sleeves were turned up just below the elbow, to show he was really getting down to work.

They sat down and he smiled and held out his hand for the rent book, ready for a quick gallop on the computer and then a rewarding conversation with the next clients, who had been studying the pictures in the For Sale window.

"Er—" said Bernice.

The young man put his head encouragingly on one side and picked up a pencil, which he proceeded to caress.

"Do you by any chance have anything else rather like our present flat," asked Bernice, "only with two bedrooms, and our own bathroom, and not too expensive?"

"And in a quiet street," added Julia. Might as well get rid of the other disadvantage as well.

"Where are you?" he asked.

They told him.

"Oh! Oh yes! Ah! As a matter of fact, we've been asked to contact you by the landlord, well, it's a lady, actually."

"We know," said Julia. "We met her."

What are we doing, we can't leave Harry and Win alone in that house. Why can you never do anything that suits you without hurting other people? We all seem to be chained together in an endless cause and effect which tugs us away from the satisfying of our desires.

The young man wriggled himself into a more comfortable position, scratched the back of his head with the pencil and stared thoughtfully at the desk. He picked up the intercom.

"Er – yes. I have some tenants from Ermintrude Villas here. Would you like to speak to them? Oh. Yes. Yes. Right." The receiver went down. "Sorry, Mr Bland is engaged at the moment. Er – ye-es – you are probably aware that there has been a change of ownership on the property?"

"Yes, we found out. Not from you, though," Julia added.

"No. Well, we wanted to clarify the situation first. Er – well—"

"Would I be right in thinking you have bad news for us?" asked Julia. When the man in the back room tells the man out front to deliver the message, it generally is bad or at least difficult.

"Well, not exactly bad. Not for you, at any rate; after all you only have a six-month tenancy and you want to move anyway, but the Grosvenors – do you know the Grosvenors well?"

"Pretty well," said Bernice, fixing her reproachful doe eyes upon him, unaware that she was making him uncomfortable. He felt as if he should be sending for the PDSA.

"The situation is this," he said with a bright smile, a breezy jerk of the head and an attempt to look like an honest man laying all cards upon the table. "Mr Rillington, who lived in the basement of Number Two, acquired the property in 1932. At that time he occupied the whole of that house, and let out the other three."

"Excuse me," Julia interrupted despite her urgent wish to

hear what he was going to reveal, "but could you tell us who owned them before that?"

"Er," he said. He flicked through the computer, concentrating with confident expectancy on the universal oracle, blue light reflecting in his eyes. "Ah." More buttons were pressed. "Uhuh?" he queried it. His fingers pattered over the keys, searching for the answer that just had to be in there somewhere.

"Lisa!" he called across to the other desk, which was manned by a girl in a pink linen suit and an Alice band, "how do we access the pre-1945 info?"

"Up in Room Six," she said. "He said not to enter anything before that." Him in the back room. The *éminence grise* of Cyprian Smith.

The young man returned some ten minutes later with a powdering of dust on his trousers, a grey streak on his cheek and a couple of index cards.

"Sorry about that," he said. "Right, one to four Ermintrude Villas, Cadogan Terrace. Right. Uhuh. Mmm. Well, obviously, we don't have any records before the properties were put into our hands, and that seems to have taken place in 1901. The owner then was a Mr Abraham Ingersall."

The girls glanced at each other.

"He lived at Number Two as well, but the entire management of the other three houses was handed over to Cyprian Smith. He seems to have remained owner until Mr Rillington took over."

"And he bought them from Ingersall?"

"Suppose so," he said, looking at front and back of the dirty, ruled pasteboard. "However he got them, we appear to have continued with the management, again except for Number Two. It seems to have been a bit of a shambles during the war with tenants coming and going, bomb damage, that sort of thing, but Mr Rillington was still there in 1964 when his agreement with us changed."

He returned to the computer, struck it a few manly blows and sent the next lot of answers rolling down the screen. Julia recognised the usual young male's need to teach machinery who was boss, even mechanism so subtle and responsive that the mere resting of a fingernail on a key could send a line of letters skidding across the screen.

"You don't really want to know all this, do you?" he asked suddenly.

"Yes, we do, please," said Bernice. "We're interested in that sort of thing. History, I mean."

"Yeah, know what you mean. I've always been interested in the sixties myself. It must have been *wild*." He mimed long hair, a drooping moustache, an ecstatic trip. "Anyway, it seems in 1964 we had some trouble with a couple on the ground floor, who were well behind with the rent, causing damage, partying all night – you name it. He had a terrible time getting rid of them, in fact he had to go to court, and after that he didn't want any more to do with the actual business and passed the management of Number Two over to us as well, except for his own flat in the basement."

He suddenly came back to the present and remembered the task that him in the back office had charged him with.

"Anyway, this is all very interesting, but not what I was going to tell you."

"You want us all to go," said Bernice.

He put on a what-a-shame face. "'Fraid so. Seems the new owner wants to sell all four houses off for development – she's probably quite right, it would cost the earth to get them back into good nick."

"Well, that's your fault, isn't it?" said Julia, stroppiness rearing up from under the weight of her inhibitions, as it sometimes did. "Aren't repairs your job?"

"Well, yes, with a normal agreement, but after the troubles in the sixties he had a new one drawn up. We were to continue collecting the rent and pass it over to him, minus a percentage of course, but he said we weren't to bother with repairs, he'd handle all that himself."

"Whatever for?"

"Dunno."

"But isn't that a bit unusual?"

"Nothing's unsual in this business. You'd be amazed at some of the things that have got into letting agreements, even with the Housing Acts. I mean, those try to cover all the situations that could reasonably be expected, but there's a hell of a lot of people out there who are way beyond being reasonable, and who do things no one in their right mind would expect."

"Did you ever meet Mr Rillington?"

"No. Don't think anyone has who's here now. We've had to write to him fairly often, specially when tenants asked about repairs, but I gather they never got done. They used to come in and complain, and all we could do was say we'd tell the landlord. He'd insisted we didn't tell anyone who he was, and if he didn't intend to do anything, you can see his point. Of course, when the Grosvenors started complaining to the Gas Board, and the Electric, and then doing things themselves and sending us bills, we had to pay them and stop it from the money we sent on to Rillington."

"What did he say to that?"

"He'd stopped answering our letters by then. What did he look like?" he asked curiously. "He never seemed to be at home when we called, and I've always pictured him a bit like Howard Hughes, with long hair and fingernails and galloping paranoia."

"Well," said Bernice, leaning forward earnestly, "he looked like just an ordinary old man, but I think the last bit may have been right. He was very frightened of something. Were the people who had our flat before ever frightened?"

"Don't think so," he said, with a surprised expression which denied all responsibility. "What do you mean, burglars? Everyone's afraid of burglars, these days."

"There always have been burglars," Julia rushed in sharply.

There were certain emotive phrases and certain alarming subjects which immediately disturbed her peace of mind, not because of their intrinsic unpleasantness, but because of the Nutley gloss upon them. 'These days' peppered all Mrs Nutley's discourse upon the world. It followed any mention of the undesirable and the problematic, and meant that those things had never existed until recently. Consequently its use by anyone at all invariably kicked Julia's neuroses into gear and produced a vehement denial of its truth.

The young man looked taken aback and almost frightened, as this calm-faced young woman suddenly turned into a possible raging feminist.

Behind the feminist's face, the mind was flooded with the frightened insecurity of childhood, when she had been born into the most wicked era in the history of the world, and resided in the only family able to guard her against it.

They ate their lunch out on the grass, just within the shade of the trees which partly veiled the sleazy shame of Ermintrude Villas. Then they sunbathed, read, talked, and occasionally turned to look at the house, as if someone might be looking or even coming out.

Cyprian Smith had only main road properties available at the moment. There was no immediate prospect of moving.

They awoke as shadows blocked out the heat of the sun and sent shivers over their bodies. All the usual sounds greeted them; traffic, radios, birds shouting their own fears down before they slept. All the usual activities were around; car-washing, playing, cycling; walking and sitting; laughing, horseplay and showing off, necking and quarrelling.

"Look at the time!" exclaimed Bernice. "Goodness, I really needed that sleep. I can't remember the last good night I had."

"There's a light on in the Grosvenors'," said Julia with immense relief.

They gathered up their temporary camp and made for the gate in the railings.

The top sash of the dark bay window was open the six inches they had left it. They slowed as they came out onto the pavement, and stood cast down and wretched to find yet another advance in the colonisation of their home.

"It's probably in another house."

"No it isn't," said Julia.

It was not a good pianist, but certainly a habitual one. He or she had got the straightforward notes, the long-drawn-out trills and the rendition as they wanted, but the smudging over of the hard bits was equally practised. Julia recognised an executant who couldn't be bothered to get things absolutely right – nearly would do. The piece finished on a last extravagant trill.

They didn't move to cross the road. What for? They had nowhere to go. They were evicted tenants – the real owners were back at home.

The music started again. A few tentative notes, not all of them right, slowly reaching down to meet a fumbling bass searching for an awkward arpeggio.

"It's *Für Elise*," said Bernice. "I used to play that."

"So did I. Better than that, though."

The pianist repeated, fumbled, pushed on regardless.

"Can you hear the piano?" asked Julia.

The two girls stood before the opening in the green velvet curtain, white-faced. Their belongings had been dropped in the hall.

Win frowned in a puzzled manner. "No, love, we've got the film on telly."

"Please come and listen."

Down below, beyond the closed flat door, the piano jangled on, slow and full of sentimental expression. This pianist was devoted to expression. The clumsy performance throbbed with it, one melody after another. It was *Arrangements of Popular Ballads for the Pianoforte* now. The performer struck consecutive attitudes, inquired where Alice was, invited Maud into the garden, proposed like a soldier to fall and felt homesick for the old rustic bridge by the mill. It was at the same time ridiculous and terrifying.

"Who is it?" said Win. "My Dad used to sing them songs,

though we hadn't got no piano. Uncle Sam used to accompany him on the concertina."

"There's no one in there," said Bernice, nearly crying, "and we haven't even got a piano. Oh Win, what on earth are we going to do?"

Fourteen

"I'm not saying they don't mean well, but I can't take to their ways. Sort of la-di-da and who-are-you, and turning up their noses when they're not much cop themselves. And they got the nerve to look down on our Trish because she weren't born in Gants Hill, and all the time she's worth three of their Colin. I never took to him from the minute he walked in the door, but Trish was just head over heels in love, poor kid, and there was no talking her out of it."

Win was pretty steamed up. The girls had started off the flood of words by a simple inquiry as to what sort of day they'd had. They knew now.

The music continued in the distance, like a piano heard across a garden on a summer evening. An amateur pianist, not necessarily enjoying what they were doing; the sound of a million homes before the days of television.

"There it goes again," said Harry unhappily. "Here, I know that tune, Mum used to sing it."

The naive melody echoed in the dark hollow beneath the flowered carpet.

"*A Boy's Best Friend is his Mother*," said Win. "Now don't cry, ducks, you can sleep up here if you like. We got one of them blow-up beach lilos if you don't mind sleeping on the floor."

"Oh thanks!" They were both in tears.

"Have you really never heard any of this before?" Julia asked incredulously, mopping her eyes.

"Nope," said Win with utter certitude. "Have we, Harry?

156

Have we, Bernice? If you ask me, I still say it's to do with Mr Rillington."

"But it must be the Ingersalls," Julia insisted. "You remember, in the Post Office directory."

"Here, that reminds me – the cemetery," said Win. "No, please don't cry, kids. Oh dear, oh dear. Pour 'em a drink, Harry."

He handed them generous measures of Scotch, in small tumblers with cocktail cherries and the naff type of champagne glasses printed all over them. "Nothing like spirits to cast out spirits," he said, with cheerful encouragement, but took a large one himself. Only Win seemed to be coping without support. She got her good, going-out handbag from under the fifties coffee table and pulled out a notebook.

"We went off specially early yesterday morning so as we could pop in and copy this down," she said with relish. "Couldn't wait another day, let alone two. There you are, see what you can make of that."

"It's stopped again," said Harry, turning his glass in his hands.

"Good. Told you it would."

"But it's the waiting for it to start again," said Bernice, tears rolling down her face. "It's the waiting for everything to start, and wondering what it's going to be next. There was even someone in Julia's bedroom yesterday morning, laying a table."

"What she look like?" asked Win sharply, the notebook drooping in her hand.

"We didn't look in. We didn't want to."

"It was partly that we were afraid what we'd see," Julia tried to explain, "and partly that we might not see anything. Living with invisible people is just terrifying."

The muffled music crept into their ears again. Slow arpeggios and mawkish trills – enough expression to draw tears to the eyes without the stimulus of fear.

"Well, blow me, that's *The Robin's Return*," said Win. "I reckon it's a long time since I heard anyone playing that."

The girls sobbed again, even Julia. Stop making an exhibition of yourself, Julia. It was difficult to remember when she'd permitted herself to cry so much, and certainly not in public. It wasn't so shaming as she'd experienced it before, because this time she wasn't alone in her bad behaviour.

Come to think of it, she did remember; it was when Laurie went. She had learned from bitter experience that emotion must be hidden or it would result in the forfeiting of respect, in ridicule, and sometimes in loss. People shrank from it, were embarrassed, disapproving, even mocking. It was the most enormous social gaffe and you were never allowed to forget it; look at how Tom had reacted.

("Oh look, Julia's crying again, she is a cry baby. Be quiet, Julia, no one wants to hear that awful noise. Oh my goodness what a silly face! Go away, no one wants to look at a face like that. Come back when you've pulled yourself together.")

"Top up her drink, Harry," instructed Win, as fresh tears welled up in Julia's eyes, "then you have a look at this, love, I think you'll be surprised."

The girls put their tearful faces together like a Victorian painting of orphans abandoned in a doorway. Win had written clearly, in capitals with dots on the Is and an occasional lower case letter creeping in.

The family grave of James Buchanan Rillington of Buchanan House South Hackney Middlesex.
In loving memory of Charlotte Mary daughter of the above who died March the fifteenth 1867 aged five years
also Sarah Elizabeth daughter of the above who died March the sixteenth 1867 aged three years
also James Henry Buchanan son of the above who died April the third 1867 aged one year
also Matilda Ada beloved wife of the above who died April the sixth 1867 aged thirty years

"Them four was his first family. Looks as if it was something infectious, all of them going down together. Now look careful at the next lot."

> also Dorothy Violet daughter of the above who died June the third 1885 aged four years
> also Edward James son of the above who died January the 1st 1890 aged five years
> also Henry James son of the above who died July the twenty-seventh 1896 aged three weeks
> also Amelia Anne daughter of the above who died May the second 1899 aged seven years
> also the above James Buchanan Rillington who died November the seventh 1900 aged sixty-four years
> also Harriet Maude daughter of the above who died February the first 1902 aged four years
> also Serena Elizabeth daughter of the above who died August the sixth 1919 aged thirty-eight years
> also Minnie Eliza daughter of the above who died May the eighth 1922 aged forty-two years
> also Ellen Edith daughter of the above who died January the fourth 1930 aged forty years
> also Florence Mary daughter of the above who died December the fourth 1931 aged fifty-four years.

"Notice something funny?" Win said, once their heads were raised again.

"Well, there's an awful lot of them, and ever so many died young, didn't they?" said Bernice. "How sad."

"Always happened, love," said Win briskly. "My mum had nine and only raised five, and that was way after the Rillingtons was born. No, what I mean is this. Who's missing?"

"Well, there's no Agnes," said Julia, studying the intricacies of the list with a frown, "but I suppose she was buried somewhere else with Lily's father. And no John who took over the shop, but I expect he'd have had his own family grave. And I can't see the second Mrs Rillington," she added with more interest.

Yet again the piano insinuated itself into their ears. *The Lost Chord*. Seated one day at the organ, I was weary and ill at ease. Snap.

"No, neither can I," said Win with satisfaction.

"Perhaps there wasn't room," suggested Bernice, sniffing. "It must have been packed solid." And what a nasty picture that summoned up before the mind's eye.

"There was room for old Joe," said Harry. He started to hum along with the music, turning his glass round and round as if he'd lost the way into it.

"Well, of course, the kids wouldn't have taken up much room," Win said, "and it is a double plot."

"Where was Buchanan House?" asked Julia. She wished he'd stop, it was only encouraging Them. ("Take no notice of Julia, it will only encourage her.") Take no notice and They may stop, too. I won't encourage you. I won't take notice. But if I don't, your frustration may increase and burst out like mine sometimes does. Maybe that's what's happening, or maybe it doesn't make the slightest difference to you whether we take notice or not. Perhaps none of you give a damn about us or what we do, or what we think, because we're not there at all in your past world.

"We'll find out," said Win triumphantly. "Back to the archives tomorrow, if they got room for us that is. Gets very busy sometimes," she explained, "and they're a bit short of space."

The piano broke into impassioned triplets, but had to slow down in order to accomplish them. "I always liked that bit," said Harry, his attention still uneasily occupied. It was nightmarish; Julia wanted to scream now, not just cry.

"It may be that Death's bright angel," sang Harry.

"Hey!" said Win. "I think we can do without *that*, thank you very much."

The pianist would have had all those rhetorical musings

160

answered long ago. When Death's angel came, and let it be hoped for their sakes that it was a bright one, *The Lost Chord* would have rung in their ears, played by heavenly executants who had bothered to get it right.

The last desultory runs faded away about ten o'clock. At half-past Harry unfolded the double lilo and blew it up with a foot pump. Win brought in pink floral sheets and green, well-washed blankets, then escorted the girls along the curtained landing to the bathroom and bustled comfortingly between her bedroom and kitchen while they used it. She had cleaned it yesterday as usual and put them to shame. The hall was unswept and dusty; they hadn't touched it for days.

Their stay in that still, pregnant room was briefer than ever. Bernice left her lenses in because her glasses were down in their flat and she couldn't face dealing with the unknown in a haze of myopia. Julia once more fled before the vicious gush of the cistern, and the terrible stillness of the blinded window, the crazed tiles and the worn linoleum. And who would have thought that brass taps, a cracked washbasin, a stained, claw-footed enamel bath and even a brand new gas water heater could come to hold such an appalling sense of threat.

They took off their shoes and skirts and crawled under the blankets. The view from the floor brought a whole new unease to their situation. The distance from floor to ceiling seemed immense, and the cracked plaster hung in the air, bearing its invisible, dangerously heavy burden of timber and tile. The mock marble fire surround seemed to lean towards them, ready to cast Shirl and Trish and their families down upon their heads. The furniture threatened to trample them. The chimney behind the electric fire could be seen to be stuffed with newspaper, so what was it keeping from coming down?

And the empty darkness of their flat existed less than a foot beneath their heads, and might be inhabited by anything or anyone.

"We've got to go to work tomorrow," said Julia with bleak incredulity. "I'm never going to sleep. Whatever will we look like?"

"Terrible," said Bernice, in the voice of a tired, weary child, "at least, I will. You'll look as cool and composed as usual."

The light streamed down into their eyes. The Grosvenors didn't go in for indirect lighting; all was revealed in one no-nonsense blast, like Win.

"I'm not turning it off," Julia said hysterically, as they sought to escape its dazzle. They pulled the sheet over their heads, but then felt blinded, and the downstairs flat seemed even more near. Supposing, thought Julia, someone knocks on the ceiling just beneath my head.

Finally, they pulled the bedding apart and climbed up onto the settee with a blanket and a pillow apiece, closed their eyes and began to doze.

It crept up on them. First the uneasiness of interrupted sleep, then the dragging of consciousness out of its refuge, then the inescapable blow of reality. They drew closer together. The sound was quite specific, though you couldn't tell where it was coming from. There was no direction to it, no identity. It was as ubiquitous as air and as eternal as human life.

A woman weeping. Low, miserable sobs, smothered snivelling, the sound you make when crying under the bedclothes so no one will hear. Desolate tears which had been shed many nights before, and which would be shed many nights again. Despair and yet resignation; tears become a way of life. The audible bleeding of a broken heart. It was a sound which Julia, at least, recognised.

They couldn't move. They couldn't speak. They couldn't even cry any more. The footsteps, the voices, the music; the aggressive, slinking cat, the busy maid; the hurrying, whispering women, the silent, smoking man. These had hinted and said, be aware, look further, we are the indication, though we dare say no more. These had been symptoms of the house's sickness.

But this was the seat of the disease, the scandal which could not be hidden for much longer, but which would escape from the close control of this mysterious family and give the whole game away.

"Morning, Mr Jones. Hi, Candice! Hello, Tracy. Bernice, have you got another aspirin? I feel like death."

"In my bag. Help yourself. Good morning, sir. Yes, it is a beautiful day, isn't it?"

Julia fumbled under the desk for Bernice's bulging bag, in which even the owner could never find what she wanted. The numerous zips scraped her fingers as she searched for the remedy for her increasing headache. The phone rang.

"Good-morning, Jones, Brown and Wilkinson."

"Julia, I've been trying to get you all over the weekend. Where the dickens were you?"

"Out with Bernice. Mum, will you please *not* ring me at work, I have asked you all before. This is a very busy firm and if anyone hears—"

"Your voice sounds odd. Have you got a cold?"

"No. I'm perfectly all right."

"You don't sound perfectly all right. Well, I think it was extremely ill-mannered of you not turning up at Belinda's on Sunday, she was most upset."

"I bet she wasn't; you mean you were."

"Of course I was, everyone was upset! Now next Sunday everyone will be coming to me, and I shall expect you without fail, Julia. I absolutely refuse to put up with your silly tantrums any longer. And Brian will be coming round to tea."

"No," said Julia, holding her head. Three laughing, hail-customer-well-met reps brushed the automatic doors aside and aimed their hilarity in her direction.

"What do you mean, no?"

"No, I'm sorry, madam, it won't be possible. I'll ring you soon. Goodbye."

"Good-morning, my dear. Can you point us in the direction

of the delightful Miss Candice Kent?"

She managed to look suitably amused by their wit. She finally took the aspirins two hours later with her coffee.

They stopped on the foot-bridge and leaned over the parapet, looking down towards Hackney Wick.

"Oh look at the state of those poor tower blocks," said Bernice, "there are workmen all over them."

"How much longer before we can get out, Bernie?"

Bernice gazed across at the Trowbridge estate. "Think of all the family life which has gone on inside those."

"Think of all the stress, and the rows and the vandalism and the nervous breakdowns. Most tenants seem to have hated them."

"But they were still their homes. And the flat's my home, Jule. I've got it just as I want it, with all my own things around me. It's going to be an awful wrench leaving it."

"Even in these circumstances?"

"And we can't just walk out on Win and Harry," Bernice continued firmly. "I think we should hang on until they've found a new place, too."

"But they don't seem all that afraid, do they?" Julia puzzled. "Shocked, yes, and put out, but not a quivering mass of nerves like us. It makes me feel so feeble." But then, most things did.

"I suppose they've been through so much already. I mean, even ghosts can't be as bad as the war, specially the Blitz. Win told me her family was bombed out, and lots of her relatives were killed. In fact, their whole street was flattened in one night – that's why there was so much building like that afterwards. You ever been inside a tower block, Jule?"

"No." What, me? A Nutley? I've never even been inside a council house. Neither's my mother. It's one of the things she's most proud of, like never having bought anything in a chain store, and never having opened a copy of the *TV Times*.

Mrs Nutley's code of behaviour was simple – right wing and middle-class, yes, left wing and working-class, no. Anything in between, take no notice. Julia had had a couple of schoolfriends who lived on a council estate and had been forbidden to visit them.

And I obeyed her, she thought, appalled at her unquestioning aquiescence. Good Lord, I was so completely under her thumb it never even occurred to me to go round to their houses anyway and not tell her. But – Where have you been, Julia? Why did you go? Why did it take you so long? Why didn't you ask my permission first? All those lies which would have been necessary—

"Wonder if they're in yet?" said Bernice, looking at her watch.

"What were they trying to find out today?"

"Where Buchanan House was. I suppose Mr Rillington would have been brought up there, with all those brothers and sisters. It sounds as if they were a very rich family, doesn't it, Jule? Funny he should have finished up in a place like this, specially when he had money."

"He may not have had much left, it could all have gone gradually over the years. In fact, that may have been why he wouldn't do repairs – he was trying to eke it out."

"But what else could he have been spending it on?" Bernice said. "And Lily seems to think there's plenty left."

"But she can't know, not till the solicitor gets going. I mean, they haven't got probate yet. She may even find all she's got is the houses, and a lot will go in tax. That'd serve her right, snobby old bat. Wonder why she and Mr Rillington had a 'misundahstending'," said Julia, putting on Lily's affected face and voice. "Perhaps she sent him threatening birthday and Christmas cards. No, I know, blackmail! That would account for him being short of money, too."

"You mean, she had a hold over him," mused Bernice. "Gosh. Perhaps she knew something about his past."

Julia's eyes wandered away from the run-down tower

165

blocks and fixed on the four neglected backs of Ermintrude Villas; the empty shell with the hole in the roof and the blackened edges to the windows; the house with the nearly closed curtains, behind which the Bangladeshi family lived out its shy, secret life; the house in which Joseph Rillington had lived, then retired into the basement as if taking shelter; and the derelict house empty except for the fey trio living their unworldly life, and sitting out the last years or months of the Villas with little apparent anxiety or apprehension; used to change, used to moving on, used to not knowing where they would be and what they would be doing, even in the near future. At least, she supposed squatting was like that – a sort of urban gypsydom. It was a lifestyle so totally divorced from her own structured experience that she couldn't even imagine it.

The upstairs window was open and the Grosvenors therefore back. The girls unlocked their home and surveyed the mess left from that morning's hasty breakfast, rummage for clothes and departure. They opened all the windows and left the flat door ajar with a chair holding it. Bernice straightened the furniture, plumped the cushions and rearranged the teddies. Julia ran water to wash up.

She opened the fridge and studied its meagre store of odds and ends. All Saturday's shopping seemed to have been consumed, apart from three small potatoes, a tomato and a slab of 'delicious' vegetarian pâté which had turned out to be a mistake.

"Take-away?" suggested Bernice.

They finished cleaning up first; it was a bright evening with lots going on outside both front and back, so the opportunity had to be grasped. They even swept and washed the hall floor, with the front door open and their backs never turned on the stairs. If you turned your back they might come alive; alive with past lives.

They were tired already, but by the time all was returned to what might be considered normal, they were more like zombies. Bernice put the oven on a low gas and picked up the old plastic carrier bag whose interior bore many indelible fast-food stains.

"I suppose we'll have to close the windows while we're out."

There was no need to debate whether both were going on the errand – neither was ever going to stay there alone again. The act of closing the flat up made them as anxious as if they were imprisoning a gas leak which could build up and reach danger point.

"There you are," said Win.

They were sitting in the bay window, the television turned down, the dirty plates and foil containers still on the coffee table, damage limited by the orange cloth. The Grosvenors had come down after *Eastenders* and *The Bill*.

Julia took the notebook while Bernice looked over her shoulder. Buchanan House, Victoria Park Road, South Hackney.

"Found it in the Post Office directory for 1872," said Win beaming. "The archives was pretty busy, but they let us just pop in and look that up."

"Gosh. Over there?" She nodded across the park, to where the tall terraces peeped through trees, and where Win's Gran had made bread pudding in the basement.

"No, the other end. There was lots of posh houses down there."

"Did you find it?" asked Julia.

"Nope. We come home on a bus to Mare Street and walked down, but that part's been built over all modern. Well, then we went down to Chancery Lane and took a look at the Census. This here's the 1881 entry. You have a read."

The photostat was produced. She sat back with a pleased smile on her face and awaited their rapture.

With the best will in the world, it was difficult to produce it immediately. Quite apart from puzzling out what the different columns meant, the writing was rushed and difficult to decipher. Win had to come and lean over them like a teacher, pointing to the words with one finger as she read them out.

"James Buchanan Rillington, head of the house, married, aged forty-five, proprieter of drapery establishment employing thirty-two people, born Clerkenwell Middlesex.

"Constance Agnes Rillington, wife, married, aged twenty-three, born City of London.

"Florence Mary, daughter, aged three, born Hackney.

"John James, son, aged two, born Hackney.

"Minnie Eliza, daughter, aged six months, born Hackney.

"Jane Scragg, servant, aged eighteen, nursemaid, born Bethnal Green Middlesex.

"And there's three more staff – a cook, a housemaid and a kitchen maid. And on the next page there was a coachman and his family, living down the end of the garden."

"So these are Mr Rillington's parents."

"That's right."

"She was much younger than him, wasn't she? Were any of these children that died?" asked Bernice, a sad, sympathetic expression ready on her face in case they were.

Win whipped back a few pages and consulted the inscription from Abney Park.

"Nope, these all grew up. The two girls didn't marry, though, died old maids. Well, seems they all did, except for Lily's mum. Might have been others buried with husbands, of course. Anyway, here's the next one."

Another photostat. Census 1891.

"See? The house has got a number, now. It can get a bit tricky when they change numbers and even street names, but luckily they was in the same house and we looked all down the Victoria Park Road entries until we found their name. He's fifty-five and she's thirty-three and they've got six kids now, one of them Lily's mum. Two more had died."

"Eight children!" exclaimed Julia with some horror. "She must have been worn out."

168

"Oh, she weren't done yet. There was at least four more of them to come."

"What about 1901?" asked Bernice eagerly, "that's the one we're really interested in, isn't it?"

"Ah!" said Win, with a grimace. "Well, now, we ain't going to get a look at that one for another six years, I'm afraid. It's absolutely confidential for a whole century."

"Oh." Their faces fell.

"So we won't find out when Mr Rillington was born," said Julia.

"Oh yes, we will, but not off the Census. Don't worry, we'll get there. I did take a look at Ermintrude Villas, too, but I didn't have time to get copies, just scribbled it down. 1881 – a couple called Brough with a fourteen-year-old skivvy. 1891 – that Mr Tarrant was a commercial traveller aged forty-two, and he had a wife and three kids. No servants, which means they can't have been too well off."

"So that's as far as we can get?" asked Julia, disappointed. It was the Ingersalls she wanted to get at, though only because of her brain's irrational insistence on the year 1910. There was no good reason for that. The invisible inhabitants of their house could just as well be the Broughs, or the Tarrants, or the John Jarvises. But she knew absolutely that it was 1910, and that frightened her.

"That's as far as we can get the easy way," corrected Win. "There's plenty other places to look. We'll be off again tomorrow. Reckon we'll try the Greater London Record Office."

Her eyes were gleaming with the joy of the chase. Harry was grinning, too. "We'll get 'em," he promised.

"Do you want to sleep upstairs again?" asked Win.

They sat with open mouths, in an agony of indecision. They looked at each other, at the Grosvenors, at the flat.

"Up to you, kids," said Harry kindly. "Look, if you decide you want to, come on up. We'll put the stuff in the living room again and we won't lock the door, OK?"

*   *   *

169

"I'm sure it's the Ingersalls," Julia insisted with compulsive certainty. "How could it possibly be Mr Rillington's family when they lived right down the other end of the park?"

"But why should it start all of a sudden," said Bernice, hugging Teddy Mary, who was the largest and therefore the one with the strongest security quotient. "I mean, before you were here, Jule, there was nothing at all like this going on."

"You sound as if it's my fault," Julia said, with an unpleasant sensation of shock in her stomach. Oh no; she wasn't still the scapegoat, was she? Perhaps the rôle had become so irrevocably built into her psyche that other people saw it as well. And perhaps there was, in fact, no means of escape, and it was just too late to try and remake herself.

"No, no, no, Jule," said Bernice quickly, giving her hand a reassuring squeeze. "I mean, Mr Rillington may have been hearing them down in his basement, and when he'd gone they moved up and started taking over the rest of the house."

Julia gave a miserable moan. "What do we do tonight?" she asked. "There's nowhere left."

"We could sleep by the open window," suggested Bernice.

"What about burglars?"

Julia was trembling. She was brought up to be afraid, and the training was certainly coming into its own now. Perhaps she attracted frightening situations, or even created them. Perhaps they were only frightening because it was she who was experiencing them.

No, anyone would be frightened by ghosts; even rock-solid, no-nonsense, life-experienced Win and Harry weren't too happy about it.

But perhaps the ghosts were only present because she was here. When she moved out, the house might return to normal, with all the past back under the carpet, and all the terrible secrets once again safely lost in the mists of time.

No. Joe Rillington had felt it – she was absolutely certain of it. All right, he was senile, but senility might strip off the protective layers of experience and reason, once more baring the mind to the terrors sensed in childhood. The fears of the young and the very old might be a shared nearness to the other world.

Fifteen

Not a thing was heard in the house that night, not even footsteps on the hall tiles. But the silence was of little use to them, because they still sat upright in Bernice's bed, watching television and waiting. If they dozed, they woke in a panic, and once Julia found Bernice in tears.

"What is it? Have you heard something?"

Bernice shook her head. "No, I just miss Tom."

Guilt clawed at Julia.

At last, Wednesday morning. What will this Wednesday bring? What will happen today?

"I really must have a bath," said Julia.

They both bathed, chaperoning each other against invisible intrusions into the narrow space amid the steam and roar of the water heater, then covering their barely dried bodies and hurrying down to shut the flat door behind them.

"What's the matter with that room?" Julia asked tensely.

"I expect it's all right really," said Bernice. "We're just expecting things to happen everywhere, that's all."

Julia braved her bedroom for clothes. Bernice investigated the prospects for breakfast.

Television, traffic, but no other sounds.

"Perhaps it's over," said Bernice, as they crossed the motorway. For the first time in what seemed like weeks, the sky was overcast and the air cool.

"Perhaps it isn't," said Julia, resisting the tempting sirens of relief; she knew they were deceivers. Never let yourself feel certain; never let yourself be taken by surprise.

*   *   *

172

"Morning, Miss Standish."

"Good-morning, girls." Miss Standish broke the habit of a working lifetime and came up to the reception desk. "How are you both? Excuse my saying so, but you're neither of you looking on top form this morning. Have you not been very well?"

It was a bit like receiving concerned attention from the headmistress, or even one of Docklands' architectural monuments. Miss Standish had never before come across to them as a human being.

"Oh no, we're quite all right," said Bernice immediately in her brightest voice. Julia said nothing. Miss Standish studied their faces; Bernice's eager, animated smile and drawn complexion, Julia's calm face and dark-circled grey eyes.

"If you had any problems you would approach the personnel officer, wouldn't you? That's what she's there for. We like our staff to be happy with us, and I can say quite categorically that you two are very much valued as the first impression our clients receive of Jones, Brown and Wilkinson. Do please remember that."

They very nearly started crying again. Oh my gosh, this is dreadful, can we hang on until we move? "Good-morning, Mr Jones." We're both at breaking point, even cheerful old Bernice. "Hi, Candice!" I wonder if the personnel officer could find us another flat – and one for Win and Harry. It's about the only thing which could help us. "Good morning, sir, welcome to Jones, Brown and Wilkinson."

It rained all the way home. Neither had an umbrella. They had shopped at the Canary Wharf supermarket, and climbed the foot-bridge weighed down by heavy plastic bags. Water came at them with almost personal intent as they plodded to the other side without even glancing at the backs of Ermintrude Villas. The nest of rubbish beneath the downward slope was inhabited by its builder, drinking from a can and puffing a probably illegal roll-up, and it almost looked cosy. Their relieved arrival on the front steps had something of the old pleasure of homecoming about it.

Julia looked out of the kitchen window as she prepared the dinner. Under the storm of rain, the garden was going to pieces altogether. Overgrown ivy and dead flowers had fallen down together on wet, brown, overgrown grass. "What do you think downstairs is like?" she said.

It was extremely alarming that there was the immediate slam of a door beneath their feet, and even more alarming that it was followed by the sound of women's voices.

"Bernice!" Julia screamed. "They're here again!"

Bernice rushed to her side and they stood listening with suspended breath, staring out into the lobby. Within seconds, steps started to come up the basement stairs, and then there was the rattle of a door handle.

"Hello? Hello?" It was a very polite, tentative ghost.

"Hello?" responded Bernice, her vocal cords reverting to toddlerdom.

"Are you all right? Can we help?" The door knob rattled again. "I'm afraid this is locked. Is the key on your side?"

"No," said Julia, feeling pretty stupid.

"Just a minute. What? Oh, I see. Ah, there it is."

The lock rattled, the mattress heaved itself painfully forward a few inches. Bernice emitted a muffled squeak and held on to Julia's arm.

"Oh dear, I can't seem to—"

Julia stepped forward, grasped the stained, grubby mattress and pulled. It collapsed like a casualty on top of her pile of unpacked belongings, the door jerked open as far as it could, and a slight figure in a pink apron lurched forward into their presence.

"Oops, oh goodness, I am so sorry. Oh dear, what will you think of me? I heard somebody scream out and I thought – but you look perfectly all right, don't you?"

She was about fifty, with soft, pale hair and a wistful, over-eager face, the eyes made more staring by a scarcity of brows and lashes. Julia received a disturbing impression that she might break if you touched her.

The woman turned and called back down the stairs.

"It's all right, Lily, just two young ladies. She lets me call her Lily," she said proudly. "Such a lady. She can't come up, it's her feet," she explained. "The poor thing has been a martyr to her feet. Fortunately I have a little runabout, so I've been able to be of use to her over the years. Now Miss Wright has come into her inheritance at last she will be able to afford her own transport, perhaps even with a chauffeur, who knows?" She uttered a shrill titter of excitement.

"What are you doing?" Bernice asked, her face still white.

"We've been sorting out her uncle's effects. The authorities will soon be granting probate," she vouchsafed with lowered voice, as if the decision were in the personal hands of the Lord Chancellor, "and Miss Wright wishes to press on with the arrangements. So many things to be done after a death, aren't there? And in a case like this! Well!"

"A case like what?" asked Julia.

"Well, in such a family! The last of the Rillingtons of Hackney! Goodness me, it's the end of an era, really."

"Did you know them, then?"

"Oh no! My family never came into contact with people like that," exclaimed the woman with becoming humility, "I've just heard about them from Miss Wright. Oh, the wonderful stories I've heard! Really, I've been so privileged to be able to share her wonderful memories. The parties, the carriages, all her aunts and uncles and their wonderful, glamorous lives."

A voice was heard below.

"I'm just telling the young ladies about your family, Lily," the woman called down the dark stairs, "and they're very interested. May I bring them down to speak to you in person?"

"Oh, no, thanks," Julia said quickly, "we're just going to cook. We won't disturb you." She was sure a strange, sinister smell was rising up from below, perhaps just damp, possibly something far worse.

"You may invite them to descend," Lily's voice rang out below.

"Be very careful on the stairs," their guide whispered, as if they were being asked into somewhere very special, "they are rather dark."

It was a thoroughly unnerving experience. The ghost's descending footsteps sounded beneath their own feet, as if she were using their bodies. They grabbed the dirty handrail and went down into the dim passage which linked the rooms of Joseph Rillington's flat, in which They had visited and tormented and frightened him for so many years.

Lily was in the front room, seated in an ancient brown leather chair by a kitchen range which had received no alteration since its installation. A red, fringed, chenille tablecover was draped over the range like a pall, and on its faded surface ornaments, photographs and the antique paraphernalia of that once respectable occupation, smoking, were laid out. A half-full packet of cheap cigarettes lay in an ashtray.

Julia's horrified attention was immediately captured by the floor in front of the bay window. No carpet, no lino, just bare boards showing through a roughly cut hole. All gone? No stain at all? And was there *really* no smell left?

The last of the Rillingtons was wearing a venerable brown silk dress covered with small, multicoloured squares. The pattern seemed gratuitous; it added nothing to the garment's attractions. Beside her on an oriental table inlaid with mother-of-pearl was a large pile of papers, both enveloped and naked, which she was barely halfway through examining. On the floor were open suitcases, and a pile of boxes labelled Cluny Lace, Silk Ribbon, Dacra Cotton, Velveteen, and other far-off memories from the days when drapery was drapery, and when white goods were not washing machines and refrigerators but household linen.

"Eoow, good-evening," said Lily. "This is my friend and neighbour, Mrs Doreen Parkin." She studied them from under a strange brown straw hat, not broad-brimmed and tidily bowed, but pummelled into a shape which seemed to indicate that it had been involved in a nasty accident. "Let me see, Jane and Barbara, isn't it?"

"Julia and Bernice."

"Eoow, really?" Lily questioned suspiciously, as if they might have forgotten their own names.

Her friend and neighbour hovered excitedly around them, making little darting movements with her head and hands, as if constantly drawing their attention to the august and wonderful celebrity in whose presence they stood.

"Miss Wright is very busy getting her uncle's affairs in order. He had been unable to deal with them properly for many years, but refused all her kind offers to take them out of his hands. Time and again she approached him, by letter and in person. She even took the trouble to write to the local welfare people, to see if they could find sheltered accommodation for him and allow her to take his burdens from his shoulders, but all was refused, and most offensively, too. I have even, on one terrible occasion, known Miss Wright to come home in tears because of his unkind words. I am afraid Mr Rillington didn't appreciate what a treasure he had for a niece."

So that's why he wouldn't have anything to do with her – she was trying to put him away.

Lily stared at them with conscious pride. "I did what I could," she said bravely. "I could do no more. It is," she went straight on, as her praise-singer opened her mouth once again, "a very great responsibility to be the last survivor of such a family as mine. It is my intention to gather all papers, photographs and memorabilia together in my home, so that their memory shall not be lost to the world. I cannot find my uncle's gold watch," she said, glaring balefully at Bernice, "can you tell me where it is?"

"No," said Bernice with some surprise.

"Miss Wright is very distressed about the watch," said Mrs Parkin, nearly bent double in sympathy with her friend's pain. "Also some jewellery which belonged to Mr Rillington's mother and a bronze bust of Shakespeare which his father left him in his will. In fact," she practically rocked with grief, "a very great number of valuables seem to have disappeared."

"Was he ever burgled?" asked Lily, this time deciding to accuse Julia.

Julia found it very difficult to turn her attention to the question, let alone answer it. Standing in that dirty-windowed, lace-curtained, under-lit basement room, surrounded by furnishings which not only seemed to have been there for most of the century, but some of which she actually recognised from her imaginings, the sensation of nightmare was enough to strike her dumb. On a small mahogany chiffonier sat an open canteen of cutlery which seemed to have a lot of gaps in it, and there was an upright piano with curly floral inlay and brass candle holders. A pile of sheet music sat on top of it among dusty china and glass. One piece was open on the stand.

But it couldn't all be the Rillingtons' stuff, they didn't come here until 1932. The chair, the tablecover – I *know* it was 1910, and he wasn't *here* then.

"Excuse me," a measured, insistent voice interrupted her hypnotised state, "I asked you a question."

"What?" Julia turned and tried to pull her thoughts out of the mire. Dare I go and see what that music is?

"Well, actually," Bernice said, "we did think we saw someone leaving the flat a few weeks ago, but when the police came they couldn't find any signs of disturbance at all."

"The police are not what they were," said Lily, shaking her ponderous head and silly hat, "and I regret that South Heckneh is also sadly changed. Indeed, Great Britain itself—"

How well she would get on with Mrs Nutley, though neither would listen to a word the other said.

"I can tell you where the bust of Shakespeare went. He threw it out of the window," said Julia. "In fact, it nearly hit me."

"Did you pick it up?" asked Lily.

"No, I was going to, but then he threw a footstool, so I didn't hang around any more."

"Where is the footstool?" Lily demanded. "Mrs Parkin, please find that footstool, it was worked by my grandmother."

"Was that Constance Agnes Rillington?" Julie asked. Twelve children in twenty-four years, five of them dead in infancy.

"It was," said Lily graciously. "I see you have heard of her. She was indeed a famous beauty, even called by some the

Belle of South Heckneh. Before she met my grandfather she had every eligible young man in North London at her feet."

How come she finished up with someone twenty years older than her, then?

"Of course, my grandfather was a most tremendous catch, even for such a lovely young gel. He had been married before, but his wife and children died. Then he met the lovely Constance and his heart lit up and his life started anew."

Julia wondered what sort of reading matter Lily Wright went in for, and whether the most highly-charged emotional experiences of her youth, or even her life, had taken place in the Granada, Walthamstow.

She looked above the mantelpiece.

"Excuse me, but didn't there use to be a photograph of your grandparents up there?"

"Yes," said Lily, immovable in her chair, with both trouble-some feet stretched out on a box in front of her. "I intend to take it home with me. Mrs Parkin, please get the photograph from out in the passage."

Mrs Parkin went with eagerness and indeed gratitude to be given such an honour. She bore its gilt frame and cracked glass into the room as if it were an icon.

"Isn't she lovely?" she exclaimed, almost dewy-eyed.

The girls looked. James Buchanan Rillington, draper, employing thirty-two people, had grey hair, a frock-coat, a stunning moustache and a positive tangle of watchchains and fobs. He had a look of old Joe about him, was rather short and more than rather plump.

Constance Agnes Rillington was wearing a dark satin dress which stretched over the bones of her stays in a way very remi-niscent of a lampshade. Her immense leg-of-mutton sleeves appeared to be black velvet, and her boned lace collar looked very like an instrument of torture. She, also, had quite a lot of jewellery on board, especially rings. Her light-coloured hair was piled on top of her head and her face was actually fairly nondescript, with pale eyes, a sharp little nose and a full, weak mouth.

"It was taken at a photographic salon by Royal Appointment in Regent Street," said Lily.

"There!" said Mrs Parkin, nodding.

Further comment seemed unnecessary, if not impertinent; one was intended to be struck dumb.

Julia got a quick glance at the music on the piano as she left. It was *Melody in F*, by Rubinstein. No, they certainly hadn't heard that the other night.

Mrs Parkin saw them up the dim wooden stairs, ready to lock the door behind them. She continued to sing Lily's praises all the way and, at the top, stood in the lobby and gazed up into their faces, cradling the key in her fingers like a chatelaine.

"Miss Wright is an old friend, a very *dear* old friend. She has been so kind, so generous to me, and allowed me to help her in so many different ways. Her other uncle was very distinguished, you know. He took over the drapery and ran it until it was burned down. Her mother married another gentleman in the drapery business, though sadly he died rather young, and her aunts were at the very centre of all the social events in the borough. They used to sing at concerts, and play the piano beautifully, and they were regular worshippers and wonderful supporters of St Augustine's church – never missed a service, you know."

But they weren't *here* then! Everybody played the piano. Everybody went to church. It isn't them!

Mrs Parkin pushed the door to behind her and whispered on.

"Did you go to the funeral? I was looking forward to it so much, but then I had one of my tummy upsets from excitement and became too ill to go. Miss Wright put an announcement in *The Times* as well as the *Hackney Gazette*, and I was so disappointed not to meet all the family's old friends and business associates. It must have been such a distinguished gathering, all come to pay their respects."

The girls looked at her silently. Whatever sort of a line had Lily Wright been shooting this gullible woman over the years.

And if she had told her one lie as big as that, how much else of her oral history could be relied on?

"And their wonderful grave in Abney Park!" She was bright-eyed, almost dazed with sheer wonder. "Miss Wright kindly let me drive her there a year or two ago, and it was such a beautiful experience. Such taste! Such sweet carving! Oh, it was enough to make you cry, thinking of all those brothers and sisters laid together in the grave, and reunited and happy together in heaven. How Miss Wright must long to be with them."

"Do you really think so?" said Julia, trying to be polite. She had the impression that Lily had quite a lot of earthly business to see to before *The Lost Chord* was played for her, and that missing gold watches and jewellery ranked very high on the list.

Mrs Parkin ran out of words with which to express her emotion and merely smiled and shook her head. "You know," she said at last, as she turned for the basement door, "it may sound rather silly, but the Rillingtons have always seemed to me like a Royal Family – the Royal Family of Hackney, setting the standards for all other local families and looked up to by everyone. Does that seem very silly of me?"

"Oh no," said Bernice, who was the better liar of the two. Julia couldn't have trusted herself to answer.

"Lily's in the basement," whispered Bernice as she let the Grosvenors into their flat.

"Oh yeah? After the spoils, I suppose," said Harry, plonking himself down on the chair in the window.

"It looks like it," said Julia. "She's got a poor little sycophant of a friend down there with her, running around looking for things and doing what she's told like a servant."

"What, you mean she's a serial killer?" asked Win.

"No, not a psychopath, a sycophant. Someone who sucks up to people," she explained.

"Oh, so that's the proper word for it. You learn something new every day, don't you?" said Win tartly.

The blush flooded up over Julia's cheeks and her whole body burned in the flames of embarrassment. They think I'm showing off, trying to prove how much more educated I am. Gosh, how awful!

"We saw the flat," said Bernice, "and the photo of Mr Rillington's parents. She does look rather snooty, doesn't she, but not awfully happy."

"Well, they never smiled for having their photo took then," said Win. "Took too long."

Julia just knew she was put out at being shown not to know something. How silly – I mean, nobody knows everything, so why take it so badly? I always say the wrong thing, I'm no good with people. She won't like me now. I don't suppose anybody likes me really, not even Bernice.

Negative thinking took her over, as so often in the past. Silly old Julia. Clumsy, leggy old Julia. Stupid Julia, the butt of the family.

"Well," said Win, plonking the notebook on the table and seizing the upper ground again, "we had a real good go today. I took the parish registers and Harry went off searching the indexes to see what else he could come up with."

"Would you like some coffee?" Julia offered in abject abasement. I'm so sorry, I didn't meant to show you up. Please forgive me. Please like me again.

"Thanks, love, that'd be very nice," said Harry, looking at her kindly. He understands how I'm feeling. Oh how *awful*. No it isn't, it's nice. He understands and feels for me because he lives with Win.

"Don't mind if I do," said Win, still a touch huffy. "Right, now, Mr and Mrs Rillington was married at the Parish Church, that's St John's up near Hackney Central Station. 1876, that was. Then Buchanan House was in the parish of St John of Jerusalem, Lauriston Road, that's where our Shirley was married. I showed you the photo, didn't I?"

"Strange that his second name was the same as the house," said Julia, leaning forward like an eager pupil. Mum, please forgive me. Come out of your sulk and say I'm forgiven.

"He named it after his mother's family," said Win, magnanimously dropping the information into her lap. "Anyway, I got the full list of their kids' christenings – twelve altogether."

"Goodness," said Bernice solemnly.

"The last one was old Joe, born on May the first 1900 and christened on June the tenth."

"So that means he was ninety-five when he died," exclaimed Bernice.

"Yeah, good going, wannit?" said Harry. He smiled at Julia as he took the mug. "Thanks, love."

"Now I worked out from the inscription on the grave, that when Joe was born he had one older brother and six older sisters still alive. You want to hear their ages?" asked Win.

It was a rhetorical question.

"Florence Mary was twenty-three, John James was twenty-one, Minnie Eliza was twenty, Serena Elizabeth was seventeen, Agnes Clara was thirteen, Ellen Edith was ten and Harriet Maude was two."

"No wonder they needed a big house," said Bernice.

"Anyway, not long after Joe's birth, his father died, and the eldest son took over the shop."

"Gosh, he must have been clever for his age," said Bernice, wide-eyed.

Fancy being able to run a big store with dozens of employees at twenty-one, thought Julia. Still, Pitt ran the country at twenty-four. Gosh, I am useless.

"Next time you look at the Abney Park records, could you find out what they died of?" she asked, looking desperately interested.

"No, it won't tell us. That'd mean St Catherine's House and six quid a go," said Win.

"Oh, really? Goodness!" said Julia. Win started to look happier, back on top, imparting information and loving it.

"So then I went for the directories," Harry put in, "and looked up Buchanan House. It was Rillington right through to 1944."

It was certainly all very interesting, but it was the Ingersalls they should really be looking into. Who were they? How many of them were there? What did they do? And most important of all, and most difficult to find out, what sort of lives did they live behind the lace curtains of Number Two, Ermintrude Villas?

"Do you think you could possibly look into the Ingersalls as well?" she asked in a pleading voice.

"We'll have a go," said Harry and smiled yet again.

Sixteen

"There's a piano down there," said Julia to Harry as she showed them out.

"Yeah, that's right, old Joe used to strum a bit, once upon a time."

"Do you think it was him the other night?"

"Nah! Never heard him play stuff like that. Used to like *Pack Up Your Troubles* and *Tipperary*, and I have heard him sing *Soldiers of the Queen* once or twice. Don't worry about it, love," he told her, "the only way you can be hurt by a pianner is if it falls on you."

"We'll leave the bedding out in case you want it," said Win, now back to the no-nonsense, heart-of-gold mother figure.

"Aren't you scared, too?" Julia asked, and waited for the answer she was almost certain was coming.

"If Hitler couldn't scare me, then ghosts ain't going to. You didn't go through the Blitz, love."

"Their generation always bring that up," said Bernice as they cleared the debris of their meal. "Like a sort of trump card, the last word on everything."

"I bet it felt like the last word on everything," said Julia.

The steps tapped through the hall at about eleven fifteen. The locked basement door was heard to open. The thuds on the wooden stairs died away as they went below.

It happened again at three o'clock. Only Julia heard it that time, as Bernice had dropped off. But they were both awake when the cleaning of the range began just after six o'clock.

They made tea. They washed in the sink. They escorted

185

each other up to the bathroom. It was raining again outside, and the hall and staircase were dim. Rain pattered on the glass in the front door and gusts of wind tried to find out whether it was locked.

They hurried down again. Their dressing-gowns brushed against the banisters and Julia's mule slippers clicked on the tiles. It's as if she's me, now. Or as if I'm her. Or Them.

"Another miserable day," observed Bernice with regret. "Mustn't forget the umbrellas this time."

"Shall we ring the estate agents?" suggested Julia.

"What about the Grosvenors? Are they looking, too?"

"And will they be able to get somewhere they can afford? I mean, it's going to mean more expense for all of us, but they're not working."

"Perhaps their Shirley can fix them up at Leytonstone," said Bernice, and they felt a touch better.

The phone rang.

"Hello there, Julia, hope you weren't in bed."

"Hello, Philip. No, I've been up for ages."

"Well done! That's the way to start the working day. Look, Julia, it's like this, darling. I mean, I'm not going to apologise for going on about this, but, well, your mother is really very upset indeed, and—"

Julia groaned. "She's taking it out on you, is she?"

"She's been telling us how she feels, yes, and it's rather stressful for Helena, in her condition. If I can just say that you will definitely be coming to see her this Sunday it will defuse everything and we can all get a bit of peace."

"I'm sorry, Philip, but I don't think I can. It'll just mean another row and more upset in the family, and definitely not the tiniest bit of peace."

"But aren't you ever going to come and see her again?" Philip sounded deeply shocked.

"Yes, of course I am. I invited her here when I first moved, you know, and I've seen her twice since. But not again just yet."

"Oh really, Julia!" Philip abandoned diplomacy and became

thoroughly irritable. "You're causing trouble to everyone, being selfish like this."

"I am not being selfish!" Julia shouted, sleepless nights and nerve-wracked days bursting out like ginger beer from a newly tapped bottle. "I am doing what seems best. I am doing what suits me, the way you've done all your life. What about all your golfing weekends? What about all those conferences and business trips? What are you going to do when you're due at a surgery or a special do in the constituency on a Sunday? Are you going to say, sorry, everyone, I have to go to dinner at my mother-in-law's? Still, that's completely academic; even if all the Government's troubles suddenly disappeared and they were back to the ratings they had in the eighties, Labour would still hang on to the East End. I don't know why you're bothering, unless it's just an ego trip."

"I bother because I care about democracy, and because I'm determined to save the country from another attack of the paralysing disease of socialism," said Philip in a ringing tone. "And if I fight a good campaign in a difficult seat I will probably be given a better one in the future. Public spiritedness, Julia. A wish to serve. A feeling of deep gratitude for the advantages I have enjoyed, and a sincere wish to see others able to buy those advantages as well."

"Oh yes, and when are they going to be able to do that?" asked Julia sceptically. "Before or after they've got a roof over their heads and some sort of a job?"

"Julia, you used to be a charming, shy young woman who was a pleasure to know. Now, you seem to be abandoning all your responsibilities to your mother, along with every single meaningful family tradition. We should value them and protect them, together with everything else we hold most dear."

"What, shares, you mean?"

"Oh yes," said Philip with counterfeit patience, "I should have expected that sort of gibe from a socialist."

"I'm not a socialist. I'm not anything." She corrected herself quickly. "I don't wear labels these days. Look, Philip, you try taking on responsibility for my mother. You get criticised and nagged and put down. You get told you're useless compared to your sisters. You get put in your place in front of strangers. Go on, enjoy yourself. Give my love to Helena and the children." She put the phone down.

Bernice pulled another oh-dear face.

"Do you think the agents' is open yet?" Julia said, her heart pounding with rage.

They tried. The answerphone invited them to try again and succeed later.

Julia caught the Grosvenors as they sprang through the hall.

"We've been talking about this moving business. You know, Bernice has only got a few weeks left on her lease, and Lily wants her out anyway. Are you going too? Because we feel very unhappy about leaving you alone with all this disturbance."

Disturbance! Talk about Nutley euphemism.

"She can't shift us, love," said Win grimly. "Been here long enough to have security of tenure. Anyway, we never had none of this bump in the night stuff before. I reckon it'll all fade away again, don't you, Harry?"

"Yeah," he said, "shouldn't be surprised. If you two want to get out, you go, though we'll miss you, mind – hope you'll come back and see us. But I don't see why we shouldn't try and get some money out of old Lily before we bother to stir ourselves. Anyway, it's been you who's had the real upset – there ain't been nothing up in our flat at all."

Julia remembered those dreadful, heartbroken tears in what had once been the main bedroom. "No," she said.

They rang the estate agent from a public telephone in Cabot Place East.

Lisa of the Alice band answered.

"Oh yes, you're from Ermintrude Villas, Cadogan Terrace, aren't you. Right. Just a sec, I think we have got one or two new lets in. Er – umm. Ah. Ray, what are we pricing Wick Road at? Oh, *right*. Yes, we've got a two-bedroom flat in

Wick Road for a hundred and twenty a week. And er, oh yes, there's another with one bed one box in Chatsworth Road for a hundred. Or what about a house? There's quite a nice terrace in Sewardstone Road, but it needs a bit of doing up. That's a hundred and thirty."

"Nothing cheaper?"

"Well, not with two beds. Large studio flat off the Kingsland Road for ninety-five pounds? One double bedroom flat behind Homerton High Street for a hundred and ten?"

"Can we go and look at some of them?" Bernice asked.

"Sure, this afternoon?"

"No, we're at work. Supposing we come straight round afterwards, will you still be open?"

"In the present climate, we're always open," said the girl.

Ray covered his gleaming shirtsleeves with the top half of his suit, packed them into his East End boy made good saloon and ran them swiftly round the moderate To Lets of Hackney. Most of them would have done from the point of view of space, but there was always a drawback, usually a fully operational main road outside the windows. One overlooked a fire station, another got the full benefit of a row of bottle banks and a late-night kebab bar.

The terraced house was in a quiet road facing the nicely tidied up canal and the even nicer and tidier Victoria Park, but it was very run-down.

"We've been trying to sell it, actually, but the owners have no objection to letting for the time being."

The back door had recently been broken in, the kitchen ceiling was covered with grease and there was a suspicious smell of drains. They left it with a shudder.

"Have you got anything else in a quiet road?"

He leafed through his folder. "New one-bed conversion in Amhurst Road – no, you've got traffic through there. Top flat in Mare Street – you really wouldn't hear a thing once the windows were closed. No? Two-bed garden flat off Church Crescent, but that's a hundred and thirty." They flinched.

"All right, let's have a look at that."

It was unbelievably quiet, in a turning shielded from traffic noise by other terraces. The present occupants' belongings were still in full possession, but brimming dustbins showed that the removal process had started. There was a shower instead of a bath, but it was all theirs; also the flats above seemed gentrified enough to guarantee no rock or reggae blasting all night. Vacant possession in two weeks. Back to Cyprian Smith's and the paperwork.

They bussed down to the Wick and walked up Cadogan Terrace. They'd done it. They'd arranged the move. Oh God, what a relief.

Bernice spun round like a little girl in a party dress and laughed out loud. "Oh Jule! Isn't it wonderful? And the windows are the same size, so the curtains will fit and we'll have a bedroom each. Our troubles are all over."

"Bernice," said Julia quickly, feeling a rush of panic, "never, ever say that. Nothing is ever all over and nothing is ever completely got away from. The best you can hope for is a new try at getting things right."

Bernice looked at her with surprise and went very quiet. They were nearly at their gate (except that there wasn't a gate) when she spoke again, and then it was in a tentative, pardon-me-if-I-say-this but surprisingly firm voice.

"You know, Jule, you're getting into an awful habit of talking things down, as if you didn't believe in anything being nice. Every time I get happy or hopeful you rush for a bucket of cold water. You weren't like that before."

"Do I?" said Julia, quite shocked and even ashamed. "Well, you've never lived with me before, have you. I suppose it's nerves, not expecting too much in case it doesn't happen."

Don't trust and you won't be let down. Don't hope in case it doesn't come true. Don't dare feel or open yourself up in case someone takes advantage. No feel, no hurt, no cry.

"You want to be kinder to yourself, Jule," said Bernice, climbing the steps, "then other people will be kinder to you.

And if you're always looking on the black side it does tend to make people back off."

"Are you telling me you're going to back off?" Julia asked carefully. "I mean, if you feel we're not getting on we could forget about sharing and get separate flats. I'd quite understand."

"No-o-o," said Bernice with equal care, "but perhaps we aren't as good for each other as we thought. I expect you think I'm a bit soppy, don't you? I know I'm not as attractive and sophisticated as you, and I'm pretty certain I'm not as clever."

"Oh don't!" Julia said in horror. "Is that how I've made you feel? I didn't mean to, I swear I didn't. I've had too much experience of being put down myself to want to inflict it on others. I suppose it's catching; you learn how to behave from the way people behave to you. I'm sorry I've proved such a liability, Bernice, but I honestly haven't been able to help it. If you'd rather be on your own, do say. Pity we didn't think of it earlier, before I frightened your boyfriend away."

Bernice's eyes filled with tears. "See, there you go again, blaming yourself for everything. Once we've moved I'm sure you'll be your old self, and then I might give Tom a ring."

"I can tell you what his first question will be," said Julia, as Bernice unlocked the front door. That's negative again, I can't seem to stop. She's quite right. I'm a power station turning out bad vibes. "Promise me you'll tell the truth if you want to be rid of me. Please promise."

"Yes," said Bernice, nodding hard. "Of course I promise." She opened the flat door and immediately they both drew in their breath at the unmistakable sense of presence.

"Who's there?" called Julie. Perhaps they'll answer this time. There was a crackling sound. Leather creaked.

They backed out onto the steps. A questioning meeaiow greeted them.

"Bubastis? Oh hello, Bubastis, darling!" Bernice grabbed the great ball of black and white fluff and cuddled it for comfort. Bubastis indulged her for a very few seconds before leaving

191

with a spitting yowl, and at the same moment Julie felt the soft nudge of furred muscle sliding round her ankles and departing to see the rival on his way.

"Smell the pipe smoke?" Bernice whispered.

The sound of a door opening on the first floor back, and then swishing and thudding advancing down the stairs. Swish, swish, swish, thud, thud, thud. Anxious whispering. A tearful protest.

"—so wicked—"

The clattering of heels. The slap and click of an umbrella opening! It came on, the voices, the hurry, the anxiety; like a force, like a brushing of winds, like something alive passing through them and tip-tapping down the steps and along the path. And the clang of an iron gate, opening and closing, and footsteps walking across the road, and again the sad, protesting words floating back upon the wind.

"—so cruel—"

They pressed back against the side of the porch, hands gripped, eyes looking across into the park as if trying to make out those who had passed into it.

"This is pathetic," said Julia, angry not only at her fear, but at the refusal of the ghosts to acknowledge them. After all, she had tried, hadn't she? "I mean, Harry's quite right, they can't hurt us. They're just getting on with their lives, and we're getting on with ours. They don't even seem to know we're here."

"The cat does," said Bernice.

"Well, it's only a *cat*," Julia argued, aware that the remark was irrational. So it's understandable for ghost cats to know the living are there, and for ghost people not to, eh? Nice bit of Mother there.

"That woman's voice, Jule; wasn't it sad? I wonder where they were all going."

"Let's go in," Julia said, anger giving her courage. "If they don't take notice of us, why should we take notice of them?"

"Did you hear his newspaper?"

"Yes."

"It's Thursday. Perhaps it's the *Hackney Gazette*."

"Was it published then?"

"Don't know. All right, Jule, let's try and be brave; we haven't got to put up with it much longer."

The smell of smoke still lingered. They opened the windows.

"I suppose it isn't real smoke? Anything been touched, Bernie?"

"Don't think so. Though we're in such a mess at the moment I'm not sure I'd notice."

Julia shrugged irritably. She must be pretty deadened if a possible burglary could be taken in her stride, and pretty exhausted emotionally if her fear of the ghosts could become anger. Her tiredness now was above all else.

"Well, we went down to St Catherine's and found a woman called Ingersall who died in Hackney in 1925, so we ordered a copy," said Win.

"Oh, you must let us pay for it," Julia exclaimed.

"We'll see about that," Win granted graciously.

"I suppose we might find out if Mr Rillington was married that way, too."

"We don't need to," said Harry, "Lily told me the other day. 'May uncle was a lafe-long bechelor,' she said. Wouldn't be surprised to find out her Dad was, too."

"What did he do for a living?"

"As far as I can tell, sod all," said Harry, "if you'll pardon my French. He told me once he'd got investments, but never said one of 'em was us. Here," he said suddenly, "do you think he'd got other property round Hackney?"

"Lily didn't mention them," said Bernice. "I wonder what she lives on?"

"Her pension and the neighbours?" Julia suggested. ("Julia's such a suspicious little thing; she's not as sweet-natured as her sisters are.")

"Oh, by the way, Harry," Bernice vouchsafed with shocked awe, "it looks as if that stuff she told us about her wonderful

193

family might not be absolutely true. She told Mrs Parkin that lots of people who'd known the Rillingtons in the old days turned out for the funeral."

"Stone the crows! How's that for a whopper?" exclaimed Harry.

"Makes you wonder about the rest of the Rillington legend," said Julia, even more cynical. "She probably got most of it from her mother and then embroidered it. Do you know who Agnes married, and when?"

"Give us a chance!" said Win indignantly. "All this looking things up takes time, you know."

That night, there was someone in the room.

The girls first noticed it at about eleven, just as they were drifting towards sleep. They sat up stiffly in the bed-settee, looking towards the fireplace. There was no pressure on the cushions and no smell of smoke.

The person stayed in one place. There were slight sounds of movement, an occasional clink of very small objects, and once, a cough. There was something particularly eerie about hearing a ghost cough. How could irritation occur in a non-physical throat?

"Hello?" Bernice said at last. Her voice was very quiet and high.

There was no response. After another few minutes a weary sigh was breathed.

They were unbelievably weary themselves. When I get out of here, thought Julia, I'm going to sleep for a whole day, then have a wonderful, leisurely hot shower, then put myself on a course of vitamin tablets. I've come from one constant cause of stress and drain on my energies to another, and I'm not sure which is the most damaging to my health.

"Are you trying to tell us something?" she asked, so desperate she really hoped for an answer.

There was not even the impression that the question had been heard. They were getting on with their lives. They didn't know that the years had moved on, and that They had moved

194

on, too. They were stuck like a seventy-eight record with a crack, or perhaps it was time which had stuck; or perhaps their everyday existence was stuck in a crack in time. Or perhaps the house had recorded their moment in time and it could not be erased, short of demolition.

Julia had a sudden vision of time as a stream of water pouring continuously from a tap and swirling away down the drain, and of something stuck in the corner of the sink, like a blob of tea leaves, in such a position that the water eddied round and left it behind. What a mundane image for a metaphysical concept. But then, everything they'd overheard had been mundane. Cleaning the grate, moving up and down stairs, smoking and reading the paper by the fire, laying the table.

And why should a next life be any more spiritual than the people who had become spirits? When they walked across the great divide they would take with them all their daily concerns and habits, their ways of thought and codes of behaviour, their worldly pleasures and their worldly anxieties. What else could they be judged by, except, perhaps, their dreams?

Although the first day of their week might be devoted to the outward exercise of a religion, it was the six others which exposed what people's spiritual standards really were.

Bernice's were obvious; kindness to people and animals, the enjoying and sharing of nice things, the attempt to spread happiness.

What occupied her own thoughts and energies the most? What seemed to her the most important things in the world?

She could give herself no very satisfactory answer, except for personal survival, and a picture of herself trying to scramble out of an emotional bog and start living.

Seventeen

J ulia went into the bedroom to collect clean clothes for the new day. It was a mess. Though both girls had been coming in and out to the wardrobe, they had got into the habit of dropping dirty garments onto the unused bed and not bothering to hang up used but still cleanish ones. There was a veil of dust over surfaces and the ornaments on the mantelpiece. One of their swift visits had knocked 'Yes you can' askew.

The room smelt stale. She pushed up the sash. Roar, whizz, scream, fumes. The tops of the tower blocks hung high beyond the parapet in the dull, damp, morning air.

They were in an awful state; broken or boarded up windows, scaffolding holding the balconies together, or perhaps apart. White sheets covered with writing hung from the roofs and draped over the upper floors; the first and largest word was 'Controlled'. I should hope they are. There was an alarming impression of instability about them – you could almost believe they were leaning.

"We'll start packing tonight," she told Bernice as they cleared the breakfast things – well, moved them from the table to the draining board. They'd woken late – again.

"We'll have to hire a van," said Bernice. "Tom moved me last—" She stopped.

"I can't drive," said Julia apologetically. "My mother never let me learn." And I never thought of doing it anyway without telling her.

"I can," said Bernice.

Another point won for her. Another point lost for Julia. No!

Stop it! Remember, this is the beginning of the rest of your
life. Cinderella, you *shall* learn to drive, so stop wallowing in
self-pity. And that's negative, too. Telling yourself off, even
with the best of intentions, only reinforces your bad self-image.
Be kinder to yourself. You need encouragement, not criticism.
You've had enough of that to last a lifetime.

"Good-morning, Jones, Brown and Wilkinson."

"Julia! Philip has just told me what you said to him! Why
the dickens are you avoiding me like this?"

"I'm sorry, I can't possibly speak now. I'll ring you this
evening." The receiver went down, as if of its own accord.
"That," she told Bernice with a tight throat and shaking
hands, "is the first time in my life I have ever hung up on
my mother."

"Will she mind?" asked Bernice in a low, apprehensive tone.
"Hi, Candice!"

"Will she mind!" said Julia.

They picked up fish and chips on their way home. There
was knocking and drilling going on in the direction of the
Trowbridge Estate. The tower blocks looked very dodgy
indeed.

"What's that written on them?" asked Bernice, squinting
upwards. "Controlled – dem – demolition. Gosh! Trowbridge
D-day – 4th of June. *Gosh*! They're going to knock them down.
Heavens, Jule, how will they do that? If they keel over they
could hit our house!"

"I think they'll be a bit more skilful about it than that," Julia
reassured her.

It was no great surprise that the phone was ringing as they got
in. Julia went straight for the receiver, metaphorically gritting
her teeth.

"Julia! For the last time, when are you coming home?"

"Hello, Mum. Well, I'm rather busy at the moment, we're
getting ready to move."

"I *knew* you wouldn't be able to stick that awful place for

197

long, not after what you've been used to!" Her voice was triumphant. "I'll put the sheets on for Sunday. Thank God you've come to your senses at last."

"I'm not coming Sunday, Mum, and I'm definitely not going to come home to live. We've found a very nice flat in a much quieter street, and there's a bedroom for each of us."

"But you must come home!" For the first time, Julia heard a touch of anxiety in her mother's ranting. "How can I stay here all on my own? I need you, Julia. I'm just not used to sitting here with no one to talk to, staring at the wall. What am I supposed to do in the evening?"

"You've got television. And you could join things. There's the Townswomen's Guild, and the local National Trust branch, and—"

"I don't *do* that sort of thing, you know I don't. I've always been a family person. I thought you were, too. I thought we were company for each other. Why do you want to leave me and this lovely house? I mean, I'm having a terrible time getting someone to do the grass – they all want an absolute *fortune*, and I need it looking nice for Sunday."

"Can't you do it?" asked Julia, trying not to weaken. "After all, you've got a Flymo, they're dead easy."

"I've not been *used* to that sort of thing. Now look here, Julia, listen to me. You must come on Sunday. It's your duty. Everyone's expecting you."

"Mum," said Julia desperately, "it would really be far better if I didn't. We've been too bound up with each other, and we've got to learn to live apart. I want to grow up. It will be good for you, too – you'll find a whole new world."

"At my age? I don't want a whole new world, I like the one I've got. And supposing I get ill?"

"You're no age at all. People much older than you try new things every day. And you're never ill."

"I've not been feeling at all well lately," said Mrs Nutley, with an accusing tone which seemed to hint at poison. "Still, you don't care about that, do you? As long as you can go off and enjoy yourself, slumming and throwing away all the standards you were brought up with, I can go to the dickens! You've abandoned me."

"If it makes you feel any better, I'm not particularly enjoying myself at the moment, in fact something very difficult is happening. But," she said firmly, before her mother could launch into an I-told-you-so about mugging, burglary, murder, rape, riot, bugs, lice and litter, "I'm learning to cope with it. You must learn to cope with things, too. If you do, and stop clinging on to me like a leech, and we stay away from each other for a while, we may then be able to meet again without tearing each other to pieces." Oh good heavens, I sound like the advice column in a women's magazine.

"It's not me who starts it," retorted Mrs Nutley, "it's you who takes offence at everything I say. I just do not see what the dickens I've done to deserve such treatment. What can you possibly have against me?"

"You don't respect me," said Julia, grabbing the chance to try and explain. "You don't even see me as a separate person, certainly not an adult person. You despise me, really. How can we ever have a workable relationship on those terms?"

"I don't despise you!"

"Well, you treat me as if you do."

"I do not! Oh really, Julia, where do you get these ridiculous fancies from, you're so *stupid.*"

"See? You do despise me. You think I'm stupid and useless and no good at anything, and you've been telling me so for practically the whole of my life. Mind you, I'm quite good at doing things like cutting the grass, aren't I?"

"Well, you do tend to leave the edges rather shaggy."

"Right, well you do it yourself, then," said Julia, reaching breaking point, "then you can get it just the way you want it. Goodbye."

"Oh dear," said Bernice almost with reproach.

"I know, I know. I always start off trying to be polite and finish up very nearly downright rude. It's her fault, I can't get through to her. She doesn't understand a bloody word I say. It's so frustrating, Bernie," she said, throwing her hands up in a gesture of despair and giving an alarmingly good performance of tearing her hair. "She's incapable of seeing any point of view but her own. You can explain how things look to you over and over again, and all she says when you've finished is 'Don't be silly.' And she really thinks it is silly. If it's not the way she sees things, it must be. She quite simply *cannot* take on board anything else – that's why she gets so aggrieved. She has no ability to put herself in someone else's shoes and understand their point of view. Tell her she's upset you and that's just a case of 'Don't be silly', as well."

"I can see it must be very difficult for you, Jule," said Bernice sympathetically.

"Yes, and it always has been."

The insensitivity. The scolding and the putting down. The complete unawareness that others possessed feelings which could be hurt. ("Oh look at poor old Julia, her knickers are drooping again. Ha! Ha! Ha!! Come here, Julia, you'll have all the little dogs after you.") Being the object of ridicule in a circle of laughing adults, her shame intensified by sheer puzzlement. Why dogs? Why should dogs run after knickers? Could one, in fact, stop dogs from bothering you by the simple expedient of keeping your knickers well up?

Like many of Mrs Nutley's stock phrases, it had a lurking coarseness in it which she was certainly unaware of; for instance, her favourite reproof to over-confidence (or any confidence): "Now then, cocky breeches!"

That one didn't bear examination at all.

Julia had often wondered what her maternal grandparents had been like, and whether they were, in fact, on the downmarket side.

Win was looking pretty grumpy.

"Well, we've had another look for them Ingersalls but ain't found nothing. It's always twice as tricky without a Census entry to start from. I mean, you can look through the births, marriages and deaths, but where do you start from if you don't know when they was born or when they died? You could be at it weeks before you dredged 'em up."

"They're not in the commercial section of any directories, neither," said Harry, "and we couldn't look up any christenings because the parish church registers for this area ain't deposited at the Greater London. Of course, we could make an appointment to go and see them, I suppose."

"Which church is that?" asked Julia.

"St Augustine's."

"Oh, that's where Lily said the Rillington girls went. Where is it?" asked Bernice.

"Gone," said Harry. "It was over there." He waved his hand towards the bay window.

The girls looked out.

"What, Victoria Park Road?"

"Yeah, but not that side. Look, you see that big plantation of trees by the lodge? It was behind there, right on the edge of the park."

Outside, a drowning sun emerged from the watery clouds, and its light dived beneath branches and touched the houses. So the Rillingtons had put on their beautiful clothes, and boarded their carriage, and driven down to a church near to the wrong end of the park, in order to hear a service high enough for the beautiful Constance Agnes.

"What happened to it?" asked Julia.

"Bombed. So that's it till Monday, kids. Sorry," said Win, slapping the notebook shut.

"Everything's closed Saturday, is it?"

"Some places are open, but not the Greater London or St Catherine's or Somerset House. I mean," she went on with irritable frustration, "we could try looking for a Will, but we don't know when Ingersall died."

"What about 1931?" suggested Bernice tentatively.

"We don't know that he *died* in 1931," Win pointed out, "he might just have moved."

"Oh yes," said Bernice, looking crestfallen.

"We could try it, I suppose," Win granted. "Yeah, all right, we'll go down to Somerset House on Monday and then have another go at St Catherine's. That'll sweat a few pounds off Harry – it don't half get hot in there when it's busy. Pity They can't tell us the answers," she added, "it'd save an awful lot of trouble."

"I don't think They're that sort of ghost," said Julia wearily. "They're not aware of us at all. We just seem to be hearing bits and pieces of what went on here near the beginning of the century, happening in no particular order, for no particular reason. Like tuning a radio, and getting brief blasts of voices from distant places. And there doesn't seem to be any reason for it to have started in the first place."

Everyone went very quiet, even Win, who was inscribing a tight little doodle on the cover of her notebook. It looked like a trail of rising smoke. Harry smiled kindly at Julia and she smiled back, without quite knowing why.

Bernice poured the drinking chocolate into the mugs. Julia hadn't drunk it for years, mainly because her mother had kept pressing it upon her.

It was none too warm tonight; the rain had lowered the temperature and Bernice had lit the gas fire. It hissed at them in duet with the television.

"I don't think I ever want to watch night-time TV in bed again," said Julia. How I should like to turn off the light and close my eyes in complete silence, and fall asleep with a sensation of total security.

"Do you want to try without it?" Bernice asked.

"No," said Julia.

"Jule?" Bernice started, after a thoughtful moment.

"Yes?"

"Have you ever thought you might be just a bit, well, you know, well, sort of, well, psychic?" She seemed to believe that the blow of an awkward question could be cushioned by extra words.

"No, of course I haven't. Why?"

"Well, you know – all this."

"Oh no. I mean, we've all heard it, haven't we?" said Julia confidently. Thank goodness I've kicked that perpetual paranoid guilt. In fact, all things considered, my fight against conditioned neurosis has been going extremely well.

"Not till you did first. And you're the only one of us who's actually seen anything. You remember, that shadow in the garden that looked a bit like a woman."

"Oh, good Lord!" Julia cried. "You think it's my fault, don't you?"

"I never said anything about fault," Bernice said quickly. "I didn't mean you'd actually done anything on purpose to bring it on, silly. Oh no, sorry, I don't mean that you *are* silly. Oh Jule, please don't get upset, that's the last thing I want to do to you."

With her calm, protective mask back in place, Julia sat struggling with her feelings. The sudden, unpleasant sensation in the chest and stomach. The trembling of shock which can trigger tears, the sudden snatching away of security, leaving the emptiness of lost confidence and demolished self-esteem.

You thought Bernice and the Grosvenors liked you, didn't you? No, approved of you, that's what you need, approval. You were daft enough to relax and let yourself go a bit, because you felt secure in their approval, and all the time they were doubting you, and suspecting you of causing this whole dreadful situation. When will you learn? You've been given the lesson enough times. Watch what you say. Watch what you do. Never be spontaneous – you'll only make a fool of yourself and regret it. And above all, always remember how vulnerable you are, and keep up your defences.

"Are you sure you want to go on living with me?" she asked, "I mean, I might do it again, mightn't I. Supposing the new flat really was inhabited by Jack the Ripper, like Tom said. I might attract him back, and then we'd really have trouble."

The speech started out being carefully calm and rigidly reasonable. By the end it sounded hard, sarcastic and offensive, and the reference to Tom seemed taunting and cruel.

Within seconds, they were both in tears again.

"Oh, for heaven's sake," sobbed Julia, "this is ridiculous! No wonder we're allowing that wretched, miserable family back into their old house; they must feel thoroughly at home."

In the night, smoke drifted into their nostrils. They awoke but didn't move. They stiffened beneath the covers and felt their heartbeats rise and their breathing grow shallow and fast. Bernice's hand stole into Julia's and she held it hard, not opening her eyes.

I'm going to see something this time, I know I am.

There was a tension in the air, an altered state of consciousness in the atmosphere of the house, a sensation of loss of balance and of lurching sideways into what could only be the past.

I'm going to open my eyes and see it all – the man smoking in the chair, the fireplace unblocked and blazing with coal, the old furniture, the sort of depressing wallpaper it's impossible to imagine anyone choosing unless they had a gun at their head.

There's going to be an upright piano, probably where this bed is. In that case, we are resting inside it, between the keyboard and the pedals. If anyone sits down and starts playing now, the sound will ring though our heads, and the performer's skirts will smother our faces.

She sat upright with a cry.

"Jule! Are you all right?"

"No!" she cried, agonised with dread.

"Is it the smoke?"

"Yes."

"There's nothing here now. I can still smell it a bit, but there's no one in the chair. How do you feel?"

"Awful," Julia said, trembling. "Did you see anything? I didn't dare look."

"I didn't look either," Bernice admitted.

"Can we move the bed?"

"Why?"

"The piano is here. We'll get in their way."

"But where?" asked Bernice helplessly.

"Further along towards the kitchen."

"We won't be able to get in there," Bernice protested.

"Well, move the television and the music deck."

"That'll be OK when it's closed, but get in the way of the fire when it's opened. And anyway," she said cajolingly, "it's not a real piano, is it?"

"It might be one day. Some day we're going to hear these things, and smell them, and then start to see them, and after that we'll feel Them touch us like the cat does, and They'll take us over and we'll be pulled back into the past ourselves and won't be able to get out again."

"Oh Jule, how could they possibly do that?"

"How can they possibly do any of it? I think you may be right, Bernice. It could all be caused by me. I'm an awful mess inside, you know, and I've never felt the same as the rest of my family. It was as if I was made differently, not just the way I looked, but mentally. Perhaps that was why my mother was always having a go at me, she sensed I was a sort of stranger in the camp. If she'd been an animal, I'd have been the member of the litter which smelt wrong and got thrown out."

"Jule! Oh Jule!" Bernice was as sorry for her as if she were indeed an ill-treated, rejected little animal. "Look, supposing you are a bit on the psychic side. That doesn't have to be dreadful, you know. I mean, lots of mediums seem to be quite jolly people. Look at Doris Stokes."

"I don't want to be a medium!" Julia cried, gripping the coverlet. "That's a terrible responsibility, a gift like that, you'd have to devote your whole life to it. All those dead people trying to get at you so you could help them, or act as a sort of telephone exchange for them, and all those live ones putting their faith in you to put them in touch with people they've lost. Supposing you couldn't do it? Supposing you got it wrong and sent them away more heartbroken than before? And just think, you'd never be alone again! All the time there'd be voices in your ear, or perhaps you'd see people everywhere who were really ghosts."

She drew her knees up under her chin and stared ahead, as

if she really was confronted by things which no one else could see. It was deeply distressing for her friend to watch her; as if she was stripping in public, and revealing ailments and even deformities from which no one could have dreamed she was suffering.

"But you're seeing it all negatively, again. You could be so useful, and so comforting to people. Though of course," Bernice added hastily, as Julia looked more frightened than ever, "you don't have to develop the gift at all if you don't want to. But just think, Jule, if what we've been hearing is really ghosts clinging on to their old lives, and it does seem to be such a sad, sad life they had together, someone with gifts like yours, well, a gift like you might have," she corrected, "could get in touch with them, and find out what was wrong, and see if she could help them. I think if I could do that I'd feel *so* privileged."

"Do you remember that time we walked across the park to the estate agents on Bank Holiday Monday?" said Julia, still staring ahead at the gas fire. "We were imagining that the whole park might be full of ghosts, people who'd enjoyed it in the past and who still liked to come and remember the nice times they'd had there. I – I've got a confession to make, Bernie. As soon as that was said, I saw some people walking a few yards in front of us. A man in a bowler hat held out his hand to a little boy in a sailor suit, and a woman on his arm turned her head and looked back in our direction. She was in a dark jacket with fringes on it, and a long green skirt. Then I panicked and they weren't there any more."

"Why ever didn't you say?" Bernice asked with utter astonishment.

"It was only for about two seconds at the most, and I wasn't sure I hadn't imagined it."

"But Jule, that's amazing! Don't you realise that if you could see the people here, and perhaps speak to them, we could find out what it was all about, and save Win and Harry all this rushing around looking things up. Still," she thought again, "they're loving it, aren't they, specially Win. Though I think

Harry would rather like to get back on the trail of the Duke of Westminster. No, Marquis."

"I don't want to be able to do that!" Julia protested, genuinely terrified. "I don't want it!"

"But you're assuming that dead people are all wicked and frightening and dangerous. If your dad came and tried to contact you, would you expect him to have turned into an evil spirit?"

"No, of course not!" Julia said angrily.

"And if I died, would you expect me to stop liking you and start wanting to harm you?"

But Julia was overwhelmed by fear of the unknown and the never-thought-about. Those disturbing little incidents in her past, particularly her childhood, when she had felt not quite alone; when she had wondered if she really had heard that, or felt that, or been right when she suspected that there was something behind that door—

No, it wasn't so.

"Don't be silly!" she shouted.

Eighteen

They had a brief Saturday lie-in to try and recharge their flagging batteries, then started packing immediately after breakfast. Bernice suggested that everything they were going to need in the way of clothes should be laid on the bed in the back room, to save the inconvenience of having to unpack the packed, and they had put quite a lot on top before they remembered the bedding should be removed first.

The washing machine was loaded and started up. Julia took her ornaments down and returned them to the cardboard box which had carried them to Hackney. Bernice started wrapping the teddies in tissue paper and tucking them up in a large, soft holdall. The books were wedged into another.

"You finished reading this, Jule?" asked Bernice, holding up *Just For The Hell Of It*.

"Definitely," said Julia.

A bareness began to spread over the flat. Undusted corners were revealed, mislaid objects miraculously came back into their lives.

Outside, it poured with rain. From the front window the park was saturated and empty, and from the back ones the motorway carried on regardless, the usual row backed by the hissing of tyres on water.

The washing was hung to dry in front of the gas fire. Its steam began to fill the air, then condense on the cold windows. They made coffee.

"We're doing quite well, aren't we?" said Bernice happily, moving the clothes-horse of plastic-covered metal back a bit so they could warm themselves.

"Are you going to wash the throws before we go?" asked Julia, fingering the arm of her chair. The coarse, cream-coloured cotton was pretty grubby, and also bore the marks of a few run-ins with coffee and curry.

"Yes, I think so, then we can put everything on fresh and new. But we'd better get this lot dry and ironed first."

"How much of this furniture is actually yours?" asked Julia, lifting the fringed edge to discover varnished, machine-carved legs and greasy tapestry upholstery which was Art Deco design at its worst. "Look at this! Can you imagine anyone wanting to buy that? I wonder who did."

"Well, either Mr Rillington when he moved in, or the last tenant, who hadn't got room for it at Jaywick."

"Bernice," said Julia anxiously, leaning towards the comforting fire with hands cosily on hot mug, "down in Mr Rillington's flat did you notice the leather armchair and the red cloth over the range?"

"No, I don't think I did."

"They were what I'd imagined being up here. Back in 1910, I mean."

"Really? Well, there'd have been a lot of that sort of thing about then."

"But the tassels on the chair arms were the same, and the woven black border round the tablecloth. And the piano," Julia went on, gripping the mug until her fingers burned. "It was just the kind I'd imagined playing that night. It even had *Für Elise* lying on the top. And I'll tell you another funny thing; can you imagine Mr Rillington playing *Melody in F*? That's what was on the stand."

"How does it go?"

Julia hummed it, then thought it might not be a good idea. She got up and switched on the radio.

"Oh yes," said Bernice, "but They didn't play that, did they?"

"They haven't yet," said Julia in a low voice. "Anyway, if those things are the ones I saw up here, and I really have got some sort of gift and was seeing them correctly, then what was Mr Rillington doing with furnishings which belonged to the Ingersalls?"

Bernice took a while to answer. "Perhaps he bought them with the house."

"But if he was that well off, he wouldn't need second-hand furniture."

"Oh well, goodness, I don't know, then." Bernice sighed and gave up.

"And the canteen of cutlery – I'm sure it was silver. That sort of thing would go down with a real thump if you dropped it."

"Well, every Edwardian middle-class household would have had a canteen of cutlery, and silver wouldn't sound any different from steel."

"But it does," said Julia.

"Oh." Bernice recognised the beginnings of acceptance in Julia's voice, and had nothing more to say.

But only the beginnings; all this probably wasn't very special, really, it was a sort of ESP, and lots of people had that. Like telepathy – just another example of the marvels of the human brain.

She had taken her first step, taken a surreptitious sideways look at an alarming fact, on a par with Beethoven accepting that he might, at some time in the distant future, have to consider very occasionally cupping his ear with his hand.

The Grosvenors gave them a knock about midday and expressed admiration at how busy they'd been.

"We'll give you a hand with painting and that, if you like," Win offered, "that is if your Tom ain't doing it."

Bernice looked stricken.

"He's away for a bit," said Julia.

"Right, then," said Win heartily, "you just got to shout and we'll be there."

"Will you mind staying here all alone?" asked Julia, feeling guilty about them for all sorts of reasons.

"Nah!" said Harry. "We got a letter from the estate agent this morning, did you? No, don't suppose you would have if you're going. We've told them we don't particularly want to, so we'll see if they'll take the hint and come up with a little sweetener. Or a big sweetener," he added with a grin.

"I wonder what she's going to do with these houses."

"Sell, I should think," said Win decidedly, "perhaps to that builder doing the conversion up the road. But there's Luke and Fern to get out, too, and where will they go, poor kids? I expect they've got the Asians on a short lease, though, they ain't been here all that long."

"We are sorry to leave you alone," Julia said again as they left, feeling acutely the predicament they were in.

"Don't worry about it," Win said, and gave her shoulder a playful, if forceful tap. "We ain't made of bone china."

"Did you ever hear Mr Rillington play *Melody in F*?" Julia called after them anxiously.

"How's that go?" asked Win, turning at the bottom of the stairs.

Julia sang it again. They shook their heads.

"Nah," said Harry, "not his style."

They carried on cleaning and clearing all afternoon, with two television films, one after the other, to keep them company. Julia got busy ironing, then put the still dampish clothes and linen back on the clothes horse to finish drying. Bernice started on the kitchen cupboards. From behind the curtain, Julia heard the clunk of tins and the clink of bottles and jars being dumped on the table, also the occasional crash and cry of, "Oh *dear*."

Poor Bernice, she was happy here until I came along. No, stop it, stop it, stop it! It's not all your fault, even if you are – I mean, Mr Rillington would still have died, and Lily would still have inherited, and Bernice would still have had only a short lease and the possibility of being turfed out at a month's notice.

And really, the new flat is so much nicer that I've probably done her a favour, apart from the increase in rent, and I'm paying half of that. It's a bit more vulnerable to break-ins, being basement – no, stop it!

But you couldn't stop all unwanted thoughts – it wasn't, perhaps, desirable that one should; awareness of danger was an essential defence mechanism, and her many apprehensions had never before included a danger as unmanageable as this.

Unexplained noises. Sensations of presence. Sudden appearances, like the woman-like shadow in the garden and the little family in the park.

Oh, that had been strange. Just an ordinary Mr and Mrs in their best clothes, taking their little son out to enjoy the air. He reaching out to offer support and affection, she glancing back as if to say, 'Look at my handsome husband. Look at my beautiful child. And do, please, look at my best velvet mantle and my freshly-trimmed bonnet. Are we not to be envied?'

Well, if it did happen again, there was no reason why she shouldn't see contented spirits like those, not the Ibsenian lot the Ingersalls seemed to be. It's not long now. Keep going, it really isn't long now.

Julia cooked – there was enough in the fridge to make a reasonable meal, and the rain was still swishing down between Ermintrude Villas and the take-aways of Hackney Wick.

She heard Bernice pick up the phone and tried not to listen, humming to herself and making noise with the implements. Immediately she changed *Melody in F* for another tune, then discovered she was embarking on *The Lost Chord*.

She stopped, not just because the associations of those melodies were uncomfortable, but because her mouth had dried and her throat had closed up. Her fingers hung suspended in temporary rigor above the half-chopped parsley, and she felt the muscles of her neck and shoulders tighten as the sick tremor of nerves rose from her stomach to her heart.

Bernice's lowered voice could be heard in the living room. It certainly wasn't that. There had been clarity, and authority, and urgency about the female voice which said 'Find it.' I thought I'd just imagined that. Once I'd got over that shameful bout of hysterics I convinced myself I'd imagined it.

Julia remained in suspended animation, her breathing coming in audible gasps. It will come again. I know it will come again.

"It must not be discovered."

It was difficult to locate where it was coming from. Perhaps behind her? Or more to the side?

She heard the phone go down and the rustling movement of someone crossing the room, and then Bernice came through the curtain. Julia turned, overwhelmed with relief and ready to share her experience, but she looked too thoughtful and withdrawn to be burdened with more trouble.

Towards evening, they heard the footsteps along the hall. Again the basement door opened and closed without moving the mattress, and again the steps went below on the bare, wooden stairs.

They never come up again, thought Julia, though she must have done as often as she went down. And the group of women always go out, but I've never heard them come back.

"You must find it and hide it."

The personal pronoun hit her like a sharp implement, piercing through the last remaining layer of her denial. She turned from the cleaning of the kitchen cupboard, ready to face the woman or women who lived in Number Two Ermintrude Villas. Nobody there; the door stood open into the lobby and revealed only the pile of belongings on the tiles.

"Find it."

This was different. This was not a slip into an unaware past, this was now and They were here. She could sense their presence. She was in her stripped, packed-up home and They were here with her. The Ingersalls. Find what? Hide what? Why?

I won't let it happen again, Julia told herself as they settled down to sleep, not in the past nor the present.

They were tired out and aching all over. They could both have done with a bath but couldn't face it, both for sleepiness and for unease.

"Let's wait till tomorrow morning, Jule. Hope you can stand the grunge and sweat till then."

I will not let it happen. I've held this off for years, though I wasn't aware I was doing it. If I go back to being reserved and uptight and always on my guard, I can stop it happening now.

Yet it seemed such a pity. It was good to be coming out of herself, and learning to reach out to people instead of holding them off. But if she did that to the living, it seemed she did the same to the dead. There must be something in her which they responded to. Understanding? Kindness? Generosity in listening? Well, if there was, she'd never noticed it, and no one had ever remarked upon it, certainly not her family. ("Julia keeps herself to herself, she prefers books to people; I'm afraid you won't get much out of her.")

Except a rise or a laugh. Silly old Julia, inept old Julia, too tall, too awkward, too shy, too – oh shut up, stop feeling sorry for yourself. That's all over now – as far as the influences which built your personality can ever be all over.

The television was on, but with the sound down to a soothing murmur. The performers looked ridiculous. I suppose that's how people look if you're deaf. I hope I never get deaf, that must be a real handicap to battle against; no use talking to Julia, she can't hear a word you say; just shout and wave your hands at her.

A coal fell from the grate and rolled towards the fender. The fender was polished steel. The chimney opening was round and edged by a garland of iron flowers. The fire was burning low at the end of a long day, and the whole room smelt of coal smoke. I don't think I've ever smelt a coal fire before – except for that time we went to the Bluebell Railway. I remember Dad saying it brought back his childhood, because all towns and all homes smelt like that then.

She closed her eyes quickly, visualising pushing the mental cupboard door shut. She saw it gradually seating back into the door frame and her fingers pressing the bolt home. She opened her eyes again.

Bernice stirred and she nudged her.

"Do you want some chocolate, Bernie?"

"No thanks, Jule," she murmured.

"I'm making some for myself," Julia insisted. "Look, I'll get one for you as well, and it's up to you if you drink it."

Boxes of kitchen equipment lay all over the floor. She stepped across them to get to the fridge.

The milk saucepan was unwashed in the sink. It took a minute or two to clean it and put the milk on to boil.

The heavy velvet curtains hung closed on their brass rings. The many pictures reflected the single gas jet on the chimney breast. There was no fire in the grate, it was masked by a vase of pampas grass.

She circled the table several times, willing the empty cupboards and the scratched, steel-topped sink unit back into her world.

The milk came to the boil. She whipped it off the gas and poured it into the mugs. She stirred, deliberately noticing their patterns – willow pattern. *Willow pattern?* Yes, it *is* willow pattern, they're still making it now. Nostalgia rules. Genuine reproduction Victoriana is on sale everywhere.

"You must find it."

"Bernie, here's your chocolate."

She slipped back into the bed, chocolate and willow pattern amulet holding off harm.

I am living in now. The wallpaper came from Great Mills. The throws on the chairs came from a mail order catalogue. The bed-settee was a special offer in a Habitat sale. The curtain material came from Ealing and they were run up by Bernice's mum.

"Find it."

It looks bare without the teddies. I had a teddy once, his name was Bucephalus – I got it out of a book called *The Glories of Greece*. Mother thought it was a silly name for a teddy bear. ("Bucephalus! Ha! Ha! Ha! Bucephalus was a horse, Julia, not a bear. Listen, everyone, Julia thought Bucephalus was a bear! Isn't she a scream?")

I thought it was such a lovely name. All those ancient names have a ring to them. Like Bubastis.

The cat stretched on the grey fur rug. It showed up so well against it, as if it had been purposely designed to show off its occupant's beauties. Bright marmalade, golden glossy with health and pampered living, long-haired and almost gross with the fat of the eunuch.

No! Not then! Now! Worn, cheap, rubber back carpet with flattened pile. A gas fire. A television. A bed-settee. Bernice.

"It must be found."

She shook her awake.

"Aren't you going to drink your chocolate, Bernice?" she begged.

"You must find it."

The voice sounded so close, as if the lips from which it issued were no more than inches from her ear.

Sunday morning, and still the rain.

Julia made tea in an atmosphere of gloom. The flat was dulled by the clouds outside, and all homely touches had been removed.

Bernice emerged from under the covers.

"What's the time?"

"Quarter to six."

"Jule! It's Sunday," she protested, rubbing her eyes.

"Sorry, I couldn't sleep. I'm too scared," Julia admitted.

Find what? The question had tormented her all night.

She opened the flat door and looked up the stairs.

And if it's found, why must it be hidden again?

Julia felt sensation on the back of her neck – a chill, an awareness, perhaps, as if her body was taking the psychic temperature of the house. She froze as she heard them descending; the swishing skirts, the patter of footsteps on carpet. Someone was crying very quietly, in the restrained, ladylike way which involved a lace-edged handkerchief, little change of facial expression and the least possible release of actual tears.

I know all that, though I can see nothing. She's wearing a very large hat; I know that, too.

The heels clattered on the tiles. "It's so wrong!" the voice protested. The front door was heard to open, though from her place peering round the door, Julia saw that it stayed closed. She heard the hollow snapping of umbrellas, and the different pitch of tiles and stone as the invisible women moved out onto the steps. The door slammed and feet hurried down.

The house's ironwork might have been at the bottom of the sea with other gates and railings collected for salvage, or remade into some other object, or merely rusted away to red dust, but the vanished gate clanged.

She stepped out into the hall and undid the chain and bolts on the front door. The flowered, frosted glass, so impossible to get clean, was difficult to see through, in fact, only to be seen through darkly. The door opened, she could look across the road to the modern park railings and the rich, wet green of the grass and trees beyond, dripping in the grey morning.

She scanned the park from left to right, and the road in both directions. If there had been a bell, it had stopped now. They might not be going to church at all, but have other urgent business calling them from the house in the early morning, and perhaps it concerned something wicked, or cruel, or wrong.

She went back into the flat. Bernice had got up and was looking through the window.

"What were you doing, Jule?"

"I was trying to follow them," said Julia, her voice tense. "Did you hear them? I think it must have been church again, though it's pretty early."

"They've gone before breakfast," said Bernice, dropping her voice as if they were still present. "My great-aunt told me it used to be considered irreverent to eat before communion, and sometimes women used to faint in the pews. Still, I expect that was partly the corsets. You ever seen an old-fashioned corset, Jule? It was like an instrument of torture. Goodness knows how I'd have got into one. Did you actually see them this time, then?"

"No. But I felt I could have done, if I'd wanted to."

They used the bathroom together again, bath and hairwash, turn and turn about, like teenage sisters. Julia still found it fairly embarrassing, being much less of an extrovert than Bernice, who didn't seem to find any problem in the situation at all.

Julia didn't actually look straight at her, but knew any comparison would reveal that she herself was ridiculously skinny.

After breakfast, it was back to the packing. Cardboard boxes had run out, it was plastic carriers now, most of them too flimsy to take the amount crammed into them.

"What are you looking at?" asked Bernice, trying to slip another unbroken bag round the one which had underclothes protruding through its side like a hernia.

"Just the rain," said Julia, staring out of the bay window. I didn't hear them come back. Why do they never come back? Is it not the coming back that matters? "Do you know where St Augustine's was?" She felt restless and unable to keep still.

"No. Harry said it was over beside Victoria Park Road."

"I'm going to see," said Julia, going out to the bedroom. "Do you want to come?"

"No thanks, Jule. I thought I'd get the throws into the washing machine, and then I'll have another try at ringing Tom."

So she hadn't got through yesterday.

Julia collected raincoat, umbrella and boots. The bedroom was now a total shambles. The dumb fan stared at her. The overmantel mirror stared. Weighed down into immobility by piles of their belongings, the furniture stared and waited to be released.

Find what?

The front door slammed and her feet clattered down the steps. No gate to clang. Not straight across into the park, she didn't know the right way.

She felt better walking through the cloudy, modern, traffic-ridden outdoors, though inevitably guilty about leaving Bernice alone. Still, it was her choice and she seemed quite happy about it. The reason being, Julia realised, that she didn't expect anything to happen if Julia wasn't there. She was now not far from agreeing with them all. Julia Nutley, that nice, quiet girl who stayed at home with her mother, had turned out to be a bit funny; you know, sort of odd; in fact, not to put too fine a point upon it, things happened when she was around. In the times when she daydreamed about her talents being developed, discovered and appreciated, she'd never envisaged that one.

She walked down to the Wick, where many lines of vehicles met and fought it out at the traffic lights, and turned left past the great Molesworth gates of Victoria Park; they were new and brightly painted, not the old ones They'd known, which had probably been drowned in the cause of morale as well.

Victoria Park Road started to rise at once; a gentle rise, but enough to start you puffing if you were agitated already. On the right, the old terraces and side turnings, on the left the park, edged by giant plane trees and sloping up. Somewhere along here. The grass looks completely smooth, there's not a sign that a building stood upon it.

Those houses are modernish, those flats are brand new. There might have been a bomb here. Perhaps it was the one which destroyed St Augustine's.

A woman with a dog emerged from Homer Road and crossed over to a small gate in the railings. She took off its lead the instant they were through, and the animal leapt and ran and barked with joy, sending drops of water flying from the grass like sparks.

One day, when she wasn't out at work all day, she might have a dog. The Nutleys didn't really go in for pets, and the cat which walked out on them was probably quite right, but dogs were programmed to worship. It was you Tarzan, me dog, and even if you treat me like dirt I'll adore you. You could see why dogs were so popular.

The green notice beside the little entrance answered her question. Within St Augustine's Gate, a row of huge trees accompanied the path until it met the Drive, and further along, another row marched in parallel. It was a fair bet that the church had stood between the two, but there was nothing left to see. If the women of Ermintrude Villas came to this church in life, it was entirely appropriate that they should come here now it was as invisible as they.

Nineteen

The great plane trees dripped onto soggy grass. The park was nearly deserted, though way out in its centre a family of cricketers were still batting away. A panting, helmeted cyclist in black, red and white Lycra swept towards her up the Drive, his legs working like the connecting rods on a steam engine. Supposing he's a mugger who'll grab me as he draws level; I haven't any money with me. Well, supposing he's a pervert.

"Nice weather!" he shouted as he whizzed past.

"Yes," she agreed, far too late for him to hear.

But she left the park and passed into the Victorian streets; why give yourself more worry than necessary? The borough was wet, traffic-ridden and not at its best; the cherished buildings would have looked a lot better in sunlight, and the neglected ones looked worse than ever. The cosmopolitan inhabitants, no matter how bright their clothing, were mostly hurrying on their way to somewhere dry.

St John, Lauriston Road was still imposing, though carriage trade no longer drove up to its west door. There were large and even splendid houses remaining in Victoria Park Road, though the site of Buchanan House had been resown with red brick flats and balconies made of green poles. Mare Street was its normal, busy, run-down, messy self, weekend or no, but if you looked past the buses and lorries and cars, and under the architectural sleaze, old buildings survived. No trace, however, of the wonderful Rillington's Repository, burned to the ground in 1942.

In upper Mare Street, too narrow for proper traffic and still with a period quaintness, the past grew nearer, and the few people sitting under the great trees of the churchyard were watched by old houses.

Julia sat down beside a pocked altar tomb, from which lichen had effaced all inscription.

Two little children stared at her, hand in hand on the other side of the path. Their clothes were bright and eccentric, their hair was long, even the boy's – well, it was back to the Seventies, now, wasn't it? The girl wore a flounced dress that made her look like a tea cosy, so completely did it overwhelm her tiny body. Julia smiled, looked away as a large, cheerful retriever bounced along the path and turned back to find them gone.

The rain started again, pattering onto the leaves above her head and hitting her straight on as she moved out into the street.

Where shall I go, what shall I do – I'm being hunted down. I should have moved into a brand new estate on a green field site with no history of human occupation.

But she'd only have been pestered by ghost sheep. It was totally useless to run away from this thing, because there was nowhere in the world where human beings had not been, and where the spirits of the dead might not linger. Very few people knew they were there, so why did she?

Because you're different, Jule. You've got a gift. You're psychic.

She didn't want to be psychic.

But there was no choice in the matter. Gifts and handicaps were as much a part of your nature as the shape of your face and the colour of your hair. You couldn't do plastic surgery on the bits of your psyche you didn't like – it was a dodgy enough business doing it on your body.

But I want to be normal. I want to be like everyone else, doing what everyone normal does. I want love, marriage, children, friends, a home, a feeling of usefulness and fulfilment – a knowledge that my life makes sense. I want to be accepted and approved of, and if news of this gift gets out, I can say goodbye to all that.

She walked home through a schizophrenic world in which any person approaching her might either pass on along the wet street or be banished from sight by the slamming of the cupboard door in her brain. Three black teenagers were real, but an aged Indian woman in a pink sari walked on dry, sandalled feet, and disappeared in the very second Julia realised there was no Kingshold Estate ahead of her.

Several times the houses became sooty, and the road filthy with horse-droppings crushed into flat, strawed pancakes by feet and wheels. People wore jeans or bowler hats, leggings or crinolines. Sometimes they ignored her and sometimes they smiled, and either way, she was not sure who was flesh and who was spirit, and whether they were in now or then.

If this is genuine, and likely to keep happening, I've got to learn to control it. I can't live at the mercy of a wandering, undisciplined mind and panic every time it gets away from me. But can it be done?

She stopped at St Augustine's Gate. How could a church harm her? She stepped just inside and stood holding on to the modern railings, like a nervous traveller waiting for a ride to start.

She stared at the empty grass in the oblong of trees, loosened her shoulders, breathed deeply, closed her eyes and imagined the door opening in her mind. And it didn't feel like a door opening at all. It was as if someone took her fingers from the handle with a reproving little shake and instead laid it on a bright, shining curtain. So easy, so natural.

Behind her closed eyes, her hand wafted the curtain aside and revealed the church; stone, plain, with its roof sliding on down over its side aisles, sitting at the foot of a wide, square, featureless tower with thin pinnacles on the corners. The hand in her mind kept the curtain open as she raised her lids and she continued to see the building there before her. She held it for several seconds, and then her untrained mind tired and the rain fell once again onto the empty grass.

So it was possible to control this gift, but it felt as if it might require the training of an athlete.

Down at Hackney Wick there were a lot of people strolling about for such a wet day, and Cadogan Terrace was heavily parked. Oh well, the English were said to like their pleasures on the sad side. Julia had always suspected one of the main objects of the family seaside holiday was to prove you could withstand freezing water and a nippy wind. It hadn't been quite the same when they went abroad – the invigoration of challenge was missing.

Win and Harry were in the hall, talking to Bernice and smiling broadly, as if in anticipation of a treat. They were in hooded parkas and Win was carrying an umbrella. Harry had a camera slung around his neck.

Something moved near the top of the stairs.

"We're going round to Mabley Green," said Win with immense gusto, "they reckon it'll be the best view from there, and there's a marquee and that, in case the rain gets bad."

"Good view of what?" asked Julia abstractedly. It had been like a dark skirt sliding round the door frame into the bathroom. Her heart started to pound.

"The tower blocks, Jule, they're blowing them up today. Don't you remember the notices? It'll probably be quite easy to see from the bridge. Shall we go?"

Anything to escape her gift for another half hour.

The foot-bridge across the motorway, on which they had rarely met more than one or two other people at a time, was full from one side to the other. Hackney Wick was *en fête*, along with its kids, in-laws, girlfriends, boyfriends, best mates, cameras, camcorders, many styles of rainwear and wide range of brightly coloured umbrellas, making the concrete structure look as if it were tethered to hot air balloons and about to take off. More people had climbed up onto the derelict railway bridge.

Below, the traffic had been stopped, and there were police vehicles parked at the side.

The Grosvenors had still opted for Mabley Green, not least

because refreshments and music were rumoured to be on tap, and the girls stood together under Julia's umbrella between a squat, glum, bespectacled old couple and a tall, chain-smoking girl with three children. It was a strange occasion, almost indecent in the anticipation of the crowd.

Julia looked over at Ermintrude Villas. Watch this, Ingersalls. You won't have seen anything like this since the Blitz, if you were already hanging around then.

The blocks looked stripped, gutted and precarious. Only three were going, the girl told Bernice – the fourth one would be in use for a bit longer. Sirens sounded in the distance.

A signal rocket shot up against the grey sky and burst in a puff of dirty smoke.

"Here we go," said the old man.

It all happened remarkably quickly. A percussive, frighteningly loud 'ba-dum, ba-dum' came at them, and smoke puffed from behind the block which was receiving stay of execution.

"Couldn't see that one," complained the old woman indignantly.

The second double explosion followed immediately and the left-hand block shook, shrank and settled down into dust which rose to meet it like a pile of red-brown pillows. Barely a few seconds, and then the third collapsed into the spreading dust of its neighbours.

There was a brief silence, then a cheer and a round of applause.

"Goodness!" said Bernice, awe-struck. Julia felt quite shocked. Deliberate destruction on a large scale does tend to shock, even if it's a good idea.

"Well, that's the end of them," said the old man.

"They was a bloody daft idea from the start," said his wife.

"Yeah, and they'll go on having bloody daft ideas," said her husband. They turned and waddled slowly away.

"I never saw that first one," the complaint floated back.

The girls remained staring at the immense clouds of dust

advancing on the motorway like mist coming off the river. The remaining block was gradually engulfed from the bottom upwards until it disappeared. The factories and workshops on the other side of the bridge had already been blotted out.

It was like fog, or the legendary smog, or what Dickens had called a London Particular, in which the old houses of Hackney had been repeatedly wrapped throughout the coal-burning centuries. Below on the motorway, traffic was being held until visibility cleared.

At last the girls turned away and moved towards the end of the bridge. Progress was slow. Camcorders were still being wielded. The lone tower block began to appear again.

Julia glanced again at Ermintrude Villas.

Someone was standing at the Grosvenors' bedroom window. It was too far away to see her clearly, but near enough to know it wasn't Win. She was wearing a dark blouse and a dark skirt, and holding back lace curtains. Win and Harry hadn't got lace curtains, they favoured pink nylon. The woman was very still.

Julia's stomach felt hollow and she drew in her breath. This is it. I knew it was going to happen.

"Is that someone in Win's bedroom?" she said, pointing, and knew what Bernice would say.

"No, I can't see anyone, Jule."

In Cadogan Terrace, everyone was trying to drive away at once, and the road was blocked within minutes. Meanwhile, family parties unencumbered by the freedom of personal transport wandered into the park or walked down to Mabley Green, where cover and entertainment would be provided until the Trowbridge Estate opened again.

It's happened, Julia reminded herself again. No question of imagination, it's definite. I've heard one of them. I've seen one of them; not a perhaps shadow in a dark garden, a clear view in daylight. I've passed the point of no return. I've accepted what They are, and what I have the potential of being. I don't think I can shut it all off again now, and I don't know if I want to.

Well yes, I do want to. If I absorb this into my personality

I will never be able to go back again. I will no longer have any chance of being ordinary, like the get-it-together people I've seen around me in droves and always envied so much. I will never again be able to hope that, one wonderful day, I will become part of the Great Normality. It means abandoning the goal of my entire life.

I will have to stop seeing the world in three dimensions and see it in four. Or five. Or six. Once open the boundaries of your mind and where will it end? How far will you be forced to look, how much will you have to try and understand? And perhaps that understanding will cut you loose from familiar reality and send you drifting away into the endless blue sky like a fragile balloon, never to see sanity again.

"Hello, that's Mrs Parkin's car," said Bernice, as they passed the mature little servant in rust-edged blue livery. "Lily must be here searching for the Rillington millions again."

They tiptoed up the side of the front step, hoping not to be seen or heard. They tried to practice equal secrecy with the front door, but it refused to co-operate.

"Oh dear, now she'll send Mrs P.," said Bernice, grimacing and getting into the flat as quickly as possible.

Julia glanced up the stairs as she followed her in. She was there – she'd known she would be. Standing still, with the light from the bathroom door silhouetting her padded, cottage-loaf shaped, upswept hair.

Julia's thigh muscles weakened and her knees bowed. She stumbled into the room and onto the settee. Bernice had gone into the kitchen. The fireside chairs were naked, dirty and deeply depressing; period fashion which had doubtless seemed an excellent idea at the time, like housing families twenty-one storeys above the ground, but whose time had passed.

The body betrays us. We don't own and direct it, it is the other way round. Against our will, the construction of flesh and bone in which we live weakens and trembles. Its central engine goes out of control and batters the walls of its veins with racing blood. Joints loosen. The digestion loses its secret discretion. We are at the mercy of our bodies.

227

How can I hope to control my spiritual dimension when I am the slave of my physical one? ("Oh look at Julia, everyone, she's made a mistake again. Julia! Julia! Come here at once. Surely you could have held on till you got somewhere.")

But I have nowhere to go. She's up there. It could be her I've sensed in that bathroom, and who turns the sniggering absurdity of sanitation into a waiting room for the fourth dimension.

She curled up in the corner of the settee, still wrapped in her raincoat. Her umbrella had fallen to leak water into the carpet. She held her hands before her and watched her fingers shaking. Her lips trembled. She pressed them together, and her teeth tapped against each other.

So I've accepted it, have I. Tell me another one, Julia Nutley. Tell your pathetic, skinny body.

"Aren't you feeling well, Jule?" Bernice looked down at her.

Julia shook her head.

"It was a bit chilly out there, wasn't it? Would you like some coffee?"

Julia nodded.

"Won't be long, I've already put it on. I'll just pop up to the loo."

Go for me, too, Bernie; believe me, my need is greater than thine.

Somebody knocked at the front door. She couldn't get up. Bernice was otherwise engaged upstairs. She rolled off the settee and started to drag herself towards the door. Her limbs were still out of her control. She was breathing in audible gasps. I'm going to have a heart attack, I know I am. This is appalling. This is the worst I have ever felt physically in my entire life.

The knock was repeated.

She prised her knees off the cold tiles and tried her weight on her feet. Her hand slipped on the Yale knob and the door snapped open, catching her knee. She doubled up and rubbed it, on a level with flat-heeled boots and a polyester skirt.

"Oh, good-afternoon," said Mrs Parkin, bending forward

with apology. Julia saw the skirt hem dip and looked up. "I'm very sorry to bother you, but Miss Wright wishes to speak to you again. She's so upset about the items which are still missing that I'm really afraid she may – these old, well-bred families can be so highly strung, can't they?"

"Why us? Does she think we've stolen them?" Julia was too distressed herself to be diplomatic.

"Oh no, no, no!" exclaimed Mrs Parkin, blushing deeply because the dark suspicion had indeed passed Lily's lips.

"We'll call in later," said Julia. She closed the door almost before the visitor turned away. She heard Bernice open the bathroom door.

"Bernie! Please stay there while I go!"

She actually cried while she was in there, trying to keep the sobs low so that Bernice wouldn't hear her out on the landing. Under the wash basin, that's where the trouble is – between the cracked, fluted pedestal and the door, along beside the lurking mess under the bath, pressing against the clawed iron feet. Quick, quick, before I find out what it is.

She rushed out, grabbed Bernice's arm and pulled her down the stairs, sobbing, "Hurry! Hurry!"

"Jule!"

"Oh Bernice, I'm so scared!"

Bernice sat her down on the settee, hugged her and fed her liquid caffeine, one cup after another.

"It's happened, Bernie," said Julia, when she had started to regain horrified control of herself.

"What has, Jule?" Bernice patted her hand. She didn't want her to, but couldn't possibly object.

"They've started appearing. I've seen one of them at the top of the stairs. I knew I would sooner or later, I could feel it coming on."

"Who was it?" Bernice whispered, an expression of appre-hension blooming on her round face. "The one you saw in the garden?"

"Well, it was a woman. Sort of middle-aged, though I couldn't see her face. Nondescript pepper-and-salt hair put up on top of her head. A dark high-necked blouse and a long dark skirt. She had a very small waist – I remember thinking she looked like an hour-glass against the light from the bathroom."

"Corsets!" breathed Bernice, as if that proved everything, whatever everything might be. "Did you see her face?"

"No, it was in shadow. Bernie, I'm horribly scared."

"It's probably the woman who comes down the stairs."

"But she wasn't coming downstairs. She was just standing there, as if she was thinking something out, or wondering what to do, or even as if she'd just come to a decision. Oh it's so silly," Julia said with disgust, "trying to imagine what's going on in someone else's head, and a hundred times more silly when they aren't even alive any more."

"I do wonder what it's all about," Bernice said wistfully, her hand caressing Julia's restlessly.

Julia drew it away and laughed with a touch of hysteria. "All we can be sure of is that it's a leftover of trouble; something swept under the carpet but insisting on creeping out."

"Well, we've tried to find out what it could be, or rather, Win and Harry have, but we haven't got anywhere, even though they say the dead have no secrets." Bernice looked troubled. "It doesn't seem right, this, intruding into other people's private lives."

"Why not, they're intruding into ours," said Julia with resentment. "If they want to keep their scandals private they should stay in their own world."

"Perhaps they can't," said Bernice, her face solemn. "Who was that at the door?"

"Mrs Parkin. She delivered what was practically a royal command to go down and see Lily. It seems all is not yet well with the inheritance of the Magnificent Rillingtons."

"That's not our problem," said Bernice.

"No, but I could hardly refuse point blank. I told her we'd look in later."

"Let's eat something first, Jule, it'll make us feel better."

Over tinned soup and rolls, Julia started to relax, and at once the square kitchen table became round and her elbow was on an embroidered black silk shawl edged with deep fringing.

She tensed and banished it.

As the plates were put into the sink, she looked down at the desolate garden and wondered how large it had been before the building of the motorway, and whether the Ingersalls tended flowers in it or merely used it as a yard; and for that unguarded moment lilac bloomed and white, lace-edged garments blew on a washing line. And when she wondered how many there were living in the house, and whether they had servants or whether Mrs Ingersall did the work herself, she heard the back door open and rushed away from the window, although she knew it had to be either Lily or Mrs Parkin. The obsessive thoughts followed her into the living room. What was Mr Ingersall's job? Was he rich or poor? How old was he? Were those whispering, frightened, neurotic-sounding women his daughters or his sisters? Was the woman on the stairs one of them, or was she his wife? *What had to be found and then concealed?*

Looking out of the bay window at the wet park, she heard something drop on the floor, and then a swish and a sigh as someone bent to retrieve it. If she turned she could find out who it was, this time. Her eyes would travel over the pale flowers on the wall and they would grow dark and convoluted, shooting up like the flora of the rainforest and turning deep green and fleshily carnivorous in appearance. And She or He would be sitting there, in a phantasm of the chair whose carcass now sat below her feet in the basement.

And what would they say? And if their eyes met hers, what would it do to her?

"Bernice, let's go down and see old Lily now. Might as well get it over with."

Such a pointless flight, when They would be downstairs as well. Everywhere she looked in this house, the past might be there instead of the present, like a wrong slide in the projector.

*   *   *

"They should be here," Lily insisted. "By rights they should have come to my dear mother. My grandmother always promised that they should be left to the first daughter who married. Had it not been for the misunderstanding they would have been in my hands many years since."

"You could see if they were listed on his house insurance," Bernice suggested helpfully.

Lily's cold eyes swivelled slowly beneath the burden of her headgear. It was the same straw hat, only she'd stuck a flabby pink silk rose under its crippled brim, in acknowledgement of the new season. "I have inquired of the estate agent and searched all my uncle's papers. I can find no insurance."

"Oh dear, lucky there's never been a fire," said Bernice, with a jolly, sympathetic smile.

Lily's gaze moved back to Julia's pale, still face.

"I believe you once mentioned a burglary."

"We told you; that was a mistake," said Julia.

"But before that? Did my uncle ever show the jewels to you? How long have you been here?"

"Just coming up to six months," said Bernice. "We're moving out next week."

"Oh! Well, I'm very glad to hear it."

"Thanks," said Julia, "we love you too."

Julia Nutley! What is happening to you!

Lily stared. "I beg your pardon?" she said.

"Do you think we took them?" Julia followed up immediately, her temper rising. She often found emotional upset was followed by this reaction. Sheer blind rage, hitting out at a world she was unable to deal with. The furious, impotent tantrum of the toddler.

("Naughty Julia! Go on, scream away. *I* won't listen to you.")

Scream, scream, scream. Howl, howl, howl. Drum your heels, beat your weak, soft little fists on the floor. Assault them all with the violence of your most extreme and terrible rage, and hear the laughter which tells you that its effect upon the world is absolutely nil.

232

Oh yes, you will listen, Mother. You'll listen now, because I've found my voice.

"I said, do you think we stole them? Why else should you think we'd know anything about it? We never even spoke to your uncle, I don't think anyone did for the last few years of his life. And by the way, this misunderstanding you had with him, was it because you wanted to put him into a home so you could get your hands on his things?"

"Oh, my dear young lady!" cried Mrs Parkin, actually bursting into tears and wringing her hands. "How terribly wrong you have got this sad situation! How little you know of the many hurtful slights poor Miss Wright has suffered, both on her own account and that of her deceased mother! If you were only to know the bitter inheritance which she has so long sought to set to rights."

Gosh, Jane Austen. No, she's modelled herself on the perfectly ladylike Lily Wright.

"Did he show them to you?" Lily repeated angrily.

"No, I never even met him, unless you count his throwing things at me."

"What had you done to him?" demanded Lily, jutting her head forward over her large, flabby body and presenting a finger like God's on the ceiling of the Sistine Chapel.

"I was stupid enough to ask if he was all right. The poor man seemed to be as mad as a hatter and I was worried about him."

"You see!" Lily cried in triumph. "He should have been in a home!"

"All those years ago? Anyway, your 'misunderstanding' is none of my business, Miss Wright, but your accusations about our honesty are, and I very much resent them. And it seems to me that if Mr Rillington's mother had intended her daughter to inherit her jewellery she would have left it to her, not to her son."

"Un-for-tu-nate-leh," said Lily fiercely, enunciating every

syllable with vehement care, "my grandmother left no will. That has been the problem. Her many valuable belongings were reft from her dying hands and scattered to the winds."

"Reft?" asked Bernice, puzzled.

"Reft," Lily confirmed.

"Utterly reft," Mrs Parkin endorsed the word breathlessly.

Twenty

"When did she die?" asked Bernice sweetly, trying to give Julia a chance to cool down. You couldn't really blame her, she'd had a difficult morning.

"I don't recall the exact date, it was before I was born. My grandfather had predeceased her, being somewhat older."

"And what did your father do?" Bernice looked absolutely fascinated.

Lily's head was proudly raised. "He, also, was in drapery." Julia found herself seeing him in a toga.

Lily sighed. "Although I never had the privilege of meeting my grandparents, I feel as if I did because of the wonderful stories I heard at my mother's knee. Oh, the pictures she painted of the great days of the past! The dances at the Hackney Assembly Rooms! The concerts! The evening parties in the wonderful house in Victoria Park Road! The beautiful fashions worn by my grandmother and aunts as they drove to church!"

"Which one?" said Julia. She was still suffering from a racing pulse. A slowly aroused temper took equally long to cool down.

"In the early days of her marriage, it was St John the Baptist's in Lauriston Road, but later she became somewhat ensnared by the baubles of Ritualism, and I regret went to St Augustine's. My grandfather did not accompany her, the service was not to his taste. But he was devoted to his beautiful wife and indulged her in all things. My Uncle John returned to moderation after his marriage, and so did my dear mother after hers. I myself," she said grandly, "have travelled even further along that blessed path."

"Did you meet—" started Julia.

"On the occasions when my mother took me to be measured for my wardrobe at Rillington's Repository, we were always entertained in my Uncle John's office, though relations were not, by then, entirely cordial. My father was associated with a rival establishment in Walthamstow."

A woman in a cloche hat and a fur-collared coat, sitting in a mahogany-fitted office, sipping tea. A fat, ugly little girl in a frilly dress and a bonnet which seemed designed to hide as much of that ugliness as possible, eating Nice biscuits with little finger crooked, the way her dear mother had taught her. The smart, moustached man in the frock-coat. The careful small talk. The volumes of large talk which never got opened at all. I can see it all.

"There was a very large staff, all of them absolutely devoted to the Rillington family. People used to enter the firm straight from school, in a very humble capacity, of course, and then gradually work their way up the ladder. The loyalty my grandfather and my uncle inspired in those who served under them was quite astounding. My dear mother said that when they came to retire, they were often overcome with tears as they left the portals of that distinguished building."

I suppose I've been pretty rude, Julia admitted to herself. Should I apologise? Should I heck.

Her eyes were drawn to the piano. *Melody in F.* As Lily passed on from the staff of Rillington's to the clientele, she moved away discreetly and turned back the faded, grey cover of the sheet music. Inside it was a brilliant green, and a dedication in sprawling black writing hurled itself at the recipient like a challenge.

'To Florence from Joseph. Easter 1919.' I suppose he'd have been just back from the war.

She raised the dried, cracking piano lid. The underside was rich golden red, and the keys were yellow. The maker was one never appearing on any concert platform in the world, and the instrument was made in the busy side streets of Camden Town.

"What sort of piano did your grandparents have?" she said,

very nearly interrupting Lily, if getting in sharp between one sentence and the next can be called interruption. Lily looked at her with annoyance, but the question was too tempting to be ignored.

"It was a full-sized concert grand made by Blüthner of Leipzig, a truly magnificent instrument."

"Did you ever see—"

"Many distinguished musicians played upon it, to the delight of my grandparents and their guests. My mother remembered leaning over the carved mahogany handrail on the landing with her nurse, listening to wonderful performances by Brahms and Paderewski and Kreisler—"

"I thought Kreisler played the violin," said Bernice, looking puzzled.

"He also played the piano," Lily said with determination, "and very beautifully, too."

"Who was Florence?" asked Julia, as Lily opened her mouth to continue.

"My eldest aunt."

"Did Mr Rillington get all her things? Her name's on that piece of music."

"He inherited from her. She didn't marry."

"And neither did he," said Bernice sadly. "He stayed alone and lonely all his life, poor old man."

"There's nothing wrong with single blessedness," said Lily quickly. "I myself have found it most fulfilling."

"Oh good," said Bernice, pleased for her. "Some people are so silly about marriage, aren't they? I mean, I'd far rather be single and happy, than married and miserable."

Mrs Parkin suddenly went for her handkerchief again. Lily pointed out her distress as if she owned it.

"My friend Mrs Parkin has suffered," she pronounced, "you must forgive her. She has not had the happy advantages it has been my fortunate lot to receive."

As they left the room, Julia kept her eyes away from the dark staircase climbing up to the lobby.

"Florence!" whispered Bernice. "Could that be the Florrie he was so afraid of?"

"Shouldn't be surprised." Julia hurried to the release of the basement door and tried to turn the knob with shaking, sweating fingers.

"Here, I'll do it. Poor old Jule, you're all fingers and thumbs."

Julia stepped to one side. There was a shabby door with a tiny barred window leading under the steps. Must be the coalhole. All that shovelling into coal scuttles and carting them up and down stairs.

"Do you really believe all those famous people came and played to the Rillingtons?" added Bernice in a low voice.

"No, I don't," said Julia shortly.

She glanced back at the basement stairs to find someone there; back view climbing up towards the first floor, her body dragged over sideways by the weight, her hair straggling out from under her grubby cap.

She pushed through the opened door and slammed it.

This time, the mere thought flickering across her mind seemed to have been enough to create the image. No, not create, because it wasn't imagination, it was seeing into the past. But she had seen the woman upstairs against a present day background; she remembered quite distinctly the ship's bell on the wall beside her. There were two different sorts of visions. Thought now seemed either to project the past onto her retina, or to spark out of her head and draw waiting spirits from the shadows.

"I'm not sure she does entirely, either," Julia said, uncomfortably breathless as they climbed the steps. "Her mother seems to have spun her enough yarn to knit a pullover with. I'd like to know why relations with the rest of the family were bad."

"And why her grandmother's valuables were reft from her. Is that a real word, reft?" Bernice unlocked the front door.

"I wondered about that, it doesn't sound quite right. Oh God."

She'd put the scuttle down for a moment. She was thin and undersized. There was a black smudge across her brow where she'd passed a hand across it. Julia bent her concentrated attention on the opening of the flat door and the hall was empty again.

"What's the matter?"

"Nothing. Yes there is, I'm seeing things again."

A whiff of smoke? She opened the window. She must keep her thoughts under control.

"Are they still here?" asked Bernice, looking round uncomfortably.

"No. What do you think happened to the jewellery?"

"I think he must have sold it to live on, don't you? I mean, if he never worked he must have had some sort of investments, perhaps in the shop, and the war would have affected them badly. And half the silver cutlery was missing. I bet he'd sold them off, one by one. It looks as if the only way Lily will get any money is to pull down Ermintrude Villas for redevelopment."

"Find it!"

Julia stiffened. She must not indulge in wondering and imagining and what-iffing. She must think of what she was doing now, every moment, and not allow thought to skive off. No slipping out of this time into another, or out of this world into the next.

This is quite awful. I wonder if it is just physical, not a psychic gift at all? Perhaps there's something wrong in my brain. Perhaps a blood clot, perhaps a neck vertebra pressing on an artery, perhaps something worse.

The young girl in the bay window stared out at the park, not lifting the lace curtain but peering through its gross white roses.

"What are we eating tonight, Jule?" asked Bernice.

"Don't mind," Julia said. Think of what we'll eat tonight.

She went for the fridge. Eggs, cheese, milk and still the vegetarian pâté. Pass. They'd better start emptying the freezer compartment.

The door stuck. Forced entry sent cold, frothy snow all over the kitchen floor. What a blessing a fridge is. We take it for granted and yet once you had to use things up in—

The album lay open on the black silk shawl. Around the photographs, its thick, gold-edged pages were printed with coloured pictures; forget-me-nots, honeysuckle, rural scenes. The young woman turned a page. She was in black. Even the handkerchief in her hand was edged with black lace.

"We must use up this frozen stuff," she called to Bernice. "Put the telly on, will you?" Her voice was strained and artificially bright.

Bernice looked round the curtain. Julia was plonking snow-covered, rock hard, plastic-wrapped packets onto the kitchen table in agitated haste.

She went and switched on the set, then came back into the kitchen. Now Julia was mopping up the wintry mess on the floor, singing loudly to herself as if to drown out something else.

"Come into the garden, Maud—"

"Jule, are They here again?"

"Not if I don't let them be," said Julia fiercely. "Bernice, talk to me. Talk about anything. Don't let my mind wander for a minute."

"Oh! Goodness! Well, let's see, what would you find interesting enough to stop that, for goodness' sake? Oh, I know. When you went out for your walk this morning, I had a few words with Luke and Fern. I've been quite worried about them, and how soon Lily would get them out, and where they would go. Anyway, I couldn't seem to get through to them how urgent it is, you know what they're like, and then their dear little baby started laughing and holding out her hands, and there was Bubastis playing with a big paper bag and really, Jule you'd have died! He got his head right inside it and couldn't get it out, and he was actually running around the front garden—"

The golden cat jumped up onto the silk-covered table and put its spread claws on the photograph. The girl's hand pushed it off quickly. It was a very pretty photograph; a young girl with her hair swept up into curls which cascaded down her back, looking back over her bare shoulder and holding her fan against the frills and ribbons of her bustled train.

"Something else!" Julia insisted.

"Oh! Well, then, Win and Harry came and told me about the tower blocks, and suggested we go round to the recreation ground on the marshes—"

She thought of the marshes; the football pitches, the canal, the high-banked River Lea, the busy main road sweeping across it from the flyover, the new Spitalfields Market on the Leyton side, the grazing cows, the ragged, barefoot boys fishing, the old White Hart Inn away over there to the right, with horses tied up outside like in a Western; the quietness, the rough, narrow roads, the carts trailing out onto its green wilderness—

"Something else!"

"I'm *trying*, Jule," protested Bernice. "Look, why not just tell me what's wrong? It's Them, I suppose. I haven't heard anything."

"Neither have I, but I keep seeing them. Every time I lose concentration and allow my mind to idle, there they are. There are quite a lot of them, and they all seem to be women."

"And what about the man smoking the pipe?" Bernice asked with wide eyes and lowered voice.

"I haven't seen him yet. They're all sitting around these two rooms, dressed in mourning. They're sad and hopeless and bored. They feel as if their lives are being stolen and wasted and frittered away, and as if they'll never ever escape. That was a bit how I used to feel," she added, the remembered mental agony returning to grip her mind.

The girl at the round table cried silently into her sombre handkerchief. No, not a girl, a young woman, perhaps even a getting-on-a-bit young woman. She was losing hope.

Julia burst into song to drown out their mutual misery.

"What's that tune?" asked Bernice.

"I've no idea," said Julia, in as near as is possible to a flat panic without actually taking to your heels. "Quick, let's play something modern. Something silly. Chopsticks! You take the bass, I'll play the tune—"

She hurried into the front room. Bernice followed her.

"Jule," she said in a subdued, little-girl voice, "there isn't a piano."

Julia fell down onto the bed-settee and cried.

The telephone rang. Bernice picked it up.

"Well, I think she's here. I'll just go and see."

She covered the mouthpiece and looked at Julia with raised, questioning brows. Her own eyes were filled with sympathetic tears.

"If it's my mother, tell her I've just died," sobbed Julia.

"No, it's a man."

"Well, if it's Philip, tell him I'm dead and buried."

"I don't know who it is, Jule. I'll tell him you've just gone out, shall I?"

"Oh, give it here," said Julia, blowing her nose. A bit of rage expressed in a few well-chosen words might clear the spectres from the house. "Yes?"

"Julia, this is quite disgraceful, you know. It goes right against the whole family spirit. Your mother's in tears."

"Rubbish. Mother doesn't cry, she just shouts or sulks, so don't try emotional blackmail on me, Philip. She's got the rest of you there, hasn't she? Three daughters, three sons-in-law, ten and a half grandchildren? What's all this panic really about, having to take the fall-out yourselves?"

It was satisfying to observe the gradual pulling in of the string which Mrs Nutley had attached to Philip without his being aware of it. More and more often, he was having to put himself out to please her, or to avoid displeasing her, and the situation was certainly going to get worse for all three sons-in-law. The family image was of obedient wives supporting strong husbands, but in truth the three men were trapped like flies in a web of womanhood.

"You sound strange," said Philip, "have you got a cold?"

"Yes," said Julia, grabbing the weapon which fate had

suddenly thrust into her hand and lying without conscience. If people couldn't take the truth they must expect lies. "I could have come down and spread it around among the whole family, including giving Helena the added enjoyment of coughing and sneezing all the way through labour, but it didn't seem a very good idea, somehow."

"No, I can see that," Philip conceded, the righteous tone of his voice subsiding into manly understanding.

The room looked so bare, and the uncovered chairs were quite dreadful; all those silly triangles and circles and zigzags. Imagine old Mr Rillington choosing something like that.

The woman in the brown leather chair threaded her needle. The long, sharp scissors in the shape of a bird slid from her black silk lap and thudded onto the fur rug. She sighed and bent to pick them up.

Bernice turned and looked in that direction.

"Did you hear that?" she mouthed to Julia, who nodded wearily.

"Well, look after yourself, Julia, but as soon as you're well enough not to pass any germs on to Grace you must come and see her. It simply *is not done* to ignore your own mother's feelings."

"She never considered mine," said Julia indignantly. Does he mean it's all right to ignore those of somebody else's mother?

"But she doesn't mean to be unkind, and you have to take her as she is. She's one of those people who speak first and think afterwards."

"But she never does think afterwards, and she never apologises either, not for anything. When I was seven she knocked my best doll off a chair and broke it, and all she said was 'You shouldn't have left it there.'"

"Isn't that rather a long time to nurse a grudge? Think of her feelings, Julia," Philip repeated firmly.

"How can you expect people to consider your feelings if you don't consider theirs? You say, take her as she is, but she doesn't take other people as they are. Everyone gets criticised and pulled apart and pushed in the direction of what she

243

considers right and proper. Do you think she'd be smarming all over you and boasting about your wonderful vocation to the neighbours if you'd had a burning, irresistible call to become a drummer in a rock band?"

"Don't be ridiculous, Julia," said Philip with weighty patience, "that is totally hypothetical. No one of our background and class would do that."

"Oh really? Well, that's all you know!" retorted Julia. "Remember Laurie Davies? Prep school, Radley, Oxford, the City, heavy metal, excommunication from the upper middle class of Worcester Park?"

"My dear," said Philip, his voice becoming deep and fatherly, like a Dutch uncle at least seventy years old, "that was for your own good, you know it was. Think what sort of a life you'd have had with a man like that!"

"Better than the life I had before I met him," said Julia, new tears in her eyes, this time of humiliated rejection.

They were all there again. Pale, hopeless females in black dresses which swept the carpets and wrapped around the legs of the furniture. Pale-haired, from fair to light brown. They sewed, read, crocheted, glanced through the sheet music on the piano, gazed like prisoners from the veiled windows of their prison.

"You think that because you have no experience of the real world, Julia. Believe me," he informed her from the heights of his whole forty years' life experience, "marriage to a person with a different set of standards from those you were brought up with is doomed from the word go."

"That happened to you, did it?"

"Of course not. I know people it happened to."

"In the Party?" asked Julia. "In Parliament? No, in the Cabinet?" She knew she was being silly and childish now, but it still hurt so much. If he expected her to behave well he shouldn't bring up subjects like that.

"Julia, you can argue with me as much as you like, but I still say she was absolutely right. She wanted to protect you. Any responsible parent would have done the same."

"Done what?" asked Julia, suddenly apprehensive. It felt as if a crater had suddenly opened up; an unmapped hazard she had previously passed without realising it existed.

"Now calm down and get yourself better. Goodbye. I'll give your love to Grace."

"What did she do?" Julia shrieked down the phone. The line went dead.

The room was undivided, although wooden doors lay folded against the wall on either side of the arch. The old-young woman stared at the family album with tears pouring down her face. The even older young woman turned from her needlework and looked down the room to press a finger to her lips.

Julia sat stranded between the two. Horrified. Outraged. Her secret pain out of the cupboard again and fit to break her heart. She wanted to protect you. She meant well.

The two rooms came and went with the turmoil of her thoughts. The stripped modern room with the piles of belongings awaiting removal; the old-fashioned room with dark wallpaper, many ornaments and long heavy curtains, with no future but eternity. Bernice stood with laced fingers and tear-stained face, sharing her pain; the women sat in mourning clothes, enduring their silent, hopeless lives on yet another cloistered Sunday evening.

Twenty-One

"**S**he warned him off!" Julia cried in agonised protest. "The only decent, interesting, likeable, fanciable man who ever showed interest in me. He was a bit younger than me but he said he loved me, Bernie, he said I was beautiful! I couldn't believe it! And I loved him so much. I came alive, because I thought my life was going to be a happy one after all. I really heard wedding bells."

The force of her distress dragged her to her feet, to stride up and down the disorganised room.

"He didn't even say goodbye. Just landed this job with a band and took off for a six month tour. I mean, for God's sake!" she exclaimed with the utmost protest and pain. "I didn't even know where he'd gone until I met his mother and she told me all about it. So I thought perhaps he might ring, then I waited for a letter, or perhaps the odd picture postcard from exotic places, but there was nothing at all. And I'd thought the two of us would be together for the rest of our lives."

"Yes," said Bernice in a low voice, "it does come as a shock. At least, I hadn't thought of marriage with Tom, but we got on so well."

"Oh Bernie, I'm so sorry about Tom!"

"It wasn't your fault, it was mine. I shouldn't have kept insisting you came along with us. I thought I was helping you, but it was none of my business, really. I expect your mother thought she was helping you, too – I mean, it was hardly the most secure of futures, was it?"

"No," Julia admitted with full acceptance, "and I expect it might've fallen apart one day, but a person's entitled to make their own mistakes and at least I'd have been happy for a while. And got the hang of it," she added bitterly.

Bernice got up wearily. She looked worn down. Yet another emotional crisis to deal with, yet another problem.

"I'll start the dinner, Jule." She went into the kitchen, slowly and with none of her usual happy ebullience.

"Thanks, Bernie. I'll come and help in a minute."

Julia sat down and buried her face in her hands, trying to bring her thoughts in line with this new understanding, to grasp that at least part of her wasted life had been deliberately sabotaged.

She watched me slowly breaking my heart and said nothing but 'He was no good.' No sympathy, no acknowledgment of my grief. ("Don't waste your time thinking about him, Julia, you'll get over it.") I thought we were going to get married. ("Stop mooning around, Julia, you've got a face as long as a wet week.") I was so wretched I wanted to die. ("Oh, for goodness' sake, Julia, how long is this silly mood going to last?")

If she hadn't gone off to visit Aunt Jean and left me enough space to do a bunk, I would still be down in Worcester Park with her, perhaps for ever, scared of everything, depressed about everything, with no hopes for the future and, no matter how many protests I might make, always eventually doing as I was told.

And what if Laurie hadn't really got tired of me or been weak enough to be warned off, but had just been told a downright lie? "Julia's asked me to tell you she doesn't want to see you again." If that was what she did, it was unforgivable.

Julia thought back into the time when love had seemed a possibility after all, and then back to the emotional paralysis he had rescued her from, and back again to the childhood which had brought on that paralysis. Her mind slipped away and the room slipped with it, into the over-curtained, over-furnished past.

Only no women were in the room this time. There was just a boy standing in the bay window and looking out, with the lace curtain crumpled up in his hand. He wore a Norfolk jacket and knee breeches, and one shining black laced-up boot swung back and forth to kick gently at the skirting above the carpet. He raised his head and listened. Down the stairs, swish, swish, swish, then heels clicking on the tiles.

The brass door knob turned and the door swung inwards.

The woman from the window. The woman from the top of the stairs. Around her long, black skirts, the ginger cat rubbed and purred and bestowed its unctuous patronage.

Julia leapt up and marched to the other end of the room, kicking boxes across the carpet and tripping over the bag of teddies.

"All right, Jule?"

"No! I can't get away from them!" Her voice was more angry than frightened this time.

"Is it the women again?" asked Bernice. Her hands pulled at her apron as she stood by the dividing curtain, her eyes were tired by the slow drip, drip of fear over days and weeks.

"Just one. And there's a boy. Did you hear her come downstairs?"

"No. What did they want?" Bernice looked at her wearily, still gripping the apron.

"They didn't know I was here. It was the past, not real. I keep seeing into the past."

Outside, the footsteps came again, click, click, click, through the lobby outside the open kitchen door, down the wooden steps into the basement. They stared at each other, then Bernice said "I heard that." She turned away and started to persuade food off the bottom of the saucepan.

It was some time later that Julia asked "Did you hear the church bell today?"

Bernice turned from the television and looked at her, reluctant, even pained to be dragged out of the escapist fiction of Sunday night entertainment, although at that moment its subject matter was only romanticised misery. She shook her head. "No, I didn't. You did, did you?"

"Not today. Several times when They went to church," said

Julia, her anger starting to rise again. "Well, it seems that wasn't real, either. How'm I going to know what is and what isn't? Supposing I say good-morning to someone at work and they're not there?"

"They always go out, don't they?" said Bernice in a dull voice. "I suppose that's what they wanted to do most of all, to get away, so the feelings they had when they returned weren't strong enough to last. They go out of the front door, and downstairs to the basement and the back door, and that woman you said you saw went towards the bottom of the garden. It's all escape. Their whole lives must have been spent longing for it."

"Not the maid, but then, she probably had no better place to go."

"What maid?" asked Bernice.

"In the basement this afternoon. I saw her climbing the stairs with a scuttle of coal. Then when we came back up here, she was in the hall."

"Jule!" Bernice looked awed and uncomfortable. "What's it like being, well, the way you are?"

"Not nice," said Julia unhappily. "It's scary, and inconvenient, and intrusive, and as off-putting as being given a medal you don't want for something you haven't done."

"I suppose a lot of great gifts must be like that. Not that I'd know," Bernice added with an apologetic grimace. "Didn't you ever guess before?"

"I suppose I wondered sometimes. Yes, I did have one or two indications, but took no notice. I was brought up with that golden rule," she said with a wry laugh. "Something nasty? Something inconvenient? Take no notice. But now I can't help taking notice. It's getting worse, Bernie, I'm seeing things all the time." She paused, expecting more on-tap comfort.

Bernice said nothing and turned away.

They made their bedtime visit; it was a great hindrance to cleanliness and health, to have a bathroom which made you feel phobic. I mean, what alternative was there? You could wash in the sink and there was old Joe's toilet out the back, but as that meant walking down to the corner, up the slip road and climbing over the fence, the name of convenience no longer applied.

Keep your mind firmly in the present day and nothing can happen. You've never actually seen anything in this room, and if you do, it will only be a poor, sad, disappointed woman, rather like you. Fellow feeling, that's why you see them.

Win was bustling back and forth between her living room and bedroom, singing loudly.

"I'll be all right, Jule," said Bernice as she came out, "you go on down."

Julia went downstairs, concentrating on the fact that the carpet was worn and that they ought to wash the hall floor before they went.

It is 1995 and there are no less than three other people in this house, all very active and wide awake. It is 1995. It is now. The cornices are dusty, we should clean those too. There must be moulded flowers under all that paint. I wonder how they made them; before they put them up or after?

As her feet left the stair carpet and struck the tiles, she heard the clatter of curtain rings on a wooden pole. She stopped, her heart immediately starting to thud. If I go in there I shall see them again. I could avoid it. I could go out into the front garden. I'll be out of here in a few days and then things like this may never happen to me again.

The swishing started down the stairs. She backed towards the front door. No, they might be coming that way. She slid over into the corner, the back of her knees pressed against the wooden umbrella stand. It might be raining out there. She hurried across to stand between the handrail and the wall. They or she could be coming down to the basement. The sounds grew, pressed on her eardrums, made her dizzy.

With no other choice, she took control. She breathed deeply, drew back the curtain in her mind and allowed the past of Number Two Ermintrude Villas to reveal itself.

The woman in black stepped off the stair carpet and clicked

across to the parlour door. As she passed in she pushed the door wide. He was sitting in the brown leather chair beside the fireplace, smoking a pipe and reading a paper. He was dark, glossy-haired and moustached; a touch too flashy, certainly pretty pleased with himself. The great orange cat was curled up on the hearthrug.

The rest of the room seemed full of women, sewing, reading, sitting, dreaming. They were all in black – it seemed possible that they would never entirely leave it off again.

She forced herself to keep the wretched Ingersall family before her eyes until Bernice started to walk down the stairs, then banished them, experiencing a new sensation of being in charge. Bernice looked at her uncertainly as she alighted on the tiles.

"All right, Jule?"

"Yes," said Julia with surprise. She felt strong and confident and somehow full of power. It felt very good.

Bernice looked depressed and even timid. Julia gave her a reassuring squeeze and ushered her into the flat; she needed looking after tonight. It had been a hell of a weekend.

"Well," Win said, as she and Harry prepared to dive out of the front door into a new week spent exploring the wonderful world of archives, "we're off hunting again! See you tonight, girls!"

"Win, can I ask you something?" Julia called as they were about to slam the front door.

"Yes, duck?"

"Do you think there were likely to be any Asians in Hackney, back at the beginning of the century?"

"Ayahs' Home," said Win at once. The answer popped out like cash from a dispenser. "It was in King Edward Road. You see, when people used to come home on leave from India, they'd bring their kids' Indian nannies with them, and that's where they'd stay. Made them feel more at home, I suppose, everyone speaking their language, instead of having to try and get on with English servants."

"Oh. Thanks."

The girls emerged into a cloudy Monday morning in June 1995. They crossed the foot-bridge with heads turned silently left to acknowledge the executed tower blocks and their bereaved brother standing among their remains. They stood on Hackney Wick station, staring at the trees of Victoria Park, with the row of old house backs in front of them.

The outside world seemed totally irrelevant and unreal – reality lay inside there. That great concrete motorway, this messy, unkempt, partly demolished industrial landscape, these casually-dressed, cosmopolitan people on the platform – what had they to do with a Victorian/Edwardian suburb? The buildings should be of sooty brick, the people should be wearing flat caps or bowler hats. There should be the sound of cart wheels and horses' hooves rising up from the streets beneath the railway embankment.

In the bright, brash, false world of Jones, Brown and Wilkinson, the fish greeted them with open mouths and the visitors approached them as if they brought gifts. It was all meaningless, like a garish television soap about the glamour of big business, peopled by over-written characters mouthing a cliché-crammed script.

Miss Standish inquired about their health again, and was told that they had had accommodation problems but that all was nearly resolved. She looked earnestly at their faces and was not convinced. Others made similar sympathetic inquiries.

"We're all right, thanks," said Julia firmly. "We've got to move flats and you know what a business that is."

Once she glanced out through the momentarily resting doors to see a man in a worn, dirty suit and muffler and a flat cap, standing in the middle of the ornamental gardens. There was no matching world around him; no warehouses or ships or cranes or thick, greasy ropes snaking across worn, dirty stone paving. He was really there, looking up at the high, shining, marble-skinned buildings. It seemed they were everywhere, those that were called dead. They visited the earth like tourists, recalling old times.

At the end of the working day, they sat down on the platform at Stratford Low Level to wait for the North London train, while soft, thin rain breathed over them. The tracks were strewn with sodden litter and obscured by a newly sprung plantation of tall weeds.

"I can't wait to get out of that house," said Julia closing her eyes on the bus station and the Stratford Shopping Centre.

"Yes," said Bernice, "it'll be nice not to have to listen out all the time."

The train trundled in, its driving cab coming to rest under a bridge still encrusted with the soot of steam engines.

Out on the marsh, the bushes were covered with plates of white flowers, and the long wet grass around them waved in the breeze. It had all been like that; just green marsh and meadow from Hackney Wick to Leyton High Road. Julia was tired and finding it quite difficult to keep her thoughts in the present. Even the old brick factory beside the canal was itself under the impression that it still made sweets. For a disturbing moment, she expected to see long-skirted girls in white caps down in its yard, before she recognised the worn nature of its lettering.

Nearly home. Here we come, ghosts. We'll be seeing you again very soon, back in your past and perhaps as you are now, sightseeing in our home, watching us as we use your house.

And that she had not got used to, nor could she even think about it without a pang of fear. What would they want? What could they do? What had to be done and what must be found?

As they came down towards the house they could see the Grosvenors climbing up the slope. They were panting with hurry and excitement.

"Oh my Lor'!" Win exclaimed when they met on the steps, "Oh goodness! Well! Phew! Let me get me wind back!"

"We just couldn't wait to tell you," Harry said, beaming. "We cracked it! We really cracked it!" The door suffered a shadow punch. "Somerset House, that's what done it. Gawd," he panted, "what I couldn't do to a cup of tea."

The hint was quickly taken.

"You tell 'em, Win," he said as he prepared to swallow the first. She was going to anyway.

"We found some wills!" she announced triumphantly. "We looked round about 1932 for Abraham Ingersall and couldn't find him, but I started working back anyway, and at the same time Harry looked for the Rillingtons. Now, I'll give it to you a bit at a time and in the right order, so as you get the picture."

The notebook was put into their hands, but with some pages shut off by a giant paper clip. Capital letters again.

Abraham Ingersall, insurance broker, of 2 Ermintrude Villas, Cadogan Terrace E9 had made his will in 1911 and died in July 1914. He left absolutely everything he possessed to his daughter Maria, consisting of property, goods, chattels, cash, securities, etc. etc. The said Maria had received probate and walked away, no, stayed put, with a legacy of the value of five thousand and twenty-five pounds, ten shillings and fourpence.

The girls's reaction was entirely satisfying, and the Grosvenors basked in it for some minutes.

"Why did he make a will in 1911?" asked Julia, riveted by the date.

"Ah!" said Harry, and looked almost coy. "Right! After we done at Somerset House, we rushed across to St Catherine's before it closed. Deaths." He mimed the pumping arms of a sprinter. "Show 'em, Win."

"Coming up," said Win, unlocking another page. "There. That's only what's in the index, of course, not full details."

In the Hackney district, during the quarter ending December 1910, died Constance Agnes Ingersall, aged fifty-two.

"She married again!" Bernice cried. "Constance Agnes Rillington married Abraham Ingersall some time after her husband died in 1900 and came to live here! So that means this Ingersall family we've been looking for doesn't exist except for Maria. Those other women *are* the Rillingtons!"

"And because she didn't make a will he inherited all her money and made a new will himself soon after," said Julia.

This was a strange feeling, discussing these long-dead people, dragging out their secrets. Never speak ill of the dead – they may well be listening.

"Well, that's what it looks like," Win granted, "but you can never be absolutely sure till you've checked things. Now!" she said with a delighted grin. The paper clip was adjusted and another page of notes was released for public perusal.

In 1925, Maria Ingersall had left everything to Florence Mary Rillington of 2 Ermintrude Villas. She in turn left it to her brother Joseph James Rillington of Buchanan House, Victoria Park Road.

"But the occupier of Number Two was recorded as Ingersall until 1932!" exclaimed Julia.

"Well, directories wasn't infallible, you know, they could only work on information received," said Harry. "If they knocked at a door asking who lived there, and the people didn't want to say, they'd just go on printing the same as before or sometimes leave it blank. And it's possible the Rillington sisters got a bit funny, like old Joe."

"But there were still Rillingtons at Buchanan House for ages," said Bernice.

"That was John and his family."

"He probably didn't approve of his Mum marrying again so soon, and it caused a split in the family and at least some of her daughters went with her," Bernice pursued. "And if Joseph was only a baby when his mother remarried, he might have been taken back to Buchanan House by his brother when she died. Gosh, we're starting to get somewhere, aren't we?"

"I should say so!" exulted Harry.

"So that's what Lily's mysterious family misunderstanding was," said Julia, "sheer snobbery. Granted, he *was* a pretty vulgar-looking man, and we can presume from the miserable life that seems to have gone on here that he was a bit of a domestic tyrant, too. And he looked a lot younger than her."

There was an uncomfortable pause in the animated conversation. Harry pursed his lips and stared at the ceiling. Win drew in her breath and let it out in a gentle snort. Then they both essayed faint, never-mind smiles, as if trying to cover up a gross piece of bad manners. Julia felt herself blush.

Bernice hurried to smooth things over.

"I wonder when Lily's mother got married?"

"Well, we can find that out at St Catherine's, too," said Win, folding up her notebook.

"And Constance and Abraham's marriage," added Bernice eagerly, "and what Constance died of—"

"See what I meant about addiction?" asked Win with a proprietorial smile. "You don't want to stop, do you? You want to know it all. Don't worry, we'll be off again tomorrow."

Twenty-Two

"They didn't like me mentioning what Abraham looked like, did they?" said Julia, laying the coffee table. "I suppose it must seem pretty strange and frightening to them."

"I got the impression it did to us, too," said Bernice, unpacking a defrosting cottage pie from her shopping bag. The elliptical, ironic, wary remark sounded more like Julia than upfront Bernie.

"Yes, but at least I'm beginning to understand it now, and I think I'm getting the hang of controlling it. You're quite right, Bernie, it's a special gift and it's up to me to use it and make the most of it." She sounded more confident, almost happy.

It was all there in her own brain, a wonderful talent, a rare gift. A very small minority of people had this. Useless old Julia Nutley was gifted and special and, at long last, feeling rather pleased with herself.

When Bernice went to the bathroom, calling up to Win to stay on the landing, Julia stood looking in through the flat doorway and tried once more to call up her newly harnessed powers. She was still nervous, but this time the nerves were more akin to excitement than fear.

She imagined drawing back the curtain and bade her eyes to see.

That young, dark, fragile-looking girl with the sulky expression sitting at the piano was Maria Ingersall. That one sewing was Florence Rillington. The woman with the album was Ellen, and the young woman in the photograph was her dead mother, wearing the extravagant 1870s ball gown of her most glamorous and probably happiest years as the Belle of South Hackney. There were two more; what were their names?

The answer was introduced into her mind. Serena Elizabeth and Minnie Eliza.

No Joseph James. This was 1910, and Constance Agnes Ingersall, formerly Rillington, was newly dead, but her ten-year-old son was nowhere to be seen. Probably up in bed.

Abraham Ingersall laid down his pipe and looked at her. He's a bit of a bully. He's challenging me. He's daring me to do something. No, it's not me; I'm standing in the same position as someone else and she's about to defy him.

She wants to marry. It must be Agnes. The others are all looking up. They're afraid, but also envious. I'm not afraid, because it's nothing to do with me, I'm just an onlooker, a time-traveller.

She released the vision and was suddenly flooded with confidence and immense pride. I have a great gift. I'll learn more and more how to control and harness it, then I'll go out into the world and use it. This is what I'm meant to do. I'll help and comfort people and they'll be so grateful. I'll do good – my mother will be amazed and put out to find out how much I can achieve. Perhaps I'll be able to get messages for her from spirits in the next world, and they'll tell her how wrongly she's been behaving. She won't believe it, of course, but at least it'll make me feel better. I can see my future at last.

And there was no longer any reason to demand a hand-holder for a simple visit to the bathroom; she was grown-up now, and with a great mission before her. She passed Bernice on the stairs, smiled affectionately and gave her a hug. Bernice stared at her.

Julia washed with her head full of hopeful dreams and turned to find a rough, white Turkish towel hanging across the side of the bath as if left there in careless haste. From side to side was stretched a white metal grid loaded with sponges, loofahs, a large, round tablet of brown soap and a wooden nailbrush with black bristles. The mahogany towel rail beside the basin was hung with smooth white cotton hand towels edged with crochet, and there was a razor strop hanging on a hook behind the door. There was a strip of perforated metal at the top of the window and it was glazed in daisy-pattern glass, the thousands of little flowers crushed into a claustrophobic meadow within the frame. The shade around the gas mantle was white glass.

It was all nearer to new, but no less depressing because the colours were so hideous. The woodwork was a hard Prussian blue, the walls a leaden green. The red and white checked border on the bath towel seemed like a stray from the larger patch of red which slid through the fabric of the white night-shirt, and escaped onto the floor around the staring head of the dark, moustached man.

Julia put her hands to her head and screamed continuously for at least a minute, by which time the other three occupants of the house had pulled her out on to the landing and borne her along to the Grosvenors' living room.

They were in dressing-gowns. Mugs of hot nightcaps stood on the table getting cold while efforts were made to return Julia to normal. It took a long time, and the revelation of what was wrong with the bathroom even longer.

"Was it Mr Ingersall, Jule?" Bernice whispered nervously, as if he were listening.

"Yes," said Julia, staring ahead of her, totally deflated, her attention continually diverted away towards the scene impressed upon her memory; the pale, waxy face beaded with sweat, the dead eyes staring at nothing, the sticky blood hardening around his head and shoulders, the two, widely separated edges of the wound in his throat.

They made her lie down on the settee. Bernice sat beside her looking deeply upset, but held her hand and regularly passed tissues from a box provided by Win. Harry insisted on Scotch, which was followed by fiercely strong tea insisted on by Win.

The phone started to ring downstairs. Bernice went, still

259

flustered and anxious, but with an expression of hope upon her face.

"Well, all I can say is, I ain't never seen nothing like that, not never," said Win, and that was undoubtedly her final word.

"No, I don't suppose you have," assented Julia.

"So he come to a sticky end," said Harry, studying Julia's face with mixed awe and alarm. "Wonder why, when there was still a fair bit of money left? Reckon he was in some other sort of trouble, to do with the police, like?"

"Don't know," said Julia. It took a very violent person to inflict such violence upon himself. It took hatred and rage, perhaps self-directed, perhaps diverted from another who could not be reached. With all her experience of self-dislike, she couldn't imagine hating herself quite as much as that. A gentle hushing to sleep with drugs, perhaps; butchery, never.

Bernice came up again.

"Jule! Lovely news! You've got a new nephew. I told your sister you were a bit poorly and that you'd ring in the morning."

"What? But I was talking to Philip only last night and he didn't even mention she was in labour!"

"Well, she probably wasn't," Bernice explained. "Apparently, your mother was trying to make little Margaret eat some bread and butter, and she went into a tantrum."

"What, Mother?"

"No, I don't think so," said Bernice, brought up short. "I *think* she said it was Margaret. Anyway, Margaret ran away from her and slipped and went into the pond, and Helena just dropped everything and ran to pull her out, but unfortunately she gave herself a nasty wrench and started things off."

"Oh poor Nell! Is she all right? Did they get her to hospital in time?"

"Well, no. By the time medical help turned up it was too late to move her, and he was born in your old bedroom."

Julia burst out laughing. Bernice looked mystified. Win poured more tea. Harry looked distressed and embarrassed.

"Oh dear," Julia giggled hysterically, "it's got a new mattress and a new carpet. Are they both all right? Not the mattress and the carpet," she said, going into further hysterics.

"Absolutely," Bernice assured her. "Rowena said the baby is seven and a half pounds and that Helena is fine, if a bit tired."

"Oh, I'm so glad," said Julia sincerely, stopping laughing and starting to shake again. "I don't suppose they've chosen a name yet?" she went on, clutching for normality.

"Either John or Michael. Or perhaps both."

More hysterical laughter. "Philip's hedging his bets," Julia practically whimpered.

They stared at her.

"No, you're quite right, it isn't funny."

Laughter is always close to tears. Julia wept.

Bernice fell asleep quickly, worn out. She lay curled up with Teddy Mary while Julia sat bolt upright, staring at the television and not bothering to strain her ears for the turned-down sound. She felt not only apprehensive but also subdued, reprimanded, put in her place. Now then, cocky breeches.

I'm back where I started. I hate this room. I hate this whole building. What an appalling atmosphere there must have been here, to have culminated in such an event and left such a lasting legacy of unease.

But all buildings were charged by atmospheres and events, every sort from happy to hideous. In fact, if its history could affect its occupants like this, it might be desirable that every piece of property should be sold with a rundown of its life history, as a sort of psychic MOT certificate.

Sleep crept up on her at last. She awoke to GMTV, got up and turned it off. Although chastened, she felt remarkably calm, considering. She'd learned the lesson; a gift is nothing to be conceited about, it's a responsibility. They surely wouldn't do that to her again.

Bernice proved difficult to arouse. Her mug stood acquiring a milky film while Julia got herself breakfast, washed in the sink and put her clothes on. It was that bathroom moment again.

"I'm sorry," she told whatever was in charge of her psychic education, "I know I can't handle this without you, but I don't want to see that again, please."

A kind of peace seemed to accompany her up the stairs, but it left her at the bathroom door. At least, the rush of dreadful recollection which overcame her probably blocked it off and sent her alone into that appalling place.

There must still be traces of Abraham Ingersall's blood in its crevices; between the skirtings and the floorboards, splashed on the underside of the bath. And in that inaccessible area behind it against the wall, the dust might contain his sloughed skin and the scum of mould his blood.

His reason for doing such a dreadful thing was in no way obvious. For some reason, he must have reached despair. After ill-treating his sick wife for years, could he possibly have missed her that much? How could it be money problems when he had plenty to leave? Whatever his trouble was, he rose from his bed in the Grosvenors' bright, cheery living room and cut his own throat. Here. No, please don't let me see him again.

She washed her hands quickly and reached for the towel. On the floor beneath it lay the cut-throat razor, stained with blood and inches from his outstretched hand.

She ran downstairs, badly shaken and even angry.

"I said I didn't want to see it!" she protested out loud.

"What, Jule?" Bernice still wasn't dressed. She was gazing out of the bay window.

"Nothing. Just talking to myself."

"Or someone else," said Bernice with something uncharacteristically like depression.

Julia rang Rowena.

"Is Helena all right?" she asked. "It must have been awful for her."

"It was pretty alarming for everyone," said Rowena with feeling. "Some of the children were a bit upset at first, but they're fine now and boasting to their friends that they were there when a baby was born."

"They weren't really, were they?" asked Julia, appalled at the thought of giving birth before an audience of children.

"No, of course they weren't. Dennis and Bradley shoved them into cars and took them off to play cricket until the light failed. It was the only thing they could think of."

"So when can I come and see my new nephew?"

"Well, Nell should be home tomorrow, then any time, I should think."

"It will have to be an evening, unless I wait to the weekend. Oh, by the way, we're moving the weekend after that."

"What, again? So it didn't work out."

"Yes, it did. We've just found somewhere nicer."

"From what mother said, anywhere would be nicer than where you are now. And I don't suppose it'll be Hackney this time."

"Yes it will. You must come and see it."

"All right," conceded Rowena gamely. "I'll see if I can buy a phrasebook."

Their last ten days at Ermintrude Villas continued to twist together the different strands of their lives. First, they went out for nine hours daily to go through the motions of being efficient, friendly receptionists in a busy, globally orientated firm. Second, they stripped and cleaned the flat, just in case Cyprian Smith and Lily Wright had the nerve to examine it for dilapidations. And third and most important strand, they constantly experienced the other dimension which came and went within their own. They listened for it and waited for it, always tensed and alert.

When the sounds came, they wondered which of them it was. Is that Florence? Is Abraham reading his paper by the fire? Is it Ellen who steps so busily down the basement stairs to see to the work of the house, or is it Agnes hurrying to a lover's meeting or a nocturnal elopement, dressed in long coat and large hat, and with a bag in each hand?

Win and Harry brought home more information each day, dug out of archives all over London. The more they learned, the more they spoke of Them as if they knew them personally. It was like observing them from the viewpoint of live-in servants.

The Grosvenors looked up the Electoral Roll for 1918, when women over thirty first got the vote. Florence Mary Rillington, Minnie Eliza, Serena Elizabeth, Ellen Edith.

They traced Abraham's birth to Bishop Auckland, ten years after his second wife's. They found his daughter Maria's birth at Stoke Newington in 1895.

Lily's mother, Agnes, had married early in 1911. The register of St Mary's Church, Walthamstow revealed that it was by special licence, that Tobias Wright was a mere draper's assistant and that his deceased father had been a bootmender. The witnesses were relatives of neither bride nor groom.

The Magnificent Rillingtons wouldn't have taken kindly to that, nor Abraham Ingersall, if Constance's jewellery was destined for any daughter who married.

John Rillington's will of 1920 forbade Joseph James from marrying Maria Ingersall – ever, or he would be cut off from the Rillington wealth.

"My goodness!" exclaimed Bernice. "There's a whole can of beans to be opened *there!*"

"Seems he opted to take the money instead of opening the box," said Harry.

"Don't be coarse, Harry!"

"I wasn't! Oh, sorry, didn't mean it that way."

With what looked like spite, John left nothing to his sister Agnes, though Lily was grudgingly allowed into the pecking order once all his children were dead. Lily never got that inheritance; one, because most of it went up in high explosive, two, because his son was granted probate on the remainder in 1944.

It was all so complicated. So much information was being presented to Julia, and yet she felt little of it really went in. Day after day she was continually aware of Their presence, standing and watching as the girls packed or cleaned or cooked or watched television. And whatever she was doing, her mind spun with dates and puzzled about what it was that had to be found.

Bernice, however, absorbed everything with feverish anxiety, as if she was cramming for an exam. Constantly, she mulled over the whys and the wherefores of the doleful existence endured by the Ingersalls and the Rillingtons, as if somewhere in that mass of information was the answer to laying their ghosts. She moved more quickly and relaxed less. Often, her hands fidgeted and her face twitched.

"I suppose Joseph would have had the tiny room over the hall and the five women would have been in the other two bedrooms. I wonder why the girls didn't stay with their brother John? There must have been so much room there and there was so little here."

"Probably loyalty to their mother. I have the impression that John was a bit of a stuffed shirt like his father, very conscious of his position and a great upholder of the family honour. Sort of Lily Wright in trousers."

"Do you really mean an impression, or are you certain?" asked Bernice.

"Well, to be honest, I don't know. But it seems a reasonable conclusion to come to, doesn't it?" Julia said, offering both an excuse and a word of comfort. Poor Bernie seemed to be shrinking visibly these last days.

"Perhaps," said Bernice doubtfully, "but surely they could have gone back once Constance died?"

"I suppose they'd become too scared of Abraham by then to leave. And John probably had a string of children and no room for repentant maiden sisters who'd sullied the Rillington name."

"You're so calm about it all now, Jule. I think you're being absolutely wonderful," said Bernice humbly.

"Find it," said the voice. "Hurry and find it!"

With all this clearing out and cleaning up, you'd have thought we'd have done so by now. Unless we or even Lily already have found it without realising its importance, and thrown it into the dustbin.

Now *that* was a thought.

They were both afraid of the bathroom again now, so Win had to stand guard, morning and evening.

"I'm sorry about this, Win, you must think we're absolutely pathetic," said Julia as she prepared to shut herself up in the nastiest sort of past yet again.

"If I was seeing what you say you are, I reckon I'd be windy myself," said Win. "Go ahead, I won't budge."

Julia concentrated fiercely on the essential components of now. Pink toilet paper. A new tube of fluoride toothpaste. Bernice's fluffy bath sheet with kittens gambolling along the hems.

Abraham Ingersall. The seeping sheet of blood moving down his night-shirt in a slow, almost controlled progress.

She left without washing her hands, thanked Win and went to finish her evening toilet in the sink. She was shaking and her feelings were hurt. "Why?" she kept asking. "Why do you keep inflicting that upon me? Why must I keep seeing blood being splashed around?"

But it wasn't splashing around, it was moving slowly. Wasn't there something wrong about that?

"Bernice?"

"Yes, Jule?"

"When somebody cuts their throat, doesn't blood fly all over the place?"

"Oh Jule, don't!" pleaded poor Bernice, who was about to go up to the dreaded bathroom.

"Oh sorry, I didn't think. I'm getting more and more self-centred, aren't I?" said Julia with shame and hugged her friend. "I'm so busy being a newly-discovered psychic these days I'm forgetting about being a decent human being. I do apologise, Bernie."

"That's all right, Jule," said Bernice faintly, but didn't smile.

Twenty-Three

A s the facts about the Rillingtons and the Ingersalls continued to build up, proving that they did this, or lived there, or possessed such and such, the central secrets remained untouched and only occasionally did an action cast light on personalities and motivations. Above all, the great mystery remained, the one which no amount of biographical research could solve, because the majority of a person's life takes place inside their own head.

What were they really like?

Win and Harry came hurrying down to pick up the latest brown envelopes to slide through the letter-box and across the tiles, opening them in the girls' flat while they got ready for work.

"Right, here we go: answers time again."

Information was extracted from envelope after envelope. Constance Agnes had died of 'phthisis' after 'many years'.

"Generally means TB," said Win, "but it could mean any sort of wasting illness. Perhaps the poor girl just pined away."

"I've never seen her," said Julia.

"But we heard her, didn't we?" said Bernice, looking upset, "she was crying her heart out."

"Reckon Abraham married her for her money," said Win with a knowing expression on her sharp face.

"He 'reft' the lot," said Julia.

"What's reft mean?" asked Harry, with none of Win's image to protect.

"It's something Lily said about her mother's belongings," explained Bernice. "I bet Ingersall had sold Constance's jewels by the time he died, and Joe never even got a look at them."

"Never heard nothing," reiterated Win strongly. "Anyway, here's his death certificate. *Felo de se* by cutting of the throat. Information reported to the registrar by the Hackney coroner. Try the local paper, do you reckon, Harry?"

"Or the inquest?" he suggested. "That'd be interesting; post mortem might have been done by the great Sir Bernard Spilsbury himself."

"Who was he?" asked Bernice, drooping over her mug of tea.

"Greatest pathologist of all time," said Harry with the expansive certainty of those who have been brought up in a firm belief. "Never known to be wrong."

"Here's Constance and Abraham's wedding," said Win. "Aha, special licence again; didn't want the game being give away by banns. St Augustine's, though, and one of the witnesses looks like the verger. The other's Florence. Reckon she was the only relative to know about it beforehand?"

"Talk about secrets!" Harry said with glee. "So much for the wonderful family spirit of the Rillingtons. Cor, I'd love to show Lily Wright this. Wonder what else got whitewashed by her dear mother?"

But was that such a terrible secret? A flutter in the dovecote then, no doubt, but enough to split the family for ever? It seemed so petty.

Julia was aware of the women to the side of her, but made no attempt to turn and try to see them. Supposing I caught their eyes, what would happen? How would it feel?

They were not the only spirits hovering on the edge of her life now. The occasional appearance of people who could not be accounted for continued. One morning, a smart gentleman in a frock-coat and top hat turned off Cadogan Terrace ahead of them and walked through the new flats to a vanished station on the viaduct. Another time, a plump, cheery sweep greeted her in the front garden.

"How do, love? I won't step in because of me boots."

A gaggle of twenties flappers screeched their way down the Drive in the park, and ragged children played in the streets of

Hackney Wick, but in Number Two Ermintrude Villas she was always aware of the Rillington sisters, and expected that at any moment they might appear before the fireplace or in the bay window, standing silent and still.

And the message kept being repeated, crystal clear in her ear. "It must be found."

At last the moment came. Wet-handed from the defrosting of the fridge and momentarily concerned only with the speedy discarding of something in a state of decay, Julia came round the curtain into the living room one evening and found them waiting for her. For a moment she thought it was another time slip, with her self safely on the other side of eighty-five years, but the figures were pale and colourless like holograms, and through them she could see the striped curtains and the open bay window which allowed in the sounds and smells of the present. She stopped short, her hands gripped around the sheer silliness of a superannuated vegetarian pâté.

This is it. They're here. They're real. They want me. She turned and ran back into the kitchen. Not now. Sorry, not now, I'm not ready.

"You must find it."

No, sorry, no, no, no, not me. There'll be someone else around soon, tell them.

"These houses are all coming down," she said out loud. "They'll be bound to find it then."

"No! Find it now!"

The woman's voice was clear and very urgent. She was almost certain it was Florence. A strong character, Florence.

She heard the familiar sound of fire-irons being moved and used. A fire in June.

Another voice came, reasonable and calm.

"You cannot see only the things you want." She was aware of the presence which had momentarily got through to her on the stairs. At the very moment of alarm, confusion and recognition, the thought surfaced like an old boot on a silver tide. Don't let it be a Red Indian – I don't think I could take him seriously. She looked back round the curtain.

I can see them and they can see me. A row of women with upswept hair and in long, dark clothes. I must not look at their eyes. If I do they may take me over and I shall belong to them.

She left the room quickly, and took the pâté on a special, personal trip to the dustbin. In the hall, someone brushed past her, sobbing with fear. Oh my God, who was *that*?

"Found the report of the inquest in the local paper," said Win, "and it wasn't Sir Bernard as opened him up. Like the certificate said, he done hisself in."

"Yeah, but you can't be absolutely sure that's the proper verdict unless old Spilsbury said so," demurred Harry, obviously a bit disappointed. "Wonder why they didn't go to him?"

"He was on holiday down in Bude," said Julia without even thinking.

They looked at her with increased unease.

"Anyway," continued Harry grimly, "it was a nasty business. Abraham stayed in bed until all the girls had gone to church and then done hisself in. Seems poor old Joe found him – imagine that when you're only fourteen? He went rushing down to his brother John's, poor kid."

"Why didn't they take Joe to church?"

"Had a cold. Don't suppose old Abraham realised he was in the house."

"And we found another will," chimed in Win. "Wasn't looking for it, matter of fact, I was just reminding meself of what me Uncle Frank Riley left and there it was, John Rillington's son. He died in 1973, widower with no kids, and the very last knockings of the Rillington Repository money went to Lily. Guess how much?"

"Well, I expect it had shrunk a bit by then—"

"Two hundred and seventy-six pounds. How about that for the mighty being fallen? No wonder she was waiting for Joe's whack. Here, wait a minute, if that was the end of the stuff entailed by Lily's grandfather, Joe's things wouldn't have been anything to do with it. She'll have to go through all the business

of proving she's entitled to it. Oh dear, oh dear. Looks like we
could be here for a while yet, eh, Harry?"

"We shall not be moved," he said, grinning.

The girls washed up after the evening meal, because so little
was left unpacked that it would all be needed for breakfast.

"Poor Constance," said Bernice, drying another lot of foil
containers ready for Guide Dogs for the Blind. "She must have
found out quite quickly that she'd made an awful mistake and
that he only wanted her for her money. And poor, poor little
Joe. You never know what people have had to put up with,
do you? I'm so sorry I ever said anything nasty about him, I
really am." She sounded tearful.

"You never did say anything nasty about him."

Julia looked at the depressing view from the kitchen window
and thought that even a motorway might not be able to destroy
the dominion of ghosts. Perhaps late at night, it might always
sometimes be possible to see Agnes Rillington, opening a
vanished back gate in the middle of the slip road and fleeing
beneath the concrete stilts, hand in hand with Tobias Wright,
draper's assistant, on the way to a new life in Walthamstow.

She went down to Leatherhead with flowers, bright blue
rompers and a white teddy from Bernice. Helena looked pretty
good, considering, and her nephew appeared to be made of pink
marzipan and sweet enough to eat. Mrs Nutley was running the
house which meant the Spanish housekeeper was permanently
offended, Philip was wearing a perpetual strained smile and
the children weren't talking to anyone. The spirit of tension
and antipathy within the family was now so well established
that there was no point in diverting any of it on to Julia.

She returned to town with a wonderful feeling of freedom
and elation. It lasted right up to the moment when she passed
the ghost gate of Number Two Ermintrude Villas and started
to climb the steps, painted rosy by the sunset.

The music came to meet her. A rich, romantic melody with a
sobbing accompaniment, singing low down in the most mellow

and resonant part of the keyboard. A tune which brought to mind yearning and sadness and a longing for passion denied. *Melody in F*. 'To Florrie from Joseph, Easter 1919.'

As she turned the key in the front door, Bernice burst out of the flat.

"Oh Jule! I might have guessed you were here. It's only just started. Tell them to stop, Jule!"

Julia put her arms around her and led her into the flat. The music stopped at once. Above, the Grosvenors' television could be heard thundering through the floor. It sounded like the real-life crime as entertainment genre.

Florence didn't greet her at the keyboard, like an Edwardian young lady showing off her accomplishments to a visitor. She was standing before the empty fireplace, with none of its gaping dustiness on show, because she now appeared as solid as poor Bernice. Her brown hair was full of grey. Her face was taut and sallow and lined by the health-draining tension of habitual stress, and her hands were clasped together across the huge, smug cat in her arms; the creature on which she had lavished all her frustrated love, so that it had become a part of her identity and perhaps even started to share her soul.

The cat looked at Julia with self-satisfaction, its neat, triangular mouth pursed amongst its white whiskers. Florence fixed her with hard, desperate eyes, and it was like looking into a pit.

"Find it and get rid of it," she said. Julia saw her lips move and heard her voice, very clear, very definite but with a lack of echo, as if it was enclosed in a soft-walled box with no resonance.

"Why?" asked Julia.

Bernice looked up at her. "What, Jule?"

"It must not be found by others."

"What will happen if it is?"

"Jule?"

"The family will be disgraced. The inheritance will be declared invalid. We will never be able to hold our heads up again."

273

"But would it matter? Nobody remembers you except Lily, and she wouldn't believe anything bad against any of you, even if she found out."

"Jule, who are you talking to?"

Bernice sat down on the settee, picked up Teddy Mary and hugged her against her breast with both hands. She looked pitifully close to terror.

Julia looked away from Florence, knowing that she might disappear, but with a strange acknowledgement of her own control over the situation. If she wants to talk to me that much she'll wait.

"They're here, Bernie," she said gently, and knelt down before her, taking her hands. "Florence is anxious about something being found. The other sisters are over there, by the bay window. Can you see them?"

"No." Poor Bernice was shivering. Julia held her, full of strength.

She looked up at the row of women, standing so still and sad in that stripped room on the point of desertion. Their hair was greying, their eyes were dulled by mental imprisonment. Their black clothes had a few little ornaments of an understated, ladylike nature; a small gold locket, a fob watch with a flowered face, a silver ivy brooch inscribed with the word 'Mother'.

"Why are you still so sad?" she asked them. "You don't want to worry about all that now, it hasn't mattered for years."

"What are they saying?" asked Bernice, her voice getting anxious. "What's it all about, Jule?"

"They won't tell me."

The sisters began to get agitated. Hands were twisted, heads were bowed. One of them leant towards her.

"It does matter, it will always matter. He was so cruel, so unjust."

"You mean, to your mother?"

"She cried so terribly, for hour after hour. He would not let us go to her. If we tried, he struck us."

"Couldn't you have told someone?"

274

There sounded a general indrawing of breath, like a deep sigh of horror.

"It would have been such a scandal!" exclaimed another sister. "We should never have lived it down. The family's position would have been destroyed for ever."

"So you allowed your mother to suffer just for the sake of the family reputation?" said Julia with shocked recognition of an idol to which everyone and everything must be sacrificed.

"Did they?" asked Bernice pathetically. "Tell me what they're saying, Jule. And don't let them hurt me, will you? I want them to be happy, poor things. I want them to be in the beautiful next world, learning how to be happy. I want you all to be happy," she said more loudly, looking round the room.

Julia was shocked that they ignored her completely. But what use was sweet, kind-hearted Bernice to them? Their vision was blinkered by their desperate, self-centred aim – the cult of the family. It was Julia who mattered, and that was only because she could help them.

"What is it I must look for? And where have you put it?"

Florence's hand stroked the cat compulsively. It purred and preened, squeezing its eyelids together in ecstasy.

"He wouldn't tell me where it was."

Julia suddenly saw Victoria Park Road on a hot July day in 1914, with a boy in a Norfolk jacket running as fast as he could up the slow gradient, crying, gasping for breath, afraid to stop until he rushed up the impressive flight of steps which led to Buchanan House and pressed the bell.

"What are they looking for, Jule?"

Bernice's head was buried in the back of the settee and she was crying. Julia leant over and hugged her hard.

"They won't say."

"Can't they tell us where it is?"

"They don't know. Mr Rillington knew where it was but he wouldn't tell them. He hid it when he was a boy."

"But what *is* it?"

"They're so ashamed of something they can't put it into words."

"Oh, Jule, tell them to go away! Please! Tell them to go away!"

On Saturday morning, the girls awoke from their very last disturbed night at Ermintrude Villas and hugged each other with overwhelming relief. It had not only been the footsteps; restless, often-repeated and chilling to the soul. There had been the sounds of doors being opened and closed, of drawers being pulled out, of scrabbling and searching and the frustrated, tearful voices of those who sought but could not find.

Bernice went eagerly for the kettle. Her face was white and tearstained, and her glasses had been knocked crooked by being slept in. Julia looked round the bare, empty room. I'm going today. You're too late. I might have been able to help you. Sorry.

Next door, Luke carried the pushchair up the steps, followed by Fern in a flowered skirt and a brown shawl, bearing Gaia in red. They said nothing to each other, but made for the park.

In the bay window on the other side, a small, brown hand hung with bangles pushed the net curtain to one side so its owner could follow their progress away across the grass, then allowed it to drop again.

Up in the first floor flat, Win and Harry put on their oldest clothes and gathered together tools and useful household odds and ends, plus a tupperware box full of special biscuits for tea breaks. Down on the ground floor, the suitcases and carriers, the bags and boxes, the strapped-up piles of folded bedding and curtains were ready and waiting. They stripped the bed and pushed the linen into yet another bag.

Julia opened the flat door, went into the hall and saw the morning sun shining out onto the landing from the bathroom. It is June the 17th 1995. It is a bright summer day and this is the last morning I need ever go up to that room. The next flat has a nice bright shower room built on the back, and I'm going to put plants all along the window-sill. I'm going to enjoy showering in there, and going back into my own room, and being able to sit out in our own little garden. In three weeks' time I shall be

276

thirty and for the first time I feel I know who I am, where I'm going and why. It's another new start, and this time it's going to go right.

The gas man came to disconnect the appliances, and Harry and Bernice lifted the gas fire and carried it out to the hall. The gap in the hardboard was full of dust, mortar, soot and cobwebs, and the grate itself had gone, but when they shone a torch within they found a round opening wreathed with metal flowers.

"Gosh, what a mess!"

"Should we sweep it up?" asked Bernice tentatively. "You never know whether Lily might charge us for damage and dirt?"

"Yes, it might be a good idea," said Julia, though not for fear of Lily. She owed it to Them to go on looking to the very last moment. She emptied the mess onto a spread-out newspaper.

"What you looking for?" asked Harry.

"I don't know," admitted Julia. "What the ghosts are looking for, actually, and that could be anything at all and any-where at all."

Harry sat down on his haunches and swirled a finger round in the rubble. "Yeah, never know what's going to turn up in an old house, do you? Found a few funny things when I was doing the repairs. Old hairpins and suspenders and other odds and ends. Just by the window frame over the porch there was a loose bit of rendering what had come away. I pulled it out to brush off the loose dust before I cemented it back and there was a sort of hidyhole there, like a kid might have had once. Found a few cigarette cards and a couple of smokes, and a few other bits."

"Harry!" Bernice cried. "That must have been Joe's room!"

"Oh my Gawd," he said, "and I'd forgot all about them."

The little hoard was in a large biscuit tin, along with rusty nails, drawing pins, perished elastic bands and crumbling shreds of sandpaper. They were emptied out, and at that very instant Julia discovered what the Rillingtons were looking for with such anxiety. Everything was covered with black, gritty dust, and she pushed a pencil through one handle to lift up the filthy, bird-shaped scissors with the long sharp blades.

"I saw Florence sewing with these," she said.

"Did you really, Jule?" asked Bernice, shrinking away from those ghosts made metal. "What's that on the blades? They're all black and rough."

"But he was killed with a razor," Win objected forcefully. She had been called down to the reopening of the inquest on Abraham Ingersall, due to the finding of new evidence.

"Well," said Julia, full of amazed and relieved excitement, "supposing Florence got in a rage with him and stuck the scissors in his throat. She left him for a bit, perhaps pulling herself together and wondering what on earth she was going to do. After a bit, when his heart had stopped beating, she went back, took out the scissors and cut his throat with his razor to hide the stab wound."

"So out she goes to church," said Win with even greater excitement, "and poor old Joe walks in and finds the body with the blood starting to flow all over the shop."

"Oh!" moaned Bernice. "Poor little boy!"

"Then he finds the bloodstained scissors—"

"No, no, no," Harry interrupted Win, which proved how excited he was, "how about he found the body with the scissors still in while Florrie was still thinking about it? "Oh my Gawd," he says, "them's Florrie's scissors, she's done him in." And he pulls them out and hides them."

"Pulled them out! But the blood would have gone all over him!" protested Bernice in horror.

"Not if Ingersall had been dead for a while."

"Which means—"

"He was killed before the women went to church, and Florrie must have done the actual throat-cutting when she come back. No wonder poor old Joe was afraid of Florrie."

Bernice looked white. "Oh please don't," she begged. "Jule, why not just ask them what happened?"

"I have. They won't answer. They wouldn't even tell me

what I had to look for, it's as if they're in that state psychologists call denial. Sort of 'Ssh, don't mention the murder.' Or even 'What murder? I don't know about any murder.' All that seems to matter to them is hiding something which could blacken the family name."

"If Sir Bernard had done the post mortem they'd never have got away with it," said Harry solemnly, shaking his head.

Bernice came back from the phone.

"That was the van-hire company. I was supposed to pick it up at nine and they asked whether we still wanted it. I said we'd been held up but'd be around in a few minutes."

She and Harry went off to do just that and Win went up to finish tidying her flat. Julia stood in the bay window, holding the pair of scissors in an old egg box.

"Now hide it."

"Aren't you going to tell me what happened?"

"Take it away and hide it."

They were all round her. She could hear their whispering voices, the swishing of their skirts, the gentle clink of neck chains as they leant forward, the clicking of heels on the boards bared by the removal of the carpet.

They all knew and they all covered it up. Even little Joe hid the scissors. They were probably not only protective of the family honour but personally frightened of Florrie. After all, any one who could lose control of themselves and stab someone to death, could presumably do it again.

What about Maria? Did she suspect? In fact, did she know? She may have been bullied by her father, too, and his death did bring her a small fortune.

It really seemed possible that the whole household at Number Two Ermintrude Villas knew the secret of Abraham Ingersall's murder and guarded it as long as they lived – and longer. With the formidable Florrie still ruling the roost, no one would have dared to spill the beans.

'Mey femily' were extremely well-bred people. Family loyalty was upheld by every member as a sacred trust –

as long as they didn't step out of line. The Royal Family of Hackney, setting the standards for everyone else, give or take a throat-cutting or so.

Abraham's death hadn't released them; it was far too late for that. The paralysis of will and enterprise created by the need to hide the scandal of a disastrous marriage was now followed by the need to hide even worse. The sterile way of life they had become accustomed to must continue for ever. Until the end of their lives they must read and sew, and sing and play, and go to church and share the work of the house. And their respectability must become more and more unassailable, and the outside world must be kept more and more separate from their private lives, because there must not be the slightest chance of the secret coming out. Even sister Agnes must remain cast out, because she mustn't know either.

Julia closed the egg box and went out of the flat and down the front steps into the road. Where? It didn't really matter, so long as it could no longer be associated with Ermintrude Villas.

She walked down to Hackney Wick, turned right and crossed the turnings feeding on and off the concrete which covered such a huge swathe of the past. Should she pitch it into the remains of the towerblocks, or might a child discover it and hurt himself? No, she knew the answer.

A few minutes later, the murderous metal bird dived over the parapet and turned to plummet feet first into the dark waters of the Hackney Cut.

When she got back to the flat she was expecting them to come and thank her. They did no such thing, and she felt a hurt sensation of betrayal at such ingratitude. This was the very first time she had ever employed her gift to help someone, and all they had done was use her and go. Well, perhaps that was the Rillingtons.

However, the sweep paid her another brief visit.

"I won't step in, ducks," he repeated, "don't want to dirty yer tiles. Give me love to our Grace, won't yer?"

It was minutes before she realised that she might have met her grandfather.

They were ready to go. Julia took the last bag of rubbish out to the dustbin and found a man hesitating outside the vanished front gate, as if not sure whether to enter in case of rebuff. His face was so familiar, and yet it took seconds to recognise him. He was too young for his formal lounge suit and carried his glasses in his hand instead of on his nose, as if their sole function now was to be shown, not used. He looked at her with touching anxiety, leaning forward but not moving, unwilling to trespass upon her private territory.

"Julia," said her father, "it's not as I thought," and was gone.

Julia sat quietly in the passenger seat. Bernice drove with the utmost consideration for everybody else on the road, and slowed down at every zebra crossing, just in case. Win and Harry walked smartly down Victoria Park Road and across Well Street Common, bearing bags full of lunch.

In their new street, several neighbours saw the girls jump out and make for the basement door through the neat little show of early bedding plants. One woman gave them a nod of acknowledgement.

They swept and cleaned and arranged. Harry mended this and that, Win insisted on scrubbing. Bernice was bubbling over with joy, right back to her old self. Soon the flat was decked in stripes and sunflowers and teddies, Julia's ornaments were spread upon her dressing table and the wall above it told her Yes, she could.

At midday, men arrived to switch on the gas and the electricity, and a picnic meal was eaten in the tiny paved garden, among shrubs longing for their care.

Julia, it's not as I thought. No, it seems it isn't, Dad. I hope you're all right. I hope you've been able to settle down in a world which is not as you thought. You look well, though, and that's a funny thing to say to the dead.

Tears threatened. She went out into the sunny road and sat on the wall, hearing distant cars in Victoria Park Road but feeling nearer to another world. I wonder if he'll meet the Rillingtons, poor miserable things, and whether they'll discuss the prime importance of the family?

Three houses down, the neighbour appeared again in her front garden, obviously longing to communicate. She was dressed in a short, square-shouldered dress and a cross-over cotton overall edged with red binding. She waved at Julia, smiled, then cupped her hand to her mouth.

"It was a blooming bomb," she called, and shrugged her shoulders in resignation. Her hair was parted in the middle and pushed back into a coarse green net. Not even the VE celebrations had brought back the fashion for snoods.

Well, at least this one looked cheerful.

Julia swallowed her tears and smiled back.